S.M. GAITHER

For Mom

ONE

Aleksander

In the dark depths of my mind, a soft voice echoed.

It spoke only my name, over and over, as though desperate to not let me forget it. Whether it rose from my imagination, or memory—or someplace altogether different—I couldn't say. Harder still to say how long it had been reverberating through the hollowed-out places where I'd once held thoughts.

I didn't remember the sound beginning.

Couldn't fathom it ending.

But, at some point, I recognized the one speaking.

Or, at least, I managed to conjure up a face to go

with the voice: Bright blue eyes. Dark hair falling over ivory skin, curtaining scars only halfway healed.

Those scars...

My stomach lurched.

Nova.

I blinked, and she was gone.

Her voice went away, too.

Without it, the darkness seemed more absolute. Impenetrable. There was nothing else—had never been anything else. The longer I spent in the inky silence, the more I began to question if Nova had ever been there at all.

Focus. My own voice, now, pleading with me to stay awake, to stay aware. To not give in to the dark. Something wanted me to close my eyes and give in. To stop resisting. A pressure coiling around my mind, encouraging me to sink deeper and deeper into it.

I fought.

I was not in control of where I looked, but I could still *see,* even if my vision was hazy.

And what I saw was the aftermath of a battle that looked to have occurred some time ago—broken buildings, bodies crumpled and coated in dust, blood dried black in the grooves between shattered flagstone. I moved without any direction through it all. Memories tried to surface, floating around me like smoke, whisking away the second I attempted to grab them for a closer look.

My feet carried me to what remained of a bridge.

After climbing over jutting support beams and leaping several precarious openings, I stood in the doorway of a circular room with a collapsed roof. A dais sat at its center, its face shattered and half-swallowed by rubble.

Standing beneath the broken doorframe, I felt something far more powerful than mere smoke and memory rise up and ripple through me. An odd, clearly magical energy lingered in the space, but there was something else beneath it—a stain of violence, raw and unfinished.

Something horrible happened here.

I tried to close my eyes. To think. The attempt was met with sharp resistance. I tried to move my hands toward my face, as if to shield myself from whatever horror stretched before me.

More resistance.

Abruptly, I realized what was happening: *I was not controlling my body.*

Lorien was.

And he wanted to see the destruction he'd caused.

He turned my head slowly, surveying the carnage with something like reverence. A feeling of satisfaction rippled through me, one that was not my own. But there was something else tainting it, I thought—something like uncertainty. Fear.

His, or mine?

I tried to pull back, to twist my body around, to take a single step out of his control—anything.

"You waste your energy, Aleksander."

My voice. Except, it wasn't me who had spoken the words. I wasn't sure they'd even been spoken out loud. They seemed to echo through my head, like something from a nightmare.

And no matter how hard I fought, I could not wake up.

TWO

Nova

The floorboards creaked and groaned beneath my boots as I picked my way through the wreckage of what looked like it had once been a grand library. Dust coated nearly every surface. The sweltering air was thick with a mixture of memory and melancholy, clinging to my body and making each of my steps feel heavier than the last; its embrace was an odd combination of comforting and suffocating.

Thalia, my near-constant companion as of late, stepped through the crumbling doorway behind me, knocking cobwebs aside as she came. She breathed out a slow, astonished breath. Her amethyst eyes widened slightly as she walked to the center of the vast room, taking in the shelves rising all around us. A thin sheen of sweat coated her brown skin, and her chest rose and fell with labored effort, despite her fitness—more signs of the strange weight this place possessed…

And more reminders that my magic wasn't enough to insulate us from the heaviness, despite how hard I'd been trying to expand my abilities over the past month.

"Your brother is going to be incredibly jealous when he realizes what we've been up to," Thalia said, making her way to the nearest shelf and reaching for a leather-bound book. Its cover was cracked, barely holding it together. Its brittle pages whispered like wind through dry leaves as she carefully flipped through them.

"No doubt," I agreed. Bastian would have been beside himself just to get his hands on that single tome she held, let alone to be *standing* here, surrounded by a thousand other books that looked equally ancient and interesting. "Eamon will be, too. But they'll forgive us as long as we bring back plenty of material for them to obsess over, I suspect."

Nodding, she placed the book gently back on the shelf and proceeded down the row, running her fingers over warped spines, trying to decide which ones to pluck from the hoard.

It was hard to know where to start.

This was my fifth trip to the ruined realm of Nerithys, and its center kingdom of Midna, in the past month—not counting the first, disastrous trip where we'd faced off with a monster known as Lorien Blackvale while vying for control of the life-giving magic found here.

The palace we were currently crawling our way through had been in rough shape before. Now, after having served as our arena during that battle with Lorien, it was worse, each creak of wood, and every shift of light and shadow making us tense for fear it all might give way at any moment.

But at least it was still here.

At least I'd been able to come back.

After our narrow escape from Lorien, the portal into this ruined kingdom had seemingly snapped shut behind us. A violent end to a violent duel.

Except, it hadn't been the end. Not really.

Days later—while back within my own realm of Noctaris—I'd felt the magic in the middle realm stirring again. Beckoning, almost. Telling me there was more power, more history, to discover here. More to make sense of.

I'd returned alone the first time. Reckless, in hindsight. But, truth be told, I hadn't expected to actually be able to pass through on my own. I'd only been experimenting with my shadowy magic when it had latched onto…*something*…and managed to pull me through the veil that separated the realms.

My first visit had been brief. Just long enough to grasp the fact that it could be done, even if *doing* it left me feeling like I was ripping apart at the seams—a feeling that persisted, even now.

I felt Thalia's eyes shift to me. "Are you sure you're okay to keep going?"

"Never better."

She gave me a long, appraising look.

"Liar," she concluded, in her characteristically blunt tone.

Maybe I was, but I was going to keep going anyway.

There wasn't really another option.

As one of the Vaelora—a being responsible for controlling cycles of life and magic between the realms—I was the only one able to carry us into Midna. This place had once been the center kingdom when the realms of Noctaris and Soltaris were still united, and legends said that the last king and queen who ruled over it had been responsible for creating the Aether-stone, along with the other apparatuses that allowed the Vaelora to more precisely control the world's cycles of life and magic.

Of course, there had always been two Vaelora. Light and Shadow. Life and Death. Both working in agreement—in tandem. Alternating where the power was directed to. But now...

Now, I was alone here.

And I wouldn't—*couldn't*—think about the Light missing from the equation. Never-mind how unsure or off-balance I felt.

Balance could be improved.

So I would just have to keep improving.

This was the deepest we'd managed to press into the palace thus far. Magic continuously coursed from my body as we moved, as I concentrated on controlling my breathing and my shadows along with it, adjusting my power so it kept the unstable energy in the air at a bearable weight against us.

"Hopefully, I'll be able to bring Bastian as well, next time," I thought aloud. "And maybe some of our other allies, too. It's only a matter of improving my magic's ability to fill in the spaces, to even out the power in the air here. At least, that's what Eamon said; he thinks the capability is well within my reach."

"Hm."

"…That *hm* sounded unconvinced."

Thalia shrugged. "Eamon is exhaustingly optimistic."

I gave her a slight grin. "He and I have that in common, don't we?"

A corner of her mouth twitched, as though she'd thought about returning my grin. "Well, hopefully you're both right," she replied, though her eyes were clouded over in doubt.

I pretended not to notice that doubt.

And, for as long as I could, I pretended not to feel the constraints of my power, either.

We moved swiftly but purposefully, gathering up as many sources of knowledge as possible. Thalia had brought along a canvas bag nearly as big as me; it wasn't long before it was overflowing with books of all sizes, along with several tightly-bound scrolls, scraps of parchment scribbled with notes, and a couple of torn, yellowed maps.

I spotted an interesting looking alcove off to my right, lined with marble busts—a few of which appeared to be mostly intact. Nothing we could bring back to Noctaris, but I was curious about who these statues represented all the same.

As I approached the space, however, the shadows that had been circling protectively around my body suddenly recoiled, slamming back into my chest with a viciousness that nearly knocked me off my feet.

It was too overwhelming, the pocket of other magic hovering here; I couldn't summon enough of my own to balance it out.

I backed away slowly, studying the way the air shifted and wavered, all too aware of the frustrating limits of my powers.

"This has been a successful excursion already," Thalia said, making her way to my side. "We should head back." Her usually stoic expression betrayed a hint of worry; I must have looked even rougher than I felt.

I nodded. Reluctantly. I knew I was fast approaching the current edge of my powers, but that didn't mean I was ready to quit.

"Ready to take us home?" Thalia pressed.

"Ready enough," I replied, swallowing down the lump that formed in my throat at the mention of *home*.

I still wasn't sure that was the right word for the palace we would be heading back to.

It was where I was born. Where I'd found my brother, after believing he was dead for well over twenty years. And yes, it had started to feel like I might be where I belonged…

But home was more than a place.

For me, home was a person.

And now that person was gone.

Still, Noctaris was waiting for me. Its people expected me. Needed me. So, rolling the tension from my shoulders, I focused on making my way back to them.

We returned to the point where we'd first entered Midna. The evidence of our arrival still shimmered in the air, spirals of violet-colored energy twisting around like a whirlpool ready to suck us back down to the Below. The energy was fainter now, moving more sluggishly. I wasn't sure how long it would ultimately last. We hadn't dared to stay longer than a few hours on any of our trips, and we were pushing the length of the longest visit, now.

Even so, I couldn't help looking toward what remained of the Aetherstone's chamber.

Thalia let out a disapproving sigh, knowing what I was going to do next, but she otherwise didn't object. She simply kept watch while I went perfectly still, willing my tired body to manage one last bit of magic.

With a deep breath of concentration, I severed a

piece of my soul from my body and shaped it into an apparition. It was an old trick that I'd been using for years, but it had grown stronger as my true self awakened over the past few months; this apparition was far more solid, aware, and capable than the spirits I used to summon.

I guided it across a partially-collapsed bridge and into what remained of the chamber holding the Vaeloran stone of legend—an artifact that had once been the most powerful conductor of magic in all the realms.

Through the safety of my shadow-self, I took in the sight of what the stone had now become: a blackened, cracked monolith, humming with faint energy. It was still alive, still pulsing with raw, obvious power…but *dimmed*. Like a dying star.

What would happen if it blinked out of existence entirely?

Nothing I'd tried thus far had brought more life back to it. Nothing increased the flow of its magic that I was trying to feed into the lifestream of Noctaris. No matter how my own powers—and my control over them—grew, I couldn't seem to gain any more sway over this most vital object.

I could only hope we'd find answers in the things we'd collected from the palace.

With this in mind, I snapped back into my body with a gasping breath, as if coming up for air after a deep dive.

Thalia was watching me expectantly. Most people were unnerved by this particular trick of mine. She wasn't one of them.

"Well?" she prompted.

"Some power is still flowing from it. I think it's getting weaker, though."

"At least it's not gone entirely dormant. That's something, isn't it?"

"It feels like nothing."

"After all the years I've spent in the Below, watching things barely cling to life, it feels like more than that to me." Thalia shrugged. "Don't underestimate what a drop of hope can do in an ocean of despair."

I only managed a nod.

It was true, what I'd said earlier—I had been exhaustively optimistic, once upon a time.

But it was getting harder and harder to see the silver linings around me.

"Maybe I should try pouring more magic into it again?" I suggested halfheartedly.

"Says the woman who currently looks like she's going to collapse right where she's standing." She poked me toward the swirling, fading portal. "Let's go. I'd rather *not* have to drag your lifeless corpse back to Rivenholt. Assuming I could even make it back with your dead self, I'd never hear the end of it from your brother."

I agreed, but not before casting one last forlorn look at the chamber.

Luckily, returning was always easier than leaving; it was simply a matter of closing my eyes and letting the magic inside of me reach for the energy of that world below us—the one I'd once thought of as *Hell*. Like called to like, so I didn't have to think about keeping my balance; I only had to allow my shadows to reach for the darkness concentrated in Noctaris's three kingdoms, in its soil, in its very air.

Feeling those energies rush over one another was like slowly stepping into the sea, letting the dark waters rise around me, drench me, then pull me down, down, down.

Once upon a time, I might have been afraid of drowning.

But no longer.

I couldn't afford to be afraid.

I held out my hand. Without hesitation, Thalia took it in a light grip, and I let my shadows wash over her as well. The portal rippled, dark and velvet smooth.

We sank through it together.

THREE

Nova

It was always haunting, coming back. Always a moment, between pressing through the portal and my feet hitting the ground, when I was like a hovering ghost, adrift and untethered to any solid realm.

Sometimes, I thought about how nice it would have been to just keep floating, ignoring all the weighty things trying to settle over me—a fleeting, blissful thought that shattered the instant Thalia and I touched down on dusty, black ground, steadying one another as our bodies regained their substance and burdens.

Phantom, in his typical black dog form, was waiting

for us exactly where we'd left him, loyally sitting atop a nearby hill next to a large tree with golden, glowing leaves.

As Thalia stepped away from me, busying herself with securing our haul from Midna, my gaze caught the glimmer of a knife in the ground beneath the golden tree. Its hilt was wrapped with bracelets featuring a multitude of beads and brightly-colored threads.

It had been a month since I'd stabbed that knife into the ground. A month without the bracelets that had once tempered my powers.

Those bindings had been a necessary evil when I lived in the Above, in the Light realm of Soltaris, hidden away with no understanding of my abilities' true depth and alignment. My former guardian and mentor, Orin—who was also Thalia's father, it turned out—had created them to help guide my magic, to keep it from overwhelming me until I was ready to embrace it.

The time for temperance, however, was well behind us.

Of course, putting those bracelets down had been easy enough… resisting the urge to pick them back up was the more difficult thing.

The temptation was there, but I didn't spare them more than a glance today, instead fixing my eyes on my beloved dog as he leapt to his feet.

(*You look terrible*), he informed me, his pointed ears twitching as his words entered my mind.

"That's rude."

He let out an unapologetic snort.

It was a relatively short walk back to the palace, but he still insisted on shifting into a larger, but still canine-like, form that could carry both Thalia and me with relative ease. I climbed onto his back without protest, happy for the chance to let him pay attention to the path while I let my mind drift to other things. Other problems.

I had no shortage of them, after all.

The world around me now was different than it had been when I first touched down in it months ago. No longer as dark and hopeless as the hell I'd once thought it to be. There were signs of life clawing its way back everywhere we looked—a glowing edge to most of the plants; the occasional chatter of birds; a sky that was easing toward the color of an old, healing bruise, and which sometimes shifted to reveal an almost proper-looking sun.

But life was a fragile thing.

What we'd managed to give back to this world—the magic we'd funneled toward it from the center power source in Midna—had not been enough to fully reverse the centuries' worth of decaying.

It had only given the struggling survivors of Noctaris a taste of what could be. What had once been.

Which honestly had caused more problems than it had solved so far.

Thalia was silent for most of the ride, focused on

keeping her balance while also keeping the overflowing bag properly secured across her body. Once we reached the main courtyard of Rivenholt Palace, she slid from Phantom's back first. I braced myself before jumping down after her. My head was pounding, my legs shakier than I'd anticipated; they nearly crumpled beneath me as I hit the ground.

Thalia shifted the bag over her shoulder, tapping her fingers against its strap. "You overdid it. You should have told me you were ready to come back sooner."

"I'm fine."

She *tsked*, but I waved off her concern, even as a rush of dizziness had me reaching for Phantom's shoulder to steady myself. My fingers clenched into his fur. He leaned closer, placing a paw on my boot, his weight a comforting anchor.

"Fool," Thalia muttered, with equal parts fondness and exasperation.

I started to protest, but my vision chose that moment to flicker, and my legs again threatened to give out. When I managed to blink back into awareness, Thalia was staring at me, her hand braced against my arm—a testament to how far our friendship had come; she didn't like touching anyone unless she had to.

Slowly, she pulled her fingers from my skin, though her eyes remained fiercely fixed on me.

"Just don't tell my brother," I mumbled.

"Don't tell me what?"

I twisted toward the sound of Bastian's voice as he appeared on the path just behind us.

Perfect.

The regent of the Rivenholt Kingdom looked tired and troubled—as though the meetings he'd been holding all morning, with various leaders of the surrounding territories, had not gone well.

I stood up straighter, suddenly hellbent on not betraying my own tiredness. Our realm faced so many problems; I was determined not to be another burden for my brother and our advisors to shoulder.

He gave me an appraising glance as he approached, just as he did every time we ran into each other now—checking to make certain I was still in one piece. He was always the first to notice any new bumps or bruises I'd sustained during my training sessions. The first to make sure I was eating enough, sleeping enough, *breathing* enough.

Sometimes, it felt like he was trying to make up for all the years we'd spent apart by cramming twenty-five years' worth of brotherly concern into every interaction.

"Don't tell me *what?*" he repeated, arching a brow.

"About all the books and artifacts we uncovered, but then had to leave behind, in the Palace of Midna," said Thalia. "You'd be devastated at the amount of knowledge rotting there. Though we brought back as much as we could carry, of course." She shoved the bag of our collected spoils into his arms.

The distraction worked; the concern in his grey eyes gave way to curiosity as he picked a book out, shouldered the bag, and then gently started to flip through crinkling pages.

"…In rough shape," he mumbled after a moment. "But there's still plenty of legible reading to make sense of, isn't there?" He seemed to be talking to himself—and he answered his own question, too. "I'll share these things with Eamon, and we'll see what we can extract from it all."

"So that's your afternoon sorted," Thalia said, pointedly. "We were on our way to go wash the dust of the middle realm off ourselves, anyhow." She poked me in the back, urging me to move before Bastian could protest.

We hurried toward the palace without looking back. We lost Phantom at the entrance, his attention caught by two squirrels who scampered across the front steps.

The rodents were a welcome sight—another sign of life returning. Little by little, creatures like these were being reintroduced into our world. They had likely come from the sanctuary in the center of the nearby city of Tarnath, where royal scholars had been raising and protecting all manner of flora and fauna during this realm's prolonged period of decay.

While the rest of Noctaris had withered into a wasteland of dust and drifting ghosts, Tarnath had been spared, protected by magic that radiated out from the palace.

Now, as other parts of Noctaris fought their way back to life, we were testing things, letting smaller creatures venture into wider perimeters to see how they fared.

These squirrels looked lively enough so far.

Hopefully, they would survive my overzealous dog, too.

Once inside, we didn't make it far before we spotted a familiar, careworn face—Aveline. Her pale hair was slicked back in a tight braid. Flour coated the bright blue, smocked dress she wore. She smelled of sugar and spice, which wasn't unusual for her; she'd likely been baking all day, making treats to coax our political visitors into calmer, more rational discussions. We certainly needed all the bribery and help we could get with that.

She swept a quick, concerned look over my disheveled appearance, just as Bastian had done.

"We've had a long day," Thalia informed her.

"I should say so," Aveline replied, propping a hand on her hip. "You look as though you were dragged from one end of that day to the next."

"I've looked worse," I pointed out.

She pursed her lips. "Nevertheless, you have several obligations to attend to this evening, and you can't very well walk into your meeting with so many important leaders while looking so...*unkempt.*"

I didn't ask how she knew who I was scheduled to meet with this evening; nothing happened in this palace without her being aware of it, even if it didn't truly involve her.

"Come with me," she ordered, beckoning and starting to walk without waiting for my reply or to see if I followed. "We'll get you cleaned up and revitalized. The pools are ready by now, I suspect."

I felt a bit like baggage being tossed from one handler to another. But my head was pounding too hard to argue, so I let Aveline lead the way toward the pools in question—warm, natural springs that flowed through several rooms carved out beneath the eastern wing of the palace. Another sign of life erupting back into Noctaris—quite literally, in this case. A week ago, the ground had rumbled, and then steaming mineral water had started to seep into the rocky, empty basins for the first time in ages.

Palace records suggested these natural baths had once been a favorite gathering place of royalty and visitors alike. Aveline had insisted on returning the space to its former glory—a plan I'd wholeheartedly endorsed.

She glanced my way several times as we walked. Her lectures weren't generally as stern as Bastian's or Thalia's, but I could tell she was biting her tongue as she looked me over, trying to keep herself from giving her opinion on my latest dangerous mission.

I kept my gaze forward. "I can tend to myself, you know. If you have other things to do."

"Never mind the other things I have to do. They can wait."

I breathed in deeply through my nose and exhaled slowly.

She stopped to gather towels and toiletries before steering me onward with a dogged determination. "That's the second time you've visited that dangerous middle realm this week, isn't it? I do think perhaps you could take a longer break before next time, if there's any chance—"

"I prefer to stay busy."

I didn't elaborate on *why*.

I didn't have to—she already knew.

She pursed her lips but remained silent.

It was the unspoken solution I'd settled on: If I filled my days with training sessions, missions to Midna, and more diplomatic meetings than I could count—all these grueling, mind-numbing, but necessary things—then I wouldn't have time to think about what I was missing.

Who I was missing.

We were passing the hall where Aleksander's bedroom had been.

For weeks, I'd looked the other way when I walked by his door. It had been a mistake, looking at it on the day after I'd lost him. A mistake I wouldn't repeat now, regardless of how weak and foolish it made me feel to not even be able to look at a fucking *door* without feeling as though a bottomless pit was ripping open inside of me.

Don't look.

Eyes ahead.

Keep walking.

I kept walking, following Aveline in a sort of trance, somehow ending up undressed and sinking into a pool of steaming water some time later.

While I piled my long, dark waves into a messy bun on top of my head, Aveline sectioned off part of the baths with the aid of folding privacy screens. She left and returned several times, carrying various scrubs and soothing oils; an assortment of fresh fruit served on a silver platter; and then, finally, one of my favorite dresses—a fitted gown of scarlet with golden accents, which always made me feel like a queen forged in flames.

Everything I needed was now here. I wouldn't have to return to my room before my meeting. I wouldn't have to walk past Aleksander's empty room again any time soon, and I wondered if Aveline had planned it that way on purpose.

Knowing her…yes.

She'd been looking out for me since the first moment I arrived in this palace, and that hadn't changed.

Warmed by the thought, I sank lower into the steaming water, trying to let it soothe away the weight of the day.

Phantom eventually trotted into the space. He didn't care for the hot water, but he was a fan of the warm stones edging the pools; he was curled up and asleep on them in no time at all. I watched his dark sides rising and falling in a steady rhythm, trying to match his calm breathing.

The heat was soothing at first, until it triggered a memory of warm light—of magic that had caressed and illuminated even the darkest parts of me.

My skin prickled.

My stomach tangled into knots.

He's not here, I reminded myself fiercely. *Your magic is the only thing you have. It has to be enough, for now.*

The problem was, no matter how hard I worked to stand on my own two feet, my power was intrinsically intertwined with his. Along with my heart.

In the quiet, lonely warmth of these pools, I felt his magic like a living memory inside of me. I saw his face when I blinked…an image that would have been a welcome sight, if not for the soft, echoing voice that often accompanied it. Not his voice, but the voice of the one who had stolen his body—Lorien.

And yet, there were also moments when I thought I could feel Aleksander's voice trying to break through. When I heard his words rising loudly, clearly over the beast that had come between us.

We are not a tragedy, he'd once told me.

I was clinging to those words with everything I had.

It was killing me, being unable to ignore all the other obligations I had to attend to—to not be able to drop everything and focus only on storming my way to wherever he was. On saving him.

But it had to be a calculated effort, I knew; we needed answers about what Lorien had truly done. What he was doing. What he was *capable* of doing.

And I had the rest of Noctaris to worry about, besides.

So for now, I would simply stay busy with what I could.

I would focus on attending to my endless meetings and other royal obligations. I wouldn't think of his closed door, or the empty room behind it, and I would ignore that infinite pit in my stomach that felt as if it might swallow me up if I dared to keep still for too long. Because this once-doomed world was now on the cusp of unfolding, poised to break or to bloom.

And it needed me more than I needed time to grieve.

FOUR

Nova

I stepped into the circular meeting chamber, my head held high, the train of my dress flaring out like ribbons of fire behind me.

Nine leaders had joined us for this particular gathering. They sat stiffly across from my brother, Thalia, and our most trusted advisors and guards, separated by a table piled high with food and drink that looked as though it hadn't been touched.

Our visitors represented varying levels of authority: lords and ladies; messengers and emissaries; even kings and queens in their own right. Most were descendants of rulers who had once controlled neighboring kingdoms. Large portions of those kingdoms were little more than wastelands now, yet the power these visitors exuded was palpable.

In the five hundred and something years that had passed since Noctaris had been cut off from the source of magic in Midna, various powerful bloodlines had been huddled away in what we called *sanctuary cities*. Protected within them, given the bulk of whatever extra magic the Rivenholt Palace and its capital city could spare—which wasn't much. It had been a desperate attempt to keep lineage and leadership intact; these chosen few were the only ones who had lived, aged, and reproduced relatively normally within their respective safe zones.

Their subjects within those so-called sanctuary cities had also been given magic to protect them from death, but only enough to allow them to continue existing in a kind of suspended state. *Wraiths*, some called them. Like ghosts, but slightly more solid and sentient. And they could all eventually be revived—we hoped—and returned to their disrupted lives.

The differences between the sanctuary cities barely clinging to existence and the palace we presently stood in were…stark.

Which was one reason for the tension hanging over the room like a storm cloud poised to break.

Unlike the world outside, we had never experienced any unnatural death or decay here, nor in the nearby capital city of Tarnath. Calista, the last Shadow Vaelora before I came along, had made certain of that, casting a spell of protection that had made this entire area a glittering island within a sea of ruin and misery.

I had often wondered how she'd chosen this spot. What set it apart? Why save the ones here, while so many outside of our protected circle suffered?

So many questions and so few answers.

Hopefully, the ones we'd gathered here would help us navigate a clearer path forward.

My appearance caused mixed reactions among them. Some looked upon me with shock—and maybe a touch of reverence—as though I was some manifestation of prophecy. Others watched with narrowed eyes, as if waiting for my mask to slip and reveal something dangerous. Something monstrous. Only one smiled a greeting at me—Lady Zara Virelle, whom I'd met a few times before. She was the sovereign of the sanctuary city known as Durnhelm, which was the capital of the once enormously wealthy Kingdom of Kaedren.

The dark-haired man next to her, who I didn't recognize, was the first to speak. "So, this is the Shadow Vaelora who failed to fully turn the stone's power in our favor."

"But who at least gave us a glimmer of hope," said Zara, and—to my relief—several of the ones seated around her motioned or murmured in agreement.

"Hope will not bring the dead back to life," the man said with a scowl.

"Maybe not hope alone, my Lord Renvar. But it plays a role."

I took my seat, maintaining my composure even though it felt like I was lowering myself into a pit filled with venomous snakes.

Renvar's gaze followed me as I moved, his dark-silver eyes calculating, as if trying to decide the sharpest words—the best weapon—to wield against me.

He started to speak, but stopped short as a man stepped from the shadows with commanding grace, his perfectly-polished armor flashing in the low light.

I relaxed the tiniest bit as my gaze fell over this man—Captain Darien Voss, leader of the most elite regiment of Rivenholt's army.

When Aleksander and I had first started to understand and test the limits of our combined powers, we'd managed to revive Voss, along with more of the undead soldiers who had been existing in stasis in the Rivenholt fortress known as Graykeep. Voss had soon after charged with us into the battle with Lorien in Midna, and he was also the one who had carried me away when that battle had descended into chaos, ensuring my safety that day—and every day since.

"Mind your tongue," the captain warned.

Renvar shrank slightly underneath his withering glare, but the man seated to my brother's right scoffed and said, "If she is truly one of the Vaelora, then why are we treating her so delicately?"

I tilted my head in the direction of the speaker, a

lean, hawk-nosed man with a voice like cold steel—measured, deliberate, meant to cut. This man, I knew. He was Marius Thentros, the King of Drynland, which bordered Rivenholt to the south. Very little of the magic that flowed out from our protected circle had reached his lands—lands that had apparently once been the cradle of most of the Noctarisan Empire's agriculture.

He had wisdom and connections that would be instrumental in the revival of our realm's food stores, and the trade centered around it, among other things. My brother had stressed this more than once; that was why he'd been invited to the palace, even though he was a known agitator.

I held in my retort as King Marius fixed his unimpressed gaze on me.

"*Mystralith*. World-shaper," he sneered. "That's the name my kingdom once called her kind. So let her take her supposedly powerful hands and keep shaping."

Eamon, who until this point had been watching the conversation unfold with his usual bright, intrigued awareness, sat up straighter and said, "Her progress with her magic over these past weeks has been impressive. She continues to expand and hone her abilities, as well as monitor the Aetherstone and all that surrounds it in Midna. Even if it takes more time to put a true guiding hand on all these things, she's already *shaped* more than enough to give us hope for the future."

"She could stand to do a lot more," Marius countered.

"She also stands alone," Eamon reminded him with a sharp smile, his bright tone unwavering.

"So did her counterpart, didn't he?"

This remark was met with a long silence. Even Eamon quieted, running a hand through his messy, reddish-blond hair, his eyes glazing over in thought.

"For over a century, Lorien Blackvale managed to keep the balance of magic and power shining brightly over Soltaris," Marius eventually went on. "He had no help in guiding the Aetherstone and its magic. Yet the Above has flourished from that magic while we've all wasted away here in the Below."

"Yes—if the Light Vaelora could do it, then why not our Shadow Vaelora?" Lord Renvar added. "It's past time for Soltaris to experience the same suffering we've endured."

My heart pounded as whispers of tentative agreement rippled through the room.

My brother shook his head. "If there's a chance for balance, then that is the better long-term—"

"Balance! *Bah*. Isn't it our turn to thrive?"

More chatter of agreement, growing bolder now.

Eamon cleared his throat. "The situation is not as black and white as some of you want to make it. The magic is changed. The Vaelora have changed. The chances of our realm returning to its former glory are slim. The better hope lies in dealing with Lorien and his corruption, and then forging something new within the rubble he's left in his wake. It's no longer a simple back and forth, an exchange of Light versus Dark."

"We brought you all here to discuss the path forward," Bastian added calmly. "A path toward stability. Rebirth. One that may mean circling inward, redefining our borders so we can more efficiently allocate resources and protect what remains."

Several people stiffened at that.

"Redefining borders," Lord Renvar said, drumming his fingertips against the shiny tabletop. "It sounds like you intend to sacrifice some things in order to shape *your* kingdom into something even more powerful than it already is."

My brother took a deep breath.

My temper was dangerously close to flaring. "No war has ever been won without sacrifice," I said, quietly but firmly.

A thick hedge of prickly silence wrapped around us.

My brother broke through it moments later. "...Whatever comes next—however it comes, and whenever it comes—we need to have things in place to endure it. Plans and agreements. Treaties. We need to be civilized about things."

Marius let out a bitter laugh. "Spoken like someone who has had the benefit of *civilized* living for his entire existence."

"And you speak as though we haven't had our own challenges to contend with," I snapped.

"You seem as though you're managing well enough." He gestured to the untouched dinner laid out on the table before us, fixing his dark eyes on me. "With your gilded halls and flowing wines and fancy dresses."

I clenched my fists, too annoyed to speak right away.

It was Thalia who answered him, her voice icy and calm. "The monsters she's faced would have utterly crushed lesser rulers." She looked him up and down, not bothering to hide her opinion of him as one of these *lesser rulers*. "So just be grateful you haven't had to face such things—that she's been facing them on your behalf, while wearing fancy dresses and all."

Several of the gathering snickered. Marius fumed. Bastian gave Thalia a slight frown, but she ignored him and kept her glare on Marius, daring him to reply.

"...I think that's enough for tonight," Bastian said, getting to his feet. "We have more to discuss, but some among us are still recovering from their travels into this kingdom. Rest is in order. Tomorrow, a small company and I ride for the camps on the outer edge of the revived circle, and we'll have clearer notes to share with you regarding how things are progressing."

With that, most of the gathering dispersed, save for King Marius, Lord Renvar, and a few of the louder naysayers. My brother lingered as well, speaking with this group, trying to further mitigate their grievances.

I started to turn around and go back to help, but

Thalia put her hand on my arm. "He's fine. He's very experienced at dealing with those assholes."

Eamon moved closer, blocking my view of the assholes in question.

"You should get some rest," he said, and Thalia added an encouraging nod toward my room as well. "We'll help keep things under control here, don't worry."

I wasted no time arguing. I *was* tired, and I still had one last duty to attend to before I could retire to my private chambers for the evening.

Bidding them goodnight, I steeled myself with a deep breath and turned left instead of right when I reached the top of the stairs outside the meeting chamber, making my way to a quiet, mostly empty hall of the palace.

Tucked away at the end of this hallway was the room where we were keeping yet another victim of Lorien Blackvale: Zayn Caldor. The cousin of Aleksander and—until a month ago—the host of Lorien himself.

Decades ago, that monstrous other half of the Vaelora tandem had possessed Zayn's body following a failed attempt to overtake Aleksander's. For nearly twenty years, he'd walked in Zayn's skin, lied with his voice, and poisoned every relationship and alliance Zayn might have had.

We'd managed to extract Lorien's essence, but he'd been in and out of consciousness ever since. Mostly out. The few times he'd woken up, he'd been entirely disoriented, unable to do more than choke down just enough substance to keep him clinging to life.

It had been several days since his last awakening.

It was impossible to say what was left of the real Zayn; what sort of rot or corruption Lorien had left in him. Not even Aveline had much hope or insight to offer, despite how gifted she was when it came to healing.

I greeted the maid at his bedside, pausing to swallow down the lump in my throat. "How is he today?"

She busied herself with changing pillowcases as she spoke. "Still very much the same, Highness—though he did seem to be trying to respond, earlier, when we were speaking to him. A weak attempt, but…"

I breathed in deep, trying to inhale the pinch of hope I thought I'd heard in her voice. "Keep trying."

She bowed her head.

My eyes shifted to Zayn once more. Fixed there. I couldn't look away. Couldn't stop thinking about how desperately I needed him to wake up so we could talk.

Like the ruined palace in Midna, I suspected he had answers buried inside of him. But much like that palace, he was broken and battered, in danger of collapsing and taking far too much of this world's complicated past with him.

"Thank you for taking care of him," I said quietly.

"Of course."

I turned to leave, but found myself lingering in the

doorway, watching him a minute more, hoping for a sign of life. A promise of return.

He remained perfectly still.

I made myself move, even though part of me wanted to linger.

And now came the hardest part of my day.

Always, always the hardest, even when my days were filled with a seemingly endless number of hard things.

My bedroom felt like a mausoleum. A tomb of velvet curtains, gilded walls, and perfumed linens. But I had to retire to it. Had to attempt rest despite the nightmares waiting for me, because tomorrow was another day full of tasks that needed doing, problems that needed solving, and I couldn't sleepwalk my way through it all.

After readying myself for bed, I went to the cabinet where I kept the wine, reaching for the largest bottle and uncorking it with slightly dazed, well-practiced motions.

A knock on the door made me jump, splashing some of the dark red liquid on my wrist.

"…Come in," I called, reluctantly.

I expected Aveline, or maybe one of her well-meaning minions. She was forever checking on me under the guise of needing to bring me clean linens or other small comforts; the stack of extra blankets and pillows in the corner of this room was nothing short of obscene at this point.

But it wasn't Aveline; it was my brother who pushed open the heavy door and stepped inside.

"Sorry to barge in so late."

I waved off the apology, focusing on pouring my glass of wine.

"There's been a slight change in tomorrow morning's plans," Bastian said. "King Marius insists on accompanying us during our trek to the edge camps."

I took a long drink.

"I thought you'd appreciate a warning."

Another long sip. Burning, bitter, comforting. Another sip, then another—until the cup was empty. I'd drained it alarmingly fast. A slight buzz was already humming at the edge of my thoughts, which was perhaps what made me bold enough to say, "Marius can bring his entire fucking army along with him tomorrow morning, I couldn't care less."

Bastian's eyes were troubled, but he acquiesced with a nod before letting his attention slide to the glass clutched in my hand, and then to the bottle on the side table, still open and waiting for me to pour myself more.

I made my way to that bottle and did precisely that.

"You're going to have a hell of a headache in the morning," my brother commented.

"I'll manage."

He didn't reply right away. A minute passed before he took a step closer and said, "Aveline tells me this is becoming a concerning ritual with you."

"It's hardly that concerning in the grand scheme of things."

"There must be something else you can use to help you get some rest."

"I've tried everything else."

He sighed. "You can't keep doing this to yourself."

I stiffened. "I wake up sober enough. And I haven't missed a beat outside of this room, have I? I've attended every meeting. Every training. Every diplomatic dance. What does it matter what I do behind my closed bedroom doors? I've played my role perfectly outside of them, despite what Lord Renvar and Marius and all the other naysayers think. So what does it matter?"

"It matters because I don't stop caring about you the moment you lock yourself away behind closed doors," Bastian said, his voice gentler now. "I don't care about you being perfect, either. Whether outside of this room or otherwise."

I made a face, lifting the glass to my lips, inhaling the wine's bittersweet aroma—but I stopped short of taking a sip as my eyes met Bastian's.

Cursing to myself, I clenched the glass tighter and walked to the window, staring out into the darkness.

"Don't be angry with me," Bastian said.

"I'm not angry."

"No?"

"No," I said, truthfully. "This sort of thing is just… strange."

"What do you mean?"

"Having so many people care about me. My life before, in the Above, it was just…different."

"You had Orin, didn't you? He cared."

"Orin." I scoffed. "Who mostly left me to my own devices, and who…"

Bastian said nothing, patiently waiting for me to find the words.

I exhaled slowly. "Who lied and withheld so much from me. And who abandoned Thalia—his own daughter—years ago. All of which makes me question every ounce of affection I ever felt from him."

"…He's a complicated man," Bastian admitted.

I snorted, looking back over my shoulder. "I don't want to talk about him."

"You don't have to, then."

Nodding, I took a sip. Habit, at this point.

It really was becoming a habit.

I heard Bastian circling the room behind me. Biting his tongue a little harder, I imagined, every time I started to lift the wine glass to my lips.

"Drinking is the only thing that keeps his voice from getting in," I said after draining the last of the soothing liquid. My words were quiet, tight from the effort of not breaking. "Lorien's, I mean. And…and sometimes Aleksander's, too."

I felt my brother's eyes shifting my direction. Restlessness overcame me. I made a few of my own laps around the room before finally settling onto the bed.

"I don't know if it's the innate bond the Vaelora

share, or something that happened during our battle… some spell residue, or something else…but I hear them more and more here lately. And it's always loudest at night, whenever I close my eyes to try and sleep." I swirled the glass, studying the few drops of red still in it. "The alcohol dulls my mind in a way that none of Aveline's sleep remedies have managed to do. It…it protects me."

Bastian started to reply only to fall silent. Letting out a soft sigh, he came to sit beside me on the bed, sinking heavily onto the edge of the mattress. He leaned forward, elbows resting on his knees. It was a long moment before he spoke.

"I wish I knew how to make all of it stop," he said.

Do I want it to stop?

The question startled me as it slid quietly into my mind.

It was torture, hearing Lorien's voice. And hearing Aleksander's—but not being able to answer him— wasn't much better.

But never hearing Aleksander's voice again would likely have destroyed me completely.

I never found the courage to say any of this out loud, but my brother was studying me as though he understood, all the same.

I stared at my hands in my lap. He put an arm around my shoulders, pulling me closer. His strength was comforting, as was his scent—like ink and old books, and something woodsy that reminded me of the little cedar chest I used to store treasures in as a child.

Something in his embrace undid me, bringing the words I'd been fighting all evening to the surface.

"I miss him," I choked out.

Bastian tightened his hold just slightly, grounding me with a simple, steady pressure. "I know," he said. "And I wish I knew how to make that hurt stop, too."

FIVE

Nova

I woke up slightly hungover, as Bastian had predicted, but my pounding head remained mercifully free of voices.

Someone had left a glass of water and a vial of pain-relieving elixir on my bedside table. I gulped both down and dressed just as quickly, refusing to linger long enough to let any stray voices find their way in—or to let myself think too hard about what I had to do today.

A short time later, I was at the stables, greeting Bastian and King Marius. Both were busy readying their scourge stallions—beasts specifically bred to withstand the harsh conditions of Noctaris and its shadows.

The stallions were like living embodiments of the darkness itself, the way their bodies rippled with power, occasionally sending twists of vaporous black energy into the air. Their eyes were like flames, burning unnervingly bright even in the relatively strong morning light.

Phantom had shifted into the shape of one of these imposing horses. But he still sat much like a dog, cocking his head as he watched me approach.

(*You're late*), he informed me.

"Then let's make up for lost time, shall we?" I said with a yawn, motioning for him to kneel so I could climb onto his back.

We rode for hours.

The distance our revitalized zone stretched across wasn't particularly wide, but there were lots of stops to make along the way to its edges—people to speak with, re-growth to observe, detailed notes to take. Bastian spoke calmly and deliberately with the stewards we'd assigned to each area, doling out measured encouragement and quiet, stoic direction in equal amounts.

King Marius observed from a distance, never dismounting, never speaking unless spoken to. I got the sense he was taking his own kind of notes—a judge witnessing evidence.

I had little hope that his ruling in this trial would be fair.

Finally, we reached the westernmost edge of our revived area. Here, the strained limits of the Aetherstone's life-giving magic quickly became apparent. There were patches of green, stunted and thin, and our people had started to rebuild simple irrigation lines and rough shelters, but the soil was still dry and crumbled between our fingers, and the air had a tightness to it—a tension that seemed to increase with every breath we took.

Beyond the edge, I could see the barren wasteland that made up much of Noctaris. I could see the ghosts within it, could hear their low, keening murmurs and smell the dust they stirred up as they drifted across the landscape. They watched from a safe distance, occasionally glancing into our sanctuary with dead eyes, and—I assumed—with no real awareness or interest in what they saw.

None of them tried to pass the threshold into the revived territory.

They didn't even come close to it.

We'd had more success gathering some of the wraiths from the sanctuary cities and bringing them into these healing zones—as many as we dared, while making certain not to exhaust the resources barely sustaining the fragile rebirth of Noctaris. Even that had proven a surprisingly delicate process, getting them to step into the light after they'd spent so long in the dark.

But these shades that haunted the emptiness had proven even more difficult to save. Most of the ones who had crossed the threshold were not ones that we'd managed to coax into salvation, but those who hadn't been given a choice one way or another; the power that surged from the Aetherstone a month ago had fallen over this area with little direction or restraint, thrusting all the shades it overtook violently back into life—or into the beginnings of life, at least.

The long-term effects of this violent reawakening remained to be seen.

Nevertheless, we carried on and hoped for the best. This western edge was where we'd decided to purposefully build out from. Over the past few weeks, we'd worked with revived beings and the soldiers we'd stationed here, laying the foundations of a proper base camp—a point from which all our future revival might expand.

But as I stood there watching the reborn shuffle through the half-built structures, toiling among the dirt, so many of them wearing oddly vacant and haunted expressions…

Well, I could almost understand the ones still in the dark and their reluctance to step across the threshold.

They might have been ghosts, but I imagined there was a certain blissfulness that came with that empty existence.

"I expected the perimeter to be wider," said King Marius, pulling his stallion up between my brother and me. "All the talk of revival and salvation was somewhat exaggerated, wasn't it?"

My brother didn't take the bait. All he said was, "It's

certainly a slow process, bringing an entire world back to life."

Marius snorted. "It's that word—*entire*—that concerns me."

Bastian ran a soothing hand along his stallion's neck as it stomped its hooves. "Why don't you tell me your exact concerns, Marius?"

Not for the first time, I admired my brother's patience.

"We're stretched too thin here, Bastian," growled Marius. "You must be able to see that." He gestured out at the expanse of grey beyond the revived zone before casting me a quick, disapproving look. "If our Shadow Vaelora here cannot expand this effort into something greater, there is no hope of rebuilding anything resembling a proper empire. *Circling inward,* as you suggested last night, will not be enough. I shudder to think about the sacrifices that will have to be made."

Despite the words, he didn't appear rattled by the idea of sacrifices at all.

"You shouldn't have told so many people of your plans, or invited them to have a say in this reawakening," he went on. "Now they've all descended upon your palace like hungry wolves, each with their hand out. And what will happen when you run out of magic to feed their ravenous appetites?"

"Should I have sent word only to you, then?" Bastian asked.

Marius smiled without warmth. "You could have

honored the long-held alliance between our courts. That would have been a start."

"Nearly everything else in this world is undergoing a process of death and rebirth," I interjected, unable to keep quiet any longer. "Why would you assume our old alliances wouldn't be subject to change as well?"

"I wouldn't expect *you* to understand the loyalties and alliances of this realm," he said, casting me another disdainful look. "As I understand it, you spent most of your life playing princess in the world Above while this one rotted."

"Yes." I gritted my teeth in a smile. "And now that princess is a queen, and if you want your *rotten* kingdom to stand any chance of revival, I'd choose your words and actions very carefully around me."

Marius laughed, bitter and brief. "A queen with no crown, ruling over a kingdom with more ghosts than people. You'll have to forgive me for not rushing to bow down before you."

"She is the destined Queen of Rivenholt whether you choose to kneel before her or not," Bastian said, somehow still maintaining his calm.

Marius laughed again. But then he seemed to be calculating his odds, his eyes darting between my brother and me. He kept silent, though the look he gave me was enough to make me want to reach for the dagger resting against my back.

Phantom bristled beneath me, his tolerance for this man clearly reaching its limit.

But I was slowly getting better at biting my tongue and choosing my battles, so I resisted the urge to grab my dagger. I merely tightened my grip on Phantom's mane and looked back to the distant shades—though I continued to watch Marius out of the corner of my eye.

"Tell me the truth of it, Regent," he said, turning his shrewd gaze back to my brother. "There is no *entire world* in your plans, is there? How small do you really intend to keep this oasis of rebirth? And with Rivenholt remaining in the middle, I presume. What a powerful centerpiece it will become, hm?"

"My plans are constantly evolving, as would the plans of any decent leader," Bastian said, his tone uncharacteristically cold.

The three of us stood, studying our surroundings, for several minutes more before the Drynland king said, "How *decent* the two of you are remains to be seen, I suppose."

With this, he pulled his horse in an about-face and trotted off to observe the rows of various, freshly-planted crops in the distance.

Phantom's voice was in my head a moment later. (*I should rip his chest open for speaking about you the way he did.*)

I exhaled slowly through my nose. "I'm not sure that would solve anything."

(*It would make* me *feel better. And that's what's important here, isn't it?*)

I gave him a weak smile and patted his neck. "Maybe next time."

Bastian moved closer to me. "An exhausting bastard, isn't he?"

"Yes. But maybe he has a point," I said quietly.

My brother lifted a brow.

"What if I *can't* draw more magic into this world by myself, no matter how many stupid practice sessions I suffer through with Eamon? The stone was barely pulsing when we checked on it yesterday. And nothing I've tried to do has reawakened it. The amount of magic trickling down into Noctaris is pitiful, really, and every trip we take to Midna feels more useless than the last."

He shook his head. "You brought back an incredible amount of information yesterday—knowledge we can use to plot out our next steps. That's plenty useful."

"Knowledge isn't going to keep war from breaking out if the other leaders of our world get impatient. Not to mention the threat of Lorien and whatever chaos he's planning from the Above. It feels like we're balancing on the edge of a cliff, doesn't it?"

Bastian ran another few soothing strokes over his scourge stallion's dark coat; the creature's eyes were wide, its ears and tail twitching. Restless and ready to bolt into the distant shadows and not look back.

I understood the sentiment.

"There are answers out there, whether in the middle realm or otherwise," Bastian insisted. "Paths to a more permanent, more complete solution. We just haven't found them yet."

I tried to believe him, ignoring the heaviness in my heart. "You've managed to decipher some of what we brought back?"

He nodded. "Eamon planned to leave our notes in your office for you to look over," he said. "He was working at a frenzied pace when I left him this morning; I don't think he slept. So, there will be lots of half-legible ramblings for you to look over, if nothing else."

I took a deep breath, looking one last time at the camp around us. It seemed so meager against the great expanse of darkness beyond.

The idea of locking myself in my office and searching for something—anything—to give us more hope suddenly seemed incredibly appealing.

"I've seen enough," I told Bastian. "Let's head back."

The palace was abuzz with movement when we returned—the patter of restless boots upon the marble floors; the voices of our visitors arguing in borrowed chambers; the guards and servants hurrying through the halls, trying to impose some kind of order over everything.

I ignored it all as I made my way toward my office

on the second floor, pausing only to duck into my room and grab the bundle of notes I'd left on my bed. Phantom stayed behind on that bed at my insistence; he was a distracting force whenever I brought him into my office, always bored and incessantly pacing or trying to get me to play fetch within the first hour I shut myself in.

I cloaked myself in shadows as I walked from my room to the office, letting darkness bleed from my skin in soft, subtle waves. The power worked twofold, both snuffing out any light I passed and helping me blend into the darkness that followed that extinguishing.

In this way, I slipped largely unnoticed into my refuge, closing the door behind me and leaning against it for a moment. The silence on the other side of the heavy door was like a welcome, long-awaited embrace.

I closed my eyes and took a few deep breaths—the deepest I'd managed all day. The scent of ink, old books, and candle wax washed over me, warming me from the inside out.

"I was beginning to think you'd never show up."

My eyes flashed open. I turned toward the voice and gasped, my notes slipping from my grasp and scattering across the floor.

Aleksander was waiting for me, leaning casually against my desk.

SIX

Nova

I tried to say his name.

Nothing but breath came out.

Once that breath escaped, I couldn't draw it back. My chest felt as if it were cracking in two, my lungs collapsing into the chasm between the halves, and…how could I breathe? How was I supposed to fucking *breathe*—

He was here.

Just… *here.*

As if he'd never left me at all.

A candle burned in a tarnished silver holder on the desk. In its soft, flickering light, he was every bit as beautiful as he was in every memory that had haunted me since we'd been separated. But there was something else in the glow—something that didn't belong. Something sinister in his eyes. Something menacing in his movements.

I blinked, willing myself to focus, to access my magical ability to see the energy that surrounded all things.

As expected, his aura was different from the one I'd memorized. Darker. A reminder that this man before me was not Aleks.

Not entirely.

He tilted his head, regarding me from under long lashes. When he spoke, his voice was all wrong, all Lorien Blackvale and nothing of Aleks.

"Hello, Chaos."

I inhaled sharply.

"I've missed you."

"No," I whispered. *No.* It was the only word I could think to say—a warning to myself. Aleks might have missed me, but *Lorien* had not. This was all a trick.

He pushed away from the desk and sauntered forward.

I swallowed hard. Held my ground. Managed a breath, and then a bit of movement, glancing to the door behind me.

My guards were not far beyond that door. They were never far from me, no matter how often I tried to dismiss them—Bastian had made certain of that.

Calling them would have been the smart thing to do. I was weaponless, exhausted, confused. Lorien had clearly been expecting me, hoping to get me alone. Probably watching me for some time before now…how else would he have known that I rarely allowed anyone else in this quiet sanctuary of mine?

I knew the kind of games Lorien liked to play.

I knew I was likely to lose if I didn't forfeit now.

So why wasn't I calling for help?

The man before me smirked as though reading my thoughts. "If you call for your guards, we won't be able to have the talk we need to have."

Aleksander's voice.

He'd spoken in Aleksander's voice, this time.

He closed the space between us.

Move, I ordered my trembling self. *Move!*

His hand fell over mine the instant I grabbed the doorknob. His fingers caged and squeezed, the strength of his grip so powerful I nearly cried out in pain.

I jerked away from his touch so hard I crashed into a small cart near the door, sending it toppling over. Piles of messages and other documents meant for me went flying in all directions.

Lorien smiled as I righted the cart and steadied myself against it. "What's wrong, Nova?"

"Stop using his voice, *thief.*"

He didn't stop. "Who says I'm a thief right now? Maybe this is him, desperately trying to talk to you once more."

"Be quiet!"

"I thought you'd be happy to hear his voice after all these weeks."

I sucked in a breath. In. Then out. I just had to keep breathing. Because of course I would have given anything to see him again, to hear him again—but not like this.

Not like this.

I scanned the room, noting everything I might be able to use as a weapon. There wasn't much. I considered shouting for the guards once more.

"You don't want to pretend?" he asked. "Not even for a moment?"

Fuck you. The words rose like a battle cry in my chest, but I couldn't seem to get them out.

"Well?"

"I don't want to pretend anything with you."

"Oh, but I think you *do*." His eyes flashed to an arresting shade of gold, like a sudden break of daylight amid clouds of smoke.

Aleksander's gold.

I couldn't help the small, distressed sound that escaped me as my chest tightened.

He chuckled. With a blink, his eyes shifted back to the burnt red shade I recognized as Lorien's, even as his voice continued to sound like Aleksander's. "Your emotions are painfully obvious, Nova. You should work on that. A queen who wears her heart on her sleeve is just asking for it to be broken."

I gripped the cart so tightly I began to lose the feeling in my fingers.

"It's interesting, being here like this." He knelt and casually began picking up some of the papers that had flown from the cart. "I wondered how Aleks would react to being in the same room with you again, and now I know; does it comfort you to know that his desire for you is still here, under the surface? It's nearly bleeding through, almost overcoming the enormous amount of *contempt* I feel for you." He placed the stack back on the cart, watching me in a way that felt entirely too familiar—the same tilt of his head, the same slight smile that accentuated his dimples.

I guess it shouldn't have been a surprise, how similar their movements were.

But it was still unsettling.

No...*terrifying*.

So terrifying, it rooted me in place for an instant. Ice filled my veins, and I could only shudder as he moved closer and brought his hand up to my cheek.

I wanted to disappear as he caressed my skin. To close my eyes and pretend that it really *was* Aleks standing before me, offering comfort. He'd been my refuge so often after my arrival in Rivenholt. A safe harbor amidst the stormy seas of dangerous politics and deadly enemies surrounding me.

I needed that now more than ever.

But I didn't let his touch become my anchor, no matter how badly I wanted that.

Instead, I forced myself, again, to perceive the magical energy surrounding his stolen body. To peer through the lies, and then to knock his hand aside.

"Why are you here, Lorien?" I demanded.

He ignored the question at first, studying the hand I'd swatted as if he was truly surprised I'd struck him. Then he stepped away, circling the dimly-lit room, occasionally picking up books and trinkets and studying them, too.

Finally, he shifted his voice back to his own true sound—low, silken, serpentine—and he asked, "Did you really think our dealings were finished?"

"No. But ambushing me doesn't seem like your style."

"Well, I tried to send a cordial message to arrange a meeting. Twice, in fact. But they didn't seem to reach you."

Confusion and doubt twisted through me.

"A certain overprotective brother intervening, perhaps?"

My skin flushed. My mouth went dry. I didn't want to believe he was telling the truth, but it sounded entirely too much like something Bastian would do in yet *another* misguided attempt to keep me safe.

Lorien let out a dark, quiet laugh, clearly believing he'd guessed right. "They underestimate you in this realm, don't they? So strange, how you are the only one who could really save them—yet they doubt and question you at every turn. The respect our kind once commanded has dropped very far indeed. What are we to do about that, I wonder?"

"There is no *we*," I hissed. "And what do you know about the respect I command in this realm?"

"Plenty." He came closer again, his full attention settling on me with an intensity that made the hairs on the back of my neck lift. "And I also know you've been visiting Midna these past weeks, desperately searching for answers about how to lead this poor, unfortunate realm forward." He circled me as he spoke, like a serpent trying to ensnare its prey.

I moved carefully, calmly out of his reach. "So what if I have?"

"Have you found anything interesting during your adventures?"

"Nothing I feel inclined to share with you."

"That's too bad." He continued his attempt to trap me, backing me toward my desk. I braced a hand against it, subtly noting how close my fingers were to the sharp letter opener in the center of the desk. I'd foolishly left my dagger in my room; the letter opener was a poor substitute, but I could make do with it in a pinch.

If only the thought of actually piercing Aleksander's body with it didn't make me want to vomit.

Lorien licked his lips, as if tasting the fear rolling off me. Savoring it. "There's so much we could accomplish together, you know. It would be easier than fighting me."

"I've no interest in being *together* with you, in any sense of the word."

"Unfortunately, I still need you either way."

"That *is* unfortunate. Mostly for you."

"Mm…but luckily I have a bargaining chip, don't I?"

My heart slammed against my ribcage. I tried to speak in the same cool, collected tone he seemed to have mastered, but I'm not sure I managed it. "I don't understand. Why do you need *me*?" The words of King Marius slithered through my mind—

For over a century, Lorien Blackvale managed to keep the balance of magic and power shining brightly over Soltaris. He had no help…

"You have Aleks, and his body and magic," I said. "You have the magic you stole from me. You should be stronger than ever."

For a brief moment, something like…*uncertainty* crossed his face. Or maybe it was regret?

But no—neither made sense.

Monsters weren't capable of feeling either of those things.

"The answer to that question is difficult," he said. "And delicate. A conversation meant for elsewhere; this room really doesn't provide the stage I was hoping for. Which is why I wrote and tried to arrange another meeting place."

I inched my hand closer to the letter opener, but I still didn't grab it.

Part of me knew better than to play his games, yes.

But the other part was desperate to know what he was planning.

Quietly, I asked, "What were in the messages you allegedly sent?"

"Invitations."

"To *where?*"

"The central throne room in the Palace of Midna. Meet me there tomorrow night, why don't you? Come alone."

"*Alone?*" I bit back a harsh laugh. "Why? So you can finish killing me?"

His smile sent a fresh shiver down my spine. "If only it were that simple."

My fingers wrapped around the letter opener's handle. I heard voices outside—the changing of my guards was underway, and they were swapping notes and orders. There would be no less than eight of them out there right now. Enough to overwhelm Lorien, maybe.

Or maybe not.

"Do I have your word?" he asked. "Or do I have to make him suffer a little more, until you're willing to submit?" His voice was softer toward the end, almost to himself—or to Aleks, perhaps. "Make your choice, Nova."

It was clear from his tone that he didn't believe there *was* a choice. He thought he had me cornered, that I would simply cower and let him have his way.

"GUARDS!" The word tore like a sob from my

throat, and the pounding of boots echoed through the hallway an instant later.

Lorien shook his head. "Your stubbornness is tiresome."

He struck with no more warning than this, grabbing for my throat.

He *missed*.

I barely moved, yet his hand struck the wall just to my left. A strangled sound, something between a hiss of pain and a cry of confusion, ripped through the air as he jerked his hand away, flexing his fingers.

I looked up and saw that his eyes had changed again —back to a bright, burning gold. The color stayed longer this time. Not a flash of battered daylight, but a rising sun, determined to chase away the dark.

"…Aleks?"

His gaze took mine.

Time seemed to collapse into nothing.

Later, perhaps I would realize that only seconds had actually passed, but in that moment, we felt infinite as I stared at him, as I stumbled forward, reaching over and over until my swiping, desperate fingers finally managed to close around his wrist.

He pulled away.

I heard my voice as if I was far in the distance, only able to hear an echo of myself crying out— "No! WAIT!"

Light bled from Aleksander's body, cocooning him. Fiery, hellish light. The floor trembled. The walls rattled. A painting fell, its gilded frame and glass face shattering as it landed.

The creature before me lifted his head, glaring at me. There was no trace of Aleks in his eyes any longer.

"I'll be waiting," he said. "You know where."

Then he was gone, the broken painting the only evidence he'd been there at all.

Everything was blurry. My vision. My thoughts. Nothing felt real. I dropped to my knees and felt my way through the pieces of shattered glass, picking one of them up, trying to convince myself of its solidness. I clenched it tightly in one hand. With the other, I traced the scars that ran along the right side of my throat, following the branches of raised skin with unsteady fingers—another grounding exercise.

A memory flashed in my mind, brutally clear: The moment I'd gotten these scars, when I'd first realized the truth about Lorien and confronted him. He'd stolen so much from me that day. I'd felt so empty. So lost. So…*broken.*

But it was nothing compared to how I felt in this moment.

I had a strange desire to rip the scars open. To feel warm blood running over my skin, to see bright, puddling proof that *I* was alive among the wreckage, if nothing else.

And this was how my guards—followed swiftly by Thalia and Phantom—found me: With a blade of broken glass pressed to my neck.

Gasping, Thalia raced forward and knocked the sharpness away from my pounding pulse. "What the hell are you doing?"

I still clenched the shard in my fist; feeling it bite into the skin of my palm woke me up enough that I managed to flick my eyes toward hers.

I'm fine, I tried to tell her.

The lie wouldn't leave my lips.

"Nova?"

I rose to my feet, and my voice was surprisingly steady, even though it felt like every other part of me was crumbling, as I said, "He was here."

SEVEN

Nova

"This is unacceptable," my brother said, turning to my guards after I finished recounting Lorien's visit. "*Completely* unacceptable." His voice boomed through the small space of my office. I'd never seen him so furious; the guards looked as though they were fighting the urge to run.

It took a moment, but one of them finally found the courage to step forward and reply. "We're spread thin, Highness. Between the visitors you've asked us to monitor, and the soldiers we've sent to aid with the rebirth projects, our numbers—"

"Do you know what the word *priority* means?"

"*Bastian.*" My tone was sharp. "It's over. I'm fine. And I asked my guards not to suffocate me—it's my fault, really. They merely followed my orders to keep their distance."

He continued to fume, his gaze shifting between the guard and a pair of marks that Lorien's magic had burned into the floor.

"You know Lorien has ways of eluding his enemies," Eamon said, abandoning his own examination of those marks before stepping back to us. "Tricks that no one, our seasoned guards or otherwise, could be expected to anticipate."

Bastian's gaze turned only slightly less livid as he fixed it on the guard lingering by the door. "Go find Captain Voss and tell him to meet me in the stateroom at the top of the hour," he ordered. "We have much to discuss."

He bowed and hurried away.

Bastian ordered the rest of the guards into the hall outside. He paused at the door after directing them, clearly trying to collect himself. His voice was somewhat closer to his usual practiced calm as he turned back to us and said, "I don't understand how he slipped past *everyone.*"

"The same way he escaped right in front of my eyes," I said, absently scratching Phantom between his ears. "The Vaelora were once able to come and go as they pleased between the realms, weren't they?"

"She's right," said Eamon. "And he's stronger now

that he's reunited with whatever magic was contained within Aleksander's body. Not to mention what he stole from Nova, and what he might have taken from his interactions with the Aetherstone." He hesitated before adding, "There's also the connection Nova and Aleks developed. As often as their powers worked together, and as close as they were to one another…"

I averted my eyes, hating the way he spoke of us in past tense.

"What of it?" my brother pressed.

"…Their magic was so intimately intertwined that it's not all that surprising Lorien was able to find his way back to her. I imagine it was simply like returning to himself."

Thalia let out a curse. "We should have anticipated him being able to do this."

There was a long, weighted pause, where we all seemed to be trying to steady ourselves against all the wars approaching from every direction.

How could we possibly guard from every angle?

"This connection between us…" I trailed off, taking several deep breaths before continuing. "Is that why I keep hearing Lorien's voice in my head when I'm alone? Why I sometimes see his face whenever I close my eyes?"

"Likely so," Eamon said.

Another line between my nightmares and reality, blurred.

Eamon appeared to be searching for an optimistic

light to shine on the situation; it took a long moment before he settled on one. "I don't think you're *constantly* connected, though, as the Vaelora of old might have been. Lorien is a corrupted entity, after all. And you came into your powers much later than normal. So he may be able to exploit the link, but the bond between the two of you is not absolute, I'd say."

"I don't like him having *any* sort of bond with her," Thalia said.

"What about Aleks?" Eamon asked. "You hear him sometimes, too, don't you?"

I nodded numbly.

"Well, that may be the very thing that's keeping him from fully succumbing to Lorien's hold. Perhaps he can hear you through the bond as clearly as Lorien can. And as long as he acts as a sort of wedge between you and Lorien…"

My heart unclenched a bit at the thought.

"I'm not convinced a connection to Aleksander is any safer than one to Lorien," my brother said.

The back of my neck burned, but I kept my voice cordial, busying myself with cleaning up the broken painting as I spoke. "You trusted him, once. You told our allies as much. Don't you remember what you said all those weeks ago? *He has sworn his allegiance to Nova. That's good enough for me.*"

"Of course I remember."

"And do you remember how he fought for this realm?"

"A lot has changed since then."

"Not to me." He was still Aleks, regardless of what Lorien did to him.

Bastian let out a soft sigh. He said nothing else, however, seemingly content to drop the matter.

But I was tired of wasting time tiptoeing around difficult conversations, so I looked him directly in the eyes and said, "Lorien told me he tried to reach me before tonight. His messages were interrupted, apparently."

Bastian didn't deny it, which only made my temper flare hotter.

"So it's true. You were keeping this from me."

"I was dealing with it in a calm, rational manner," he replied. "Looking into the origins of the notes, making sure they were legitimate, that sort of thing. I was going to tell you about them soon enough."

"*When?*"

"When I thought it was safe to do so."

"Will you *please* let go of this foolish idea of keeping me safe?" I seethed.

He set his jaw.

I glared.

Thalia settled into the chair at my desk. Phantom followed her, placing his head in her lap and demanding pets, while his bright blue eyes remained sharply fixed on me.

Eamon—predictably—ignored our sibling spat and continued his speculating and examining, returning to the marks Lorien's magic had left behind. Running his fingers over the shimmering indentations, he said, "This three-way connection is interesting, to say the least. What I still can't figure out, though, is how Aleksander keeps managing to break through Lorien's hold on him."

"Is he breaking through, or is Lorien *releasing* him just long enough to further torment Nova?" Thalia muttered.

"Another fair question," Eamon admitted. "Though he also did it as a child—ousting him more or less completely back then. And this was before Nova came along."

I went back to cleaning up the painting, an abstract masterpiece that had been hanging in my bedroom originally. Aleks had always liked it; he said it reminded him of the courtyard where we'd first met as children, and I agreed—the swirls of yellow and white made me think of the flowers that had once grown in that yard.

I lifted it up, shaking away the bits of broken glass clinging to its face. The art itself was undamaged. Still bright, still beautiful, even as everything around it had shattered.

"There's clearly more to Aleks that we don't understand," Eamon said.

My brother opened his mouth, as if to agree, but hesitated when I shot him a withering look.

Luckily—or unluckily, maybe—we were interrupted

before our argument could go any further; a servant stumbled into the room, looking flustered.

"I'm sorry for intruding," he said, breathlessly.

Bastian waved the apology off. "What is it?"

"The Elarithian lord is awake." The servant darted a harried glance my way before lowering his eyes to the floor. "He asked to speak with Lady Nova, alone."

My breath momentarily seized.

I could feel the immediate objections building among my companions. But I was tired of people making decisions on my behalf, trying to keep me safe in a world that was decidedly *not safe* for anyone. So I quickly but carefully placed the painting on my desk and said, "If that was his request, then I will speak with him alone."

ONLY ONE NURSE STOOD AT ZAYN'S BEDSIDE WHEN I entered his room. There were two others skirting around the edges of the chamber, occasionally whispering to one another while casting wary looks in the direction of the bed. Afraid of whatever could happen next, I guessed—that there might be some lingering trick Lorien had left in his former host.

I was wary, too, but I didn't let it show.

With my head held high, I crossed the room, fixing

my gaze on Zayn. I had to fight the urge to recoil as I approached and fully took in the sight of him.

Or what was left of him, rather.

He'd always been lost among piles of bandages and blankets during my former visits, the low lighting hiding the worst of his condition. But now he was sitting up, his gaunt face fully on display. The curtains over the nearby window were drawn back, the late afternoon sun shining brightly over his emaciated body.

Gone was the handsome, always laughing young man I'd come to know. There were tired lines around his eyes, his mouth. His skin was pale. His muscular frame was alarmingly thin, distorting the tattoos that covered his arms. Among those inked designs, I found myself searching for a circle with a crescent curving away from either side of it—the mark of the Light Vaelora.

I was relieved to see that mark had disappeared along with Lorien's claim on Zayn's body. I used my magic to briefly study the energy his body gave off, too, making certain it wasn't Lorien's.

Nothing was visible, at least. But I would have been a fool to think Lorien hadn't left any lingering effects on his former vessel—even if I could no longer see them—so I still approached with caution.

Zayn's warm brown eyes were unfocused, staring in the direction of the nurse who had moved to the foot of his bed, yet clearly past her, even though nothing was beyond her except a blank wall.

I swallowed away the lump in my throat. "Zayn Caldor, Lord of the North Reaches."

His eyes continued to stare at nothing, but his mouth curved in a way that made him look a bit more like the man I remembered. "So formal," he chuckled, "even after all we've been through."

I pulled a chair up to his bedside, forcing myself to sit calmly in it despite the anxiety raging through my insides. "…Do you actually *remember* what we've been through?"

"You might have to fill me in on the finer details." He still didn't look at me as he spoke. "And feel free to skip over the more gruesome parts."

"That would leave little story to tell."

"Yes." He stretched, wincing as he did. "I was afraid of that."

The sound of a metal cup hitting the ground startled me; the nurse at the end of the bed picked it up only to nearly drop it again.

"Leave us," I commanded.

She looked only too happy to do so, curtsying before joining the two maids now hovering by the door. Those two grabbed for her as if snatching her from the depths of hell itself. With one last distressed look in our direction, they hurried away, the sound of their whispering voices echoing long after they were out of sight.

"Skittish things, aren't they?" Zayn commented.

"In their defense, they've just witnessed a man essentially come back from the dead. A man who was recently possessed by a horrible demon, at that."

"And yet, *you* don't seem fazed by it."

I shrugged. "I've never feared death. It comes more naturally to me than life."

"That much I do seem to recall."

"What *else* do you recall, though?"

He was silent for a long time.

"Zayn?"

He sat up more fully, wincing again even with his slow, gentle movements. But whatever pain he was in, he pushed through it, remaining upright. "I do have one very clear memory. One that's played over and over while I've tried to sleep."

I waited patiently, despite wanting to grab him and shake him until all the answers I was desperate for fell out.

"A vision..." he began slowly, squinting in thought, "of a crumbling palace. And a bridge leading away from it. Swords...two swords in a door. That's all clear enough, but then it gets very loud, very chaotic, and there's pain. You're there, sometimes. A shadow in the corner of my vision. Aleks, too—a brighter force directly in front of me. Then I see a knife plunging into his chest, and he disappears. I never get a clear image of it, but several times I've woken up with a strange weight in my hands, as though I was the one holding the blade."

I clenched the cushion beneath me, steadying myself.

"Maybe just a nightmare, though," he said, almost hopefully.

"No." I swallowed hard. "That is… What you've described is what happened in Midna, in a way. You didn't stab anyone, though. It wasn't really a knife, and it wasn't your fault. But Aleks…"

He tilted his face toward me.

I couldn't bring myself to finish my sentence.

He closed his eyes. A heavy moment passed. Then he said, "He's gone."

Not a question—a pained acknowledgment.

"He's still alive," I whispered. "But he's…"

"Taken?"

I bowed my head, hiding my face until I managed to blink the tears away. "We thought we had Lorien contained within Luminor, after driving him out of you. But the blade shattered. Shards of it nearly impaled me, and if Aleks hadn't stepped between us…"

Zayn exhaled a long, shaky breath. "That *does* sound like something that idiot would do."

I almost laughed despite the bitter weight in my chest—mostly out of relief, because the words were so typical of something I would have expected from the Zayn I'd gotten to know. The one I still wanted to believe I *knew*. Maybe some of our conversations, some of our interactions, had somehow been genuine and untainted by Lorien's hold.

But how to tell the difference?

How could we possibly know what of our relation-ship was real and worth keeping?

As if he could tell my thoughts had crashed in, circling around Lorien, Zayn suddenly asked, "He was here, wasn't he?"

An explanation struck me. "Did you sense him? Is that why you woke up?"

He angled his face toward the window. "I felt… something. An itch beneath my skin. An ache in my bones, like from something broken long ago. And…yes. I think that's why I woke up."

"Your connection to him could be the key to getting Aleks back—and to countless other things." I tried to sound calm. Regal. A queen interrogating a witness for answers, rather than a confused little girl trying to make sense of her trauma. "I need you to tell me every-thing you know about Lorien's true nature."

He averted his eyes again, a sudden darkness falling over his face.

"Zayn. *Please.*"

He shook his head. "Trying to slip back into his mind…it's like sinking willingly back down into the water after only just managing not to drown in it."

"I know it can't be easy. *None* of this is easy. But I—"

"You should leave." It sounded like a plea. One so tired and so heartbreakingly desperate I couldn't make myself argue with it.

Slowly, I stood up. The room seemed to expand, the

door sliding away from me. *Everything* I needed to reach felt so damn far away from me. I didn't want to leave, yet I was afraid if I pushed Zayn too hard, I might lose him entirely—again.

I would send more nurses to tend to him, now that he was awake. His strength would return, and then we would be able to talk more. I had to believe that.

I *would* believe that.

I was halfway to the door when I heard: "I'm sorry."

I stopped short of asking *for what?*

There were so many things we *both* could have been sorry for. None of them were truly his fault. Maybe I should have told him that, but I couldn't seem to speak.

The apology hovered shakily between us.

I nearly kept walking away—until I finally managed to clear my throat, and a question slipped out. "Can I ask you something?"

No reply.

"About Aleks, not Lorien."

He turned his face toward me.

The image of Aleksander's eyes meeting mine in that brief, desperate moment in my office spurred me onward. I closed the space between Zayn and me before I even realized what I was doing.

He didn't look away, so I kept talking. "I just need to know that he's still whole, somewhere within that monster's hold. I...I need to know that he can come back to me."

Zayn closed his eyes for such a long moment, I

thought he might be going back to sleep. But then he opened them and said, "I don't know how whole I am now. I don't know what I'm returning to, really. But I haven't forgotten everything from when my body was not entirely my own. And we were the same cousins we'd always been, as far as Aleks knew. He told me things he wouldn't have told Lorien, obviously—maybe things he didn't have a chance to tell you, even. And…"

I was holding my breath, I realized.

I loosed it, gripping the bedpost as I started to feel lightheaded. "…And?"

"And I know that he'll fight to get back to you, no matter what it takes."

THE KNIFE WAS THE LAST THING I HAD TO PACK.

It was Aleksander's—a beautiful white blade with sapphires inlaid in its handle—and one of several things he'd left behind in his room on the last fateful day we'd had together. I hadn't disturbed much in that room since that day. Partly because I could barely bring myself to go inside it, but also because I wanted him to return and find it all waiting for him exactly as he'd left it.

Maybe it was foolish to think I could bring him back as if nothing had happened.

But I was still going to try.

"Are we preparing for something I should know about?" came Thalia's sudden voice, making me jump.

I quickly tucked the knife into the inner pocket of my satchel and turned to face her.

Thalia looked between the bag and me, her lips pursing. "I get the feeling I've stumbled upon a secret."

"You startled me, is all. You didn't knock."

"The door was open."

"...I must have been too distracted to close it," I said, more to myself than her.

"You're planning something," she accused.

"So? I'm the *destined Queen of Rivenholt*. My days are filled with making plans."

"Yes, but you have that look in your eyes that tells me this *isn't* a plan you've cleared with your advisors. Or with anyone who cares about you."

"It's very sweet that you're finally admitting you care about me."

She scowled.

I moved on to adjusting the baldric strapped across my chest.

"This has to do with Lorien, I assume?"

Rather than answering her, I took Grimnor from where it lay in its ceremonial casing on my dresser, and I situated it at my hip.

The legendary Sword of Shadow hummed as it settled against me, the subtle pulse of its magic falling into rhythm with my heartbeat. Faint shadows skipped across my skin as if excited by the sword's presence. I briefly took hold of Grimnor's handle, guiding those swirls of darkness into its blade, letting them become one with each other.

I hadn't wielded this sword since the battle at Midna, save for a few brief practice sessions. I hoped I wouldn't need to wield it tonight.

I would be prepared, either way.

Thalia stared at it, her expression tight. "Explain yourself."

As often as she'd stood by my side here lately, I owed her as much, I decided.

With a sigh, I took the knife I'd just hidden from my bag and fixed it into a sheath at my thigh. As I did, I also revealed the only part I'd left out when recounting the visit Lorien had paid me yesterday. The last words he'd spoken, inviting me—no, *commanding me*—to meet him in the throne room at the Palace of Midna. To come alone.

Unsurprisingly, Thalia didn't agree with this plan.

"You can't do this alone, Nova. It's foolish to even think of it."

I closed my bag—filled with survival basics I might need in the unpredictable realm of Midna—and I slung it onto my back.

My mind was already made up.

"I'm afraid of what he'll do if I don't listen to his instructions," I said.

"And you'll let that fear control you?"

"It isn't just *fear* that's driving me. If our roles were reversed, I know Aleks would walk into any hell he had to in order to save me, even if he had to do it alone."

"That's not the point," she said fiercely. "He wouldn't want you to risk yourself, either."

Then he shouldn't have made me fall so hopelessly in love with him.

I shuffled the weight of my supplies and weapons, trying to find balance. "He would understand."

She shook her head.

"And this is bigger than just the two of us and my desperate need to get him back," I pressed. "You heard what Eamon said—something strange is at work between the three of us. Our power, our bonds, the broken cycle of magic…the more I think about it, the more I fear it's all related. We can't save Noctaris without fully dealing with Lorien. Which just so happens to mean saving Aleks, too."

The scowl she'd worn since we started our conversation only deepened.

"You know I'm right."

"I know you're annoyingly hardheaded when you've made up your mind about something."

"Some people would consider that a virtuous trait in a person."

"I'm not *some people*," she mumbled.

I gave her an apologetic smile. "I have to go."

"You won't get me to agree with you on this."

"I didn't expect to. I just wanted you to know I was leaving. In case…"

"There is no *in case*," she hissed. "You'll come back in one piece, if you know what's good for you."

"Your threats are oddly comforting."

"I'm serious."

"I know. I'll be back—I promise." My voice cracked slightly on the word *promise,* and her face softened, just a bit. We both knew there was no certainty when it came to Midna or Lorien. Even worse when a plan involved *both*.

Nevertheless, Thalia slowly lifted her hand and tapped it twice over her heart, a gesture we'd come up with some time ago. A way of showing affection—a promise—without touching one another.

My hand rose and mirrored the motion without hesitation.

"You better be quick," she said. "I'll be waiting."

EIGHT

Aleksander

I didn't want to see her.

It wasn't safe.

I wasn't safe.

I shouldn't have been here, waiting for her like this. Baiting her. But the alternative…

You know the alternative, came Lorien's reply, his voice a soft hiss in the back of my mind.

I sank down on one of the thrones and tried to calm my pounding heart, focusing instead on studying my surroundings.

The ruins of the Palace of Midna looked oddly

impressive in the setting sunlight. Interestingly, this middle kingdom cycled normally through cycles of day and night, despite the chaotic energy dominating the air here. The throne room I waited in seemed to have been positioned to embrace the fall of twilight, its arched windows catching the last golden rays and casting long shadows across the cracked marble floor. Tapestries of old battles and forgotten lineages looked less dusty in the fading light, their colors briefly revived by the sun's parting glow. Part of the ceiling had caved in, but it had fallen in a way that framed the fiery orange and indigo-swirled sky like a painting.

One could almost forget this place was a crumbling echo of something far grander—at least until the wind slipped through its broken bones, howling in a way that was unmistakably empty and eerie.

My gaze slid to what remained of the doorway. After weeks spent without Nova, it was impossible to keep my eyes off it, knowing she would be walking into this room at any moment.

I knew why Lorien wanted her to see me. I was a tool he was using to bend her to his will, to his plans— plans I still couldn't clearly grasp, despite the disgusting way we were twisted together.

I wasn't sure which would be worse: Greeting her myself, or letting Lorien greet her. It was torture, either way.

She was in danger, either way.

She knew all of this too, surely. Not that it would

stop her. For as much as she'd changed over the past months, some things remained constant: She was still my fearless, stubborn, chaotic little beast.

So, here we were.

Restlessness overcame me. I got to my feet and paced the room, kicking aside piles of dust and the tattered remains of rugs and fallen banners as I went.

My mind was the clearest it had been in weeks. My step was light, my movements smooth—because they were entirely my own. Lorien had sworn to stay dormant so long as I stuck to the script. Thus far, he'd mostly kept his word—slithering back into the recesses of my mind, a heavy, but silent, coiled presence tucked just beneath my thoughts.

It was tempting to believe I could make him stay there.

But how did you escape an enemy who had its claws in your very existence?

I couldn't even focus on the question long enough to truly contemplate it; he would have known I was plotting.

After memorizing nearly every crack in the walls, every dip in the floor, and every cobweb spun between broken pillars, I sank back into the musty cushions of one of the thrones once more. I thought of heavy crowns and heavier choices, of the ones who had once ruled from these thrones— supposedly under the guidance of the gods themselves.

Midna was a place of desperate beginnings and violent endings.

I wondered which one we were on the brink of now.

Whatever was to become of us, the instant Nova entered this forsaken realm, I was aware of her. Her magic—her very essence—washed over me like a tide returning to a familiar shore; steady, relentless, ready to pull me under.

Desperately, I again tried to warn her through the mental bond we seemed to have developed over the past weeks. I didn't understand how it worked, I only knew that I'd heard her voice, sometimes—even in my darkest, most fractured moments—and I hoped with everything in me that she could hear me, too.

Stay away. Please, gods, just stay away. I don't want to see you. Not here, not like this.

I didn't.

I *swear* I didn't.

But then I caught sight of her stepping through the splintered arch of the ruined doorway. Her silhouette was sharp against the last flickering threads of daylight, her body haloed in gold and dust.

The way she carried herself—head high, shoulders tense—stole the breath from my lungs.

And I forgot, for a moment, that I didn't want to see her.

I was on my feet.

I was across the room, reaching for her like the

weak fool I was, my hand taking hers, pulling her close. She went stiff in my hold, hope and fear clashing in her gaze as she studied me. Faint shadows swirled on her skin as her eyes took on a darker shade of turquoise.

Magic.

Of course—she was using her magic to try and reveal the truth of me.

I felt in control of myself in that moment, yet I was still afraid of what she might see. Afraid I was more gone than even I realized, that she wouldn't be able to find me among the shifting, treacherous layers of Lorien's power.

Who am I, if even she *can't recognize me?*

The seconds ticked by like a blade swinging back and forth above our heads, getting closer and closer to cutting.

Then, finally, she lifted her hand to my cheek and whispered, "It's you."

My mouth tipped automatically toward hers, but I somehow held myself back, my lips not quite brushing hers as I said, "You shouldn't have come here."

"I know."

"I didn't *want* you to come here."

"I don't care."

"It isn't safe."

Her gaze narrowed defiantly. "As though that could have kept me from you."

I kissed her. It was fucking *stupid,* but I kissed her

hard enough to make all the warnings pounding through my head go silent. Deeply enough and fiercely enough that all I heard was the sound of her breath catching, her heartbeat quickening.

Her tongue met mine in a wild, heated dance. My hands tangled in her hair. Her fingers dug into my back, clutching tightly, pulling me closer. As our bodies pressed together, something dangerous and determined unfurled in my chest—something that belonged to the two of us and no one else.

Something Lorien couldn't take.

I felt his looming presence like a knife at my back, threatening to sink in. Before it could, I took Nova's face in my hands, pulling back just far enough to whisper, "Listen to me, Chaos."

Her eyes went wide at my tone, the fear from before resurfacing. It killed me to see it. To know I was the one causing it. But I forced myself to keep talking:

"Whatever deal he tries to make with you, don't do it. Not for me. Don't let him use you against me. That's all he's trying to do. You understand?"

"Aleks—"

"Swear it to me."

Her mouth opened but nothing came out.

"Swear you understand."

She tried to shake her head, but I only held her more tightly, my gaze desperately fixed on her face, like it was my last glimpse of shoreline before the waves carried me under.

Then I was drowning in a furious rush of *power*.

Like a hand wrapping swiftly around my throat, Lorien's control surfaced, choking the breath from my lungs. *Our* lungs. His lungs.

The words I'd planned to say next died in mid-air—

I love you.

Over and over, I thought the words but couldn't speak them.

Nova stumbled backward, realizing what was happening.

"Such an uncooperative host." Lorien's words slithered from my mouth, low and poisonous. "It's getting exhausting, really."

Nova took another step back before abruptly halting, forcing herself to stand her ground, her back straightening, her chin lifting. "You bastard." Her hand went to the hilt of Grimnor, her grip trembling but sure. "You monster. You thief. You…you… *curse.*"

Lorien smiled, his gaze sweeping over her sword. "If I am a curse, then it's only because your predecessor made me this way."

"Blaming someone else for your crimes," Nova snarled, withdrawing Grimnor and holding it threateningly between us. "How predictable."

"Yet painfully accurate." The words hung in the air, inviting questions—another trap laid. "The part about her cursing me, that is."

After a long pause, she asked, "What do you mean?"

"Isn't it obvious?"

"No. Could you speak plainly for *once* in your miserable existence?"

He bared his teeth in a smile. "As you wish," he said, walking to what remained of a window that looked eastward, out over the bridge that connected this throne room to the Aetherstone's chambers.

Nova kept her distance, but I could feel her watching us, Grimnor's power pulsing eagerly in her grip.

"I thought this particular curse would end after I managed to access the legendary chamber," Lorien said, nodding toward what we could see of that battered place. "That's where I assumed she'd buried things. So, you can imagine my disappointment when I didn't find what I was looking for, even after you opened the last of the chamber's sealed compartments."

"What are you talking about? You were looking for nothing except power and control within that chamber."

"Wouldn't *that* be the easier narrative? The simpler one, most certainly. Light versus dark. Life versus death. The heroine overcoming the villain." He chuckled darkly. "But no—unfortunately, I was looking for more than that. I was looking for *myself*."

"…Yourself?"

"A seemingly impossible thing to find, after what *she* did."

Another long silence stretched between us, until

Nova said, "*What* she *did*…you're talking about Calista, aren't you?"

His anger rose in waves at the mention of the former Shadow Vaelora. The feeling was so intense, it swallowed up all other sensation for a harrowing moment, eating away at the line I'd been trying to keep drawn between us.

The waves calmed quickly, though his fury continued to smolder just below the surface as he quietly said, "I would have moved on from this world long ago, had Calista not been such a sadistic, vengeful bitch. Every bit of instability this world and its magic have faced is because of *her*."

"You lie," Nova snapped.

"I don't. Myself, there's nothing I love more than a painful truth. But do you know who *does* lie? Everyone in that infernal palace of yours. Your brother. Your advisors. The ones who want to keep you *safe*, even if it means keeping you in the dark about some of the more unsavory parts of our world's collective histories."

Nova averted her eyes.

"…But your magic won't lie, will it?" Lorien closed the space between them, taking hold of her chin and forcing her gaze to his.

She winced at his grip, and I wanted to break my own fingers to make him let go.

"You've gotten very talented at divining the past from things, haven't you?" Lorien murmured. "Talented enough to make an entire room reveal its secrets to you, I'd say."

A muscle twitched in Nova's jaw.

Don't listen to him, I thought.

She blinked, looking confused for an instant—as if she'd heard my voice, somehow.

Before I could try to reach her again, Lorien asked, "Do you know why I asked you to come to Midna?"

"Because you're a coward who was too afraid to face me in my own kingdom, I assumed."

He laughed, the sound low and dark. "Not quite."

She scoffed, but curiosity shimmered in her gaze. "Why, then?"

"Because this is where it happened." He let her go, freeing his hand to gesture toward a pair of doors in the back of the room. "Just beyond the throne room, there."

"Where *what* happened?"

"Why don't you come and see?" He moved toward those doors, not waiting to see whether or not she would follow his invitation.

Again, I wished she wouldn't.

Again, it did no good.

She followed at a distance, Grimnor still tightly clasped in her hand.

Lorien paused at the threshold, waiting for her to join him. We stood before a medium-sized room with glass walls covered in dust and grime. It was bright despite the layers of filth, the orange glow of the passing day forcing warmth over tattered chairs, broken vases, and worn wooden floors…though not enough warmth to chase away the distinct feeling of melancholy hanging over the space.

I felt Lorien tense with anticipation as Nova moved closer—the excitement of a predator whose prey was coming within pouncing distance.

"We're stronger together," he said, glancing her way. "Which means I can magnify your powers, and you could do the same with mine. If you wanted to see anything and everything this room remembers, I could help you. There's nothing we couldn't unravel together. Unless, of course, you're afraid of the truth you might reveal."

I sensed Nova's magic shifting with those last words —the shadows beneath her skin lifting in indignant protest, ready to prove they were not afraid.

She knelt and ran her fingertips over the warped floorboards.

After a brief bit of concentration, she quietly said, "Something cataclysmic happened here. There was blood. Pain." She inhaled sharply, as if personally feeling a stab of that pain. "Anger. Despair."

It wasn't really a question, but Lorien nodded anyway. The rage that had overtaken him at the mention of Calista was back, only this time he made more of an effort to rein it in. It settled around us like a heavy, itchy cloak.

That heaviness sank in deeper and deeper, until it was difficult to tell who it belonged to—myself or him.

The legends that surrounded Lorien and Calista, the stories that haunted all our histories...I'm not sure I would have been able to resist the urge to see it for myself, either.

So I already knew what Nova would say next.

As did Lorien, a smile curving his lips, even before she said, "Show me where to look."

Nova

I stood, and then Lorien touched a hand to the small of my back, guiding me toward the center of the room while pointing to a symbol embedded in the floor.

I'd seen this symbol in a few other places throughout Midna—one of a circle divided diagonally by a vine-wrapped sword. The circle was usually in alternating colors of light and dark; this particular one was stamped in gold and silver—gold throughout the top half, silver in the bottom. The sword, and the vine and the leaves along it, alternated in color as well.

Despite the way it all gleamed, it was nearly lost underneath the dust.

I knelt cautiously, pressing a hand to it.

A tingling sensation crept up my arm. I blinked, and the room seemed to break apart and scatter around me. It happened slowly, then all at once—like standing at the edge of a cliff as it crumbled, piece by piece, before finally collapsing completely.

I fell.

I tumbled down, weightless, only to land again in the same room we'd just been standing in. Except now, it was whole, untouched, shimmering with brilliance. As my boots hit the polished wood floor, my eyes began to water and burn.

Another hard blink, and I was fully submerged in a vision of the past—actually *living* it in a way I'd never experienced with any of my other visions. I recognized things I shouldn't have. Knew details I'd never been told.

Lorien's power and memories were merging with mine. And though I didn't want this bond, I couldn't deny that I wanted to see where it took me.

So I stepped fully into it.

This place we stood in was an opulent sunroom, a favorite dwelling place of Queen Octavia, the last sovereign of Midna. Its glass walls featured a dazzling array of stained designs, each one casting new patterns of color with every shift of daylight. Warmth permeated the space, which smelled of honeysuckle and sage.

It was a space reserved for the most honored of guests; few had been allowed to bask in its beauty.

On this day, however, that beauty was marred by blood.

A trail of scarlet wound its way over the wooden floorboards, its terminus the center of the room, where it pooled over the emblem inlaid in the wood.

Lorien stood at the end of this trail, surrounded by bluish-white light, his shoulder bleeding profusely. He was in his own, original body. Proud shoulders and a powerful stance despite the obvious blood loss. Dark brown hair that curled damply against his temple, pressed to his beige skin by a combination of sweat and blood. More blood was speckled across his cold but handsome face. Luminor floated at his side, tethered to his being by a tendril of light that pulsed erratically.

Calista stepped from the shadows, her raven hair shining in the sun. Her voice was soft. "You've made your decision, it seems."

Lorien turned, startled. His expression flickered between several emotions—anger, uncertainty, guilt— before softening into something bordering on affection.

"Was there ever a doubt?" he asked. "Ever a real decision to make?"

"Maybe not for you."

Lorien shook his head. "Not only me. I made these choices for *us*."

Calista fell silent. She kept perfectly still as Lorien

stepped closer to her, though the green of her eyes seemed to deepen as she drank him in, hardening into emeralds darkened by rising Shadow magic.

"I've seen the threads of our future," Lorien said. "I've seen what we become—together. The Order vanquished. The Below lifted into light. You love me, and all that we could be…" He stepped past her, moving to the glass wall and peering outside, dripping blood as he went.

"I did love you," Calista whispered, watching him go. "But your visions are not absolute."

Lorien didn't seem to hear her, too lost in his own plans to listen. "The realms will be remade," he continued, gesturing to the world beyond the glass. "You and I reshape it all. Can't you see it?"

Calista lifted her right hand. Dark sigils ignited along her palm and spiraled into the air.

Too late, Lorien looked at her.

Truly, fully looked at her.

"What are you doing—"

"What I must." The words came heavy and thick, wrapped in sorrow but forged in steel. She took a step forward.

Her shadows surged with her.

Light exploded through the room. Not the warm gold of day, but the desperate, harsh brilliance of Lorien's power. He cried out as the shadows met it, as the two powers collided in a violent display of blinding brightness and cold, desolate darkness. The glass walls rattled. The wooden floors splintered and popped. The air hissed.

The tumbling powers dropped abruptly away, revealing Calista and the dark symbols that had now spread beyond her palm, twisting all along both arms and creeping up her neck.

She still didn't raise her voice. "Lorien Blackvale."

"Don't do this."

Her face remained unchanged. Resolved. Her hands clasped together over her chest, and she spoke her next spell into existence as if reciting a lesson, tight and without feeling:

> *"I unmake your Light*
> *and all you covet,*
> *Your only hope now bound*
> *to Shadow's forfeit*
> *Mind carved into one realm,*
> *Heart into the next,*
> *Body to drift where gods forget..."*

There were more words spoken, but they were lost within the sound of warring magic.

Lorien's light flared again, a final push, trying to drive Calista back. Her shadows pressed relentlessly through. Over and over, their divine magic collided, until she finally forced him to his knees.

His breath shuddered, his light dimming to a singular fragment in the center of his chest. He clutched that fragment so tightly its light was nearly lost within his fist. "You think this will end me?"

Silent tears slipped down Calista's cheeks. "No."

The fragment slipped through his fingers, hovering between them for a breath.

"But that is not my intention."

The light splintered and shot up like three arrows through the circular skylight in the middle of the ceiling, shattering it.

As glass showered the vision, I flinched, jerking back to the present with a gasp. The first place I looked was to the ceiling, noting the glinting, jagged teeth in the center—all that remained of the once impressive skylight.

Shattered so long ago, but the evidence still remained.

What other lingering effects of that day still haunted this world?

I knew the stories of Lorien and Calista's doomed love. Of how she'd chosen the human king, Argoth, over him. And then Lorien had supposedly murdered her in a fit of jealous rage, and he'd spent the following centuries making certain Noctaris paid for her choices —that no Shadow Vaelora would easily rise up and take her place.

Everyone in the Rivenholt Palace and the royal city knew these stories; they'd been reciting them to me ever since I'd crash-landed among them months ago.

None of them had mentioned the scene I'd just

witnessed. They didn't speak of curses, or of Lorien being struck down while bleeding from…what?

What exactly had happened that day?

My head was swimming. No part of me wanted to see Lorien as a victim of any kind, yet I heard myself ask, "Why did she do it?"

Lorien hesitated.

"She must have had a reason."

"…I wanted to change the way our kind were treated. She—or that foolish human king she loved, rather—didn't agree with my plans."

"Which were…?"

"Unimportant."

They seemed important to *me*, but I had far too many other questions to let the conversation stall there. I looked to the center of the room—to the circular symbol in the floor—and asked, "When she spoke of scattering your flame…that fragment I watched split into three, was that your…your…"

Soul.

The word was right on the tip of my tongue, but that was where it stayed. Maybe I didn't want to acknowledge the possibility that he even *had* a soul— much less one that Calista had so viciously ripped away from him.

He folded his arms across his chest, tapping his fingers against his bicep. "It's why I've been unable to move on, even after all this time. Why I've been forced to crawl from body to body, like some fucking parasite, rather than the divine creature I was meant to be."

"Why didn't she just kill you?"

"I assume because she was afraid it would violently disrupt the magic of Soltaris, and then her beloved King Argoth might have suffered the consequences. So I was made to suffer instead."

I shifted uncomfortably under the weight of his words, trying to settle on the meaning behind them.

I'd never considered his immortality might be a *curse*.

"Of course, it ultimately disrupted the flow of magic anyway, didn't it?" Lorien looked to the broken skylight, his eyes glazing over. "The balance was forever altered that day…likely in ways she didn't intend."

I thought of my current struggle to bring life back to Noctaris. A chilling possibility struck me: Was this another reason why the Aetherstone would not release more magic, no matter what I did? Why everything felt so…*messy?*

She had cursed him.

He had killed her.

Even though I was stepping more and more fully into my power, the Vaeloran Cycle still felt damaged in ways I couldn't understand, and I was afraid I was only beginning to grasp how ruined our world and its magic *truly* were.

I gave my head a little shake, trying to rid it of a

creeping sense of despair. There had to be some way to salvage things. Some spot of hope, however tiny.

Hope.

"She mentioned a hope *bound to Shadow's forfeit*," I said. "What did she mean by that?"

Lorien tilted his face toward me expectantly, as if waiting for me to answer my own question.

Realization slowly dawned. "Shadow…*magic?* Like mine? That's the only thing that could restore what she took from you?"

He looked back to the sky. "Of course, you pale in comparison to Calista. But one assumes even a weak little Shadow such as yourself could manage to figure out *something*."

"Insulting the one being who could help you?" I said, dryly. "That's a bold strategy."

He continued as if I hadn't spoken. "I thought it would be enough to steal your sword, and then to open all the sealed compartments within the Aetherstone's chamber. I *thought* the pieces that witch ripped away from me would all have gathered there over time, drawn in by the magic resting in that space. I'd seen signs pointing to this, I believed. But…"

"You were mistaken."

"So it would seem."

Of all the things I could have felt in that moment, what overcame me was a strange, tingling sense of… *power.*

He couldn't even find his scattered pieces without my help.

But what was I supposed to do with this power?

I circled the room, thinking. Plotting. Glancing back at him, I said, "And you summoned me here because you actually think I'll help you after all you've done?"

"What happens if you *won't* help, I wonder?" Lorien smiled. "Tell me: How are things in Noctaris now that you're embracing all of your Vaeloran power? How many times have you been to the Aetherstone's chamber, trying to squeeze more magic into your dead world?"

I had a sick feeling he already knew the answer to that question.

"It won't yield to you alone, will it?" he asked.

"I'll find a way to make it."

"And if you don't?"

I glared at him.

"If you'll recall, I've wanted to work together from the beginning." He moved closer, but paused once he stood over the symbol in the middle of the floor. "It seems powers greater than us both want the same thing," he said, using his boot to brush aside some of the dust covering that symbol. Frowning down at it, he said, "We can keep up this violent dance between us, leaving everything beneath us unstable. *Or* we could finally work together and…who knows?"

"*Together.*" I clenched Grimnor more tightly. "As though I would ever trust you."

"You shouldn't trust me." The words were easy and smooth—an unsettling contradiction to the predatory sharpness that gleamed in the gaze he fixed on me. "But you must realize the more immediate consequences of *not* doing what I ask."

I had so many more questions.

So many more doubts.

But then his eyes flashed briefly to Aleksander's gold, and all my words died in my throat.

"I will destroy him," he said, his voice still chillingly smooth and casual. "And when I am finished with him, there will be other hosts to carry on with—and as long as *I* am forced to suffer, I will make sure your precious realm of Noctaris continues to suffer, too. I don't need my true body and my full power to do that. You've probably realized by now that I'm perfectly capable of destroying things with others' hands."

"And what if Soltaris suffers as well?" I asked, fighting to keep my voice steady. "If the instability between us continues to grow?"

"Then so be it."

"An entire world held hostage for your sake? Really?"

"I think very highly of my own existence."

"Monster."

He chuckled darkly. "*Survivor. Monster.* The line between the two often blurs, I've found."

I couldn't find the words to dispute this, so I stayed silent.

"Well? Do we have an understanding?"

No, I thought, dully. *This is foolish.*

But instead of telling him to fuck off, as I knew I should, I heard myself say: "I have a demand of my own, first."

He regarded me curiously for a moment before answering. "Of course."

I didn't hesitate. "Give him back to me."

"I will, once—"

"No. Not eventually. *Now.*"

"And if I don't?"

"Then we go back to dancing that violent dance between us."

"Even if it means the entire world suffers?"

"Even then."

His brows lifted. "You would risk the whole world for him?"

"I think very highly of his existence."

His smile was almost...proud. "You drive a hard bargain, Little Shadow."

I bristled at the nickname but kept my head held high, refusing to show anything but determination in that moment.

He rolled the tension from his shoulders and said, "We have a deal, then. Of course, the world will need proof of our agreement."

"...Proof?"

"Give me your hand."

Hesitantly, I offered it.

His smile turned sly. His eyes met mine, and a hundred lifetimes seemed to flash within their dark crimson depths. I saw—no, *experienced*—centuries' worth of powerful, painful emotions in the span of only breaths.

When he finally let go, I watched, dizzily, as the mark of the Light Vaelora appeared on my wrist: The two crescents, each curving away from either side of a centered sun...except all of it was faint and shimmering, like a scar that had been there for years.

Above the symbol, a darker, x-shaped sigil pulsed faintly.

The heat radiating from the *x* and shooting up my arm was immense, but I forgot it an instant later as I watched Aleksander's body go alarmingly still. His head bowed. Light bled from every inch of him, outlining his frame with searing brilliance. The air all around us turned strangely heavy with magic, blurring all but his figure; it was like watching the sun trying to fight its way through a thick fog.

That light eventually shuddered and collapsed to a single point in front of Aleksander's chest, hovering there for a moment...

And then it dove straight into Grimnor, colliding with it so violently that I nearly dropped the sword.

The blade flashed, briefly covered with blinding bolts of bluish-white, before settling back to its usual velvety black shade. I stared at it, breathless. The faintest whisper had hissed from the metal as the light diminished, so quiet and distant that I wanted to believe I'd imagined it.

Yet, somehow, I knew I hadn't.

Had Lorien…*bound* himself to my sword?

Would he be able to shatter it, as he'd done to Luminor all those weeks ago?

I quickly sheathed Grimnor so I could catch Aleks as he stumbled forward. The weight of both of them settled against me, and with them came the heavy realization of what I'd just done. The risk I'd just taken.

A thousand questions about what came next exploded in my mind, but I couldn't focus on any of them.

Aleks was finally back in my arms, so I thought of nothing else in that moment beyond my shadows, wrapping them carefully around us both, and willing them to take us home.

TEN

Nova

"Your brother will not be pleased," Eamon said, frowning as he lifted my wrist again, turning it over and inspecting the mark Lorien had left behind.

"The understatement of a lifetime." I fixed my gaze, not on the mark, but on my bed, where Aleks was resting peacefully.

I still couldn't believe I'd managed to bring him back.

It had been a minor ordeal, slipping him quietly into the palace in the dead of night—one that had involved a grumpy Phantom and an incredulous Thalia. They'd helped me carry him and distract the servants and guards we encountered, but we'd still attracted too much attention. Whispers about what I'd done were already flying, most likely; I was surprised Bastian wasn't already knocking on my door, demanding answers.

Eamon, meanwhile, had been minding his own business, still awake and busy translating Midnasian texts—as he so often was here lately—when I'd stumbled past his room supporting a half-conscious Aleks on my shoulder. He'd followed us like a curious puppy who'd caught an interesting scent, and now he wouldn't leave my side.

Not that I was complaining. Because if anybody could help me puzzle through the strange things Lorien had said and done, it would be Eamon.

He followed my gaze, frowning in Aleksander's direction. "And I have to say, this seems a bit reckless, even for you."

"Did you really *have* to say that?"

His frown deepened as he returned his attention to the mark on my wrist. He spent a long moment tracing it, during which I grew more and more tense. I was desperate for him to give me more details, more lectures—anything. His silence was disconcerting; he *always* had something to say when it came to magic.

"Well?" I pressed, nervously. "What do you make of it?"

"I…don't know." The words sounded strange, coming from him. "This is beyond my knowledge, Nova. Likely beyond *anyone's* knowledge. This isn't typical Vaeloran magic; we're way past that. And if the curse Lorien spoke of is real, if Calista laid her own corrupted magic over him, then the powers we're dealing with are…" He trailed off, shaking his head.

He wasn't even *attempting* optimism, for once.

Another knot joined the impressive collection I already had in my stomach.

"…He didn't just speak of it, Eamon," I said, fighting to keep my voice steady. "I saw the very moment Calista struck him with it. And my visions have usually been trustworthy in the past."

His attention shifted from my wrist to my sword, which I'd propped next to the window. He moved toward it. Meanwhile, I could barely stand to look in its direction; it had felt unbalanced ever since Lorien had seemingly bound his life force to it. I was just waiting for him to shatter it—like he'd done to its counterpart, Luminor—or to do something even worse.

Picking it up, Eamon carefully unsheathed and studied the blade. Normally, its dark steel only pulsed with twists of smoky-white energy. But now there were jagged lines of light blue occasionally disrupting it. It was like watching two storms battling for dominance over the midnight sky.

Quietly, I asked, "Do you think it's ruined?"

"…Both sides of Vaeloran magic are rooted in the

same power, so it's certainly not a given that they'll destroy one another. In fact, given enough time to properly combine, it could potentially make Grimnor *stronger.*"

My chest tightened at the thought of gaining strength from the likes of Lorien.

"There are even some legends that say Grimnor and Luminor were once a singular blade," Eamon added. "Verinor, the True Blade, which was broken. None of the stories can agree on *how*, but they all say that pieces of it were used to forge the two separate weapons."

"I can't imagine he intended to help forge Grimnor into something stronger. There's a catch, I'm sure."

"Well, the catch is that he needs you to go on this little restoration quest for him, right?"

I think I was still in denial about that part, so I said nothing.

"It seems like a desperate move, binding himself to Grimnor. To you. And to even reveal this curse, this weakness..." Eamon paused, considering. "I can't think of a reason he would do that, unless he truly did believe you were his only hope."

I walked over and took the sword from him, sliding it back into its casing. Gripping the red gemstones on its hilt caused a crooked bolt of cobalt to crackle around the blade. I did my best to ignore the ensuing tingle of warm energy that trailed up my arm.

It felt...*wrong.*

Looking out the window, I quickly found a distraction: The sky was lightening in the distance, and not merely because of the approaching dawn.

It was because of magic.

Magic that was coming from the Above.

From Midna.

Standing in the palace, I couldn't see the distant land beneath the lighter sky, but I suspected—hoped—that the increased magic was having a positive, rejuvenating effect on Noctaris. Though my body desperately needed sleep, I was already planning to go inspect it for myself as soon as possible. Maybe there would be enough new life to silence my doubters for a while.

Plus, my brother couldn't be furious with my risky decisions if they'd led to more rebirth, right?

Never mind *how* they'd led to it.

Eamon was staring at the distant, potential sign of hope, too. "Whatever comes next," he said after a minute, "it seems the flow of energy is reacting to the closer alignment of you two. So that's a gift, at least."

A gift.

I wanted to believe that.

But it felt more like Lorien was taunting me, dangling a sign of what could be, if only I managed to hold up my end of our bargain.

Aleks stirred, suddenly. He rolled over with a cough, his hand feeling for the glass of water beside the bed. He managed to take a sip and to clear his throat. My name tumbled from his lips a moment later.

My heart leapt at the sound.

Eamon glanced back and forth between us. "I'll leave you two alone, shall I?"

"…Yes. Thank you."

He gave a small bow before slipping out of the room. As soon as he was gone, the space seemed to shrink, some unseen force pinching in and pushing me toward the bed.

I was afraid, bracing myself for whatever lingering effects Lorien had left, but I made myself keep moving.

As I settled onto the edge of the mattress, Aleks slowly blinked his eyes open. Then tightly closed them. Again and again, he did this, until he finally seemed to accept that he was truly seeing me.

"I'm in your room," he mumbled. "In the Rivenholt Palace."

"Yes."

"How long have I been…"

"Not long. A couple of hours."

"No. I mean…how long…how long did he…"

"Oh." My mouth felt incredibly dry, all of a sudden. "Four weeks, give or take."

His brow creased as he shut his eyes tighter, as though trying to squeeze the memory of those weeks from his mind.

I was tempted to do the same.

Words slurring a bit, he asked, "How did you drive him out?"

I couldn't bring myself to answer.

"Nova." He clenched a fistful of the bedding, as though bracing himself. "What did you do?"

I gave him a tired smile. "Something chaotic, of course."

It took a long moment, but he finally returned my smile with a weak, crooked little one of his own.

Gods, I'd missed that smile.

It was gone quickly, replaced by a serious expression that made my heart sink in my chest. His eyes fluttered open only to fix on the ceiling, cold and calculating.

That look reminded me of the Aleks I'd first met in this realm. Back when we were both desperate, angry, and confused, with far more questions than answers about our future. It was hard not to feel like we were back there, standing at the beginning with nothing except darkness ahead and curses looming above.

"How do you feel?" I asked.

He didn't reply.

Maybe it was a stupid question. The answer was obvious enough to guess: *Like shit.* But I struggled to think of anything else to ask, anything comforting to say.

I slipped a hand under the covers, finding his and weaving our fingers together.

"I feel…hollow," he finally replied, his gaze flicking briefly toward me. "Like he's gone, but he took pieces of me with him. Pieces I should have been able to hold on to."

I inwardly recoiled at the thought. Outwardly, I remained calm, intertwining my fingers more completely with his. That didn't feel like enough, though, so I crawled into the bed beside him and pressed my body into his, as though I could anchor us both, somehow.

Not long after, he fell back into a fitful sleep.

I lay awake, knowing it was only a matter of time before I had to leave the relative safety of this space. Before everyone in this palace would be waking up with all of their questions and expectations for me.

My fingers absently brushed through the messy, pale waves of Aleksander's hair. I would have sworn I could hear his thoughts when I touched him like this, as if the Vaeloran bond that had heightened when Lorien took over still remained.

Like my own, his head seemed to be filled with a tumbling mass of questions with no clear beginning or ending.

He never managed to fall into a true, deep slumber.

Eventually, he gave up, dragging himself upright and leaning against the headboard instead. He pulled me to his chest. It was bare, and slightly damp with sweat—he'd been feverish ever since we returned to Noctaris—but I didn't care that his skin was almost unbearably hot to the touch.

I would have stayed against him even if it burned me alive.

Still, I couldn't make myself relax as I so often had in his embrace. In hot, uncertain silence, we watched the sunrise painting the walls in deep shades of crimson and gold, until I finally gained the courage to ask, "Do you remember anything that happened in Midna?"

He shifted, bracing himself more completely against the headboard. His arms tightened around me, his heat searing into my back.

I expected him to say *no*, but then he quietly recited, *"Mind carved into one realm, heart into the next, body to drift where gods forget..."*

He must have felt the shiver that went through me, because his hold grew even tighter, as though he could protect me from whatever came next.

"There's more, I know." His lips rested against my hair, his words vibrating over my ear, causing an altogether different kind of shiver. "I can't make sense of it all," he said, "but those words have been haunting him for a very long time. And the desperation that overtook him whenever he thought of them…"

"I know. I saw the memory playing out, the moment Calista laid that curse over him, his desperation, and… well, it almost made me feel…*bad* for him."

"Hm."

"*Almost*," I emphasized.

He didn't reply.

I tilted my face so I could see his. "So, what do we do about this curse?"

His chest rose and fell with a deep breath. "I don't know."

With a sigh, I settled more fully against him. The morning sun grew brighter, warmer, but even with that—and even combined with the heat of Aleks—I still felt as if I were sitting at the bottom of a cold, dark pit with all the answers I needed impossibly high above me.

I sat in that pit for several more minutes before I found the strength to try and climb my way out.

"I'm going to go talk to my brother," I told Aleks. "You should just rest for now."

He caught my hand as I tried to stand.

He said nothing at first. He only held me with a steady, assured grip, the sunrise washing over his face and making his eyes gleam like polished gold.

I gave him a bemused look. "What is it?"

"I love you."

I went perfectly still.

"I tried to tell you in Midna last night," he said. "And I should have said it much sooner than that."

Slowly, I relaxed, warmth melting through me and coaxing my lips into a small smile. "For what it's worth, I think that love was implied when you took multiple blades for me a few weeks ago. And that wasn't even the first time you'd saved me."

He shook his head. "That isn't enough. And now isn't the time, maybe, but I just needed you to actually hear those words. I need you to hear them over and over again until you can't possibly forget them, no matter what happens next."

I twisted more fully around, straddling his lap and looking him directly in the eyes.

It hit me in a rush that left me dizzy: All the times I'd rehearsed this conversation in my head, waiting for him to say those three words to me. How many times I'd thought them myself. How I'd fallen in love with every part of him—the good, the bad, the messy—and how desperately I didn't want to lose any of it.

No matter what happens next.

I leaned forward, pressing my lips to his. He pushed his hands through my hair, weaving his fingers into a tighter grip against the back of my head, pulling me more fully to him.

For several minutes, we were lost in a sea of soft kisses and sunlight, in waves of warmth that carried us far away from the horrors and questions of the night we'd just fought our way through.

It was the sound of a familiar, distant horn that eventually brought us back to reality—guards at the gatehouse announcing visitors. Likely a sign of a long day to come, and a reminder that I needed to speak with my brother before he got swept up in more meetings.

I closed my eyes against the thought. When I opened them again, Aleks still held on to me, his hands resting on my sides with a possessive grip. But he was staring out the window.

And maybe it was merely a shift in the light—the morning sun moving on—but his gaze seemed darker.

Another horn sounded from the gatehouse, jolting me into action.

I planted one last soft kiss on Aleksander's cheek, whispering as I pulled away: "I love you, too."

I RAN INTO PHANTOM AFTER LEAVING MY ROOM. HE WAS sitting in the middle of the hallway as though he'd just been waiting for an opportunity to fix me with one of his judgmental stares.

Typical.

"What?" I demanded.

(*How long do you really think you can hide him?*)

"I'm not *hiding* him, I just…"

He snorted.

Noticing a group of servants coming our way, I ducked into the next room I came to—one of several small studies evenly spaced along the hall. Phantom followed closely behind, settling down and stretching and kneading his paws in and out of the plush velvet carpet.

"If you're so concerned about this latest development, you could go guard my bedroom door," I said, "and make sure no one bothers him. You know, if you wanted to be helpful for once."

(*I am* always *helpful.*)

"*Always* is a generous word choice," I replied, scratching him between the ears.

Something shifted in the corner of the room, and I realized we weren't alone.

"Still doing the weird talking to your dog thing, I see," Zayn said. He was reclining in a worn armchair, his feet propped up on an equally threadbare ottoman.

Maybe it was the warm glow of the fireplace beside him, but I thought he looked much healthier. Much more...*alive*.

Phantom stalked toward him, cautiously sniffing at his boots.

"He's still starting conversations with me." I shrugged. "It seems rude not to answer him."

Zayn smiled a bit at this, sitting up and holding out his hand for Phantom to smell. Phantom's fur bristled, but he finished his inspection and then ultimately relaxed, allowing Zayn to stroke the white patch of fur on his forehead; he wasn't one to turn down head scratches, regardless of who was giving them.

"He seems anxious," Zayn commented. "And so do you, for that matter."

"It's been an eventful night."

"So I've gathered, based on the bit of gossip I've overheard."

"That didn't take long to spread."

"It never does." His voice dropped slightly as he studied me and asked, "So...what have you done this time, Princess?"

"Most are calling me *Queen* now, actually." I fixed a twist of hair that had loosed itself from the crown of braids I wore. "Though there's been no official coronation yet."

"Duly noted." He cocked his head. "But we're changing the subject, aren't we?"

"What if I am?"

"It makes me all the more curious about what you're hiding, that's all."

Phantom gave another knowing little snort, as if to say *I told you so.*

With a sigh, I sank into the chair opposite of Zayn, hesitating only a moment before telling him about nearly everything that had happened.

Maybe it was foolish, being so open with him. After all, I still didn't know how much of him was...well, *him.* But it was that connection to Lorien that made me so eager to talk, too—because I wanted to know everything he could possibly tell me.

And trust had to go both ways.

He didn't seem surprised to learn that the rumors about Aleks being back were true.

"I thought I'd felt a surge of Light magic," he said.

Aleksander's, or Lorien's?

I was afraid to ask who it had felt like.

Could he tell the difference?

"Aleks said something that's been bothering me all morning," I told Zayn. "That he feels *hollowed out,* as if Lorien took pieces with him when he left." I forced my gaze not to waver, my voice not to shake. "Is that how you feel, too?"

Zayn considered the question for a moment. "Kind of the opposite, really. It's more like I've been suddenly flooded with all the things I lost during the time he had a hold over me. The heaviness of an entire lost life, hitting all at once, and now I'm trying to learn how to carry it all again."

Hollow, heavy...I didn't know which was a worse sign.

All I knew was that both felt like a threat to the very ground beneath our feet, and I didn't know how to fix *either* of them.

"Speaking of heavy things we carry..." Zayn's gaze fell to my wrist, to the mark Lorien had left. "What, pray tell, is *that* about?"

Running my hand over the mark, I lowered my voice and more fully explained the deal Lorien and I had made.

I was hoping he would have some insight into the curse, and all the cryptic words accompanying it. When I'd finished speaking, though, Zayn only stared at me, shaking his head in disbelief. "You willingly chose to strike a deal with him."

"I didn't have much of a *choice*."

"Right. Of course. And this was obviously the best path to take."

I arched a brow.

"Yes, I'd say there's no way it could end poorly." He

coughed. It sounded like he was trying to cover up a laugh.

"It isn't funny," I said.

"Not in a *haha* kind of way, no. But in an *oh wow, we are so fucked* kind of way, it is."

"We'll be fine," I insisted, stubbornly.

"Your optimism is admirable. Stupid, but admirable."

"I think I liked you better when you were unconscious," I mumbled.

"Honestly, so did I," he said, yawning.

"I was joking."

"I wasn't. Do you know how easy it was, being in a coma?"

"I'll admit, it's tempting to try it myself."

"But you won't."

"Won't I?"

"No. Because you have a foolish, valiant streak in you. Aleks does too. Yet another reason you morons are perfect for one another."

I wasn't sure whether to take his words as an insult or a compliment. Either way, they reminded me of the Zayn I wanted back, so my tone was a bit warmer as I said, "You should go talk to him. He'll be glad to know you're safe and recovering."

He stiffened. It was barely noticeable, but I still picked up on it. The silence that followed was thick enough to suffocate.

I cleared my throat. "…It won't be an easy conversation, I'm guessing."

His reply was perfectly deadpanned. "Though likely easier than the one you need to have with your brother regarding the cursed, immortal demon that's bound himself to you."

I grimaced. "Thanks for reminding me."

His grin returned, wider than earlier. "Shall we place bets on which one of us finds the courage to speak first?"

I cut him a sideways glance. "What are we wagering?"

He pretended to be deep in thought for a moment. "Loser dances naked through the main courtyard of the palace."

I huffed out a laugh. "All of my detractors would *love* that. It would help their arguments that I'm unstable and unfit to rule any part of this realm."

"…Something less potentially damning, then," he conceded, lifting a shoulder and letting it drop. "Loser buys the other drinks."

"Challenge accepted." I held out my hand, which he shook with all the seriousness of a king agreeing to a major trade deal. "After you talk, try to get him to actually *rest*."

"No promises. I couldn't get him to listen to me when I had the manipulative powers of the aforementioned cursed demon on my side. Doubt I'll manage to persuade him of anything on my own."

"Well, just give it your all."

"I'll give it my some," he replied, getting to his feet and cracking his knuckles.

I rolled my eyes, but truthfully, I was grateful for his humor; it felt good to laugh about something again, even if our jokes were grim.

But that laughter was a distant memory by the time I made my way to my brother's office and knocked on his door.

ELEVEN

Nova

I was relieved to find that Eamon and Thalia were already with Bastian—which meant explaining *everything* wouldn't fall to me, at least.

A good thing, given the current state of my thoughts.

From the look on my brother's face, it seemed Eamon and Thalia had already told him the worst of it. I approached slowly, still trying to find a way to put the events of the past hours into something like a coherent speech.

Bastian spoke first. "So. Aleksander is here."

I looked between him and the other two. "They've already explained everything?"

"As much as we could," Eamon said, frowning. "There are still too many questions, though; it doesn't feel like we've really made sense of anything."

My brother massaged the space between his eyes—eyes that were bloodshot and accented by dark circles from lack of sleep. "It all sounds like another dangerous trick Lorien is attempting to pull. Are we really going to play right into his hands?"

"What do you think is the alternative?" I asked. "Ignoring him is just as dangerous."

"I didn't suggest we *ignore* him."

"Then what *are* you suggesting?"

He didn't reply.

"The world would be better off if we could just kill him," Thalia muttered. "But nothing can ever be that easy, can it?"

We fell silent, thinking.

Eamon ran a hand through his hair, occasionally, absently clenching the wavy strands and tugging them, as he often did when his mind was racing. Cautiously, he said, "There's a chance that taking up this quest is also our only way of truly killing him."

Bastian looked more awake all of a sudden. "What are you talking about?"

"...Well, according to the memory Nova saw, Calista told Lorien that she didn't intend to end him with this curse. It seems to me that it was the opposite—she made him immortal by scattering his essence. Dooming him to wander in pieces, to suffer indefinitely…weakening him, but not completely *ending* him."

"So, if we gather him completely, we can end him completely?" Thalia theorized.

Eamon gave a barely perceptible nod of agreement; his gaze was troubled, though, as if he knew this theory was far too simple.

But I couldn't help seizing on any and all hope, however precarious it might have been. "This might reset the Vaeloran Cycle, too," I pointed out. "He said something to me after I witnessed that memory: *And thus the balance of the realms was forever altered.* I don't think Calista meant for it to happen, but it's a side-effect of him being broken and unable to pass on: The Vaeloran Cycle broke as well. There should have been another Light Vaelora by now."

"Putting him back together will also put all of his power back together," Bastian pointed out. "And there's no guarantee we'll be able to control that power, or finish him off before he does something cataclysmic with it."

"We'll have time to figure out how to deal with that," I insisted. "My own powers are growing stronger, too. And Aleks is back, which—"

"Which only complicates things further."

"He's on our side."

"He's even *more* connected to Lorien than he was

before. And there's the question of his cousin, as well. They're both unpredictable."

"I trust them."

My brother shook his head. "I understand why you *want* to, but...this is all incredibly risky."

"More risky than letting Nova continue to venture back to Midna and try to force more magic into this realm?" Thalia asked, bluntly. "Because that wasn't working particularly well, either."

Bastian gave her a withering look.

Never one to apologize for speaking her mind, Thalia only folded her arms across her chest and stared right back at him. "Everything is a risk, given the crumbling foundations our world sits upon," she added.

"...The more immediately pressing thing," Eamon put in, "is that we have no idea where to begin, should we choose to undertake this task. I've been wracking my mind, trying to think of any clues I might have come across in my studies, but I can think of nothing that suggests where Lorien's so-called *mind, body,* and *heart* might be hidden. There are no maps to follow, and the words of the curse suggest we'll find these pieces in more than one realm, which makes it all the more daunting."

I started to agree, until an idea *did* occur to me—a memory of the strange energy I'd felt when Thalia and I had been exploring the ruined library in Midna the other day. That library was very close to the room where Calista had cursed Lorien. Could there be more clues waiting there?

I'd been overwhelmed by the clearly powerful magic saturating that spot, but maybe with Aleks and his power beside me…

"I still don't think pursuing this will end well," Bastian said. With a resigned sigh, he added, "Though I can't deny that it all warrants closer consideration, if nothing else."

"Yes," I agreed, quick to seize on any chance at hope once again. "And I think I know where to start looking, at least."

AFTER LEAVING MY BROTHER'S OFFICE, I HEADED straight for my room to prepare for another trip to Midna.

The less time Bastian had to overthink our plans, the better.

I was beyond exhausted, dangerously close to delirious from lack of sleep. But I had a plan now. A target. A purpose that carried my feet forward with little need to think.

I walked past the study where I'd spoken with Zayn earlier, ducking inside to see if he was still there—he wasn't. I wondered if he'd gained the courage to go speak with his cousin. And what happened next?

Would he come with us?

Should he come with us?

Was my brother right to be concerned about whatever invisible marks Lorien had left behind on both Zayn and Aleks?

Of course he's right.

He was right more often than I wanted to admit, and it was annoying.

I shook my head to rid it of the doubts creeping in. Caution was fine. But we'd taken them back, hadn't we? Zayn was entirely free—I could still remember the violent way we'd ripped Lorien out of him; I'd had far too many vivid nightmares about that moment to forget it.

And as for Aleks…

I braced my hands against the chair Zayn had occupied earlier, gripping its worn velvet so tightly my hands started to go numb. Staring at the dying embers in the fireplace, I made a promise to myself: Aleks was mine, and I was his, and there were some things that couldn't be taken from us, no matter what came next.

As I turned back for the door, I nearly collided with Lord Renvar.

He'd clearly followed me in—and silently, at that. Even now, he moved with the quiet, stalking grace of a predator as he stepped into the room. He stopped entirely too close to me, blocking the path to the door in a very deliberate way.

"Lord Renvar." I lifted my chin. "You startled me."

He gave a slight—somewhat mocking—bow. "My apologies. I would have announced myself, but you seemed too caught up in your thoughts to notice me, anyhow."

"The past day has given me a lot to think about."

"Yes; the chatter in your halls has given *me* much to consider as well."

I swallowed hard. "I should be going."

"What has you in such a rush this morning? Another trip to the camps at the Edge?"

"No."

"Then perhaps there's something more pressing we need to discuss?"

"I'm afraid that's between my advisors and me for the moment."

"Such rudeness, keeping secrets from your guests."

My gaze darted to the door, sizing up the tiny space not blocked by the lord's large, powerful body. He had a very obvious size advantage over me, but maybe I could slip through if I caught him off guard and knocked him off balance.

"You know," he said, "There was a time when the Rivenholt Court was considered among the most gracious and forthcoming of all the royal courts."

"Much has changed these past centuries."

"Indeed, it has." He moved even closer to me.

I held my ground. "Get out of my way, Renvar."

"Answer my question first. What are you plotting this morning?"

Cold energy swept between us, summoned by no more than my tense breath. Shadows bled across my skin like watercolor paint, little tendrils slowly rising up and arching back in a threatening manner.

Whether he'd been hoping for an excuse to fight, or he simply panicked, I don't know—but Renvar reacted quickly, one hand pressing against the wall beside me, caging me in, while his other hand took hold of my jaw, squeezing tightly as he forced my gaze to his.

My shadows swirled chaotically.

But before I could truly retaliate, the fireplace flared brighter. The sconces along the walls ignited in a flash, and a violent surge of energy followed, so sudden and so intense it took my breath away.

Lord Renvar spun toward the doorway, wincing in the sudden brightness.

Seconds passed before the light settled enough to reveal Aleks standing there, glaring.

The lord's mouth opened and closed several times before words came out. "Is that…"

"It is," Aleks replied, sauntering inside.

Renvar's head swiveled back to me. "So it's true. *This* is the secret—another reckless, questionable choice you've made, inviting this beast to walk freely in your halls."

"Get away from her," Aleks warned, his voice low and deadly.

Renvar didn't listen. His hand fell to the same place as before, crowding me back against the wall. Except, this time, his other hand moved toward my throat.

A mistake.

In the span of a heartbeat, Aleks had crossed the small room and taken hold of the back of his neck. With terrifying ease, he ripped him away from me and threw him into the nearest wall.

The lord immediately started cowering, scrambling to brace himself against that wall, but Aleks didn't stop there. He took Renvar by the throat and jerked him upward, his hand a noose hanging him in place.

I was so stunned by the violent movement that it took me a moment to choke out a command. "Let him go, Aleks."

His grip only tightened as violent light crackled around his body.

Lord Renvar coughed and sputtered, his feet sliding and stumbling for purchase, trying to stretch to the ground in order to take the pressure off his throat.

"*Stop!*" I pleaded.

Aleks went perfectly still. The light—both around him and all throughout the room—dimmed. But his grip remained fixed. And the *power* that emanated from him didn't feel dimmed at all. It felt like it could have swallowed us whole, burned us up into nothing but dust.

"Aleks. *Please.*"

Slowly, he removed his hand and took a step back.

Lord Renvar dropped to his knees, glaring up at us in hatred and rage. He took a moment, seemingly gathering what remained of his dignity, before slowly rising to his feet and leaving without another word.

Once he was out of the room, Aleks tilted his face toward me. "Are you okay?"

I stared, heart pounding, unsure of how to answer.

I'd missed having him here to fight for me, yes. But the look in his eyes a moment ago had been... frightening.

And that power *still* radiating off him...

A thought crawled through my mind, raising a chill along my spine.

This isn't the same Aleksander I lost.

I brushed it off. Because of course he'd come back different. How could he not? He'd said it himself: Lorien took pieces of him when he left. It would take time to fill in those empty spaces, to fully come back to his normal self, his normal control.

"I'm fine," I said. "But Lord Renvar isn't worth such violent energy—or *any* energy, for that matter."

Aleks looked to the doorway, as though he was still thinking about chasing that foreign diplomat down and making him pay a higher price for touching me.

Another shiver crawled down my spine.

"Come on," I said, hastily taking hold of his arm. "We have bigger things to worry about."

A muscle in his jaw twitched, but he relented, allowing me to steer him out of the study and toward my room. He seemed to relax quickly once my hand was against him, though his magic continued to throb in the space around us.

Dangerous.

It felt dangerous.

"You were supposed to be resting," I reminded him, trying to force a calmness into my voice that I didn't truly feel.

"Your magic felt anxious. I couldn't ignore it, so I came to find you."

My cheeks warmed as I wondered, again, at the depth of our magic and connection.

"And the moment I saw that man touching you..." He trailed off, shaking his head and slipping his hand into mine, his thumb tracing my palm as we walked. Then he abruptly pulled me to a stop, his grip on my hand tightening as he brought us face-to-face.

"...I'm fine," I repeated. "It's all fine, and I... I'm glad you were there." I stared into his eyes, trying to reassure myself, to convince myself that nothing about them had changed.

I couldn't stop replaying what had happened in my head, thinking of how disastrous it would have been if he'd actually harmed Lord Renvar. Or worse.

I *wasn't* fine.

None of this was, really.

But I couldn't dwell on it along with everything else.

Eager to change the subject, I instead recounted the meeting I'd had with my brother and all the plans we'd made.

"We need to pack for Midna," I told Aleks. "I can't say I'm thrilled at the thought of going back there already, but..."

He gave my hand a little squeeze. "We'll be fine," he assured me, "as long as we're together."

As long as we're together.

I managed a nod. Even as the memory of his violence continued to storm through my mind, I stretched onto my tiptoes and kissed him, and I refused to think about all the things waiting to tear us apart.

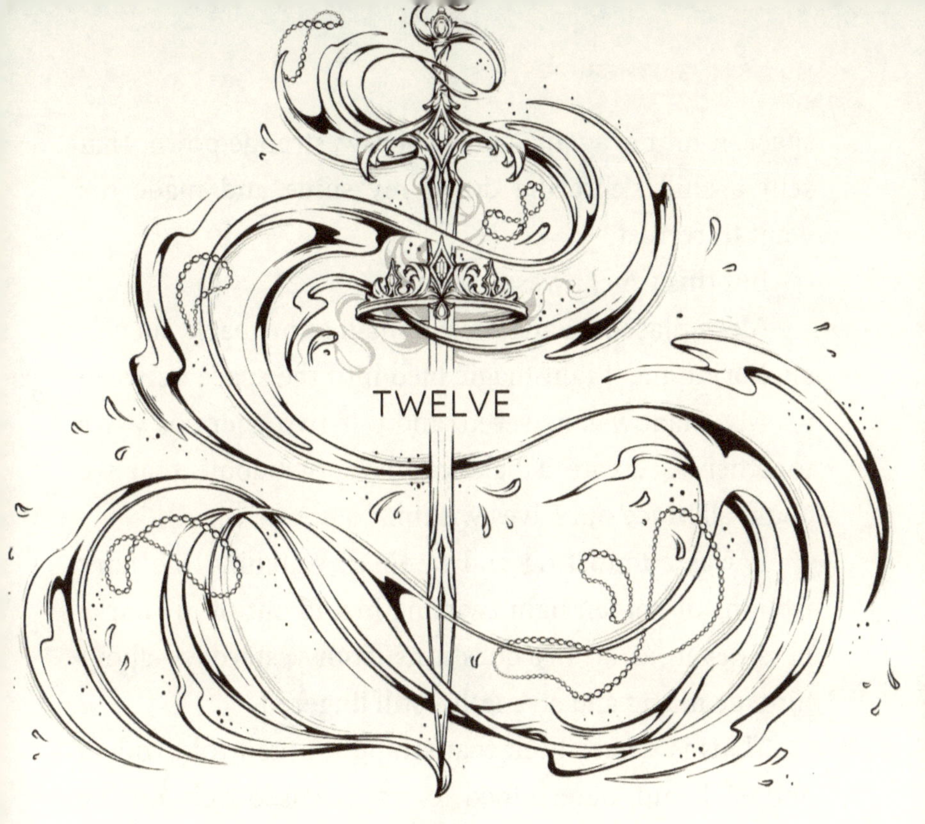

TWELVE

Nova

It was extraordinary, how much easier it was to move through Midna with Aleks at my side. How much it felt like the exact place I was supposed to be, the exact path I was meant to walk—even if I didn't yet know where it would lead.

I clung to that feeling as we moved deeper into the haunting, ruined palace

I led everyone—Aleks, Thalia, Zayn, and Eamon—to the spot in the library where, just days ago, I'd been overwhelmed by that sudden, uncontrollable surge of energy.

Just like before, the moment I stepped into the

space, it hit me again: a pulse of raw, strange power that sent a chill skittering down my spine and made me want to retreat.

But this time, I wasn't alone.

Aleks placed a hand on the small of my back, silently anchoring me. Light magic bled into the space between us. My shadows answered, and our two energies wove together to create a balanced sort of bubble that we could all brace ourselves within.

It was comforting and familiar, watching the faint ribbons of golden light twisting in and out of my darkness…even as all my questions from yesterday—about his true magic and strength—still lingered.

"This is where I felt that strange surge I told you all about," I said, determined to stay focused only on the problems directly before us. "And I felt it, again, just now. There's something significant tucked away in this corner, I'm certain of it. Something that's trying to knock us off balance and drive us away."

We explored the space for a moment, studying the busts that had intrigued me on my last visit, and the artwork hanging on the wall across from them.

"These statues…they're the kings and queens of Midna, I assume?" Aleks asked.

Eamon nodded, running his fingers over one of the plaques fixed below a bust, translating the ancient words etched into the shiny metal.

"Solemn looking group, aren't they?" Zayn commented.

"Most of Midna's history is made up of bloody wars and desperate schemes to keep their power as the central kingdom of what was once known as the Nerithys Empire," Thalia said. "And, after the realms split into the Above and Below, they were stuck in the middle, and so tasked with trying to keep the peace between them. The gods asked much of these kings and queens; you'd be serious-looking, too."

Zayn appeared to be only halfway listening to her. He'd gotten distracted by the row of paintings hanging across from the statues, which featured several colorful beasts and elaborate, beautiful figures surrounded by swirls of what could only be magic. Divine beings, if I had to guess—and more evidence of this kingdom's deep ties to the gods.

"I doubt he'd be serious-looking, even then," Aleks said under his breath.

Thalia rolled her eyes in Zayn's general direction.

I smiled, attempting to fend off the ominous feeling creeping in as I reached for one of the stone-faced rulers.

To my surprise, the statue moved even from just the light brush of my hand. Cautiously, I tried to pick it up, and I found that it was light—hollow, almost. It lifted easily from its pedestal.

And there, underneath it, half-covered with bits of plaster and dust, was the same symbol I'd seen in my vision of the past, etched into the floor of the queen's glass-walled sitting room.

"What is this?" I asked, wiping it off. "I saw it in the room where Calista cursed Lorien. And I've noticed it in a few other places in Midna, as well."

Eamon spun to face me. His gaze darted between me and the uncovered mark, and his eyes widened. "Where else have you seen it?" he asked, drawing excitedly toward me, so close our noses nearly touched. "Give me *exact* details."

"I..."

Thalia grabbed the hood of his coat, dragging him back to a more socially-acceptable distance. "Not all of us are walking record books," she reminded him, dryly. "Or diligent note-takers, like yourself."

"Yes, of course not. But, Nova..." He gave me an imploring look. "Try to remember."

"Um...well...it's never been in particularly noticeable places, I guess?"

"...Yes, that makes sense."

"It does?"

"Yes. But I do wonder..." He let the thought hang in the air for a long moment.

Zayn cleared his throat. "Are you going to enlighten the rest of us about whatever is going on in that frighteningly brilliant little head of yours? Or should we just start throwing out guesses?"

Eamon still didn't answer immediately. But I could tell from the furrow of his brow and the gleam in his grey eyes that his silence wasn't because he didn't know the answer; rather, he was trying to remember every detail he could before speaking.

"The Void Order," he finally said. "It's a name that's shown up—alongside this symbol—in a few places throughout the texts and other artifacts that I've been studying from this realm. Mostly only mentioned in passing…but in important places. Like in correspondence from the kings and queens of Midna, for example. My understanding is that this Order secretly helped oversee the Vaeloran Cycle."

"Something like the Keepers of Light?" Aleks asked.

"…It's possible some of those Keepers were once members of this order, I suppose—Aetherkin who took their servitude in a different direction." He considered for another moment before adding, "Yes, at least some overlap certainly must have occurred."

"Were there Keepers of Shadow at some point, too?" I asked. "Or some sort of corresponding group, whatever they might have been called? I've always wondered about that."

"Maybe not as well known, but there were organized sects of Shadow-aligned Aetherkin, certainly. Orin once associated with one of the largest groups I'm aware of—the Umbral Hands. Though these groups all disappeared during the long stretch between Calista's death and the birth of her next successor. Long before Orin undertook his mission to protect Nova in the Above, in other words."

He still could have mentioned something about all these things, I thought, bitterly.

But I said nothing; I still didn't want to talk about my former mentor. I doubted Thalia did, either; she had suddenly become very interested in adjusting the jewels on the magical staff she carried.

Eamon moved on, oblivious to any emotional wounds he might have re-opened. He was still talking in an enthusiastic rush, only growing silent whenever he stopped to more closely examine the artifacts around us, searching for more marks from this mysterious order.

"I think this Order was more concerned with the overall cycle of magic than with any individual Vaelora," he said. "There are references to them being *god-touched*—divinely chosen, just as the Vaelora themselves were. Though not with power, but with wisdom. Of course, whether that was true or not…"

"If the Midnasian leaders were desperate for more help to fulfill their role as balance-keepers, it makes sense that they'd want to *believe* it was true," I said.

"And they likely welcomed them into the palace with open arms," Aleks added. "Which would explain the marks."

"But were they a force for good or evil?" I wondered.

"I need to collect more data before I can say for certain," Eamon said.

"If one can ever be *certain* about something like that," said Zayn, with a shrug.

"Well, one can always do more research," Eamon countered, looking longingly in the direction of the main room of the library.

"And you seem entirely too excited about the prospect," Zayn replied.

While they fell into a spirited argument about the merits, burdens and shortcomings of knowledge, Aleks and I drew closer to the mark I'd uncovered moments ago.

Aleks reached for it first, light dancing from his fingertips and further illuminating the symbol.

I was paying attention to what he was doing, but I was also watching Thalia out of the corner of my eye. She had withdrawn into herself—likely still thinking about the father who had abandoned her.

We'd have to see Orin, eventually. He was too tangled up in the history and magic of our world to be ignored forever. And part of me *did* want to confront him and demand explanations for all he'd kept from me —which made me look forward to our reunion with a strange combination of longing and dread.

I jumped as the wall before me gave a violent rumble.

We stared at it, holding our breath, watching a thin crack splitting all the way up to the ceiling.

Nothing else happened.

When I dared to glance away, though, I noticed the top half of the Order mark was glowing—as if it had absorbed some of the magic Aleks had been using to illuminate it.

"...Try adding Shadow magic?" Aleks suggested, pointing to the bottom half of that circle divided by the vine-wrapped sword.

I sent a swirl of black into it, to no effect—

At first.

But as I started to take a step back, the floor beneath me rumbled even more violently than the wall had. Another crack appeared, joining with the first. It was enough to make the fissure in the wall expand, giving us a glimpse of something on the other side.

I thought maybe I was seeing things, until Aleks said, "There's a room hidden behind this wall."

The symbol on the pedestal blazed brighter and brighter with our combined power, and I wondered how many other secrets might be revealed in this way—by a balance of darkness and light.

After a brief search, we uncovered more Order marks hidden around the bases of the statues. We activated them in the same way as the first. One by one, they responded, humming faintly as they lit up. Soon, cracks began to split through the entire wall, outlining the shape of massive double doors. Then those doors pulsed with a dull light, slowly sliding apart and into hidden channels on either side, rattling and groaning like stone giants waking from a long sleep.

The space beyond seemed small, though the exact

edges were lost to shadow and the swirling dust kicked up by the shifting walls; for a long moment, we saw nothing definite—just the air glittering with old particles, disturbed after who knew how many years.

Then, the dust began to settle, and light poured in through three narrow skylights cut into the high stone ceiling. The pale beams revealed a room with walls scorched black in places, and with strange, crooked veins etched into the floor, some of which were faintly glowing. There were claw marks as well—and these were *everywhere*. Deep, violent grooves that made my stomach flutter anxiously.

The brightest beam of light fell directly onto the center of the chamber, locking on an altar slick with what looked like dark and long-dried blood.

A corpse slumped against this altar, head bowed low as if in mourning. Or shame.

We all slowed to a stop, staring at it.

Thalia whispered something under her breath; it sounded like a prayer.

Eamon appeared to be trying to work up the courage to take a closer look.

Zayn coughed and said, "Leave it to the necromancer to lead us to a creepy dead body."

He let out a grunt as someone jabbed him in the side—Aleks, probably—but I was too focused on slowly making my way forward to pay much attention to what was happening behind me.

There was something...*off* about this dead body.

It was strangely proportioned, with arms and legs that looked mismatched in length, and a neck that was bent in a way that made its head hang oddly low against its chest. It wore a robe of white, which was bunched up along its back, heaped there as if hiding a mangled spine.

"The body Calista spoke of?" Aleks suggested hopefully.

I wasn't surprised when Eamon shook his head. "This isn't Lorien's body."

"Of course not," Thalia muttered. "That would have been too easy."

The longer I stared at it, the less I was convinced it had ever been human…*or* one of the Vaelora. The energy surrounding it was similar to the energy that clung to graveyards. But there was something much less…*peaceful* about it.

Something much more powerful.

Much more chaotic.

One after the other, we found ourselves looking to Eamon for an explanation.

He hesitated, but eventually said, "I think this might be…a *sentier*. Or what's left of it."

"What's left of a *what*?" I asked.

Eamon didn't reply.

Thalia frowned, chancing a step closer. "I remember one of my magic instructors talking about these. But I thought such things were only a legend. Nobody I know of has ever seen an actual manifestation of one."

"Yes, but what exactly is it a manifestation *of*?" Zayn questioned.

Eamon didn't seem eager to explain, for once, so Thalia continued: "Sentiers are a by-product of extremely powerful Vaeloran magic. Such magic leaves a permanent mark on the world, and the residual energy left behind often forms into a living being. Usually, they're semi-divine, intelligent creatures that serve a purpose tied into whatever spell the Vaelora cast upon a particular place."

"So this one is more proof that Calista *did* use extremely powerful magic in this palace?" Aleks asked.

"Seems like it."

I studied it more closely. Its limbs, unnaturally thin and oddly jointed. Its skin, a ghastly shade of grey and hanging too loosely in too many places. Its face, hidden in shadow and by the tilt of its head… From this angle, I could just make out a mouth hanging open, frozen with sharp rows of teeth on display.

It didn't look like a divine being.

It looked like a monster.

And, not for the first time since I'd learned of the curse on Lorien, I found myself wondering about the motivations and consequences of what Calista had done.

"If it's a by-product of the spell Calista used against Lorien, then it likely knew details about it," I said.

Aleks cast an uneasy look at the doorway. "Which may be why someone trapped it behind these walls and left it to die. Someone didn't want that curse undone. Our mysterious Order friends, I'm guessing?"

"My thoughts as well," Eamon agreed, grimly.

It took me only a moment to decide what to do next. "I want to try and read its memories."

A ripple of uncertainty swept through the others, but I remained insistent.

"It shouldn't be difficult, right?" I said. "It isn't as though it has a lifetime of complicated thoughts to sort through. And if it's truly a living embodiment—well, *was* a living embodiment—of the very curse we're trying to make sense of, then I have to try."

No one managed to come up with a convincing argument against this.

"…Be careful," said Aleks.

"I always am," I replied.

He let out a quiet, disagreeing laugh at this before gently weaving a spiral of light around me.

With his protective warmth pressing against my body, I closed the remaining space between me and the sentier's corpse.

The rest of the room seemed to fade away until it was only me and that bundle of white robes and ghastly limbs. Me and the air that seemed to be growing colder by the second. Me and the pungent taste of ash and salt that suddenly coated my tongue…

I placed a hand on the creature's long neck.

Somehow, I kept my arm steady, even though touching the sentier was like plunging my hand into a bucket of icy water. My fingers went numb. The sensation slowly swept up to my head, threatening to freeze away my thoughts.

The warmth of Aleksander's magic became a distant memory.

Steady, I commanded myself and my shadows, which were starting to bloom beneath the surface of my skin.

Just before I attempted to delve into the sentier's memories, a sudden, twisting pressure closed around my heart and lungs. Then released. Then grabbed again. It was as if I held one end of a rope, and something else was swiping at the other, desperately trying to get a firm grip on my magic.

The moment it truly latched on, my feet were nearly jerked out from under me by its sudden, violent hold.

"Let go." The words trembled through my lips.

The pulling grew stronger, and I would have sworn I heard a whisper of a voice speaking into my thoughts. It said only one word—

Mine.

This creature was the by-product of powerful necromancy; was some part of it still clinging to existence, desperate for more Shadow magic to feed it?

Did it have my magic confused with Calista's?

The air around me felt like it was closing in.

MINE!

Release me! I thought back, fighting to remain calm. *You have no claim to these shadows!*

The feeling in my chest tightened one last time

before finally relenting. As the pressure slipped away, I exhaled a tense breath, blinking several times to try and bring my focus back.

The sentier was moving.

Its robes billowed. The body beneath it bulged. The hump at its back was shifting, breaking through the folds of white cloth to reveal…something. Not the mangled, protruding spine I expected to see, but…

Wings.

It had *wings*—though they were mostly bone, and covered in a membrane so papery thin that I couldn't imagine them lifting even its emaciated body.

Its muscles flexed and shivered. Its ashen skin glistened. Its eyes opened, two bright slashes of molten silver glaring directly into mine.

As I stared back, I heard that whisper in the back of my mind again, only clearer now, its voice haunting and wild and full of warning—like the creaking branches of a forest caught in the breeze of an approaching storm.

So. You have come back to free me.

"…Back?"

It stretched its wings before giving several quick flaps, stirring up dust and bits of my shadows.

"I'm not the one who created you."

Another haunting whisper grated through my thoughts: *You created my prison.*

"Wrong again."

I am no fool. I remember your eyes. You watched from the other side of the wall.

Arguing seemed pointless. So, I tried a more direct question: "Do you know *how* you were created? What you came from?"

It tilted its head, the motion almost birdlike. Two more words slipped into my thoughts.

Curse Keeper.

"...That's right," I said carefully. "You are. Which means you can help me."

It cocked its head further. Then its mouth split into a horrible grin, sharp teeth parting to let out a noise caught somewhere between a bark and a yowl. Laughter, maybe. It made me want to drop to my knees and clamp my hands over my ears.

With a single flap, its wings proved more functional than anticipated, propelling it upward in a wild, ungraceful leap. It careened toward the ceiling only to twist violently and dive back down, heading straight toward me.

I rolled aside, landing in a crouch just outside of its reach.

It hit the stone floor, its too-long arms stretching forward, bracing and bending and then immediately launching it back into flight. Letting out a guttural cry, it shot higher, perching in the corner, balancing on a wooden beam that buckled and groaned under its weight.

With a snap of its long neck, the creature expelled a

breath of shadow-tinged mist. The taste of salt and ash once again filled the air. My own shadows billowed as the mist met them, seemingly absorbing it. I felt the weight of both our powers rolled into one, so heavy it nearly made me panic, until I realized…

If our magic was born of the same darkness, then why should I fear it?

I spun around to warn the others away—to assure them I could handle this—only to find they were already gone.

THIRTEEN

Nova

There was a thick veil of black separating me from where my companions had once stood. It tumbled and raged, a wall of shadows shot through with chaotic pulses of purple and blue.

When had that shown up?

"Just me and you, then," I muttered, turning back to the sentier, holding up my hand and letting more dark ripples of power pour from my palm.

I'd left Grimnor behind in Noctaris—concerned about how the sword and Lorien's essence might react to the magic here—so I instead formed my shadows into a sharpened point and brandished it like a blade.

The sentier's shiny eyes narrowed on it.

In the next heartbeat, it shot toward me, its horrible voice filling my head as it came.

I am the Curse Keeper!

"Yes," I snarled, ducking to avoid its clawing, skeletal fingers as it swooped low and made a grab for my hair. "We've established that."

It hit the wall and ricocheted off it, doubling its speed. I couldn't avoid it a second time; it grabbed both of my arms in a violent hold. Like its wings, its long fingers proved much stronger than they looked, circling my wrists so tightly I quickly lost the feeling in my hands.

It stretched its grip wide, pulling as if it intended to rip my arms straight from my body. I curled this way and that, trying to loosen the pressure while also trying to somehow keep my throat angled away from its mouth full of sharp, glistening teeth. Its hold tightened as it brought that mouth terribly close to me, breathing the foul stench of rot and damp earth directly into my face.

Why have you revived me, necromancer?

The question briefly stopped my struggling.

That odd pulling sensation I'd felt earlier…

I hadn't been *trying* to revive it—I'd never managed magic as advanced as that. The closest I'd come was reversing Phantom's death, but that hadn't been a complete spell, nor had it been on purpose.

But what I'd done moments ago had felt different. I'd been aware and in control of the threads of my power slipping in, and maybe I *had* unconsciously encouraged it to grab hold so that I might pull it up from the grave. I'd been so desperate to get answers, whatever it took, so maybe…

Why have you revived me, necromancer? it repeated.

Instead of replying, I went back to trying to break free.

Why? it howled at me.

Catching a flash of an Order symbol etched into the altar it had once rested against, I deflected with a question of my own: "Why were you locked away in this room and left to die?"

It let out another howl, its words unintelligible this time. The shadowy energy swirling all around us grew more dense. More chaotic. I focused on summoning even more, calling it forth with a violence I hoped would knock the sentier off balance.

It worked; it twisted away, screeching and throwing me to the ground as it went.

"Who left you to die here?" I demanded again, staggering to my feet, reforming some of the shadows into a blade for each of my hands this time. "And *why?*"

The sentier stopped its screeching. Slowly, it swooped back to me, landing with the full force of its weight and rattling the ground as it did.

I parted the dense magic surrounding it so I could

look more fully into its eyes. It rose to its full height within the clearing, those silver eyes darkening. Calculating. Its wings stretched wide again. Cold energy washed over me as it exhaled a slow, rattling breath.

I willed myself not to cower beneath its glare.

"*And why?*" it repeated, speaking out loud, this time—though its voice had changed to something entirely different. Something almost human-sounding, as though parroting some other being; maybe the one who had killed it. "Why? *Because the dead keep their secrets.*"

I sidestepped as it lunged.

"Not from me, they don't," I said, gritting my teeth and guiding one of my blades into something more flexible—a whip of shadow that snapped out and caught the sentier's long neck, jerking it to a stop.

I dug in my heels and pulled. I didn't have the strength to draw it in, but my shadows did; with another violent flex of my magic, we were standing inches away from one another.

I wasted no time darting a hand toward its gruesome face, digging my fingers into its hollow cheeks. Its skin felt bumpy and slightly slimy, like a toad's.

"You will reveal what you know," I commanded. "Show me the knowledge they tried to bury about the curse you keep—whoever *they* are."

It closed its eyes, breathing out another cold wave of energy. The entire room was abruptly overtaken by dense fog. All sound disappeared.

Everything disappeared for a long, tense moment.

Then I felt a vibration rumbling toward me, spreading like a ring out from a drop in still water. I blinked.

The room changed.

Before me was the sentier as it must have been when it was still alive: A powerful creature pacing restlessly, like a lion in a too-small cage. Less emaciated, more muscular. Eyes like starlight rather than tarnished silver. Still monstrous looking…yet with an unmistakably divine glow around its entire body.

The sound of voices rose from somewhere. Visions of bodies, swirls of magic, and a storm of different emotions rushed around us—a sampling of all the many things this creature had seen and survived, I realized.

A ghostly apparition of the present, corpse-like sentier appeared alongside the memory version. I fixed my gaze on it, my mind focused only on what I had commanded it to show me.

As my thoughts honed in, I felt its gaze do the same. Its silver eyes bored into mine, and more pressure grabbed at the reservoir of magic inside me. This time, I didn't resist it; I let this beast born of my same shadows tangle itself fully with me.

It crept forward and laid its forehead against my palm.

And, suddenly, I could *see*.

The chaos rushing around us stilled, and I saw a brief, but clear, memory of Calista standing tall before the sentier, looking down at it with an anguished expression as she gave her command.

Keep them safe.

Then I saw what she was referring to: The same fragments of light I'd witnessed in the vision Lorien had guided me to. But, this time, the scene didn't end with them shattering their way through glass; instead, I saw a world rushing beneath them as they flew, the fragments dipping and diving for miles before twisting back into one piece…

Only to divide once more into three shards that raced off in different directions, curving and falling like shooting stars to the earth.

One landed in a grove of trees with trunks that looked like brittle, sun-bleached bones.

Another fell into a pool of silver-blue water surrounded by polished, gleaming walls etched with words I couldn't make out.

I was holding my breath, anticipating the landing of the third, when I felt the sentier's head jerk away from my touch.

I blinked, and it disappeared.

"No," I said, voice echoing in the space that had gone abruptly silent. "No, there must be something else! There's a third piece, another resting place you aren't showing me—"

The fog rolled in again, then away just as quickly, carrying me back to the present. The reanimated sentier was before me, solid once more, arching its neck like a snake preparing to strike.

But it seemed to have lost whatever fury had been driving it—or maybe my magic really *had* revived it, and now the spell had reached its limit. Whatever the reason, it seemed near-death once more. Its voice was quiet, almost mournful as it slipped into my thoughts.

You should have let me keep my secrets.

I couldn't catch my breath.

The weight of my knowledge is too much for this world.

As if to drive its point home, *weight* was all I was aware of, suddenly—a heaviness on my chest that made it even harder to breathe. It sank deep into my stomach, pulling me down to my knees. The thought of ever standing again, of carrying this weight with me, dragging it back into the world outside of this room…

It is too much for you, the sentier said, breathing out another frigid breath.

As the cold overtook me, I decided it was right: This all *was* too much.

Darkness edged my vision. I was sinking fast into a mire I likely wouldn't be able to rise from, and I didn't care; I wanted to rest in it. I wanted to die and take all the knowledge of Calista's curse—all its awful weight— with me.

I looked over my shoulder. Saw the wall of dark, tumbling energy still separating me from the others. Maybe they would be safe on the other side of it, at least.

Stay on the other side, I thought, dully.

Light parted the veil an instant later.

It slammed into the cold entombing me with a suddenness that made my head burn and throb. The darkness around my vision caved in completely.

When I finally blinked back into awareness, I found myself cradled against Aleksander's chest. His light hovered around us, its warmth coaxing my lungs into deeper, steadier breaths.

Breathe.

I hated it. Hated *him* and everything else in that moment.

But I knew I had to inhale, no matter the heaviness.

After several moments, his face grew clearer. The room took on a clearer shape, too, though it continued to spin around us. I clenched his shirt, trying to make the churning stop. Once it did, I fought my way out of his embrace and back onto my feet, taking in my surroundings, searching for the sentier.

It was gone.

The light surrounding Aleks and me had spread throughout much of the room, gathering toward a single scrap of wispy white cloth in the very center of the floor. It looked like the same material the sentier's robes had been made from.

Eamon was staring at that scrap, his brow furrowed in concern, while Thalia was circling the room, her staff clenched tightly in her hands.

Zayn was avoiding looking at any of us.

And I realized, all at once, what had happened: Aleksander's light had *obliterated* the sentier.

His hand, pressing against the small of my back, nearly made me jump. "Are you okay?"

I nodded. But I felt strange as I stared at all that remained of the sentier. Oddly…drained. As if pieces of me had been obliterated along with it.

And I wasn't sure how to get those pieces back.

FOURTEEN

Nova

"I recognized the first image that flashed through the sentier's memories," I told the others. "I'm sure of it."

We were back in the Rivenholt Palace, gathered in the courtyard outside my brother's room. Tall hedges rose on either side of us. A vine-draped fence with a wrought-iron gate blocked off a third side. An exceptionally private space, yet I couldn't help the hush of my voice, nor the paranoid glances I kept darting toward the shadows just beyond the reach of the lanterns' glow.

"And you're certain it was somewhere in the Above?" my brother asked.

"Yes. I used to practice magic within the white trees of that grove; the small forest around it is usually called the Hollow Wood, though it has an older name I can't remember. Orin always said the grove was the safest place to practice, because something about the soil and air made it resistant to any potentially wayward spells. And he once mentioned that it was also warded against watchful eyes—even divine ones. Whatever that meant."

"…The place *where gods forget*?" Aleks wondered.

My pulse quickened. "It's not far from Rose Point."

Bastian paced along the flagstones, his expression unreadable.

Phantom let out a restless grumble, rubbing his face against my leg. He was still annoyed about being left behind on another excursion to Midna.

I knew he would insist on joining me on any trip I might take to the Above, too. The thought alone made me nervous. He was so much more solid in Noctaris—and for good reason; before we'd found our way into this realm, he'd spent much of his existence in the Above as a ghost of the dog I'd been given as a child. He'd 'died' there, but my magic had managed to sustain his life-force because he was a *vaehound*—born of the energy of Noctaris and shaped by the hands of former Shadow Vaelora. That link to the Vaelora made him resilient and capable of existing in multiple realms, in multiple forms, but he was truly meant to reside *here*.

We had that in common.

And I wasn't sure I was ready to venture back into the light of Soltaris, with or without him.

But it was looking as though we might not have a choice.

"Let's see what information we can gather about this grove, then," said my brother with a pointed look in Eamon's direction. "If some of us have to pay a visit to the Above, then so be it. But no decisions need to be made tonight."

The discussion continued for several more minutes, but everyone ultimately agreed with my brother's plan.

I knew they were right not to rush into Soltaris unprepared.

Still, I hated the idea of waiting. Whatever had to be done, I just wanted to get it over with.

The others dismissed themselves one by one. Phantom followed Eamon out—likely to go pay a visit to Eamon's little sister, Brynn, who was notorious for spoiling him with treats. I couldn't find the energy to get up myself. Aleks fixed me with a lingering, concerned look as he started to leave with his cousin, but I waved him on.

My brother and I were soon alone in the courtyard.

To my surprise, Bastian didn't insist on talking more about our plans, or lecturing me about any of the latest rash decisions I'd made.

We sat together for another hour, mostly in comfortable silence. He pulled weeds from the beds of white and silver flowers, muttering occasionally to himself. His focus remained razor-sharp even as the hour grew late, but I nearly dozed off watching the moths fluttering around the torches by the gate.

Finally, I peeled myself off my chair and trundled back inside, heading for my room. I'd nearly made it to my hall when I heard Eamon's voice calling my name.

I didn't want to stop walking. I just wanted to collapse face first into my bed and ignore all of the questions and uncertainties circling us.

Plus, I had a bad feeling I knew what he wanted to talk about.

Steeling myself, I turned to meet him, all the same. "What is it, Eamon?"

"There's something else I think we need to discuss, regarding what happened in Midna."

I kept my face as impassive as I could.

"I didn't want to mention it in front of all the others, but…"

"But what?"

"It's about Aleks."

"What about him?" The words came out harsher than I meant them to.

He was unfazed by my tone, his own voice calm and deliberate as he said, "A sentier is an echo of the most powerful magic any Vaelora has ever been capable of. And he destroyed the one in that palace with hardly any effort at all."

"So?"

"So, he shouldn't have been able to do that, Nova.

Not if he's merely a hollowed-out victim that slipped out of Lorien's hold. That sort of skill lies with the Vaelora alone—only one of their own could unravel such a creature. And even then, I wouldn't think a Vaelora of the Light persuasion would be able to undo a divine Shadow creature so easily. Which means *something* is making Aleksander more powerful than he should be. And something about the alignment of that power seems…*off*."

I thought, unwillingly, of the encounter with Lord Renvar. Of how Aleksander's magic had seemed alarmingly powerful then, too.

Eamon's expression darkened. "There may be more of Lorien still clinging to him than we'd hoped. That, or something else is going on. Something stranger. I just…I just want you to be careful around him, that's all."

"I can read the energy of objects and organisms," I reminded him. "And I know what Aleks and his magic feel like; I know these things better than I know myself."

"Magic can play tricks."

"Yes, but he's proven strong enough to break through in the past," I insisted. "He wouldn't let Lorien play such a trick on me. I can tell the difference between the two of them."

"I hope you're right." I could tell he didn't think I was right at all. "But…remain cautious."

"I will." I tried to keep the bitterness from my voice,

knowing he was only trying to look out for me. "Thank you."

He gave a respectful dip of his head before walking away.

I stood alone in the hallway for a long moment, willing the tension out of my body through several deep breaths.

I wanted to believe I was right. That there was no chance Aleks wouldn't find a way to warn me if he posed any danger to me or to all the others I cared about.

But what if I was wrong?

And what if I didn't realize it until it was too late?

What if *he* didn't realize it?

I leaned against the wall, clenching my fist and knocking it against the plaster in frustration. The more I thought about it, the more it seemed like the only way to be certain Lorien no longer had a hold on Aleks was to put that bastard back in his own respective body. Then I could deal with him on a leveled playing field— no more guessing or worrying about who I was actually fighting.

I made it to my room but hesitated with my hand on the doorknob.

I was far too restless to sleep.

Aleks had walked away with Zayn, but that had been some time ago; hopefully, he was back in his room by this point.

Without a second thought, I decided to find out.

As I drew closer to that room, I felt his presence without even trying; it washed over me like a sudden burst of sunlight in the middle of a dreary winter day. It stood out within the dark halls of this palace in a way I'd never really noticed before.

Had it always been so easy to feel him?

Or was this another facet of his apparently unexplainable, stronger magic?

His door opened before I had a chance to knock, and there he stood, shirtless, with his pants hanging low on his hips. He didn't look at all surprised to see me. Butterflies fluttered in my stomach, though all my questions and anxious thoughts weighed down their flight.

"I sensed you coming," he said.

"Is that why you're half-naked? Because you were preparing for me?"

"I was preparing for a bath, actually." He gave me a sly grin. "Though you're welcome to join, of course."

Heat flooded me, but I shook my head and told him, "I know of someplace better to take a bath."

He arched a brow, a curious gleam in his golden eyes. He shrugged back into his shirt, leaving it casually loose and partially unbuttoned. "Lead the way, then."

I took him to the thermal pools beneath the palace.

"These were once the center of all royal socialization in Rivenholt," I informed him as we wound our way through steam-filled paths. Our hands were clasped together, our skin growing damp and lungs growing heavy from the humid air. "Several of the more private pools were sacred meeting and mediation spots, where rulers would apparently go to try and feel closer to all the divine beings who shaped our world. So, I'm probably violating all sorts of protocol and sacred tradition, bringing royalty from Soltaris down here. But, oh well."

"It isn't as though I have much claim to Soltaris anymore."

"I suppose that's true." I mirrored the wry grin he gave me, though my chest tightened when I thought of what had become of our respective kingdoms in the Above. "Either way, it's not the worst thing I've done as the would-be Queen of Rivenholt."

I lost my bearings at some point, too distracted by other thoughts, and the path we were following ended up bringing us to a dead-end—a small, cave-like room barely large enough to fit us both.

Small as it was, there was an impressive display of art etched into the rock that made us both stop and stare. I recognized some of the symbols and the inscriptions carved beneath them—the insignia of various noble houses that had enjoyed power throughout the history of Noctaris. This particular cove seemed to be a visual record of a treaty agreed upon by several of those houses, however long ago.

"It's haunting to think about all the ones who came before us, isn't it?" I asked, tracing the time-worn carvings.

"Yes," Aleks agreed. He took a step closer, as if to better study the etchings himself.

But when I turned, I found him studying me, not the walls. My pulse raced as he pressed a hand against the stone above my head, leaning forward and caging me in.

"Now I *know* we're violating some sort of palace tradition," I said.

His smile turned conspiratorial as his mouth tipped toward mine. "As long as we're desecrating sacred places, we might as well make a show of it."

Then he kissed me.

No matter how many times our lips met, it always managed to take my breath away. To make my body feel light enough to float away, yet somehow grounded at the same time. I closed my eyes and sank against the wall, dragging him with me. He tangled his hands through my hair, leaving my partial updo increasingly disheveled as our kiss grew deeper, hungrier.

I felt like I couldn't kiss him back hard enough to make up for the time we'd lost.

I was still willing to try.

His body was nearly flush against mine, but I yanked him even closer, my fingers kneading into the strong muscles of his back. His tongue plunged deeper in response, pulling a soft moan through my lips. The sound only made him more hungry, more desperate to seal his mouth completely over mine until we were a single being sharing the same magic, the same rhythms, the same air.

I was dizzy when he finally leaned away—just barely —so we could catch our breath. I lost mine again as his touch slid downward, mapping out the curves of my body before settling at my waist, slipping beneath the hem of my shirt and finding skin. His forehead came to rest against mine while he traced lazy, mesmerizing movements against me with his fingertips.

He lifted his gaze, meeting my slightly-dazed stare.

My heart thumped faster, remembering the way he'd looked at me in my room the other morning, right before…

"Say it again," I whispered. "Now that you aren't delirious from a narrowly-thwarted demonic possession."

He leaned a little farther away, a hint of a smile on his lips, his eyes shining with amusement, but also with a clear understanding of exactly what I wanted—*needed* —to hear.

"I love you," he whispered, gripping my chin and guiding my lips back to his for a slow, gentle kiss. "Though, for the record, I wasn't delirious when I said it before. Were you?"

I hesitated but decided to tell him the truth. "I constantly feel like I'm walking a line between insanity and reality, here lately."

His smile faded slightly. He brushed his hand across my cheek, taking hold of a strand of my hair and twirling it thoughtfully around his fingers for a moment before meeting my eyes again. His gaze was unflinching, full of promise and the sort of desire that made everything else glide to a stop.

"This is real," he said. "Trust me."

I managed an exhale.

A nod.

I took his hand again and led him onward. It was late enough that the area was entirely deserted, but we still wove our way deeper, as far as we could get from the stairs leading to the upper palace—all the way to the darkest, quietest pool we could find.

Aleks dipped his hand into the water and summoned a faint pulse of light, allowing us to gage the depth. He let the glow linger, but even then, the space remained dark and private enough that I didn't hesitate to strip off my clothing.

He followed my lead with perfectly casual grace, and I stumbled a bit at the sight. I'd seen him naked before, of course, but something about seeing him in this setting was different. The darkness, the steam, the stone walls glittering faintly in the light…

And we were alone.

Finally together, and finally *alone*, after so many long weeks.

Desire raced from the top of my scalp down through the tips of my toes—until Eamon's warnings whispered through my mind again.

I turned my back to Aleks, at least for the moment, focusing instead on scrubbing myself clean.

He didn't pressure me into anything more than this. We merely existed together for a half hour, maybe longer. The peace, the warmth, the closeness…it was quiet, simple bliss. A rapture that felt unearned—or maybe just strange underneath the weight of everything happening in the world outside.

The heat eventually started to make me feel dizzy, so I hoisted myself out and sat on the edge of the pool, feet still in the water. There was a cool breeze drifting in from somewhere; refreshing, at first, but I soon grabbed Aleksander's shirt and slid it over my chilled, pebbling skin.

He continued to swim in the basin. His magic ebbed and flowed with his movements, though overall his light remained faint. The darkness and the murky, mineral-rich water hid much of his body, but I was still entirely too aware of his nakedness.

I tried to keep myself from staring at him. To convince myself to be *cautious*, as Eamon had insisted.

I was…not particularly successful.

After a while, Aleks waded over to where I sat, wrapping his arms around my bare legs and pulling them together so he could rest his chin on my knees. Another wave of peaceful bliss overcame me, because *he* seemed so at peace. He studied me from underneath his lashes, occasionally planting kisses on my thighs. The movements were gentle. Sweet. Much more wholesome than what I *really* wanted him to do in that moment.

Caution, I reminded myself, cheeks burning as I glanced away.

"What are you thinking about?" he asked.

"Nothing."

He gave a quiet laugh.

"What?"

"You're a terrible liar."

I bit my lip and lifted my gaze to the ceiling. I didn't want to tell him about my conversation with Eamon, so instead I picked one of the dozens of other fears running endless circles in my mind.

"If I'm right about what I saw, it will mean returning to my old home, facing what's become of Rose Point, reliving all that happened on the night of my eighteenth birthday…and I'm just wondering what I'm supposed to do, going back there with all I know now. With all the new magic I'm capable of. My mother and half of my old palace were still frozen under a spell when I left. I set out to save them months ago, and even with everything else I'm facing now, I need to somehow fix that, too. I wonder if there's any hope of reviving them?"

I didn't expect an answer; he surprised me by giving one.

"I think there is." He stood up straighter, moving his hands to my hips. He was tall enough that we were eye-to-eye even though he stayed in the pool. My knees parted so he could move closer, and my thoughts strayed again to how little clothing separated us. I regretted the shirt I wore; I wanted to feel his warm skin against mine.

"We've worked our magic to revive beings here in Noctaris, haven't we?" he pointed out. "We can do it again."

"The spell over my old home isn't like anything we've faced here. And our magic isn't exactly predictable, either. It definitely won't work the same in the Above as it does in this realm… Need I remind you about the *last* time we collided at Rose Point?"

"It will be different, this time."

"Will it?"

"*We're* different."

For better or worse? I couldn't help wondering.

"Trust me, Nova."

There were those words again. He made it sound so simple. And I knew it was anything but simple—*we* were anything but simple—but his attempt to reassure me still made my heart flutter.

He leaned even closer, sliding his hands around to the small of my back. His hold was gentle, yet strong. I draped my arms around his neck, drawing his face closer to mine. I couldn't help it; I wanted to steady myself against him and no one else, *caution* be damned.

We stayed that way for I don't know how long, lost in each other's gaze, tied together by the same thoughts and fears.

At some point, his lips found mine again, pressing

against me with the same gentle certainty as his embrace. His fingertips dug into the base of my spine, pulling me forward and deeper into the kiss. I braced one hand against the warm stone for balance and brought the other up to the back of his neck, gripping and crushing his lips more completely to mine.

This is real.

I'd believed it when he said it earlier.

Why couldn't I hold on to that belief?

Mere inches existed between my body and his, but I still feared the emptiness between us. Within us. Part of me longed for the alcohol I'd been using to fill the spaces, or maybe for the endless meetings and royal duties that I loathed, but which felt like smaller, easier battles to occupy myself with, at least.

I'd pulled away without realizing it, drifting off into my thoughts; Aleks was staring at me, his brow furrowed with concern.

"I'm sorry," I said.

"Why are you apologizing?"

"Because I keep slipping away like that. Going numb without meaning to. I just…" I trailed off with a shrug.

"Numb?"

"Trying to protect myself from something, maybe."

He was quiet for a moment, and then, "…From me?"

There was no hint of accusation in his voice, yet the words still cut like blades through my chest.

My reply was shaky when it finally found its way out. "I missed you. These past weeks without you, I…I haven't been handling it all very well. I just tried to keep myself from feeling things."

"How?"

"It doesn't matter." Concerned disagreement flashed in his eyes, but I continued before he could speak. "I was starting to get addicted to numbing away the pain. It was easier than thinking about my feelings for you. Even now, there's a part of me that thinks it would be easier to keep my distance. You know, in case…"

In case Eamon is right, and this is all a trick.

I couldn't breathe, suddenly.

And I hoped with everything in me that Aleks couldn't read my mind in that moment.

He took my hand in his, thoughtfully tracing the lines along my palm for a minute. "I would never force you to feel something you aren't ready to feel."

I shook my head. "That isn't what I meant. I don't *want* easy. I want to feel. I want…"

His gaze shot up to mine, the intensity of his stare making my breath catch again.

I forced myself to exhale. "You," I finished in a whisper. "Just you."

He went back to studying the lines of my palm, the hint of a crooked smile curving his lips again. "Is that so?"

I heaved out a sigh.

His smile inched higher. "You seem conflicted."

"In my defense, I'm never able to think particularly clearly whenever you're naked in front of me."

"I know what you mean." His gaze flicked to the shirt draped loosely around me, and his hand followed, giving the fabric a little tug. "This thin bit of cloth might be my last tether to anything resembling control."

Untether yourself, then.

I don't know if he'd heard those words through our connected minds, or if he sensed the desperation behind the thought, but he pressed even closer to me—as if in response.

I tensed, eyes closing, as he gathered a fistful of the shirt. He used that grip to keep me steady while his other hand slid between my legs, coaxing them farther apart.

"Open your eyes," he said, voice low and dripping with desire, "and watch what I'm doing. No slipping away."

I did as he'd commanded, watching his fingers drag across my inner thighs. I shivered. He cocked his head, as if questioning whether or not I was in danger of slipping away.

A divine warmth rippled and curled through my belly. It still seemed timid, afraid of unfolding into something bigger and risking an equally bigger loss, but I didn't want him to stop what he was doing.

Again, he moved as though I'd spoken my thoughts out loud. He didn't stop. He confidently cupped a handful of water, drizzling it over my bare legs. I inhaled sharply at the splash of heat against my chilled skin. He did it again, sprinkling it higher up my legs this time. Then again, and again, dripping the warmth closer and closer to my center.

There was no numbness, now.

And that much was obvious, judging by the knowing smile that crossed his face. "You still seem to be feeling this, at least."

My chest rose and fell with quick, shallow breaths.

I managed a nod.

He dipped his hand back into the water, swirling it around for a few beats. Without taking his eyes from mine, he applied the warm water directly with his fingertips, tapping dampness onto my thighs with a smooth, purposeful touch. "And this?"

"All of it."

More thoughtful taps soon turned into unhurried strokes, smooth caresses that edged closer and closer to the most sensitive parts of me.

He knew precisely where to touch. Where to tease. Where to worship. Whatever time we'd lost, whatever hell his mind had endured these past weeks, he hadn't forgotten the maps he'd made of my body.

He undid the single button of the shirt that I'd fastened, opening it to reveal my breasts. Cupping each one in turn, he kissed and sucked the already-stiff peaks until I was writhing beneath him, growing more and more desperate for release. I gasped in both pleasure and pain as teeth joined tongue in a wicked fight for dominance.

At the sound, he pulled his mouth away. I started to protest but quieted as he cradled my legs and sank partially back into the pool, easing me down with him, angling his face toward the pulsing ache between my thighs.

He wasted no time before claiming me with a slow, savoring lick. My head tilted back. My vision blurred. I pressed both hands against the stone, fighting for balance as my body shook.

Once some of the dizziness subsided, I tucked my head back toward my chest, watching Aleks through eyes heavy with lust.

His gaze met mine as he came up for air just long enough to say, "I've missed your taste."

Another wave of dizziness. I don't know what my response was; something unintelligible, I'm certain. Something he understood to mean *don't stop.*

Please don't stop.

His hands gripped my knees, once again shoving them farther apart. I shifted my hands from the stone to his head, my fingers curling, clutching into the damp waves of his hair. At first, it was for balance, but soon I was pulling him in, driving him deeper, desperate to leave no emptiness between us.

He exhaled a soft laugh, the warmth of his breath nearly sending me over the edge. "I believe you've gone from *numb* to full participant."

I rolled my hips in answer, which earned another breathy burst of laughter.

"Good girl," he murmured.

I turned shameless at the praise, riding his face with reckless abandon, chasing wave after wave of my building release. He matched my eagerness without hesitation. His tongue was merciless, yet precise. His breath was hot. Heavy. Hungry. His fingers clenched so tightly into my thighs they were likely leaving permanent marks—and I *wanted* them to.

I wanted to be able to touch those marks later, to remember what he'd done to me.

To remember the way he slipped his fingers in alongside his tongue; the way he shifted so smoothly between savoring me with reverence and claiming me with savagery; and to not forget the moment I finally shattered—how I cried out, the sound echoing off the stone walls, and the way his grip grew even tighter in response, forcing me to be still while his mouth continued to work, to wring every last drop of pleasure from my body.

I was lost for some time after that moment, spinning in a sea of color and warmth that I never wanted to leave.

With powerful ease, Aleks pulled my tingling body into his arms and down into the warm water. He didn't say anything, but soon I heard his voice in my head again, as clearly as if he'd spoken out loud: *I love you.*

"…I'm not imagining it, am I? I keep hearing your voice in my thoughts."

His head tilted, curious. *You hear this?*

"Yes," I breathed.

Can you feel this? he asked, sending a wave of warmth cascading through my skull, briefly re-igniting the last embers of my orgasm.

Again, I whispered, *"Yes."*

He studied me for a few moments, tucking my wet hair away from my face, his fingers thoughtfully tracing my ear and then cupping my jaw. Words brushed my mind, just as tender as his touch: *Keep feeling it.*

I nodded. My heart was pounding. My numbness a distant memory. I was afraid of what came next, but I was *alive*. More alive than I'd been in weeks.

And it was worth the fear.

So I drew closer to him. I thought the same three words he'd spoken earlier, the only belief that seemed capable of anchoring us—*this is real, this is real, this is real*—and I pressed my lips to his again and again, until I could think of nothing else.

FIFTEEN

Aleksander

The next morning, I rose before the sun, startled awake by the sensation of something crawling over my skin.

No—not *over* it.

Inside of it.

A cold sweat washed over me as I sat up. The room spun. I closed my eyes until faint movement to my right made me open them again, reminding me I wasn't alone.

I breathed out a soft sigh, taking in the sight of Nova curled under the blankets next to me. Memories of last night—of staying up until an ungodly hour talking of nothing and everything—flooded my mind, calming it. Watching her body rise and fall with peaceful breaths brought me even further back to my senses, stopping the room's spinning, helping me remember why I was here and where I was going.

I wasn't sure when it had happened, but my internal compass didn't point north, any longer; it pointed to her.

Quietly, I slipped out of bed and went to the wash room. After splashing handfuls of freezing cold water on my face, my gaze ended up transfixed on the ornate mirror above the sink. After weeks spent in Lorien's clutches, the reflection looking back at me still seemed like a stranger.

I stared at it for a moment, half-expecting to see movement underneath my skin; the crawling sensation hadn't lessened.

But no matter how long I stared, my reflection didn't change. My skin didn't split apart, revealing some heinous beast underneath, trying to make itself known…

I was merely myself again.

For now, at least.

Walking back into Nova's room, my eyes automatically drifted to Grimnor. It was leaning against the far wall, reflecting none of the rising sunlight that was glinting off so many other things around it. It always seemed to absorb light, instead. I could sense Lorien's presence hovering within the velvety dark blade—a brand of magic I feared I would never be able to *not* recognize, however faint it was now.

That wasn't what had woken me up, though.

The crawling in my skin was different. It didn't feel like something separate from me, trying to gain control. It felt more like something...*waking* within me. Like an old wound I'd aggravated somehow.

Movement seemed to help settle it, so I dressed and headed for the armory and training grounds on the opposite side of the palace.

As I made my way into the space, helping myself to one of the swords hanging in the armory, I heard voices coming from a meeting room along the grounds' edge. A tense conversation, from the sound of it. I recognized the voice of Nova's brother, among others, but I paid them little mind, turning my attention instead to the pile of practice dummies leaning against a nearby partition. I arranged a small army of opponents and went to work.

The next hour passed in a blur.

The meeting continued to rumble in the background, raised voices occasionally distracting me from my practice.

Eventually, the loudest exclamations thus far were accompanied by several people storming from the private room and angrily making their way back toward the main palace.

I drew closer to the scene, curiosity getting the better of me.

Moments later, three more people exited the room —Lord Renvar, flanked by two guards. Bastian followed them out but paused in the doorway, his mouth set in a hard line and his body tense as he watched them go.

Renvar threw a wary glare in my direction but walked by me without saying a word.

A smart choice.

Bastian didn't move until long after they'd disappeared, at which point he silently made his way over to the battalion of dummies I'd been working against. He unsheathed the short sword at his belt and twisted it back and forth with methodical, balanced precision before launching into a rush of powerful swings and strikes.

I considered calling it quits and leaving him to practice alone, that is until he stopped me with a pointed glance—right after cleanly slicing the head from one of the dummies. It bounced once against the dusty ground before rolling to a stop at his feet.

"There are rumors that you attacked Lord Renvar the other night," Bastian said.

"*Attacked* is a strong word."

He lowered his sword, studying me.

I tensed but said nothing else; if he was hoping for an apology for what I'd done, he wasn't going to get it.

Because I wasn't sorry.

If anything, I wished I'd done more than just frightening the bastard.

The regent knelt to pick up the decapitated head,

calmly and precisely balancing it back on the figure's body. I got the impression that he spent a lot of time in these grounds, relieving these practice mannequins of their heads.

Rolling some of the tension from his shoulders, he said, "He was overdue for a good humbling. So, thank you."

I could hardly contain my surprise at his unconcerned tone.

"…Happy to help," I said.

Light was starting to break through the hazy canopy of clouds above us, brighter than I'd ever seen it over this palace. It still wasn't a morning like the ones I remembered in Soltaris, but after so much time spent down here in the dark, it seemed almost like a normal sunrise.

There were swaths of black marring the sky far in the distance, though—places where the awakening sun clearly didn't reach.

"Renvar is growing impatient," Bastian said, "and he's not the only one. With every ounce of magic that rains down from Nerithys, they only want more." He shielded his eyes from the breaking light, focusing on the farthest patch of brightness we could see. "They don't understand Nova's power. Or its limits. They don't *want* to study the history, the nuances of Shadow and Light, how they intersect, or the warning signs within these erratic ebbs and flows of magic—all the things I'm desperately trying to make sense of. They want easy answers. But nothing about this is *easy*. Our world isn't as it once was."

I settled on the steps in front of the meeting room, laying my borrowed sword down beside me.

"Meanwhile, my advisors want to focus on a coronation," Bastian continued. "Crowning Nova to further secure Rivenholt, at the very least. All of our potential allies are counting on her to carry on the tradition of the first-born taking the throne without question." He sighed. "But now she *also* has the matter of Lorien's curse to deal with, on top of everything else."

I found myself understanding his exact point, even though he never outright said it—because I felt the same thing.

There was so much he couldn't carry for her, even if he wanted to.

Quietly, he said, "I've made the mistake of asking too much of her in the past."

I thought of how she'd fought her way into the Kingdom of Midna, alone, and forced Lorien's hand. Of how she'd walked willingly into death at the start of all this. Of everything we'd talked of last night before going to sleep: her kingdom here in the Below; the mess that remained of the middle realm; the looming shell of Rose Point above, with all of its ghosts—her mother among them.

All the things she was desperate to fix.

I said, "She asks too much of herself, too. It runs in your family, apparently."

Bastian let out a humorless chuckle.

"She isn't fragile," I reminded him.

"No. But strong things break, too." He was silent for a moment. "All these wars..." he eventually muttered, raking a hand through his hair. "I hate the idea of sending her off to face *any* of them without going alongside her. But it can't be helped, can it? I'll have to continue to hold the line down here. You all will have to return to the Above. And maybe we'll manage to balance it all before the end."

I nodded in agreement with this plan, even though he seemed to be holding a private council, trying to convince himself rather than me.

He shifted his attention to his sword again, swiping and slicing through the air with heavy but smooth motions. The blade's handle caught a piece of sunlight, and I noticed a familiar symbol in the center—a circle divided diagonally by a vine-wrapped sword.

The mark of the Void Order.

Noticing me staring at it, Bastian said, "Another war I'm trying to figure out." He held the weapon up for me to inspect. "This is one of the many relics Nova and Thalia have brought back from the middle realm over these past few weeks. I'm noticing, now, just how many things from that realm carry this symbol, even though it's often much smaller and less noticeable than this. I think that Order may have been more involved in the Vaeloran Cycle, and all its workings and weavings, than we previously guessed."

For some reason, whenever I looked at the symbol, I was struck with a wave of unease. Bastian didn't seem to want to meet my eyes all of a sudden, either, which did nothing to settle the anxious churning in my gut.

Was there something he wasn't telling me?

Before I could venture a guess as to what it might be, he cleared his throat and said, "Answer a question for me."

"What is it?"

He glanced my way, but still didn't quite meet my eyes. "Nova claims you are back in control of your own body, your own magic. And yet, my servants who witnessed the magic you used against Lord Renvar seemed terrified when they reported it to me. It apparently lingered in that room long after you'd left, so powerful that most of them refused to even go inside for a closer look." He inhaled deeply. "So, before I send you off on this quest with my sister, I'm forced to ask: How much of our enemy still lingers within you?"

I stared at the symbol on his sword for a long time.

"I'm not sure," I replied, honestly.

"Do you still feel him?"

"I feel…different. Not like him, though."

"But do you feel like *yourself*?"

The question sank like a stone into the pit of my stomach. I didn't know how to answer it, and Bastian didn't seem surprised by my silence.

He moved to face the line of practice dummies once

more. "It's a dangerous thing, to not know who you are."

I couldn't disagree.

"How do you know there isn't a chance of his control returning at the worst possible time?" he asked.

"I don't."

I could sense the tension that roiled through his body, even from where I sat, but a resigned sigh soon followed it.

I got to my feet. "There is one thing I *am* certain of, though."

He angled his face toward me.

"I would die before I let any harm come to her, from my hands or otherwise."

He finally met my eyes, holding my gaze for a long moment before readying his sword once more, preparing for another assault against the practice dummies.

"For her sake," he said, "let's hope it doesn't come to that."

FOUR MORE DAYS WENT BY.

I saw little of Nova. She spent most of her time doing what she could to prepare Rivenholt for her potential absence, whether it was meeting with every noble that demanded it; visiting the rebuilding sites across the kingdom; or using her power to guide and shape the magic trickling over the land, trying to settle and soothe as many places as she could.

Every evening, she collapsed into my arms and fell asleep almost instantly, while I did my best to settle and soothe *her*.

Even with the warmth of my magic cocooning her, she rarely slept through the night.

I spent my days being as useful as I could elsewhere, which typically meant serving as an assistant to Eamon while he scoured the materials they'd collected from Midna. We compiled and cross-referenced stacks upon stacks of notes. Zayn helped, as well—though he only made it midway through the second day before threatening to hurl himself from the library window out of boredom. Eamon then ordered him to go be dramatic elsewhere, and we carried on without him.

The mark of the Void Order kept showing up, seemingly everywhere we looked. Most notably, we came across it on a tattered letter, stamped into a corner in ink the color of blood. The contents of the letter were innocuous enough, with no actual reference to the order aside from its symbol…

But it was signed *Argoth*.

As in, King Argoth.

My distant ancestor, and the Soltarisian ruler who had, according to legend, come between Lorien and Calista.

I puzzled over the connection between it all, but Eamon didn't seem to want to linger on the subject. I thought of the way Bastian had averted his eyes when we'd discussed that mark the other morning, and I wondered, again, if there was something I wasn't being told—some theory they weren't sharing with me.

I could only guess at most of it.

But one thing I *was* certain of was that everything continued to point to an inevitable trip to the Above.

So, as soon as morning dawned on the fifth day, we began to pack. By that evening, our small company was prepared to leave. Zayn and Thalia would be joining us, along with a group of soldiers who would see us to the edge of Rivenholt's revived territory, where we planned to set up camp before continuing on to our next destination.

That destination was the Nocturnus Road—the same path Nova had taken when she'd first descended into this realm months ago. She had grown skilled in her ability to move herself and others freely between the middle-realm and this one, but traveling all the way back to the Above was another challenge entirely. The established road would be safer. Easier on her. And while there were other alleged pathways between Noctaris and Soltaris, we opted for this one because it was familiar, and because it would bring us as close as possible to our ultimate target of Rose Point.

We gathered by the stables once the sun began to set, saying goodbyes and rehashing our plans one final time. It would be two days of hard riding to reach Nocturnus, through lands caught between death and revival that would be, at best, unpredictable.

Bastian and Thalia stood alone off to the side, deep in conversation. Nova walked through the ranks of our accompanying soldiers, giving final orders. Phantom trotted closely at her heels, shifted into his usual dog form; he seemed very pleased with himself—likely because he'd talked Nova into letting him come along on this mission.

Zayn had just finished adjusting the tack on one of the massive scourge stallions we'd be riding. His eyes lingered on the beast even as he made his way over to me; their powerful, monstrous appearances were hard to look away from.

"It's going to be strange, being back in the Above after all these years," he said, gaze drifting upward as he approached. "But I'm looking forward to feeling a warmer, brighter sun on my face again. You know, without the whole someone-else-inside-of-my-skin thing."

"I'd be more enthusiastic if we had any idea of what actually awaited us underneath that brighter, warmer sun."

"Forever the voice of reason murdering my excitement," he said with a crooked smile.

"It's not a vacation we're embarking on," I reminded him, unapologetically.

"Well, I'm personally still going to focus on the feel of the sunlight on my face."

I acquiesced with a little shrug, trying to appear unbothered—even though the thought of such light had been stirring unpleasant, long-buried memories in me all day.

I was far removed from the life I'd lived in the Above kingdom of Elarith. The Keepers of Light, who had once controlled and judged my every movement were buried deeply enough in the past that I rarely thought of them or the scars they'd left.

But now, here we were, returning to the scene of one of the disasters they'd helped orchestrate.

Questions about their connections to Lorien—to *all* the wars we faced—swirled in my head. And if there was potential overlap with the members of that ancient Void Order, as Eamon had said…

What was I walking back into, exactly?

As soon as the question crossed my mind, the crawling underneath my skin struck again. It was accompanied by burning, this time—like the heated ends of a hundred needles prodding, trying to poke through. I fought to keep myself from flinching.

Zayn seemed to notice; his smile remained, but his voice was slightly more serious as he said, "Are you all right, by the way? Any more strange, internal rumblings I should be aware of?"

I'd mentioned the strangeness to him days ago, mostly because I'd wondered if he was experiencing—

or had previously experienced—anything similar. But, although we'd both been subjected to similar torture, we seemed to be recovering in different ways. No unpredictable magic plagued him. In fact, though he was still unusually attuned to the presence of it in others, he didn't seem to possess *any* for himself.

I was glad he didn't have to carry the weight of it any more. But it only made me more concerned about what was happening to me.

If Zayn had managed a clean break, then why hadn't I?

What about all the years I'd possessed magic following my first escape from Lorien's possession, when I was only a child? What if some part of him had actually lodged itself in my soul decades ago and had been poisoning me ever since?

Where did he end?

Where did I begin?

"Aleks? Are you alright?"

I gave my head a little shake. "I'm fine."

Zayn looked prepared to call me out on the lie, but Eamon joined us before he could.

"A condensed summary of the notes we've been compiling over these past few days," Eamon said, handing me a bundle of twine-secured parchment.

I arched a brow as I took it. *Condensed*, he claimed; yet, the stack was several inches thick.

Nevertheless, I dutifully tucked it into the bag slung over my shoulder.

"If you do come across Orin, he might be able to give more insights about it all," he added.

"Are you sure you don't want to join us?" Zayn asked him. "I was looking forward to watching you be entirely too enthusiastic about every rock and tree we encountered in the Above."

Eamon pursed his lips, looking as though he was considering giving a matter-of-fact lecture about those various rocks and trees we might come across.

Nova saved us from that particular horror, interjecting herself into the conversation as she joined us. "He's staying," she said. "We aren't leaving my brother entirely alone down here."

"It's an honor to remain by his side," Eamon agreed, quickly. "Thalia will be the better companion to you for this excursion, anyhow." He looked in her direction, watching as she secured the last of her riding gear. He seemed relieved at the sight of her preparing to leave.

We all were, I think.

She'd been missing for most of the day. I'd worried that she would refuse to join us, but it seemed her loyalty to Nova now surpassed whatever misgivings she had about journeying to the Above and facing her father—and whatever else awaited us there.

She caught me staring and threw me one of her typical cold, borderline suspicious looks. Her glare lingered briefly before she exchanged a final word with Bastian, then she mounted her scourge stallion, Uldrin, and immediately trotted toward the gates.

"That's our cue, I suppose," said Zayn, following her lead.

Bastian's gaze shifted from Thalia to our group, darting between Nova and me before settling on me. The quiet, unspoken plea in his eyes was obvious: *Keep her safe.*

I acknowledged it with a slight nod, then I followed Thalia's lead as well.

The first day of riding passed in a haze of quiet determination and exhausting, constant vigilance.

Nova alternated between riding with me and riding on Phantom, who shifted between a larger version of his canine self and a beast that resembled the stallions the rest of us rode. We traveled at night because it allowed us to remain largely unnoticed as we passed through the clusters of Rivenholt's reviving population —although an unsettling number of this population still called out, still tried to get Nova's attention, even when I attempted to hide her.

"It feels strange to just ride by them without speaking," she said, miserably, as we passed the last of the revived strongholds.

I tightened the arm I had around her waist. "You'll be back to them soon enough. One battle at a time. If we stopped for them all, we'd never get anywhere."

She settled back against me, disgruntled but silent.

As planned, we came to a stop just beyond the edge of that last site of revival. We attempted to rest. To eat. Nobody spoke much. Wandering shades skulked at the edges of our camp, a few of which seemed unusually sentient and far more watchful than I liked.

But they kept their distance, thankfully.

The day proved largely uneventful, and when night fell again, we wasted no time saddling up and pressing onward into the dark.

Nova had spent much of our break studying and trying to communicate with the shades—instead of sleeping—so I wasn't surprised when exhaustion quickly overtook her once we were moving again. She slept against me while we rode. I navigated the uneven terrain as smoothly as I could, trying not to wake her.

Even though most of the magic from Nerithys hadn't reached this far out, there were signs of life trying to find its way into the bleak landscape: occasional, pulsing veins of pale blue; glimmers of wayward light; the scent of crisp water and something floral breaking through the more prevalent stench of dirt and decay.

After hours spent making our way through twisted paths and ridges cloaked in darkness—a darkness that lingered, even after what should have been dawn—we finally came to the access point of the Nocturnus Road. Its energy rolled toward us in a wave, growing more intense with every step we took toward it, as if waking to our presence.

As a particularly violent wave washed over us, Nova sat upright with a gasp. She took only a moment to orient herself, and then she was jumping from my arms and striding toward the road.

Phantom followed her while the rest of us dismounted. Thalia started to remove her stallion's riding gear, wrapping it in protective cloths, as planned; we would stow our equipment in the safest spot we could find, and the half-feral beasts would roam this area until we returned.

"Hate to part ways, now," Zayn said as he removed his mount's gear. "He was finally starting to warm up to me, I think."

"*Was* he, though?" said Thalia, offhandedly. "They don't usually take kindly to beings without any trace of necromantic magic." Raising a brow, she added, "Although, I suppose it's a small miracle he hasn't ripped any of your limbs off."

As if to prove her point, Zayn's stallion bared its teeth and gave an ominous snort.

Zayn merely patted its nose, earning himself a snap, which he narrowly avoided. "I'll miss you too, friend."

"You're sure they'll be okay on their own?" Nova asked, circling back to us.

"Uldrin is smart enough to keep them safe and together until we get back," Thalia said, referring to her own trusted steed. "He knows the way home, too, should we take longer than planned. They'll probably enjoy racing freely in the meantime; this darkness is nothing to them. They probably prefer it, actually."

While they continued to discuss the wellbeing of the beasts, I found myself wandering closer to Nocturnus.

The road was covered in a tumbling mass of energies—lingering residue from all the spells used to cross it in the past, as well as the restless memories and powerful emotions left behind by the spellcasters. I wasn't as skilled at seeing these things as Nova was, but they were obvious enough here that they were hard to miss.

My eye caught a particularly bold streak of golden light, brighter than anything we'd seen on our journey thus far. It made me think of the brighter realm we'd soon be stepping into.

Soltaris is so close.

An odd pang struck me at the thought. Not exactly homesickness—how could it be, when I had absolutely no desire to return to the place I'd once called home? Yet, there was a hook in my chest pulling me toward it. An instinct I couldn't ignore.

Without thinking, I reached my hand out, as if to grab hold of that golden current of light. Though I didn't touch it, it twisted with the same motions as my wrist. Subtle movements whipped it into a frenzy, brightening it to an eye-watering intensity. Its intensity chased away some of the competing energies on the road and absorbed others. Then the radiance gathered into a spherical shape, floating in my direction, hovering before me like my own personal sun.

Another odd feeling rippled through me as I stared at it.

A violent, unsettling feeling.

I took a deep breath and extinguished the sphere of energy with a mere clench of my fist, leaving behind nothing but a dusty, barren road stretching into the distance, reaching toward a faintly pulsing portal.

The portal that would take us back to the Above.

Somewhere far behind me, I heard Nova gasp. The conversation between her and the others abruptly ended. I could sense the questions firing through her head, though I couldn't make out any distinct words.

"…Even I have to admit, that's helpful," Thalia finally said, cautiously stepping closer.

"I do what I can," I said with a shrug.

But now the crawling in my skin had returned, more insistent than ever. It focused toward my hands, as if it wanted to control them. As if it wanted—*needed* —to grab more energy from somewhere and destroy that, too.

All around us, an odd, echoing stillness was spreading.

In my mind, visions of destruction bloomed. Of an explosion of light spreading outward, flooding the world in beauty and ruin alike…only to collapse in on itself, creating a void that swallowed all sound and color. I started to sink into the possibility. Could feel the heat blistering beneath my palms, could smell the hints of ash and burning dust, could see the darkness overtaking it and leaving behind a brutal, empty cold. Light and Dark. Dark and Light. Both seemed equally dangerous, both were—

A hand came to rest on my arm.

Nova's voice was in my mind a moment later.

Aleks. Look at me.

She could have spoken out loud.

I was glad she hadn't. I don't think I would have heard her. And it was more comforting to *feel* her voice falling over the images of destruction, extinguishing them like a cool rain over a building wildfire.

If she had seen or heard any of my disturbing thoughts, she said nothing about them as I glanced her way; she only tightened her grip on my arm and asked, "Ready?"

"Yes," I replied. Even though every part of me was fighting to keep the memory of her brother's words from my mind—trying to keep her from hearing what he'd said to me at the training grounds the other morning.

It's a dangerous thing, to not know who you are.

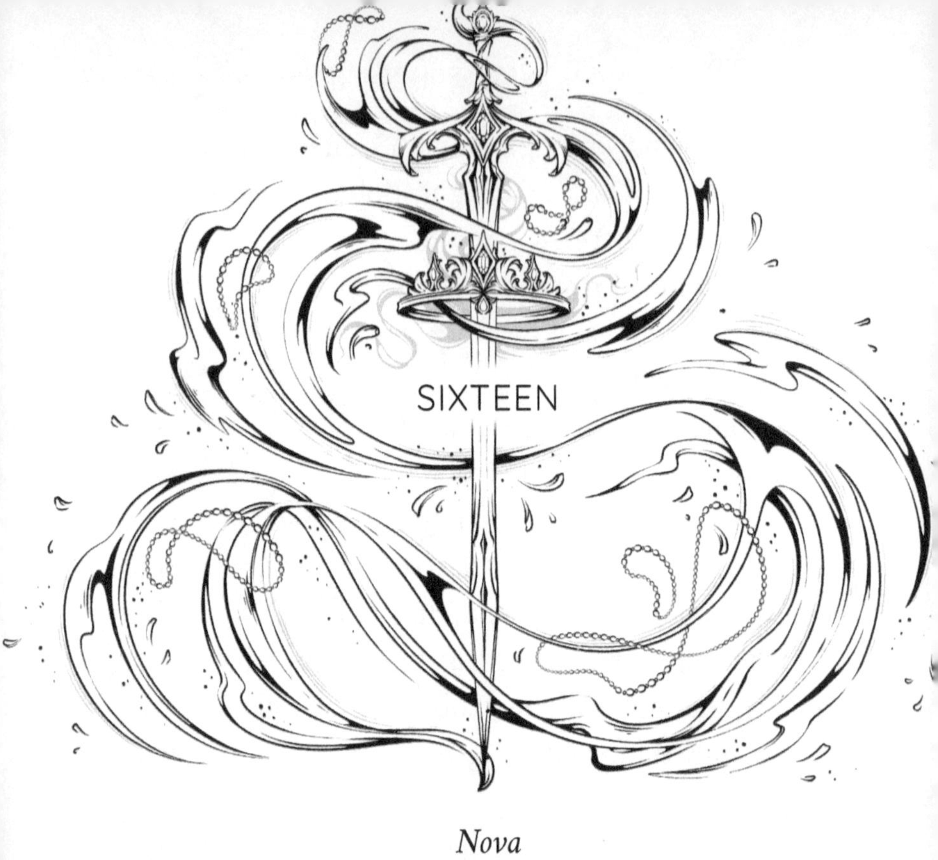

SIXTEEN

From the outside, Orin's house looked exactly as it had when I'd left it months ago. Wild, barely tamed flowerbeds; a door covered in peeling yellow paint; dusty windows open to let in the sounds of the stream bubbling nearby.

Birds chirped. The sun peeked in and out of puffy white clouds. A warm breeze ruffled my hair. It all brought back memories of beautiful days spent sitting in the creaky chairs on the back porch with Orin, discussing everything from magic to politics to dinner plans.

I'd forgotten how much I'd missed this place.

But I was not here to reminisce.

I wound my way down the cobblestone path to the front door, eyes scanning for threats. I'd seen too much these past months; I couldn't help feeling paranoid.

Phantom was my only companion. He was little more than a wisp of shadows shaped like a tiny, lanky dragon, curled up in the pocket of my coat, his head occasionally popping out and sniffing the air. Stable and aware enough, but struggling to hold a more powerful physical form, as I'd expected.

Thalia, Zayn, and Aleks waited in the woods close by. It had been Thalia who suggested we not crowd the house, at least initially—that Orin might be more willing to talk and reveal things if we didn't all confront him at once.

I suspected she simply wasn't ready to face him.

As I crept closer to the house, I started to wonder if *I* was ready to face him.

He'd kept so, *so* much from me. The more I thought about it, the more angry I felt. Anger eventually overtook any sense of caution or paranoia I felt, making me march up to the door and shove it open without any hesitation.

I was prepared for the familiar scent of books and old parchment, blended with woodsmoke and various herbs.

Instead, the stench of something rotten assaulted my nose, so pungent it made my eyes water. I found the culprit quickly: A dinner plate featuring molded bread and some sort of meat swarmed with flies. Beside it sat a cup of tea, ice cold and completely full, along with a small bowl of spoiled fruit.

The windows had clearly been open for some time, through both sun and storm alike; the curtains hung heavy and damp, leaves and other outside debris littering the floor all around them. Several weeks' and countless storms' worth of debris, it looked like.

Heart pounding, I made my way to Orin's room, to the closet where I knew he kept most of his traveling equipment.

All of it was still there.

My heart continued to race faster and faster, my magic pounding right along with it. It was so loud, so obvious, that I wasn't surprised when I felt Aleksander's power rise up in answer. His voice was in my mind a moment later.

Are you okay?

I wasn't sure. It didn't seem like Orin had planned to leave—but then again, he could be absent-minded and unpredictable. Maybe he'd simply wandered off some-where and lost track of how long he'd been gone?

Nova?

I closed one of the windows, my hand bracing against the latch, and I took a deep breath.

He's gone.

I ENDED UP SITTING ON THE BACK PORCH AFTER ALL, JUST as I had on so many beautiful days before this one, letting the noise of the creek and the woods lull me into a calmer, more thoughtful place.

Orin never showed up.

Instead, it was the four of us talking, arguing, trying to decide what to do next.

"You know the way to this Hollow Grove place, don't you?" Thalia asked.

"...I think so." I frowned as I tried to picture the paths I'd last walked more than a year ago. "I've never been without Orin leading the way, though."

"But do we really *need* him?"

"We don't know what sort of magic is actually at work in said grove," Zayn pointed out. "His guidance would be nice."

"Lots of things would be *nice*," Thalia countered. "It would be *nice* if he'd told Nova more about this grove to begin with, for example. Or if he'd properly warned her about *any* of these things we're facing. But that's not the reality we're dealing with, now, is it?"

Zayn settled into a sun-bathed chair and stretched out, tucking his hands behind his head. "Someone's in a bad mood."

Thalia fumed in silence for a moment before

storming down to the creek, mumbling something about *annoying Soltarisan assholes.*

I watched her leave, the pit in my stomach widening. "Of course she's in a bad mood," I said. "Her relationship with Orin aside, the very air of this realm is unsettling for a Shadow wielder. It feels strange to me even after only a few months of getting acclimated to Noctaris, and despite my Vaeloran blood that gives me power in both realms; I imagine it's worse for her."

Thalia was a Shadow feyth. Incapable of creating magic from nothing, but able to draw out the dark energy of a given place, or to channel the magic summoned by higher divine beings. In the Below, where Shadow magic was more abundant, she and her staff were often a force to be reckoned with. Up here, there was much less material for her to work with.

Zayn considered this for a moment. "Her father was your teacher, right?"

"Yes."

"He was Aetherkin?"

I nodded.

"So, a step above the feyth when it comes to the hierarchy of magic, but still technically out of his element here. Because I assume he was Shadow-aligned too, like his daughter. Or necromancy-inclined, or whatever you want to call it."

"Yes…which is maybe why he taught me by way of lectures, more than anything. When it came to magic, his skill lay more in creating potions and trinkets and occasional weapons. Things like the bracelets I once used to temper my power."

Yet, I'd never wondered much about his magic. Never thought it strange that he knew so much about my shadows despite not being able to fully wield them himself. It had never crossed my mind that he could possibly belong to another realm entirely.

I should have asked more questions; I felt like such a fool, standing here. A stranger in my own home. An ignorant—

No.

This wasn't my home.

And I couldn't afford to get weighed down by the memories and mistakes haunting the life I'd once lived here.

"The Hollow Grove is one of the few places he allowed me to actually practice my power," I said. "We started visiting it regularly after what happened on my eighteenth birthday. It became a kind of…sanctuary."

Aleks walked to the edge of the porch, his arms crossing over his chest and gaze narrowing on something in the distant woods. After a couple minutes of tense silence, he said, "Whether we go to that grove now or not, I don't think we should linger here. There must be a reason Orin left in a hurry and didn't come back, right?"

"Another thing that would be *nice* to know," Zayn said, "is what that reason might have been." He threw a pointed look in my direction.

I frowned. I knew what he was suggesting—that I could use my magic to divine the past events that had taken place in Orin's home.

Reluctantly, I got to my feet and went inside. I didn't know where to start, so I simply made a few laps around the kitchen, dragging my fingertips across the scuffed and scratched countertops, waiting for the tell-tale pressure in my head that meant the past was trying to make itself known to me.

But no matter how hard I tried to visualize what had happened, I kept seeing nothing but an empty canvas of grey fog.

Maybe some lingering, messy spell of Orin's was interfering with my ability to divine. Or maybe I wasn't seeing anything because I was afraid, and I didn't truly *want* to see anything.

Whatever the reason, I never managed to get a clear picture of whatever had happened.

I did manage to uncover emotions, though: a fresh, poignant wave of panic mangled with despair. I did my best to put that feeling into words for the others.

"Seems like we have more than enough proof that *something* isn't right here," Aleks said, "and we should leave while we can."

Within the next few minutes, it was decided: We needed to move. And there was no point in going back to Noctaris empty-handed, so we would just have to find our way into the Hollow Grove without Orin's guidance.

I was confident about the general direction to travel, at least. We made our way toward it, sweeping wide around the grounds of Rose Point, staying outside the perimeter affected by the curse that had trapped my mother and so many others on that fateful night seven years ago.

Even with everything else I had to focus on, the ache to make sense of that night pulsed like an old wound. My heart raced as we walked along the curse's edge. As I fought through the guilt, the fear, the urge to pass beyond that edge and see my mother again, whether in my physical body or as a projected spirit.

Aleksander's hand brushed against the small of my back. "One thing at a time," he reminded me.

Reluctantly, I nodded.

We came to an area blanketed with withering blue and white flowers. Just beyond it, the Hollow Wood's wall of tall trees loomed. A narrow path led into those trees. There were footprints that made me think it had recently been trodden upon, yet there was a tangle of briars and vines stretching across that same path, making the route impenetrable. It almost looked intentional—like a spell woven to block our way.

"This looks familiar, but…it's more overgrown than it should be," I said, frowning. "I remember this area being clear, but these thorns and vines look like they've been growing without interference for years."

"If there's magic at work, the growth here could be accelerated, right?" Zayn suggested.

"It certainly wouldn't be the strangest thing we've seen," Aleks said.

I nodded. "I think this is the right path," I said. "We just need to get through this tangled mess."

Thalia led the way, using her staff to twist and rip aside the vines and briars. Aleks summoned a floating orb of light, trying to guide our movements as the day grew increasingly darker underneath a thickening canopy of overarching trees. I moved methodically between them both, unsheathing Grimnor. Despite it being weaker here than in Noctaris, merely tapping the blade against the foliage caused it to recoil, and occasionally to shrivel up entirely.

The deeper we pressed, though, the less this trick seemed to work. The air was growing thicker with every step. Resisting us, wrapping around and settling like a too-tight embrace around our bodies...

Almost like it was trying to trap us.

But the thought of turning around and fighting our way back to the world outside seemed even more uncomfortable. So we pressed on, eventually reaching a clearing that looked strangely manicured compared to everything else around it.

At the back of this clearing, several trees bent and twisted together in a way that resembled an arched doorway.

"Is it just me, or is that terribly suspicious looking?" asked Zayn.

"Does it look familiar?" Thalia asked me.

A throbbing pain struck between my eyes as I tried to reply.

Did I know this place?

And, if so, why couldn't I clearly remember anything about it?

"Nova?"

"I've been here before, I think. But it's slightly... *wrong*, again. Like it's all been rearranged somehow..."

A branch creaked above us, slow and deliberate, as if the forest was craning closer to hear.

Thalia gripped her staff tightly in both hands. "It feels oddly aware of us, doesn't it?"

"A sentient forest." Zayn let out a cough. *"That's* a horror I wasn't entirely prepared for," he said, cracking his knuckles. "And I was prepared for *a lot* of different horrors the moment I agreed to come on this little adventure."

Cautiously, we approached the arched trees. A strange glimmer pulsed just beyond them, bright but obscured, like moonlight viewed from underwater.

A short distance away, Aleks had stopped in his tracks. The magic he'd been using to light our way grew dim, and the forest fell silent, save for our tense breathing.

Then, it started: A song. At first, I thought it was merely the wind scraping branches together and rattling pinecones in a strangely rhythmic way...until I heard a soft, sparkling voice joining in.

I fell into a trance, listening to it.

I don't know how much time passed before I managed to break free, my eyes finding and focusing on the faint orb of light still hovering next to Aleks.

"…Do you hear that?" I whispered, inching closer to him.

He didn't answer right away. He didn't have to; he was looking in the exact direction the song seemed to be echoing from, his fists clenching and unclenching, his entire body rigid.

Zayn and Thalia didn't seem to hear anything; they'd moved on to exploring the area on the far side of the clearing.

Aleks gave his head a little shake and walked toward them. I started to follow, until I was distracted by a different sound: Footsteps shuffling through the brush, somewhere off in the opposite direction. The movements sounded heavy. Weary.

Phantom poked his head out of my pocket and let out a hiss as the noise drew closer; he was so small, so weak, that I felt him more than I heard him. I urged him deeper into my pocket and squeezed Grimnor's handle, preparing to spin and strike if necessary.

"Late for your lesson, as per usual," said a familiar voice.

I turned to see Orin standing less than a dozen feet away, leaning against a walking stick that barely seemed to be keeping him upright.

He looked…*awful*.

There was no other word for it. His skin was waxy

and drawn tight over sharp bones, his lips pale as milk, and his eyes—once bright amethyst and constantly shining with curiosity—were clouded and rimmed with dark lines.

His voice wavered with a bit of uncharacteristic emotion as he said, "I expected I'd be seeing you much sooner; Bastian wrote to me a few days ago, telling me you intended to return. The vaekin that carried his message into this realm barely arrived in one piece."

I stepped toward him, torn between embracing him and shaking him, demanding answers.

"I had hoped we'd meet again," he said, quietly.

Despite my irritation with him, I couldn't help but say, "Me too."

"Our worlds are in quite a perilous state, aren't they?" he mused. "What exactly have you been up to these past months?"

"I think you could probably guess." I failed to keep the hurt and venom from my voice as I added, "And you could probably explain all that's been happening better than I could. If you cared enough to, that is."

"…We *do* have a lot to talk about, I suppose." He sighed. "Though I think that conversation is going to have to wait. The trees are restless; your mere presence has woken them up, reminding this grove of its purpose."

"Its purpose?"

"Mm."

Speaking in riddles again.

Typical.

Before I could voice my annoyance, I followed his gaze to the arched trees, and my breath caught as I realized Aleks was making his way underneath them without hesitation.

I took a step toward him, but Orin snatched my arm and held me back. "Don't be reckless."

I looked to the others for help, only to see that Zayn and Thalia both seemed to be in a trance; Zayn's head was tucked against his chest, as if he'd fallen asleep on his feet, while Thalia leaned on her staff and massaged her temples, grimacing as though fighting some invisible pressure.

I watched Aleks disappear, the light he'd summoned growing fainter and fainter. Frantically, I called his name. The only answer was a brief pulse of his light...

And then it was gone, too.

"What is going on?" I demanded of Orin, jerking free of his grip. "Why isn't he answering me? And that...that song we both heard..."

"So you *both* heard it?" He didn't seem entirely surprised by this, though his tired eyes did flash with that familiar gleam of curiosity, if only for an instant.

"Explain," I snapped. "You know more about this place than what you've told me in the past. I believe there's something buried here that we need to find, and I need to know how to navigate this grove before it's too late."

He hesitated.

"Orin. *Please.* I need your help."

The trees creaked and groaned, as if moving closer to the conversation once again.

Orin shook his head sadly and said, "If you believe nothing else before this is day is over, believe that I only wanted to help you."

My heart thundered in my throat. His words carried a heaviness I didn't understand—didn't *want* to understand.

"Explain," I said again, quieter this time. "*Quickly*," I added, with a harried look at the last place I'd seen Aleks.

He took a deep breath, like the sort he usually took before preparing to lecture me about something that he knew I would only halfway pay attention to. Only, this time, my attention was absolute.

"This wood serves a great purpose," he said, walking toward the arched trees and beckoning me to follow. "It's a place where divinely magical things can be safely contained. Buried, in some cases. Forgotten entirely, in others."

"…A graveyard?"

"Something like that. But not just for divine-touched *creatures*. All sorts of magical things, living or not. They don't break down here, though; mostly, they go into stasis. Time stands still in the deepest parts of these woods, and the air and soil throughout the forest nullifies all but the strongest divine magic. The Hollow Grove was created as a sanctuary by those who feared that the Vaelora—and the things they could create—might grow too powerful. They also used it as a meeting place that they believed was relatively safe from divine eyes."

The place where gods forget.

"They...who are *they*?" I asked.

"Figures who once served the gods and their chosen Vaelora, but who later began to question their power—who outright rejected and sought the destruction of them, in the most extreme cases."

My mind went back to the sentier, locked away and left to die, taking any chance of Lorien's revival and return to power with it. The symbols that had marked its prison…

"Figures connected to the Void Order, by chance?" I asked.

Orin stiffened and glanced over his shoulder, as though he expected members of that order to come crashing through the trees at any moment.

"You've been doing your research for once. Very good." He cast another wary look around the trees before continuing. "We used to practice your magic on the outskirts of these woods because I knew the spells here would intervene if your power ever raged beyond what I could channel into safer outlets. But it seems we've come to the point where that power can no longer be chained." His gaze briefly went to my wrists, now free of all the bracelets he'd made for me. "The Order you mentioned…they're organizing and moving in greater numbers than they have in some time, stirred into action by what you've done these past months. They're hunting you, Nova. And Aleks, too."

The words didn't come as much of a shock; I'd already feared the worst where this veiled organization was concerned.

I eyed my weary mentor. He knew so much…and there was no way he was safe with the knowledge. And again, as angry as I was with him, I couldn't help but worry, wondering if that was why he looked so tired, so ragged.

"They're hunting you, too, aren't they?"

He gave me a sad smile. "It's complicated."

I winced as the strange voice sang out from the wood once more, briefly making me forget all the questions I had for Orin.

"Are you alright?" he asked.

"That song, it's getting louder. It's…"

"A spell meant to lure divine beings into a state of confusion," he explained. "Most people can't hear it. Or, they don't notice it, at least—though it can have a calming effect on normal beings who haven't taken precautions." He nodded toward Thalia and Zayn, who I was now almost certain had fallen asleep standing up.

"You should be powerful enough to shake it off, at this point," he added, "even if you venture deeper. You just need to brace yourself."

"What about Aleks?" A second question got caught

on the tip of my tongue: *Why did he hear a song meant for divine beings, if Lorien was truly exorcised from him?*

Orin didn't answer, shaking his head. "There's a lot concerning him that we can discuss later, if…" He trailed off.

I was afraid I already knew what he'd been about to say.

If he makes it back out again

Panic bubbled in my chest, but Orin had that stern look in his eye that he always did when I started to stray from his intended lesson—a look that demanded focus.

"I know what you came here for." He lifted his tired gaze to the tiny patch of blue sky visible through the thick trees. "The forest knows, too. But it won't let it go without a fight; that sacred piece you seek is deeply entwined with the spells here, now. It's too powerful to have been extinguished, so it's likely the grove has been feeding off it instead, while dispersing and redirecting it into something relatively less dangerous. Cutting it free will have consequences."

"…Consequences?"

"Destabilizing ones."

I swept a gaze over our surroundings. Though I couldn't see Rose Point any longer, it was the only image I had in my mind. My stomach clenched. "How far will that destabilization reach?"

Quietly, Orin said, "You can't turn back now, either way."

Again, an evasive non-answer.

But I didn't press for more. There was no time. And it had just struck me, again, how awful he looked. Like he hadn't slept in weeks. Like he'd been clinging to life just long enough to meet me here for one final lesson, to point me onward and say, *Go, before it's too late.*

Phantom streaked out of my pocket as I walked closer to the spot where Aleks had disappeared. His spectral figure wavered like smoke caught in a vortex, twisting this way and that. Clearly struggling to hold his form. I could only imagine it would get worse if I dragged him deeper into the unpredictable maelstrom of magic and strange spells that lay ahead.

"Stay here," I ordered. "I'll be back soon."

I hurried forward before he could protest.

As I stepped under the archway into the deeper, darker part of the forest, branches shifted and roots lifted in my wake, snapping violently at my heels. Once I was inside, it all twisted and snarled together, cutting off my exit.

I inhaled, tasting a strange mixture of pine and rot and ash on my tongue, and the world went utterly silent.

Nova

The silence was shattered by laughter coming from somewhere far in the distance. It was so faint, I wondered if I was imagining it, yet I still found myself stumbling toward the sound.

I didn't make it far before a hand closed around my arm. I instinctively tried to jerk away, but my captor's grip remained firm, forcing me to twist around and face him.

"Whatever you heard," Aleks said, calmly taking my gaze, "I'm fairly certain it's not real."

I slowly exhaled the breath I'd been holding.

"And I doubt it will be the last trick this forest tries

to play," he added, casting a wary glance at the twisting tree limbs around us. They were paler on this side of the archway, like walls made of gnarled bones.

"Let's stay close," Aleks said.

I nodded, stopping just short of pointing out that *he'd* been the one who had left *me*. He'd seemed so completely overcome by the song, that lure meant for divine beings...

But now he didn't seem bothered by it at all.

Yet another shift in him that I couldn't make sense of.

The forest loomed, full of overgrown trails that looked foreboding, at best. I glanced over my shoulder, briefly considering turning back for the others—strength in numbers seemed like a good idea—but the trees were moving, rattling and twisting, obscuring the trails until it was impossible to say which way was *back*.

"Maybe we could try to sense the energy coming from the fragment?" Aleks suggested. "If it's here, I'd think it would feel obvious to us and our magic."

I agreed. Neither of us mentioned what we'd do after that, how we were going to make our way out of this place once we found the fragment...*if* we even managed that first part.

I exhaled slowly, letting shadows lift and curl from my skin. Their cold was comforting. Familiar. Blinking a lens of magic over my eyes, I scanned the white trees for some sign of the powerful object we sought.

I'd never seen so many different energies competing for dominance in one place.

"This could get tricky," I muttered. Quickly, I explained what Orin had told me about the purpose of the grove.

Aleks frowned. "So, I imagine this place is a mess of residue from all the magic buried in it, and from the spells used to contain and absorb that magic…"

"It is. I don't even know where to start looking for the fragment. It could be—"

The mark on my wrist started to itch, startling me. It had all but faded on my skin, and I'd given little thought to that outward proof of the bargain I'd struck with my enemy. But now it stung in a way that couldn't be ignored. Grimnor rattled violently as well, not stopping until I withdrew it to find bluish-white energy twisting along the blade.

Lorien?

My chest tightened.

I couldn't stop what happened next; Grimnor lifted on its own, the tip pointing and pulling as if to encourage me forward.

"…I guess that's a start," I muttered, staring past the blade, eyes narrowing on the path it had indicated. Rolling the tension from my shoulders, I started to walk. Aleks hesitated, but then he withdrew his own sword and walked side-by-side with me down the darkening path.

As we made our way deeper into the woods, even the light Aleks summoned didn't pierce the dark haze around us. What little birdsong there was disappeared. The breeze stilled…but *something* was still making the skeletal tree limbs rattle and dance in a haunting rhythm.

We'd been walking for several minutes when a low, resonant hum rippled through the grove. We drew closer to one another, standing back-to-back, weapons raised, as the ground began to tremble faintly beneath our feet.

Something tickled my cheek.

Glancing up, I saw pale blue flowers dotting the branches above. More bloomed in slow waves, petals glowing faintly in the half-light. A few of those petals shook free and fell over us, their touch soft and cold as they brushed over my skin.

I continued to watch the falling blooms as Aleks took a few cautious steps onward, his expression fixed on the path ahead. I realized quickly that the flowers were unfurling in sync with his steps—following him, almost, like watchful eyes opening as he passed.

"Aleks…stop!"

He slowed for an instant, glancing back at me in confusion.

I never heard his reply.

A thick swirl of petals descended, engulfing me. As they pressed against my skin, an exhaustion unlike any

I'd ever felt overcame me, sinking deep into my bones until all I could think about was how much easier it would be to just keep still. To just *stay.*

An instant after the thought crossed my mind, the cyclone of petals froze in mid-air before dropping straight to the ground.

I felt something else wrapping around my body—a gentle pressure that slowly increased, like a hesitant embrace. For some reason, I imagined my mother's arms circling around me, her body rigid with shock and disbelief after so much time spent apart.

Then, she was actually *there.*

And my father somehow was, too. Alive. In one piece. We were complete. Astonished to see each other, and certain, at first, that it had to be a trap. But then we slowly accepted what was happening, and tears of relief trickled down my cheeks as our embrace grew tighter.

Tighter.

Tighter.

The laughter from earlier returned, closer this time. With a gasp, I realized it was *mine*; a faint, ghostlike version of me was moving through the forest. Mesmerized, I watched her approach. My mother and father abandoned me and turned her way, stretching out their arms to her.

"No," I whispered—though I'm not sure any sound came out. "No, *she's* the ghost. I'm real. I'm…"

I frantically stepped toward my spectral self, pressing closer and closer until we became one; it was like fusing back into myself after using one of my projection spells. I didn't remember using any spell, but maybe I had. Maybe I'd actually severed myself in two long ago, without even realizing it, and that was why I'd felt so off balance for so long.

But now I was whole again.

We were whole again.

So I laid down my sword.

I let my mother take me in her embrace once more, melting into her as my father wrapped his arms around both of us.

I don't know how much time passed before something ripped them away from me—something that jerked hard enough to knock me off balance again. I landed hard on my hands and knees, my fall painfully broken by sharp rocks and pine needles.

I blinked, snapping out of a daze I didn't remember falling into.

Thalia stood in front of me, staff in hand. Torn vines hung from the weapon—the weapon that had just freed me from a potentially deadly embrace of the forest, I realized. Zayn stood near Aleks, similar evidence of ripped bindings hanging from his sword.

"Th-thank you," I told them, getting to my feet and hastily swiping away the last bits of vine clinging to my arms and shoulders. "But how did you…"

Thalia twisted a newly-acquired bracelet around her wrist. It was woven with threads in various shades of silver, with a faintly pulsing grey stone in its center.

Zayn had a similar one; they looked like Orin's handiwork.

"Gifts from my—from Orin," Thalia confirmed. "They won't fend off the grove's entrapment spells indefinitely, though, so we need to keep moving." She swept a concerned look over me. "He seemed to think you wouldn't need one…and that it would be better if you weren't encumbered by any protections that might interfere with your power."

"We're fine. We just got sidetracked," Aleks told her —and I eagerly agreed.

We'd been caught off-guard, but I was determined not to let it happen again.

"Let's hurry up, then," Zayn urged. "Any ideas on where we should go next?"

Grimnor—still on the ground, several paces away— shuddered with enough force to rattle the dead leaves around it. It flipped onto its edge, spinning once before settling back against the forest floor.

We all stared at it for a moment, silent and uneasy.

"…To wherever it's pointing," I said.

Zayn gave me a dubious look.

"I think it's able to sense the shard of Lorien's soul better than any of us," I explained.

"And we're just going to trust it?"

"Unless you have a better plan."

"He rarely does," Aleks said, picking up the sword and handing it to me.

Zayn ignored the jab. "Gentle reminder that there's an evil demon contained within that blade."

"Yes, which is what's making it capable of giving us directions to the soul of said evil demon," I said, dryly.

"He could very well be leading us into a trap."

"I love a good trap," Thalia muttered, starting to walk. "Keeps things interesting."

I let out a nervous laugh, falling into step beside her. Aleks followed closely behind—as did Zayn, eventually.

The path narrowed to a ribbon of sandy white dirt, hemmed in by an increasingly tangled mass of over-grown roots and branches. Everything glistened as if coated in a thin frost, despite how suffocatingly warm the air was quickly becoming.

Deeper and deeper we went, until a massive tree came into view, stunning us to a stop. It stood out—a dark giant among ghostly white trunks, its bark smooth as marble and streaked with veins of deep gold. It was as tall and wide as any tower at Rose Point. Wider, really, if one counted the roots that rose all around it, curling and knotting into shapes that, at first glance, almost resembled creatures caught in a web.

Grimnor shook once more, the energy along its blade brightening.

On a whim, I tapped the flat of the sword against the closest tangle of dark roots. We all drew back a step, tensing, as a crack of sound split the silence. Light bled from one of the veins of gold in the tree trunk, shimmering just brightly enough to give us a better look at all the things around it.

"There's something at the center of its base," Aleks said, pointing, then aiming a sphere of his own light toward it a moment later. With the added light, we all saw it clearly: A half-buried, partially broken structure made of stone slabs. Like an altar, almost. The tree's roots had grown around it, forming a cage.

Something inside of that altar pulsed with the same golden light that crisscrossed the trunk.

Aleks made his orb of light grow brighter. Parts of the tree seemed to recoil in response, limbs creaking and clattering in protest.

Or in warning.

I swore I saw the roots moving, too, tightening around the altar and its golden treasure, protecting it.

"Could that really be it?" Zayn asked.

"…I can feel power coming from it," I said, breathlessly. "And it's building."

"But is that power coming from the shard, or from the spelled tree that's protecting it?" Aleks wondered.

"Either way, it doesn't look like they'll be easy to separate," Thalia said. "Not without cutting through the wood, or whatever this strange material is." She knocked her fist against the smooth black tree; it sounded hard but hollow. "And who knows what will happen if we do that? Something tells me the forest won't like it."

A cold sweat washed over me.

Cutting it free will have consequences.

"Orin warned me about this," I said quietly.

Aleks glanced my way, concerned for a moment, before stepping forward to more closely inspect our target. Panic shot through me, but he moved with perfect calm, leaping over wayward branches and scrambling gracefully across the massive roots before finally placing a hand at the base of the trunk.

I shivered as I felt his power rising, taking on a similar energy as when I used my own power to obtain visions of the past. Except, Light magic didn't divine the past. It saw the future—a much trickier spell, and not one he attempted very often.

Because the future is always fluid, he often said.

But he seemed determined to pin it down, this time. Several tense moments passed before his eyes opened and flashed in Thalia's direction.

"She's right," he said as he made his way back to us. "The forest won't like it at all if we try to cut these things apart."

As if it had heard us discussing the mere possibility of slicing into it, that forest shuddered even more convincingly to life; this time, I was certain I saw deliberate movement—and not just from the restless root system.

Vines slithered like snakes. Branches twisted sharply toward us, curling downward like claws groping for prey. A limb struck for Aleks, but he leapt away at the last possible instant, rolling aside as it hit the ground with enough force to shatter into dozens of tiny splinters.

More limbs rattled and shifted threateningly around us. Roots rose up from the ground like living beasts, arching their backs in threat. The air grew heavy and electric, humming with waking power.

I scrambled out of reach of the deadliest-looking branches, Thalia and Zayn following my lead.

Aleks rejoined us without taking his eyes off the golden glow at the base of the tree. Power rolled off him in waves, enveloping me in warmth. I expected his thoughts to follow, like they so often had here lately. Instead, it was an image that dropped into my head as his fingertips brushed my palm: A vision of Grimnor cutting through the gnarled limbs, loosing the glowing fragment from its altar.

I realized what he was doing—trying to show me the future he'd seen, whether it would ultimately prove true or not.

While he kept his eyes narrowed and his sword raised toward the center tree, I took his hand more completely. I bowed my head, focusing. I saw images of the forest bending and breaking, collapsing altogether in some places, as a wave of unstable-looking energy raced outward from this center point. That wave stretched beyond the edge of the forest, draping like a shimmering, black veil of mourning, toward…

"…Rose Point?"

I squeezed my eyes tightly shut, trying to hold on,

to see more of the vision. The angle of it shifted higher, as though I'd scaled the center tree and was looking down upon everything. From this vantage point, I could see the black veil stretching toward the magic that had long surrounded my childhood home. Clawing at the edges, as if to claim some of that magic. Drawing it inward and stabilizing the forest again, it seemed…

But at what cost?

A rumbling sounded through the vision—though I would have sworn I could feel the vibrations of it in the present. My knees buckled. I braced myself against Aleks, opening my eyes to find Zayn and Thalia staring at me.

"What about Rose Point?" Thalia asked.

I shook my head, unable to put what I'd just seen into words.

Aleks quietly said, "The magic that's surrounded that manor for all these years…the stasis spell…I think its origin is this forest."

Tense silence followed his words.

I swallowed hard. "Orin told me that the purpose of this grove is to nullify dangerous divine power."

Zayn frowned, considering. "When so much divine Shadow and Light magic violently collided at Rose Point seven years ago…"

"It must have triggered a protective spell from this grove," I finished in a whisper. "One powerful enough to reach beyond its usual borders, wrapping around

Rose Point and leaving it in the strange, semi-frozen state it's been in for the past seven years."

"So, what happens to Rose Point if we disrupt things?" Zayn asked.

I didn't want to guess.

No one did.

Stasis.

Things don't live or die here.

Was the magic of this grove really the reason my old home, my mother—all that remained of my old life— had not decayed? Because of whatever spells the members of the Void Order had woven here?

How had that Order created something so powerful, so…*impossible?*

The more I learned about them, the more questions I had. And the more I feared they might prove an even more dangerous enemy than any we'd faced thus far.

The darkness around us deepened as the seconds passed. The wind rose and fell with a strange rhythm, as if the grove was breathing. The trees bent inward like a fist closing around a heart. Around *my* heart. More blue blossoms were drifting down from somewhere, a mesmerizing rain falling over me.

"We have to choose…let's either cut it free or get the hell out of here." Thalia's voice seemed to come from very far away. She raised her staff, shadows gathering at its tip, but she looked uncertain. "Nova. We have to choose. *Now.*"

But the grove seemed to be offering me another option.

Stay.

A scent tickled my nose: cardamom and bergamot, the perfume my mother wore. Laughter echoed through the trees—my father's laugh, high and bright and alive. Somewhere in the dark, I heard music. A waltz from my birthday. The last song before everything had gone so wrong. Before so much had ended.

But what if it didn't have to end?

This was the grove's gift, after all: not death, but suspension. I could stay here, wrapped in the warm memory of what I'd lost, and never have to face what came next. Never have to fail again. Never have to watch another person I loved slip through my fingers.

Moving forward meant accepting that they were gone. Really gone. Not cursed or sleeping or waiting for me to save them.

Just...*gone.*

"Nova." Aleks's voice cut through the dream I was slipping into. He was right beside me, suddenly, magic flickering unsteadily beneath his skin. When I met his eyes, I saw the same terrible temptation reflected there.

He wanted to stay, too.

Of course he did. Here in this frozen moment, we didn't have to think about his past. About what the Light Keepers had done to him. What Lorien had done, what he was still doing, what might become of us and our magic and everything else.

"We could just stay," I whispered, quiet enough that only he could hear. "We could be safe here."

"Safe…" he repeated. But then he gave his head a hard shake. "Is that what you call this? Nova, look around. This isn't safe."

But I *was* looking around. I was watching as the nearest vines and roots began moving again, inching closer and trying to overtake us. To embrace us. My companions hacked relentlessly at them, but I kept still.

I'd spent seven years running while carrying the weight of my failure—the curse I couldn't break, the family I couldn't save, the world I couldn't seem to find my place in. That weight had twisted itself into my spine, wrapped around my ribs, squeezed until I couldn't remember what it felt like to breathe without it.

What if I just…*set it down?*

What if I let the magic of this grove take me in and hold up that weight for a while?

Vines were encircling my wrists, lifting me onto my toes. Already, I felt lighter. I started to tuck my head toward my chest, exhaling slowly. But before I could drift entirely away, Aleks shouted my name. He spun toward me, sword flashing, cutting through the vines and catching me as I stumbled forward.

"I'm so tired, Aleks." My voice broke as I pressed my forehead to his chest. "I'm so tired of moving forward."

His hand found mine. His skin was fever-hot, magic burning just beneath the surface. "I know, Nova. Gods,

I *know*." He squeezed my fingers, and I felt the tremor in his grip. "But you can't stay here. You know that. Too many people are counting on you."

"What if I can't save any of them?"

I took a step back. A root snaked around my ankles and tightened, pulling me down to my knees. More vines snagged my wrists. These were covered in thorns and delicate white flowers—jasmine, my mother's favorite. I stared at them as I whispered, "What if I'm not strong enough? What if it's not just Rose Point I can't save, but *everything*? What if I fail? What if…"

"Then you fail." His answer was immediate, unflinching, as he dropped to his knees before me and again started to cut me free. "You try, and you fail, and you get back up and you try again. Together, we can—"

His words choked off. The vines were claiming him too, now, one of them taking his throat in a violent, silencing grip.

Something shifted inside me of me at the sight, as I realized: the grove wasn't giving us a choice anymore.

It was going to keep us whether we chose to stay or not.

Zayn and Thalia were still fighting desperately against the encroaching forest. Their shouting, and the clash of steel against wood, seemed distant, muffled. The tempting memories returned with an intensity that seemed to be trying to drown them out—the music swelled. My mother's perfume grew stronger. I blinked and I would have sworn I saw her smiling face watching me from deeper in the woods. And my father was there, too, laughing and holding his arms out to me like he had when I was still small and the world made sense.

Just let go, the grove whispered. *Let go and rest here with them.*

For one desperate heartbeat, I considered it.

Let go.

I want to let go.

Then, Aleksander's magic surged—wild and blazing—burning away the vines that held him. His eyes locked on mine. "Don't you dare, Chaos."

The memory of my mother's smile flickered.

I'm sorry, I thought. *I'm sorry I can't stay.*

I reached for Grimnor.

The sword resisted at first; it was caught just as I had been, vines wrapped around the hilt, flowers blooming from the guard. But when I closed my hand around it, Shadows surged through my veins, cold as ice.

Death, not stasis.

I was Death, and it was time to embrace my power.

Because sometimes it was the only path forward.

I raced for the center tree.

Limbs shot toward me from every direction. I knocked aside two only to spin around and find three more stabbing toward my chest. Zayn caught one with his blade. Aleks knocked the second one aside while

Thalia swept around me, beating back the third, along with the grasping branches, and clearing a path.

"Hurry," she said, nodding toward the altar at the base of the tree.

I moved even faster than before—too fast to allow myself any time to think. I could focus only on my target, on the swing of my blade, on the choice I was making.

The grove cried out as Grimnor cut through the spelled, ancient wood, the sound like a thousand birds screeching as they took flight.

The fragment tumbled free, landing in the dead leaves at my feet.

I picked it up. It was light as a feather and cold as snow. Images flashed through my mind as my fingers closed around it: a garden at night; a woman running; a palace looming in the background.

All around us, the forest began to wilt. Leaves curled into themselves. Flowers blackened and fell. The trees bent backward, bark peeling, thick branches snapping as easily as dried twigs.

In my hands, the fragment of Lorien's soul was soon doing the opposite, waking with a fierce heat, becoming hot and bright. I held it to my chest, as if I could use its warmth to fill the emptiness I felt as I scanned the dying grove, searching for the comforting ghosts of my mother and father, for some sign that I'd made the right choice.

"Put that out of sight," Aleks said, appearing so

suddenly at my side it made me jump. Fear burned in his eyes, and his voice was strange. Angry, almost.

Startled as I was to hear him speak to me like that, I couldn't seem to do as he asked; even as the shard burned against my palms, I couldn't let it go.

"Nova, *please*—"

Then the sound of a building collapsing roared in from the distance, loud enough to rattle me to my core.

I shoved the soul fragment into my pocket and started to run.

EIGHTEEN

Nova

Shaking and breathless, I walked through the remnants of my childhood home.

In a few places, the structures remained largely intact, showing only the normal dust and wear of seven years' time.

In others, the damage that the combination of Shadow and Light magic had done on the night of my birthday was finally apparent—finally *real*. The entire area around the grand veranda, where I'd watched my father meet his end, had now collapsed. The worst of the destruction swept inward from this point, forming a haphazard trail of cracked tiles, chipped plaster, and crumbling stone.

I followed that trail to the room where my mother had once been frozen.

For seven years, I'd visited this room in hopes of understanding the spell that had trapped her. Of finding a way to break it. A way to save her.

Now, the spell was finally broken.

But she was gone.

I wondered briefly about what had become of her body—was it buried under the rubble, crushed beneath this fatal reality that Rose Point had finally caught up to?

Was she nothing more than dust and bones by now?

In the end, I decided I didn't really want to know.

After searching through several more equally empty rooms, I dropped to my knees, overcome by an exhaustion both mental and physical. Phantom darted down from the perch he'd claimed on my shoulder, a shadow that materialized into a small dog who bounded from room to room.

He found no signs of any life, either.

Eventually, he returned and sat sadly beside me, his pointed ears pinned back against his skull.

I staggered to my feet, and we kept moving—though to where, I wasn't sure. Orin caught up and silently fell into step with us. When I finally found the courage to ask him my questions, he tried to help me make sense of the world, as he always had.

They died that night. The manor was wrapped in a protective spell, preventing the fall that should have been. The grove kept feeding into the spell, year after year, keeping it all frozen in time.

It was only an illusion.

"How?" I heard myself ask. "How could the Order have created spells powerful enough to freeze Vaeloran magic in its tracks?"

I drifted in and out of whatever explanation followed. No matter how hard I tried to focus, my mind kept playing the same four words over and over.

They died that night.

The magic I'd inadvertently summoned up from the Below, and its collision with Lorien's power…

It had killed them.

Nothing else truly registered.

And this must have been obvious, because Orin finally shook his head and said, "We can discuss more details later. This conversation is one we should probably save for somewhere safer, anyway."

"Is anywhere actually *safe*?"

His tired eyes looked troubled, but he nodded. "I have an associate waiting in the wings. We'll move on as soon as I see the signal from him, telling us that the path is clear and our hiding place is ready. For now, let's just lay low." He scanned the wreckage, and I again got the feeling he was expecting members of the Void Order to ambush us at any moment.

While he ventured off to watch for signals from this

'associate' of his, I made my way to what had once been the eastern courtyard. I sat on a cracked bench in the darkest part of it, a tall hedge at my back and a relatively unobstructed view of the manor before me.

Thalia found me a short time later. She leaned against a cracked, moss-covered column, staring in the direction of the manor for a minute before she said, "So…it was all an unstable disaster just waiting to finish unfolding."

I didn't reply.

She shifted her weight from one foot to the other. I could tell she was struggling to find words of comfort; it was another testament to our growing friendship that she stayed and attempted to offer any commiseration at all.

"You know there was nothing you could have done to save this place, right? It wasn't meant to be saved. Some things aren't, in the end."

I shrugged, reaching for one of several withered flowers scattered across the bench. Holding it flat in my palm, I focused on the decaying energy surrounding it, letting shadows twist from my wrist and latch onto that decay. As I pulled it out, the flower brightened, its edges perking up. It was an old trick I used to spend hours performing in these gardens; I could take the energy from dead and dying things, and, in doing so, I could make them look like they were alive again, if only for a moment.

But my magic never lasted very long in this realm.

"This wasn't even my real home," I told Thalia. "They weren't even my real parents." It sounded harsh, but I just wanted to detach myself even further from these crumbling surroundings and all they represented.

Thalia shook her head. "Real or not...absent or present...they still shaped you. And they'll go on shaping you, even now."

I crushed the flower in my fist, watching its brightness fade through the cracks between my fingers. "For so many years, I was obsessed with saving this place. It's what led me to Noctaris to begin with. It was a purpose that kept me moving even when the weight of everything became crushing. And all this time, there was nothing truly here for me to save. It was all a lie. My entire life here was a lie."

Her brows knitted together in thought. "Maybe not a lie, but more of a...detour. One that ultimately led you to the destination you were meant to arrive at. To the things you were truly meant to save."

I exhaled a long, slow breath. "...Maybe."

She started to reply, but we were interrupted by the sound of someone kicking aside debris and muttering to himself—Orin.

Even with the space between us, I felt the tension ripple through Thalia's body at the sight of him.

"Maybe you should go speak to him?" I urged, softly.

She gave a dismissive snort, turning away. Orin

carried on without paying us any mind at first, holding up what looked like a piece of a broken mirror, angling it to catch the dying light and twisting it in deliberate patterns; maybe part of the signals he had apparently planned for.

His daughter was quiet for a long time, just watching him, before she said, "It was easier when he was just a ghost that haunted my memories."

I nodded, understanding.

She wrapped her arms tightly around herself, warding against the chill of the rapidly approaching evening. We quietly watched the sun sink more fully behind what was left of Rose Point. The brilliant display of reds and oranges made me think of fire—of the last vestiges of my old life going up in flames.

Let it burn, I thought. *Let it all burn.*

As shadows overtook the final rays of sunlight, Aleks and Zayn came into sight, walking close together and talking in hushed voices. They were too far away to properly hear, and no matter how hard I tried, I couldn't seem to access the mental bond Aleks and I had been sharing, either.

"Aleks is keeping his distance, isn't he?" Thalia asked. "And here I thought the two of you were inseparable."

I said nothing, but I couldn't help replaying the strange moment we'd shared in the woods, just before I'd heard the towers of Rose Point crumbling down. The anger in his voice. The fear in his eyes.

Thalia's expression darkened. I suspected she was biting back a disparaging comment—or three—about Aleks. I braced myself, but she only shrugged and begrudgingly said, "I suppose this is hard on him, too. Whatever role he played in summoning the Vaeloran magic that destroyed this place, it can't be easy to truly see that destruction. To see what it's done to you."

I slipped my hand into my coat pocket, feeling for the shard of Lorien's soul. It hummed against my skin as my palm pressed against it. "I don't think it's merely bad memories bothering him," I told Thalia.

She tilted her head toward me.

"I think it's…this." I held up the shard. "He couldn't stand to be near it earlier, or to even look at it."

She considered it for a moment, her fingers tapping restlessly along her staff. "Can't we just destroy it?"

I clenched it back into my fist. "That wasn't the deal I agreed to."

She let out a *hmph* but didn't argue. We both knew there were consequences to breaking deals with demons—and we could only guess at what they might be.

I slid the shard back into my pocket.

With a sigh, Thalia gripped the edge of the bench, leaning back and lifting her gaze to the sky. "One down, two to go," she muttered.

WE TOOK REFUGE SEVERAL MILES AWAY, IN THE HOME OF someone I recognized: Alistair Finch. This was the same man who had brought me to the entrance of the Nocturnus Road all those months ago. I'd seen him several times before that, too—mostly while I was half-heartedly eavesdropping on clandestine meetings he'd had with Orin. Meetings I should have been listening more closely to, I guess; yet again, I found myself feeling like a fool for overlooking so many clues about the grander picture and greater destiny I was apparently meant for.

Finch was aware of who I was. *What* I was. And there were several other figures like him who had been secretly helping Orin protect me throughout the years —an entire network of connections, a web far more intricate than I could have ever imagined.

It made my head hurt just thinking about it all. So I didn't focus on it for long; instead, I took the shard we'd obtained in the Hollow Grove and put some distance between myself and the others. The flickering images I'd seen when I first picked it up had been haunting me all day.

I needed to see more.

Similar to Orin's house, the one we were hiding in backed up to a narrow creek that cut through dense woods. I settled down on a secluded stretch of that creek's bank and took out the crystalline shard. Glancing around one final time to make sure I was alone, I wrapped it in my shadows and let my magic sink deeply into it.

I opened my eyes.

My heart lurched. My surroundings swirled. A vision washed over me just like it had during my encounter with the sentier—much more immersive than my usual fleeting glimpses of the past. Maybe because of our Vaeloran connection, or because it dealt with my magical predecessor again…I didn't know.

I only knew I wasn't sitting beside the creek any longer.

Instead, I stood in the shadow of a grand palace. Moonlight gleamed off white marble columns and terraced gardens blooming with bright flowers. It was so perfect and intact that, at first, I didn't realize where I was. Then I noticed the banners fluttering from the highest towers. Black and white banners featuring three stars along the bottom, curved beneath three swords—one standing straight in the middle with two others crossed over it.

This was the Palace of Midna.

The sound of boots striking the stone path made me jump.

"Only a memory," I reminded myself in a whisper.

But it all felt so immediate, so…*real*. Real enough that I had no problem locating the source of the noise; a group of palace guards moved through the gardens, their armor glinting in the moonlight. They were calling out a name, splitting up to search different paths.

Lorien was walking among them—of course. This was part of his soul's memory, after all.

He looked younger here than he had in my last vision. A boy, really; he couldn't have been much older than fifteen, with softer features that hadn't yet fully matured and eyes that were an arresting shade of deep brown rather than the reddish color I knew, and which still held something resembling innocence. He lagged behind the others, his gaze sweeping the gardens with poise and purpose.

Then he saw it, and so I did, too: a flash of a white dress racing behind a hedge.

Someone clearly trying to avoid being found.

The company of guards didn't seem to notice anything, even as Lorien slowed his step, separating himself from the group.

I slowed to a stop as well, watching.

Lorien waited until those guards were well ahead of us, then he casually sauntered in the direction of the fleeing figure. Winding his way through a short maze of sculpted hedges, he rounded a corner and found himself facing a young woman as she huddled in an ivy-draped gazebo, attempting to make herself small and unnoticeable. Darkness shifted unnaturally around this woman, cloaking her further.

Lorien chuckled at the sight. "Calista, my Shadow...you're going to need a better hiding place if you're planning to avoid them all night."

She rose to face him, eyes wide with alarm. Then annoyance. The shadows parted, fully revealing her striking figure that was draped in an elegant, plum-colored gown, its elaborate beadwork shimmering like trapped stars.

Like Lorien, she was much younger than I'd ever seen her; this must have been one of the first times they'd met. It used to be customary for the Vaelora to train separately during their youth—though I'd heard stories that these two had corresponded by way of letters and such long before they'd ever seen one another in person.

But only once they had matured, mastered their magic, and taken their own respective vows, would they present themselves together before the leaders of the realms—an occasion usually marked by a grand ceremony in this central kingdom of Midna. And, judging by their elegant clothing and the hum of activity echoing from the palace, I wondered if that ceremony was imminent.

"I'm not hiding," Calista snapped.

"No?" Lorien arched a brow. "What are you doing, then? Inspecting the hedges? Taking notes for the gardeners?"

She scowled.

He clasped his hands behind his back, a grin playing

at the corner of his mouth as he strolled along the hedge line. "The northeast corner looks like it needs trimming. And there's a broken fountain near the rose arbor—you should make a note of that, too."

Folding her arms across her chest, Calista gave a curt nod toward the palace. "Don't you have somewhere to be? A royal court to go show off for, perhaps?"

"I'm only half of the show, unfortunately. And the uglier half, at that."

She scoffed, but her cheeks flushed pink; it was obvious she didn't believe any part of him was ugly.

Lorien's expression softened. "We can't keep them waiting forever, you know."

She lifted her chin. "Yes, I do in fact know my duty, thank you very much."

"And you've committed your sins and vows to the Chamber of Echoes..."

She stiffened. "Of course."

"So now all that remains..."

She fidgeted with the silver bracelet at her wrist—a simple band that looked out of place against her ornate gown.

Lorien's crooked grin didn't falter, but his hand twitched, as though he'd thought for a moment about reaching it out to her.

You're afraid of what comes next, aren't you?

Calista didn't answer him—and I soon realized it was because Lorien hadn't actually said these words out loud. It had been a thought. One wrapped in something tender, and the stirrings of what felt like concern. Protectiveness.

I recoiled, once again uncomfortable over the intimate connection I had to him. The vision wavered a bit, but I managed to stay focused enough to keep watching.

Lorien took a small step closer. Calista held her ground, though her breathing quickened.

Voices echoed from deeper in the garden.

I could feel her pounding heart as she backed into the shadows, dark green eyes wide, delicate fingers anxiously twisting themselves up in the long, flowing sleeves of her dress.

Lorien's gaze lingered on her for an instant longer before he strode away, intercepting the group of searching guards as they approached.

"No sign of her around here, I'm afraid," he told them with a shrug. "But one of the groundskeepers said he saw her heading toward the southern gate."

They gave a respectful nod and changed direction.

Subtly, he tilted his face back toward the spot where Calista hid.

Her shoulders relaxed. The smallest of smiles crossed her face, and that tender feeling bloomed even stronger in Lorien's chest.

He walked away without another word.

The scene dissolved into a grey fog. I gave my head a little shake, clearing it, and just like that, I was back in the present.

I wasn't alone, though; Orin stood a few feet away, watching me curiously.

"See anything interesting?" he asked, nodding at the shard, which was still wrapped in my fist—and my shadows.

I told him about the vision. How Lorien had looked so...*human*. Calista, too. Human and vulnerable. And he'd protected her.

Orin considered things for a long time, mumbling to himself, drawing his finger through the air as if making notes. I finally gave him a little poke in the side, reminding him that I was there.

He regarded me with a small, tired smile. "Your abilities really have stabilized. And improved. I'm not surprised—but still immensely proud."

I frowned; that wasn't the interpretation of the vision that I'd been hoping for.

"What does it matter if I was able to divine the past?" I asked. "I still don't know what to think about any of it."

He scratched his chin, eyes clouding over in thought for a moment. "I'm afraid we're still missing a lot of pieces to this puzzle. I will say, though, that your vision supports some theories I've been working on these past months..." He trailed off, looking reluctant to admit to whatever he was about to say.

"Theories?" I pressed.

"That Lorien isn't the enemy we thought he was, for example."

"He's a monster," I insisted.

"He's done monstrous things, certainly. But it isn't only monsters who are capable of monstrous things. And there may be greater enemies to contend with soon, anyway."

"Greater enemies…are we talking about the Order again?"

He nodded. "I fear they may have created something far more dangerous to you than Lorien."

My stomach twisted. I had theories too, of course. I just wasn't ready to talk about any of them.

"Have you had a chance to talk to Thalia?" I asked instead.

He arched a bushy brow. "Changing the subject remains one of your most reliable tactics, I see."

"Thalia is an important subject, too," I insisted.

He didn't argue, but he also didn't move.

"Go on," I said, nodding back toward the house, where I knew Thalia was resting. It was a strange role reversal, the way I was now the one pushing him to confront difficult truths.

He chuckled softly. "You really have gotten much stronger."

I shrugged, but I also mumbled a quick *thank you*. He left me, and as I watched him walk away, my mind was immediately overrun with thoughts of our latest battles, and eventually all the ones that had come before. All the things that had torn me down and built me back up, forging me into something harder than what I'd once been.

"Stronger…" I muttered, summoning a small tendril of shadow and watching it coil around my fingers.

I was not the same person who'd left this realm behind months ago, that was true.

I only hoped I could be strong enough to face whatever came next.

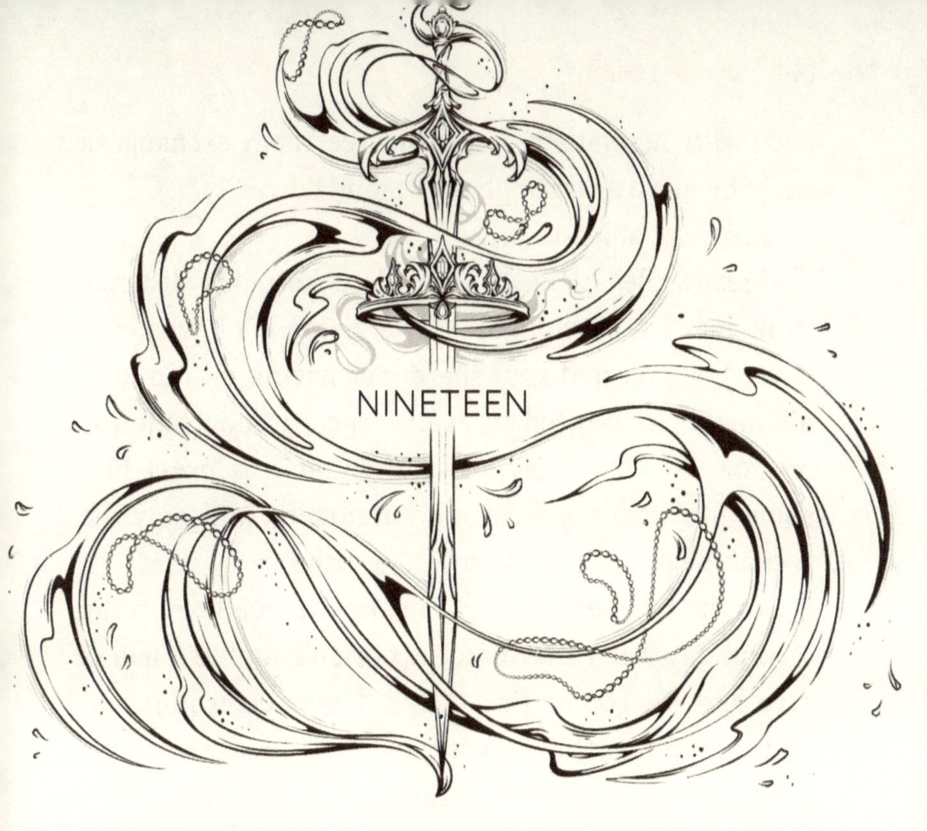

Nova

A day passed. I was eager to get back to my kingdom—back to a realm where my magic was much easier to wield—but there were reports from Orin's other allies that the route we'd taken from the Nocturnus Road was being watched. We needed to be cautious, prepared for the worst, and the ordeal at the Hollow Grove had stretched us thin enough that we decided it was safer to wait.

In the meantime, there were plenty of things I needed to discuss with Orin, anyway. Plenty of things he and Thalia needed to talk about, too. She was less than thrilled about essentially being forced to reconnect with her father, but I did see them exchange a smile by midway through the second day.

Progress, at least.

Meanwhile, Aleks continued to keep his distance from me. I still thought it was because of whatever effect the collected soul shard was having on him and his magic; he refused to even inspect it alongside the rest of us. When Zayn had attempted to press him about it, it had resulted in an argument, and now the two of them were hardly speaking either.

As the sun began to sink below the tree line on the second day, I left the shard of Lorien's soul in Thalia's care and set off to find Aleks. I was determined to understand his strange behavior, and to make sure our group didn't continue to unravel.

To my surprise, it didn't take long to find him; he sat on the edge of the rickety wooden porch, his gaze fixed in the direction of Rose Point.

I came to stand beside him, leaning over the porch railing. It creaked and swayed a bit, but seemed sturdy enough, so I let it support even more of my weight while I tried to decide what to say.

Aleks ended up speaking first.

"I imagine people have started to swarm Rose Point by now," he said. "I wonder what they'll make of it all?"

"They'll be glad to be rid of it and the spells surrounding it, I'd guess. They'll probably finish tearing it down. Burn it, cleanse it through some bizarre ritual...whatever they can do to rid themselves of the memory of me and the shadows I brought upon that place."

He glanced up.

"...They never liked me much," I said, quietly.

"Their loss, wasn't it?"

My cheeks warmed a bit. Looking back toward Rose Point, I lost myself again in thoughts of what had been —and what *might* have been, if things were really as simple as I'd once believed them to be. My political betrothal hadn't seemed simple at the time, but I would have taken it over what we faced now, no questions asked.

"I was truly prepared to marry you that night, you know." The words slipped out before I could stop them.

"Really?"

I took a deep breath, steeling myself just as I had on that fateful night. "For the sake of my family and this kingdom that I so desperately wanted to prove myself to, I would have done anything."

Aleks laughed. "*Anything*? Well, that makes it less of a compliment to me, doesn't it?"

I shrugged. "I might have been somewhat attracted to you, too."

"Only somewhat?"

"Fine. *Very* attracted."

He got to his feet, amusement still lighting up his features. "Interesting."

"You might not be aware of this, but you're an incredibly attractive person."

He drew close enough to kiss me but stopped just short of doing so. My heart skipped a few beats as I stared into the golden depths of his eyes. Those eyes always seemed to catch the moonlight in the most beautiful, intentional way, as if that heavenly sphere couldn't help being captivated by him, too.

"I'm actually very aware of it," he said.

I gave him a little shove.

He laughed again, and it sounded so real—the only real, meaningful thing in a day filled with unraveling truths and crumbling beliefs. It also sounded more like the Aleks I knew, making me forget about the odd way he'd been acting.

He looped his arm through mine. We walked for the better part of an hour, following a little offshoot of the larger creek I'd sat beside earlier. It was dangerous to venture too far, so we simply traveled in a circle, doubling back again and again, talking and teasing one another as if we were far more careless than we actually were.

I'd spent so much of these past months walking in frustrating circles, it seemed like. But I didn't mind this. It felt good to be directionless with him. No thoughts of beginnings or endings, no fears about where we'd come from or where we had to go next.

The few stray clouds across the full moon parted, bathing us in bright blue light. We paused beside a relatively deep pool of the otherwise trickling stream, taking in the sight of our reflections. In the glassy water, I watched his arms circling around me from behind, his head coming to rest on my shoulder. The warmth of his body and the feel of his heart beating against my back made me feel steady. Safe.

Taking my hand and spinning me around to face him, he asked, "Would you still marry me?"

I grinned. "Are you proposing?"

His smile was softer, less teasing this time. He didn't answer right away. Instead, he crouched beside the stream and ran his fingers over a few sprigs of green shooting up through the mud. I watched with a mesmerized little smile as those shoots blossomed into full flowers.

Every movement of his hand made more bloom around us, until an entire carpet of glowing flowers stretched before my feet. He collected a few handfuls, taking care to arrange them just so.

Rising back to me, he said, "I think of it sometimes, too. Not the pomp and ceremony, or the political maneuverings of it all—I never cared much about any of that. But the possibility of waking up beside you every morning?" He handed me the bouquet he'd collected. "I would have been the luckiest man in the world."

"You *are* proposing to me, aren't you?" I teased. "Aren't you supposed to be down on one knee?"

"You know I rarely miss an opportunity to kneel before you, but...no. I'd like to think I could plan a better proposal than this."

"I think a spontaneous proposal would be lovely."

"You would, wouldn't you? Chaotic little beast."

"What would you do without the chaos I bring into your life?"

"I don't know." He took my hand, lifting it and brushing a kiss across my knuckles. "And I don't particularly want to find out."

I melted at the words. At the way he was looking at me as he said them. He still wore that softer, more vulnerable smile that I so rarely got to see, and everything around us blurred as I stared at him. I could only think about kissing that smile—so that's what I did. I pulled him closer, throwing my hands around his neck, dragging his mouth down to mine.

It was several minutes before we pulled away from the kiss and returned to our hideout, quietly slipping away to the room Finch had prepared for me, which was tucked away at the very back of the house.

I locked the door behind us.

The small room felt like its own world. A single oil lamp flickered on the bedside table, casting dancing shadows above us as we collapsed onto the bed. Through the thin walls, conversations occasionally drifted in from the main part of the house. And there was movement out there—so much restless movement —but we somehow ignored it all.

Aleks turned to face me. I closed the distance between us, reaching to cup his face in my hand. He leaned into my touch, eyes closing for a moment. When they opened again, the desire burning in them ignited my entire body.

His lips crashed into mine with dizzying force.

And just like when we'd walked in circles outside, we no longer cared about all the plans waiting to be made or the battles looming ahead.

But we weren't directionless in this room.

Every brush of his body against mine felt intentional, weighted with meaning. We shed our clothes slowly, reverently, as if following the steps of something sacred. He trailed his fingertips across my bare, trembling skin. Swiped his tongue over the peaks of my breasts with the same torturous intent before finally taking them into his mouth and sucking until I gasped out his name.

As I tried to catch my breath, he slipped his arm around my waist, yanking me closer. Our hips pressed together, his desire hard and obvious as it throbbed against my own pulsing need.

He took one of my legs and draped it over his body, opening me more fully to take him in, then shifting his own position until we were perfectly aligned.

With a slow, powerful thrust, he buried himself inside of me.

As he pushed deeper, his gaze met mine. Held it. Even if he hadn't been moving inside me as he did it, it still would have felt devastatingly intimate—the way he was watching me as he claimed me. As if he saw every bit of me. All the messy, unraveled parts. The fears. The uncertainties. And he still wanted to bind himself to me despite it all, to push deeper and deeper until there was no chance either of us could ever deny our connection.

I didn't last long under that intimate stare. I didn't *want* to last. Didn't want to hold anything back from him.

I wrapped an arm around his neck for leverage and met his deep, powerful thrusts with increasingly desperate thrusts of my own. He moved his fingers with expert strokes across my center while his arm shoved against my thigh, pushing my legs farther apart, all while he continued to pound into me, and the combination of it all quickly sent me over the edge.

My cry of release likely would have been loud enough to concern the rest of the house, had Aleks not pressed his mouth over mine as it came. The sound faded into gasps of pleasure, swallowed up by his own answering groans as he spilled himself inside of me.

I was lost for several moments in a floating, peaceful euphoria. When I blinked back into awareness, I found Aleks watching me with nearly the same intensity as before. Another wave of release rolled through me, curling my toes and making the corner of his mouth quirk.

He pulled his fingers from between my legs and traced the curve of my shoulder, the dip of my collarbone, the line of my throat. His lips followed the trail of his touch. When I shivered, he paused.

"Cold?" he murmured against my neck.

"No." My voice came out breathless. "I'm never cold with you."

He smiled against my skin, and warmth bloomed through me. I huddled closer to that warmth. Closed my eyes and focused on the feel of his heart beating rapidly in time with mine.

After a moment, I started to turn, thinking of repositioning myself for sleep, but he placed a hand on the small of my back and held me in place. His other hand brushed against my cheek as he said, "Let me fall asleep inside you."

The thought made me blush, but suddenly, I wanted nothing more in the world than to do exactly what he'd asked. I settled halfway on top of him, straddling his body and sinking down into a position that was surprisingly comfortable. He was already growing hard again. The feeling of fullness, along with the occasional twitch of desire against my inner walls, rendered me into something soft and boneless, all warmth and sensation and utter contentment.

I never wanted to leave.

I looked up at Aleks from under my lashes. He cupped my cheek and angled my face toward his.

"I love you," he whispered against my lips.

I repeated the words back to him several times as we drifted toward dreaming, reveling in the way they made his heart beat faster and his arms circle me more tightly every time.

We slept for an hour, at most, before a combination

of heat and arousal stirred me back awake—but it was the most blissful hour I'd had in a very long time.

His eyes fluttered open shortly after mine. For a moment, we just stared at one another, the smoldering embers of desire rekindling.

But there was something else stirring beneath that desire, now: Uncertainty. Fear. My stomach knotted. I rolled off of him and onto my side, facing the window, watching drops of rain slide down it. Aleks followed my lead, loosely draping an arm around me.

"I wish we could stay like this," I whispered.

"I know." His hold tightened, pulling me closer once more. "Me too."

Several minutes passed in silence. I concentrated on the steady thrum of his heartbeat against my back. Out of habit, I soon found myself trying to listen to his thoughts, to connect as we'd managed to do in the days prior…

Only to hit a wall of silence.

Just like I had when I'd tried to connect with his thoughts outside of Rose Point—and several times after that.

Was he blocking me out on purpose?

Or was something more sinister at work? Was it part of the effect Lorien's soul was having on him? I wanted to stay in a state of ignorant bliss, but suddenly all I could think about was the reason I'd sought Aleks out in the first place, hours ago.

Sitting up, I quietly said, "I think we need to talk."

"…About?"

"About how you've been strange since we collected that piece of Lorien's soul."

"I was strange long before that." He yawned. "So were you. Maybe that's why we fit so well together."

"Maybe." I tried to smile but didn't quite manage it. "It seems like something new is bothering you, though."

He shifted, rearranging the blankets tangled around us. For a moment, I thought he might wrap himself up in them and roll away from me. But he seemed to decide against it, releasing a soft sigh and taking my hand instead. He draped a blanket around us both and pulled me to his chest.

Tempting as it was to simply nestle closer to him and disappear beneath that blanket for a while, I forced myself to keep pushing for answers.

"You're…you're scaring me, Aleks."

He went still. Every muscle tensed. I'm not sure he was even breathing.

"I just need to know you're okay."

With obvious effort, he made himself exhale. He brushed a strand of hair from my face. "I'm fine. Just a little off balance. It will pass, I'm sure."

I started to lift my eyes to his, but my gaze snagged on the downward curve of his lips. I didn't know what else to say, so I kissed him instead, just trying to get back to the way things had been only an hour before.

He returned the kiss, but there was a distance to it. A hesitation that hadn't been there earlier.

"We should rest while we can," he said as he pulled away.

Reluctantly, I agreed.

He settled down into the pillows, taking me with him so that my head rested against his heartbeat. I wanted to keep pushing, to demand answers, but exhaustion was pulling at me—the kind of bone-deep weariness that came from too many battles fought and too many truths uncovered in too short a time.

His fingers traced slow, thoughtful patterns against my skin, the touch soothing despite my concerns.

"You wouldn't keep secrets from me, right?" I whispered against his bare chest, my eyes growing heavy.

He just pulled me closer, pressing his lips against the top of my head. Warmth cocooned me, a combination of his strong arms and his magic both wrapping tightly around me.

I waited for his reply, fighting against sleep. But the only sound was his beating heart and the soft whisper of his breathing.

I drifted off before I heard his answer—if he gave one at all.

I WOKE IN THE MIDDLE OF THE NIGHT TO FIND MYSELF

cold and alone, with no sign of Aleks or the warm blanket of magic he'd used to help me fall asleep.

Something didn't feel right.

I crawled from the bed, pulled on my clothes, and silently made my way through the house, searching.

He was nowhere to be found.

I eventually made my way into the kitchen, where Orin sat nursing a mug of what smelled like peppermint tea. We weren't in his house, yet it still felt like I was walking into a familiar scene—like one of the countless times I'd woken up, gone to pour myself a glass of water, and found him sitting at the kitchen table lost in the labyrinth of his own mind.

A sweet for your thoughts? I used to ask, and then I would take one from the ample supply he kept in the frog-shaped jar on the counter, give it as an offering, and we'd usually spend the rest of the night talking about anything I had on my mind.

I probably could have benefitted from one of those long, comforting talks now. But my gaze kept sliding toward the door; I was eager to keep searching.

Orin shifted in his seat, the creak of the old chair splitting through the dusty kitchen as he turned to me. "You're looking for Aleksander."

"…It's not like him to leave without telling me where he's going."

"Has he been doing a lot of things that are *not like him* lately?"

A chill swept down my spine.

"Sit for a moment," said Orin.

He was using his stern mentor voice, so I sat. But I couldn't keep my anxious gaze off the door.

"Are you certain it's safe to go looking for him on your own?"

Something told me he knew the answer was 'no'. He was just trying to get me to realize it—to admit it to myself.

"I don't really care about *safe*," I said.

He snorted. "Well, nothing has changed there, now has it?"

I drummed my fingers against the worn table. "Can we get to the point of this lesson, please?"

"Earlier, I mentioned other monsters. Other enemies you needed to be wary of, aside from just Lorien."

An uncomfortable thought slowly snaked its way through my mind, making my scalp crawl, but I didn't say it out loud.

Orin watched me silently. Expectantly.

"Where is Aleks?" I demanded. "What have you done to him?"

"He left of his own accord, don't worry. And he likely hasn't gone far." He lifted the steaming mug of tea only to set it back down again. Anxious. Clearly anxious.

Orin never looked anxious.

What was going on?

I glanced again to the door, but I couldn't bring

myself to get up. "No more riddles. Tell me what you know about him, the Order—all of it."

A flash of lightning lit the room, followed by a distant rumble of thunder. Orin's eyes darted to the window as he gripped the edge of the table, bracing himself as if to stand. I thought he might rush outside, but then he fixed his gaze back on me.

"I've been speaking with your other allies," he said. "Having them fill in some details and answer questions about the notes Eamon sent. I'm starting to get a somewhat clearer picture of the mess surrounding you, Lorien, and Aleksander."

"And?"

"And you know that Aleksander is a descendant of King Argoth?"

I nodded slowly, confused.

What did Argoth have to do with any of this?

"It was the Void Order who ultimately drove Calista and Lorien apart," Orin explained. "But this was done at King Argoth's command. He was one of the Order's most powerful founding members."

"A command he made out of jealousy?" I asked. "Because he loved her, and he was afraid Lorien might interfere with that love?"

"That's always been my belief."

I turned this over in my mind several times. "Did Calista actually love Lorien, though?"

"Once upon a time, maybe." Orin's expression tightened. "Love is a fickle, complicated thing, isn't it? We can only guess at their true feelings for one another. And you'll find that much of their history—all history, for that matter—changes depending on who's telling the story. King Argoth wanted her to kill Lorien. Of that much I'm sure, at this point. But I believe it was more about his desire to control the Vaeloran Cycle than anything else."

"She didn't kill Lorien, though. She just…scattered him. Cursed him."

"Yes. Much to the disappointment of the Order—and Argoth—I'm sure. One could surmise from this that Calista didn't truly *hate* Lorien, at least. But that's conjecture on my part. Whatever the reason, she spared his soul even as she cursed it." He glanced up, studying the wooden plank ceiling for a moment before continuing. "And so the Order was forced to create other weapons who would keep working to dismantle the Vaeloran Cycle."

"…Create?" Something about the word made the hairs on the back of my neck lift.

Orin's eyes flicked toward the window again, another flash of lightning highlighting the tired lines of his face. "Most of the Void Order are brilliant students of Vaeloran magic. They have extensive knowledge, and some even have traces of that magic for themselves—the chosen Aetherkin like me, you know."

"But Aetherkin who stopped being loyal to the Vaelora, in this case?"

"Correct. Instead, those who pledge themselves to

the Order have spent generations developing their own corrupted kinds of power. An occult science, a twisted alchemy, rather than the divine-blessed power that governs so much of our world. But much of what they've done—and are doing—is experimental, part of a fanatical attempt to establish a new world order. The spells you witnessed in the Hollow Grove are examples. The roads that have been forged between the realms, like Nocturnus, are a result of their experiments as well. And…" He trailed off, gripping the mug tightly in his wrinkled hands as he bowed his head.

Though I didn't want to, I asked, "And what does this have to do with Aleks?"

After a weighted pause, he finally met my eyes again. "I believe Aleksander is another one of their experiments. A corrupted entity—a weapon whose ultimate purpose is to consume and nullify Vaeloran power."

All of the air seemed to leave the room.

Orin continued before I could catch my breath enough to reply. "Actually, I believe *all* the descendants of Argoth have been heavily subjected to this weaponization. *The Void King,* Argoth was sometimes called by those closest to him—by those who knew his true plans and desires. Because he was hellbent on draining away the powers that sustained the balance between realms. And the Order has honored his vision and legacy by continuing to try and create the ultimate destroyer out of his bloodline."

I stared at him, my vision blurring at the edges. "Aleks is not a destroyer of anything. He wasn't created like some kind of…of…"

"*Molded* is the better word, maybe." He paused. "A being that isn't truly Shadow or Light, but capable of manipulating both."

"He isn't *any* of those things. He hasn't manipulated me, he—"

"What do you know of his past? The things he endured, and was shaped by, as a child?"

Anger flared through me at the question. At the way it sounded more like an accusation.

But I found myself fumbling for a reply.

Orin waited patiently.

I forced myself to look him in the eyes as I quietly said, "We…we don't talk about his past much. Because he doesn't remember most of it."

There were tortures he'd endured, I knew. Things that had left scars both mental and physical. Things that the so-called Keepers of Light had done to him that he never really managed to tell me about. I'd always assumed the silence was trauma leaving emptiness in its tracks, as it so often did. I rarely pried. It was his story to tell when he was ready to tell it—that's what I'd always believed. But what if…

What if the emptiness wasn't just from trauma? What if they'd deliberately erased parts of him? The parts that didn't serve their plans for him?

Orin was watching me with something like pity in his ancient eyes.

I got to my feet, the chair scraping harshly against the floor. "You're wrong. His magic strengthens mine. Compliments it. It doesn't *void* it."

"Maybe not yet."

"Not ever."

He studied me for a long moment, his weathered face unreadable. "He's certainly...an enigma. I'll give you that. One who's managed to fight his programming in many instances. And I don't think the Order counted on you being as powerful as you are, either, or the two of you developing the bond that you have. But things are shifting back toward their ultimate goal, now. And Aleksander's true purpose and power—"

"You're *wrong*," I repeated. "You have to be wrong about all of this."

He continued as though I hadn't spoken. "As Lorien and his life are restored, I fear Aleks might change even more. If both Vaelora are fully awakened to their power, the true purpose he's been molded for is likely to awaken as well. His own power will become even more unpredictable—a void that hungers for what it was designed to destroy."

"Then I won't restore Lorien. I'll stop that quest this very instant."

"I think we both know it's too late for that. The Order is already on the move. They may have lost track of Aleks while he was trapped in the depths of Noctaris, but now he's in their sights again. So they'll be wanting him back."

I started to argue, but the heaviness in my chest and lungs made it impossible to force words out.

"You must have realized, too, that without Lorien whole, you can't fully restore Noctaris. Calista was short-sighted in her decision to fragment him; as long as he's scattered, the balance of magic and the survival of the Below remains in jeopardy. You can't shift the flow of magic entirely on your own. He has to play his part."

Thunder rumbled closer this time, shaking the windows.

"So I have to choose between saving the world or losing Aleks." My voice came out hollow. "And if Aleks truly does awaken into this monster you're describing, I might not be able to save either. That's what you're telling me?"

Orin gave me another sympathetic look, but it only made me angrier.

"How do you know all of this, anyway?" My tone was bitter. Furious and bitter and determined to find some flaw in his logic that would unravel this nightmare. "You said yourself that history changes depending on who tells it. How do I know you're not just another manipulator? Another person using me for their own ends?"

He didn't flinch at the accusation. "I know all of this

because I've spent a very long time studying the Order and their methods. Intimately, in some cases."

"Intimately…" It took the meaning behind his words a moment to sink in—because I didn't *want* it to sink in. Didn't want to acknowledge yet another lie of omission. Another betrayal.

He sighed. "The problem with living a very long time is that you see all the sides occasionally blurring into one another. Lines get crossed. Allies become enemies and enemies become…*complicated.* "

"You've been working as a double agent, in other words."

He met my eyes steadily. "I had to infiltrate their ranks to follow their movements. To understand what they were planning."

I backed away, shaking my head. "The Light Keepers, the Void Order, the network of allies who've supposedly been protecting me…" I tried and failed once more to truly catch my breath. My voice cracked as I said, "How am I supposed to know who's really on which side?"

He didn't answer.

"Orin. Whose side are you truly on?"

"Yours." He held my gaze without wavering. "It's made a lot of people very angry but…I'm certain I was always meant to be on yours, in the end."

A pause hung between us, heavy with a thousand unspoken things.

I didn't like the way he'd said *end.*

I swallowed hard. "If you're on my side, then tell me how to fix all of this. Tell me there is hope."

He offered a sad smile. "There is always hope."

My hands shook. I stepped to my chair, gripping its backing, trying to steady myself. "Tell me I can save everything I love."

His smile faded.

Before he could answer, a crash echoed from somewhere outside, followed by shouting.

"What was that?"

He jumped up, suddenly moving with the speed and purpose of a much younger man. "Go get your sword, Nova."

He was already pulling knives from hidden sheaths in his coat.

"Orin?"

"There's no time to explain anything else." His eyes met mine one last time, and I saw something in them I'd rarely seen before—fear. "They've found us."

TWENTY

Aleksander

The forest seemed darker than it should have been, even accounting for the storm clouds that had been gathering all night.

I moved through the trees with determined, silent steps, though I wasn't entirely sure what I was running from. Or running toward.

I just knew I felt restless.

I'd lost track of how much time had passed since I'd left Nova sleeping peacefully at the house.

You wouldn't keep secrets from me, would you?

I *was* keeping secrets. But not because I wanted to.

Only because my own mind seemed to be keeping secrets from *me*.

My thoughts tumbled and twisted. That strange itching beneath my skin was getting worse—like something stretching to an uncomfortable point and getting ready to snap. My magic…I trusted it less and less. Trusted *myself* less and less.

And gods help me, it all seemed to be at its worst whenever I was near Nova's shadows. And whenever I was close to that shard of Lorien's soul, the itching, the restlessness…it turned into something that bordered on violence. A violence that somehow felt both foreign and terrifyingly natural. Something a sick part of me wanted to unleash, just to see what it would do.

But I was terrified of doing something I couldn't take back.

So I was running away. Like a fucking coward. Putting space between myself and all the apparent triggers I now had.

I could only run so far, though. Only so fast. Not to mention, I had the unnerving feeling that something was chasing me down, following me no matter which way I turned. I kept hearing footsteps. Whispers. Cracking branches and shuffling leaves.

"Just paranoid," I muttered under my breath.

Just a paranoid fucking coward.

Then lightning split the sky, illuminating the path ahead for a brief, brilliant moment, and in that flash, I saw them: three figures blocking the narrow trail. Four more materializing from the shadows between the trees.

They all wore black clothing with no flourishes, no telling insignia; just layers of leather and cloth that blended with the night, making their true shape—and number—difficult to pick out against the dark forest background.

"It's been a long time, Aleksander." The smooth, sharp voice came from the center figure on the path. His face was shadowed by his hood, but I sensed, with unnerving certainty, that he was smiling. "We were hoping we'd run into you during this little excursion."

"…Who are you?" I demanded.

"You don't remember your former teacher?" He clutched a gloved hand to his heart, the motion exaggerated and mocking. "I'm hurt."

I gripped the handle of my sword, stopping just short of withdrawing it.

"Severin Thane," he said, pushing back his hood with a slow, deliberate flourish as he stepped into the light of the lanterns that some of his companions carried.

Cautiously, I took a few steps closer, trying to place his face.

His eyes were the pale greyish blue of winter ice, and they studied me with a cool, detached curiosity. His hair was dark and streaked with silver at the temples, pulled back in a way that emphasized the severe angles of his face. Despite the silver, there was something unsettlingly ageless about him. Something that reminded me of the ancient look in Orin's eyes—which I also found unsettling.

I couldn't sense magic around him, but I didn't think he was entirely human, either.

Then I caught sight of the symbol tattooed on his neck—a circle with a sword cutting through it—and my blood ran cold.

The Void Order.

We met at last, then.

"We were good friends, your younger self and me," said Severin .

"I very much doubt that." There was no shortage of gaps in my memories, but I remembered enough to know that my younger years had been sorely lacking in anyone I would have considered a *friend*.

And yet.

Something in this man's quiet but commanding voice was familiar in a way that made my stomach turn. The precise enunciation. The patient cadence, as though he had all the time in the world and enjoyed watching others squirm while he took it…

I was certain now that there was crossover between the Order and the Light Keepers; was this man really someone who'd taught me when I was younger?

So much of my torturous magical training was a blur. So many memories of those brutal years slipped and fragmented whenever I reached for them, resisting my every attempt to grab hold.

Why couldn't I just fucking *remember*?

Severin cocked his head, his pale eyes gleaming with something that might have been satisfaction. As if he knew I was feeling an unsettling flicker of familiarity but couldn't understand it. As if my confusion was exactly what he'd hoped for.

"I don't know who you are or how you know my name," I snarled, "but I'm not in the mood for games. Tell me what you want from me or get the hell out of my sight."

"Want?" Another figure stepped forward—a woman with white-blonde hair and eyes that blazed an unnatural silver with the next flash of lightning. "We want nothing from you. Not yet. Though that time is coming." She studied me with unnerving intensity. "Yes; it's coming very soon, I think."

My magic stirred uneasily beneath my skin. Shifted and coiled, and—not for the first time—I felt like it was something alive, something separate from me that wanted out.

The woman with the strange silver eyes seemed to sense it, too. "What a restless little thing you've got living inside you," she murmured, pacing like a beast sizing up its prey.

My grip tightened on my sword.

"You feel it, don't you? Something waking. Something—"

Severin held up his hand in a languid gesture, and she fell silent immediately.

"That isn't why we're here tonight," he said, his voice taking on a note of mild reproach, as though correcting a student who'd spoken out of turn. "Tonight, we've come to deal with a traitor. We only wanted to say hello to you in the meantime. To check on your progress." He folded his hands together with clerical composure. "Two birds, one stone and all that."

"…Progress?"

"Aleks!" Nova's distant voice cut through the darkness like a blade.

Severin turned toward the sound, smiling.

I instinctively circled around, putting myself between him and the direction Nova was approaching from.

His gaze slowly trailed back to me. Something like amusement flickered in his expression. "I have to say, it's disappointing to see you still wanting to protect her. But Maris is right." He tossed a cursory glance at the white-haired woman. "It's only a matter of time until it all shifts. You can't fight what's been written in your blood, after all."

I withdrew my sword, channeling a thread of light through the blade until it glowed faintly in the darkness.

The entire group before me unsheathed their weapons in response, the sound of metal on leather whispering through the damp air. I saw more figures emerging from the shadows—at least two dozen in total.

Severin *tsked* softly as his gaze swept over my weapon. His smile faded, replaced by something colder —though no less composed. The change was subtle, like watching frost creep across glass. "Why don't you put that away?"

I lifted it, pointing the glowing tip directly at his chest. "Why don't I run it through your fucking heart instead?"

"How valiant." He didn't flinch at my blade, didn't even bother to shift his stance. He only clasped his hands behind his back and said, "You want to believe you're the hero who will find a way to protect her no matter what, don't you? But deep down, you know the truth, Aleksander. You can't protect her. You aren't *meant* to protect her."

My pulse quickened. This felt like a nightmare. Like I'd fallen asleep and dreamed that the greatest fear I had —the fear that I might end up a danger to Nova—might be coming true.

I just needed to wake up.

Somehow, I needed to wake up.

"I suppose it will make it all the more satisfying when you finally do admit the truth," said Severin.

I sent another pulse of light through my weapon, brighter this time. A warning.

Nova sounded as if she was getting closer—and she clearly wasn't alone.

Maris looked to Severin as if asking for permission.

He cracked his knuckles one by one, the sound

sharp and deliberate in the stillness. "Maybe we have time for a bit of fun after all. Something like a test, perhaps."

In the next instant, Nova burst through the tree line, Grimnor in hand, shadows writhing around her like snakes.

Phantom followed closely at her heels, a blazing black cloud that would have been lost in the dark if not for the eerie glow of his blue eyes. Thalia was right behind them, staff raised and ready. Zayn came from the opposite direction, moving with lethal grace.

My gaze lingered on Thalia. She had the sliver of Lorien's soul in her possession—I couldn't see it, but I could *feel* it. That familiar pull, that hunger in my magic that I'd been fighting all night…

"Aleks!" Nova's voice again, right beside me this time. I flinched at the sound; my vision had blacked out for an instant, maybe longer.

"Aleks? What's going on?" She sounded confused now. Maybe a bit frightened—of me, or for me, I couldn't tell.

I didn't have a chance to reply.

The attack came from all sides at once.

I moved on instinct, my sword finding its first target before I'd consciously decided to act. The Order member crumpled with a choked gasp, blood blooming across his chest.

Zayn withdrew his own sword, while Thalia readied her staff, using it to pull in some of the shadows drifting around Nova and channeling them into something more solid—into whips made of pure darkness.

Nova drew closer to my side, Phantom gliding after her. She glanced my way for only an instant, and I saw the uncertainty in her gaze shifting into fierce determination. Whatever was happening with me and my magic didn't matter just then; we had to survive this ordeal first.

The five of us moved as one.

Thalia's whips cracked through the air, wrapping around limbs and throats with brutal efficiency.

Zayn became a blur of lethal precision, his blade finding gaps in armor with practiced ease.

Phantom tore through the ranks like a living shadow, his form shifting and multiplying into a dozen identical silhouettes. Not solid, but still creating chaos that left the Order members slashing at ghosts.

I parried, struck, dodged. My sword sang through the air, light and steel both flashing in a violent dance.

I kept trying to slice my way toward Severin. To get rid of that unnerving feeling he gave me by simply cutting him down. But he evaded every attempt I made, continuing to watch me with interest and amusement—as if this was all part of some grander game he was playing—and that only made me angrier. More reckless.

My strikes became wilder, less controlled.

My magic started to surge in strange ways. To twist into something that didn't light the forest with its usual warm glow. Something that instead pulled at the darkness itself, absorbing stray shadows and ultimately leaving me surrounded by an odd twilight haze.

I slowed for a heartbeat, circling among this strange haze, trying to get my bearings.

Out of the corner of my eye, I saw an Order member lunging at Nova from behind. He caught her off-guard, swiping her arm with a small, jagged knife. As she grabbed her bleeding skin, he pressed his advantage and lunged for her throat.

I intercepted him, my blade striking him through the chest.

His blood splattered across both Nova and me, warm and copper-scented. She wiped the bulk of it from her face with the back of her hand, grimacing. Shadows lashed out from her body in automatic defense, the greatest concentration pouring out from around the slash wound on her arm.

I tried to guide my own Light magic into the wound. To heal her the way I'd done a dozen times or more.

But something went horribly wrong.

Instead of soothing her, my magic ended up latching onto her shadows like hooks, pulling them toward me. I felt her power flowing into mine, being absorbed, consumed. My vision briefly flared with a sickening violet hue. The moment was intoxicating and nauseating in equal measure.

I jerked back, severing our connection, but the damage was already done.

"…What was that?" Nova took a shaky step back, a flash of fear crossing her face. The look in her eyes was like a dagger to my chest.

There was no time to explain, no time to apologize. Movement caught the corner of my eye—another attacker closing in.

We went back to the battle at hand, fighting side by side despite the tension and uncertainty crackling between us.

After several minutes of brutal combat, the Order members began to retreat, melting back into the shadows as suddenly as they'd appeared.

"Retreating already?" Zayn called out, breathing hard. "Maybe they aren't as confident as they—"

"They aren't retreating." Orin's voice cut through the clearing. He'd appeared at some point during the fight, moving with surprising stealth for a relatively fragile old man. "This is a trap."

His hand shot out, pointing at Thalia.

His eyes went wide.

At first, I didn't know what he was looking at. Then I noticed the ground where Thalia was standing—the strange symbols glowing faintly in the dirt, arranged in a perfect circle around her.

"Run!" Orin's voice cracked with panic. "RUN!"

But she couldn't move fast enough. Something seemed to be holding her feet in place. Maybe the same something that made the symbols in the dirt flare bright and violent a moment later.

"THALIA!"

Orin made his choice in the space between heartbeats.

He ran toward his daughter at full speed, throwing himself forward, shoving her out of the circle's perimeter. He grabbed something from the ground—whatever was anchoring the magic—and attempted to fling it into the trees.

He was too slow.

The spell detonated with a flash of blinding power that sent shockwaves through the trees. His body was thrown no less than fifteen feet through the air before he struck a massive oak tree and tumbled down to the base of it.

He let out a painful groan and then went limp, his chest barely rising and falling.

"NO!" Thalia's scream tore through the night.

Two Order members materialized from nowhere, blocking her path to her father. Nova raced toward her and cut one down immediately, but more were already appearing.

They were calm.

Organized.

As though this had been their plan all along.

Severin emerged from the trees as well, moving toward Orin's fallen form with unhurried grace, each step measured and purposeful. He held a dagger that gleamed with strange light. A dozen others fell into step behind him, forming a protective barrier, their movements synchronized as though they'd rehearsed this moment countless times.

"A traitor's death," Severin said, stopping and looming over Orin. "As planned."

Thalia remained frozen, staring in horror at her father's crumpled form.

Nova broke into a sprint, shadows gathering around her—

I didn't think. Couldn't afford to think.

I just ran.

My arms closed around Nova from behind, dragging her back even as she screamed and fought against me. Even as her shadows lashed at me and I felt that terrible new side of my magic stirring in response. I managed to resist its pull, but the contact between us was agony—my power wanting to devour her every shadow, every cell in my body screaming for me to just let go and let it take what it wanted.

But I held on. Held on and held back with everything I had.

"Let me go!" She thrashed in my grip, tears streaming down her face. "Orin—I can save him—let me GO!"

"You can't." My voice was strangled from the effort of trying to restrain both her and my own power. "Nova, there are too many, and if you—"

"I don't care!" She was nearly sobbing now, still struggling with a strength born of desperation. "I have to try, I have to—"

She broke free for just a moment, stumbling forward.

Desperation flooded me as well, and my power responded without my permission. An odd, purplish light exploded from my hands in a wild, uncontrolled burst. It slammed into Nova, spiraling through her shadows and pulling them to a center point in front of me, into a small galaxy of writhing darkness, and then into…nothing.

With no real effort from me, the shadows dissipated.

Only that odd, dark violet light remained, crackling around my fingers.

Nova stumbled, knocked off balance by the force of…of whatever the hell I'd just done to her.

The fear in her eyes was more pronounced now. Undeniable.

"You did it again," she whispered.

We stared at one another for several horrible, uncertain seconds, until our attention was jerked back to Orin and the Order members—

Just as Severin's dagger descended in a smooth, practiced arc, impaling Orin's heart.

TWENTY-ONE

Nova

Thalia let out a soft, guttural cry—a raw, broken sound, a mixture of grief and confusion and anger.

I made no sound at all. I couldn't breathe. The world tilted and spun.

Nothing seemed to make sense.

Orin's eyes stayed open, moving between my face and Thalia's. In the end, he ended up locked somewhere between the two of us. Unseeing. Unfocused. A man caught between worlds, between duties, between the two people he'd tried desperately to protect until the end.

He went still.

The entire world did.

And in the stillness, the helplessness, I felt like a child again. Like I was back in the gardens of Rose Point, trying and failing to take a commanding hold on death. To will the flowers back to life. To stop the inevitable decay of everything I loved.

Failing.

I was failing, and all around me, things were withering.

The last echoes of my childhood, of my safety, of the home I'd once known…all fading to nothing but ash and memory. I was losing everything, one piece at a time.

Why the hell couldn't I save any of it?

TWENTY-TWO

Aleksander

Two Order members remained beside Severin, while the others faded back into the forest like smoke. Their target was eliminated—the *traitor* Severin had mentioned, apparently, though I could only guess at what Orin had done to earn such a fate.

Nova took a few more stumbling steps forward before freezing in place. Phantom circled anxiously around her, his body shifting between ghostly and solid forms.

Thalia was kneeling in the dirt, hands outstretched toward her father. Zayn stood close to her, his weapon still raised as he studied the places where the Order members had disappeared.

And Severin was looking directly at me. At the space between Nova and me, at the hint of violet magic still crackling in the air. His expression was smug. Triumphant.

I clenched my fist, feeling trails of dried blood on my hands. My magic still churned beneath my skin. Hungry. Violent. Wrong.

"Well, this has been a very successful night," Severin said, his voice quiet but still carrying clearly across the distance. He gave a slight bow. "I'll be looking forward to our next meeting, Aleksander. Trust it will be soon."

Rage overtook me. I stepped forward even though I knew it was foolish. One, two, three furious steps and then I was sprinting, sword drawn and glowing with a light that flared through several different shades—from its usual pale golden color to that new, sickening, bruised shade of purple.

The Order members on either side of Severin threw something onto the ground—something that sent up plumes of thick, acrid smoke. Lightning flashed bright enough to blind me for several seconds.

When my vision cleared, they were gone.

I scanned the area for any lingering enemies, my chest heaving as I tried to catch my breath, to settle the storm building inside of me before I turned back to the others.

Thalia had crawled to her father's dead body, her

eyes wide in shock. She was silent, save for the occasional quiet, agonized sound that escaped her.

Zayn had followed, and now hovered close to her, still watching the shadows for threats. As the sound of too-close voices and footsteps reached us, he urged her to get up, guiding her back toward Nova, who was kneeling with her weight propped up by Grimnor.

Thalia tried several times to turn back to her father's body, but Zayn stopped her every time, whispering urgently into her ear.

Finally, she turned her back to Orin and bowed her head, body trembling as she collected herself.

A sudden commotion in the nearby trees sent me racing back to Nova's side, readying my weapon as I went.

The new arrivals turned out to be Finch, along with half a dozen other allies. Or who I assumed to be allies, anyway. But if Orin was a *traitor* to the Order, then he must have been working for them at some point.

So how could we trust *anyone* he'd aligned himself with, really?

Whatever side they were on, they formed a protective circle around us for the time being.

Finch's gaze swept over the scene and landed on Orin's lifeless figure. His body went rigid, his jaw working as he struggled to maintain composure. He bowed his head for a long moment. Then, with visible effort, he forced his attention back to us. "These woods are swarming with Order members. You need to leave, immediately."

There was nothing I wanted more than to leave this place.

But Nova was still kneeling, gripping Grimnor like it was the only thing keeping her tethered to reality. She hardly seemed to notice Finch at all.

"We can't stay here," I said, reaching for her shoulder.

She threw off my touch, and the unusually violent rejection seemed to trigger that new, devouring side of my magic.

I forced it down.

Barely.

"I could have saved him," she choked out, glaring up at me. "Why didn't you let me save him?"

I didn't answer, still too busy trying to corral my violent surge of power. Cold sweat broke out across my forehead. Phantom's glowing eyes fixed on me, a low growl rumbling in his chest, as if he knew something wasn't right.

"Something…" Nova held her hands out in front of her, studying the shadows that flickered weakly around her fingers. *Anything. Why can't I save anything?"*

Before I could find the words to reply, Thalia appeared in front of Nova, wearing her characteristically stoic expression despite the tears staining her cheeks. "You can save plenty," she said, bluntly as always. "But only if we live to see another day. Now stop wallowing and let's move."

Nova opened her mouth to argue but stopped as she seemed to register the raw pain in Thalia's expression. She rose slowly to her feet, dripping a trail of scarlet as she did. Her arm was bleeding more profusely than I'd realized; the cut that Order bastard had left was deep and jagged.

I caught her as she swayed, and she leaned against me, clearly dizzy from the blood loss.

Finch shifted anxiously from foot to foot. "We've secured and stationed more help along the path to the Nocturnus Road," he informed us, his voice edged with grief. He seemed to be trying—and failing—not to look toward Orin's body. "We'll hold off anyone who tries to stop you. But you need to go. Now."

Nova lifted her head and cast one last look at her fallen mentor. Her breaths came in short, ragged bursts. Her fists clenched into my shirt, her balance still teetering on the edge of loss.

"*Now,*" Finch urged, and Nova's broken gaze moved to me. Her eyes were oddly vacant, looking through me rather than at me. The weight of all that had happened over the past days seemed to be catching up and crashing down on her all at once.

It had been far too long since that mental bond between us had worked properly, but for whatever reason, her thoughts reached me now. Scattered, fragmentary, but the message was clear—

I don't know how much more of this I can take.

With considerable effort, I managed to send a thread of my magic around her and her wound—not the new, corrupted, consuming side of that magic, but something closer to what I was used to controlling. Something brighter. Warmer. She sank more completely against me. The bleeding slowed, but the skin around her wound had already taken on a greyish tint. She would need proper healing, and soon. Healing I couldn't give her.

You want to believe you're the hero who will find a way to protect her no matter what, don't you? But deep down, you know the truth.

You can't protect her.

You aren't meant *to protect her.*

I shook off Severin's taunts.

For now, at least, I could keep her safe.

I lifted her into my arms and started to walk, and I tried not to think about the blood on my hands or the feeling that something monstrous was waking up inside me.

TWENTY-THREE

Aleksander

We made it back to the Rivenholt Palace unscathed.

But three days later, we were still moving in dazed circles, still trying to pull ourselves together after all we'd endured in the Above.

The shard of Lorien's soul had been locked away for safekeeping in a vault beneath the palace. It helped me regain some semblance of control, not having to feel its constant pull—a small mercy.

My magic still seemed confused, though. Restless. It twisted beneath my skin like a caged, unpredictable animal, growing especially uneasy when confronted with Nova's shadows. Close proximity to Grimnor made it doubly worse.

It made me sick to admit it, but the dynamic between our magic was undoubtedly shifting in ways I couldn't explain.

She continued to train with Eamon and pushed her own abilities further each day. The stronger her magic became, the more the wrongness of mine seemed to intensify. It was reaching a point where I found myself questioning if she'd be better off if I kept my distance, hard as that was to do.

We'd barely spoken these past few days, although we did quietly find our way back to one another most evenings. We sat together while we studied maps and reports in weighted silence. I would recline on her bed while she played the violin I'd given her—one of the few things that still managed to calm her agitated mind. I listened while she vented her frustrations and fears. I made sure she ate something before bed, and I held her while she fell asleep.

It was a delicate dance. We were surviving, but the time we spent apart during the day was still creating a chasm between us. Too many things were going unsaid. The mental, magical bond we'd briefly shared was fraying. And my questions about what she discussed in her private council meetings largely went unanswered.

Boring political things, she assured me.

But she had always told me every detail, boring or

not, in the past. And, judging by the way some of her allies and advisors looked at me, I suspected there were other conversations happening.

Maybe it was mere paranoia, but it seemed like Nova knew something I didn't about the corruption of my magic—like there was something she wasn't telling me.

Something they *all* weren't telling me.

And I hadn't missed the glimmer of fear that occasionally flashed in her eyes when she glanced my way, particularly when she thought I wasn't looking. The same fear I'd seen the night we'd fought those Order members, when my magic had clearly unbalanced her.

Of course, I couldn't blame her for that fear.

Not when I could barely trust myself anymore.

Last night, for the first time since we'd reunited, I'd slept in my own room, alone. Although very little *sleeping* had occurred; I'd tossed and turned for most of the night, trying to keep the unsteady surges of my magic at bay, all while replaying Severin's haunting words over and over in my mind.

You can't protect her.

You aren't meant *to protect her.*

The worst of my unstable tremors had subsided by the time I woke up, but I still avoided Nova for most of the day. It was simpler. Safer. At least until I could understand what was happening with me.

I wandered outside of the palace for most of the morning and afternoon, only making my way back as the sickly orb that passed for a sun in this world began its descent toward the horizon. Even then, I didn't go anywhere near Nova's chambers, or the office where she spent many evenings holding meetings.

Instead, I made my way to the training grounds; the familiar rhythm of combat drills was soothing. Zayn joined me after a while. We sparred without really speaking, our blades clashing in the fading light. He could clearly sense something was wrong, but for maybe the first time in his life, he managed to stay silent.

Because what was there to say?

It felt like we were living in the shadow of a slowly-approaching catastrophe, like acknowledging it out loud would only bring it crashing down more quickly upon us.

After Zayn left, I returned my sword to the adjacent armory, lingering there instead of heading back into the palace proper. Severin's words snaked through my mind, yet again, as I moved restlessly through the room, running my fingers over the other weapons on display.

I'd been there for several minutes, moving in aimless circles, when my magic suddenly stirred with awareness.

I turned to find Nova standing in the doorway, her figure backlit by the setting sun.

She wore a sapphire dress with delicate silver embroidery along the neckline and sleeves. Simple and elegant, but she was still marked by the symbols of her noble position as well—by a brooch featuring a silver tree with red blossoms, and a small silver circlet resting in her dark hair.

I wondered what *boring political things* she'd been getting up to today, but I didn't ask. I could tell she was tired enough without my pressing.

"You managed to escape your council earlier than usual, I see."

"I had to." She stepped farther into the room, the soft rustle of her dress the only sound in the armory's stillness.

I placed the sword I'd been examining back on its rack.

She closed the distance between us slowly. There was the tiniest hint of fear, of uncertainty in her expression, even as she met my gaze. "I had to get away from all of them, and I just…" She shrugged. "I missed you."

The words settled uneasily over me. I'd been avoiding her to make things easier for her. Safer. But now it felt as if I'd let her down.

Damned if I did, damned if I didn't.

She picked up a dagger from the table, turning it over in her hands. A minute passed. Then another. She gripped the weapon tightly and said, "Something has shifted between us, hasn't it?"

The obvious answer was *yes*, but I couldn't bring myself to say it. To say anything.

"I've had a lot to think about and deal with over the

past days," she continued at my silence. "And I keep coming back to what happened during that last battle."

I tensed.

She took a deep breath, setting the dagger down carefully. "That man who led the Order's attack outside of Finch's house…he knew your name. He said he'd be looking forward to your next meeting." She lifted her gaze to mine. Like she wanted an explanation.

I didn't have one.

I'd spent the past days trying to remember anything and everything I could about Severin Thane and the Void Order. About my younger years, so full of gaps and fragmented memories that refused to coalesce into anything clear or useful.

Nova continued to watch me with careful, assessing eyes.

"He seemed…familiar," I admitted. "Though I don't know why."

She nodded as though she'd expected this answer, hugging her arms around herself, brow wrinkling in thought.

She was quiet for several minutes, and I found myself staring at her again, memorizing the way the waning daylight caught in her hair, turning the strands almost copper where the sun touched them.

"Our magic was balanced before," she said, voice barely above a whisper. "Now it isn't."

The words hung in the air, taunting us. Daring us to try and make sense of them.

I didn't want to keep secrets from her. I never did. I'd spent most of my life keeping things locked inside. Emotions. Doubts. Pain. Whatever I had to suppress so I could survive. But she had always had a way of pulling all of my buried things—even the frightening things— back into the light.

So I tried to explain the shift in my magic. Its sudden wrongness, and the way it felt like it was lying in wait for hers, oddly eager to devour any shadow she manifested.

After I'd finished, she didn't reply right away. The silence stretched between us, heavy with unspoken implications. When she finally spoke, her voice was small, almost fragile. Not like her at all.

"And when you're near me?" she asked. "Does it get worse?"

I hesitated, but there was no point in lying. "Yes."

She closed her eyes against the words. A shudder went through her—another tremor of fear, barely suppressed. The sight of it cut deeper than any blade could have, and the words that followed were even worse: "Do you want me to leave?"

I exhaled slowly, shaking my head. "I never want you to leave."

She stepped closer, close enough that I could see the exhaustion etched into the fine lines around her eyes, the grief still lingering from all she'd lost over the past days.

"How can I help you?" she asked, softly.

The question caught me off-guard.

All the other things she was trying to endure…how could she possibly have any strength left to worry about helping *me*?

A surge of confusing emotions overcame me. Awe. Love. Guilt. But above all, I felt worthless, like I didn't deserve her concern—given the way my magic had tried to hurt hers, the doubt I'd been feeling since we returned, and the seeds of distrust I'd been letting take root between us.

"You're already helping, just by being here," I told her.

She studied me for a moment. Then her lips quirked in a tired smile. "Well, that's easy enough."

I took her hand, pulling her even closer. "Just stay with me for a little while, then." I stroked her hair, my fingers coming to rest on her jaw, tilting her face up to mine. "Ignore the politics. The magic. The Order—all of it."

She curled more tightly against my chest. "Tempting."

"Yes," I murmured, pressing a kiss to the top of her head. "You are."

She let out a noise somewhere between a soft laugh and a sigh. Her hands slid up my chest, fingers curling into the fabric of my shirt. That touch, and the way she looked up at me through her lashes…

Tempting wasn't a strong enough word for what she was, honestly.

There were plenty of places we needed to be besides here, but neither of us felt like leaving, suddenly. There were several smaller rooms around the perimeter of the armory, war rooms and meeting spaces with varying levels of furnishings and comforts. One had an inviting fireplace at its center, though the hearth was cold and dark.

We shut ourselves in this room and went to work building up a fire.

As she knelt beside me, feeding kindling into the growing flames, she asked, "How long until my advisors and such notice I'm missing, I wonder?"

"They've already noticed, I'm sure."

"…You're probably right."

"I'm honestly surprised they haven't sent a search party. Especially since I'm *also* missing."

"They should know I'm safe with you."

I yawned, tossing a larger log onto the fire. "Or they'll think I've abducted you to have my wicked way with you."

"That sounds far more enjoyable than enduring more meetings with them."

"I would hope I can bring you more pleasure than politics," I said, grinning slightly. "A low bar to exceed, isn't it?"

She smiled back, though her amusement was short-lived. Shaking her head, she leaned against my shoulder. "*Wicked ways.*" She scoffed. "My point is that I don't care about what's happening with our magic; wicked or not, I'd still rather be here than dealing with another round of kingdom and council disputes."

Her voice was soft, fading a bit toward the end. The firelight danced across her features, drawing my attention again to the exhaustion written in them. She hid it so well most of the time. But now a memory dropped into my head—that moment in the Hollow Grove, when she'd nearly given in to the vines and visions that had tried to trap her in place.

I'm so tired, Aleks. I'm so tired of moving forward.

It shattered something in me to remember those words. To think about the unfairness of it all, and how I'd been keeping my distance all day when she'd clearly needed me at her side.

I hooked a hand under her chin and pulled her toward me, angling her lips to mine for a slow, deliberate kiss. She was tense at first—the side effect of an entire day spent keeping her guard up—but she soon relaxed into the warmth building between us.

Before long, she was crawling on top of me, straddling my lap, balancing on her knees as she deepened the kiss. I wrapped one arm around her waist. The other gripped the back of her head, fingers raking through her hair, taking her in a commanding grip and crushing her mouth so completely to mine that I could barely breathe.

But I didn't need to breathe.

I only needed *her.*

She squeezed her legs against me and rolled her

hips, moaning softly at the delicious friction the movement created. Wisps of shadow curled around us both. It wasn't an unusual side effect of her arousal, and it wasn't particularly powerful, threatening magic…

But it still made me pause.

Because what if my magic reacted?

What if I knocked hers off balance again—or worse?

She paused as well, sensing my hesitation. "I meant what I said earlier," she said quietly. "I don't care about whatever is happening with your magic. I'm not afraid of it. Or you. I never have been, and that isn't going to change."

And yet I've seen the fear in your eyes.

I didn't say it out loud, though. I only brushed a strand of hair from her face and said, "There's a fine line between fearless and foolish."

"Yes, and some might say we've been walking it together since the beginning of all this."

"You're not wrong about that." My fingers stilled in her hair, my hand framing her face. She leaned into my touch. We stayed like that for a long moment, suspended in uncertainty.

"We are not a tragedy," she whispered. "Isn't that what you told me?"

I frowned at the words, even though she was right: I was the one who had said them. And then we'd faced tragedy after tragedy, uncertainty after uncertainty.

But somehow, we were still here.

She crawled from my lap and stood, pacing the

room a few times before coming to stand before the blazing fire. She glanced back at me, her gaze unflinching, her eyes reflecting the fire in a way that seemed natural—like she was something ethereal and inhuman, an extension of both shadow and flame. "It's still true, isn't it?"

I didn't hesitate this time. "Yes."

It was still true, and I still couldn't resist her pull, even knowing the risks. Which was why I rose to my feet as well. Why I stood right beside her and stared into the flames.

She tilted her head. "If you don't want to—"

I pulled her to me, pressing my lips to hers once more, cutting her off. She looked dazed when I finally drew back, a slight smile playing across her lips.

"It's more than a fucking *want*. You should know that by now." The words left me in a rasp. "I need you, Nova."

She glanced up from where her hands rested against my chest, her eyes heavy with desire. The look made my abs tighten and my cock twitch with a sharp ache.

I gripped her hips, pulling her body more flush against mine. "You have no idea how badly I need you right now."

She stretched taller, her nose brushing mine, and whispered her reply directly against my lips: "Have me, then."

My mouth claimed hers in answer.

I may not have deserved her concern or anything

else she offered, but I kissed her anyway, hard and demanding, taking my fill of her taste, her softness, her warmth. Because maybe this was the answer. In the past, I'd never felt more balanced than when we were connected like this.

She kissed me back even harder than I'd kissed her, her fingers tangling in my hair. As if she'd had the same thought.

This is how we make our way through the dark.

This is how we find our way back to each other.

I guided her away from the fireplace, shoving her against the wall. My mouth never left hers for long, and my hands soon joined in the claiming. Every inch of her. I needed every fucking inch of her soft, perfect skin; her breathless sighs; her arching body.

She let out a gasp as my tongue flicked against the throbbing pulse of her neck. My lips closed over that pounding spot, sucking until she was squirming beneath me.

"*Gods*, Aleks."

"You are far closer to a divine being than me," I replied, face still buried in the warm curve of her neck. "But you're welcome to pray to me if you'd like."

"And you'll answer those prayers?"

I drew back, returning the playful smirk she gave me with one of my own. "I suppose it depends on how devout this mouth manages to be," I told her, cupping her chin and tracing my thumb over her lips.

Those lips parted, her tongue swiping over them.

Her hands moved from where they'd been braced against the wall to my chest, undoing the buttons of my shirt. She trailed her fingers very deliberately over my stomach, following the lines of my muscles lower and lower.

"Keep that up, and there's only one way this ends—" I inhaled sharply as one of her hands slipped beneath the waistband of my pants.

Her bright eyes flicked to mine.

"With you on your knees in front of me," I finished, "practicing a very specific kind of devotion."

She gave a sinful little smile. "Tempting me, again."

I grabbed her face and planted a punishing kiss against those wickedly curved lips. She moaned into my mouth, her tongue dancing with mine for a teasing moment…then she pushed me away.

Only to switch places, twisting me around and shoving my back to the wall.

The desire that surged through me nearly knocked me off my feet. It only grew as she dropped to her knees before me, her fingers hooking around my belt as she went. She unbuckled it with deft fingers before pulling my cock free with equally nimble hands. Her lips were there to meet it, their softness a maddeningly perfect contrast against its stiffness.

I pressed one hand to the wall beside me. The other formed a fist in her hair, pulling it out of her face as she took me into her mouth.

Divine, I'd called her.

An understatement.

The gods were nothing compared to the chaotic, beautiful creature kneeling before me, devouring me as if she'd been starving for this moment—as if she'd thought of doing nothing else all day.

My head tipped back as she took me deeper, deeper, *deeper*. Her hand joined in, circling the length she couldn't take in her throat, moving with her head to a rhythm that was torture and ecstasy rolled into one.

I lost track of time, of reason, of the world around us.

There was nothing outside of her and the need consuming us both.

I breathed out a curse when she eventually, slowly dragged her lips from around me, her gaze lifting and staying fixed on mine the entire time.

"Is this the *devotion* you had in mind?" she asked with an innocent flutter of her lashes.

I stared down at her in a daze. At her wet, glistening mouth. At the way her breasts pressed together to form such a tempting valley in between, and the way her head tilted, as if truly questioning if this was what I'd needed.

As if she didn't fucking know.

The temptation to drive deep into her throat once more was nearly overwhelming.

Instead, I pulled her back to her feet, guiding her hand to my length, closing it over the slickness she'd created.

While she stroked, I reached around to the clasp holding her dress in place, undoing it.

I removed that dress—and everything underneath—slowly, savoring the sight being unveiled; I imagined this was how sculptors felt when they freed the figure of their dreams from a canvas of precious stone. She was a godsdamned work of art, and it was tempting to just stand and stare at her.

But I needed more than that.

"Back on your knees," I ordered as I finished undressing myself.

She knelt eagerly on her discarded dress, and this time I knelt with her, pushing her forward onto her hands and sliding my cock between her legs. I was painfully hard by that point. I needed to be inside of her. To feel her clenching around me as I filled her.

But I took my time, dragging my throbbing length over her sensitive folds, occasionally sliding my hand between her legs as well.

"How wet can we make you?" I wondered aloud.

She only moaned in response.

I gave her clit a gentle pinch. "Should we find out?"

This time, she reached for my hand in answer, pressing it more firmly against her as she rose up and sank backwards into my lap.

I held her hip to help her balance. My other hand stayed tangled with the one she had between her legs, encouraging her to keep using me, to keep touching herself exactly the way she wanted to. "Go on," I breathed against her ear. "Get yourself nice and ready for me."

She didn't need any more coaxing than that; she took more control, using not only our hands but her hips, grinding against my lap with increasingly desperate movements.

Before long, I felt my own control slipping. I bent her forward onto her hands once more, dragging my fingertips along her spine as I positioned myself behind her, and then I grabbed her thighs and spread them wider.

Her entire body trembled. "Aleks, *please*—"

I slammed into her before she could finish.

I don't think I could have waited another second.

Her back arched as I gripped her hips and pushed deeper, words spilling from her mouth that were mostly unintelligible, save for one: *Yes*.

Yes.

Yes.

I slipped a hand around her throat. A gentle squeeze, and she gasped and arched more fully, pulling me even deeper inside.

I kept one hand bracketed around her throat. The other clutched her shoulder as I leaned back slightly, giving me the leverage I needed to drive harder. Faster.

There was nothing gentle about either of our movements any longer.

She met me thrust for thrust in a way that felt primal. Animalistic. Like we were meant to collide, to claim one another. Like we were a force of nature that couldn't be stopped, regardless of consequence or reason. Wave after wave rose from this collision, pushing us higher, closer, until finally, we reached the inevitable shattering point.

The cry that escaped her as she came ripped away what little remained of my own restraint. With one final thrust, I followed her into a place that was familiar by now, yet still impossible to properly put into words—an ecstasy that was somehow both light and dark, both a wild unraveling and a perfect becoming.

As we floated back down from our high, we both ended up lying on her wrinkled dress, bodies curved around one another.

At some point, I reluctantly blinked my eyes open. The relief coursing through my veins congealed into something heavier as I saw the bits of dark magic peeling from her skin.

After that initial display when I'd first kissed her, there had been no other erratic magic between us. She had been suppressing her shadows up until this point, I realized. An impressive display of control that had only slipped at that last second, when her emotions crescendoed along with everything else.

Slowly, silently, we pulled apart.

She rose into a sitting position, calling her shadows back with easy, beckoning motions. My eyes followed her every movement, memorizing the way the darkness settled against her skin. Watching it disappear. I'd witnessed it a hundred times before; I don't know why I couldn't take my eyes off it now. Or why that dangerous itching was once more starting beneath my skin, claws of my magic trying to pull toward the surface. Toward her. A very different kind of desire than the one I'd given into earlier.

I pushed this desire down, and I turned away—even though I wanted nothing more than to just sit and stare at her, to study the flush still coloring her skin, the rise and fall of her breathing, the way she ran her fingers through her disheveled hair.

Getting to my feet, I started to dress. I could feel her watching me, the blissful fantasy around us continuing to unravel.

"Are you okay?"

I paused with my shirt in my hand, tilting my head toward her. "Yes. You just have a way of rendering me speechless, that's all."

It wasn't a lie.

We both knew there was more to it than that, but we didn't say so. Not just then. Instead, I sat back down beside her, and we both stared into the dying fire until we found the motivation to finish dressing, to make our way back to the palace and slip away to a proper bedroom.

I still had my doubts. It still felt like we were dancing on the edge of a precipice, testing our balance every time we got too close to one another. But I didn't object when she asked me to stay. Couldn't bring myself to.

"I sleep better when you're here," she said, turning down the layers of soft blankets and silk sheets. Her voice was so quiet I barely heard it. Like a confession, almost.

"Then I'll stay," I assured her, nodding toward the bed. I followed her into the covers after only a moment of hesitation.

Of course I'll stay.

But I remained awake long after she'd fallen asleep, watching the clock tick away the hours and wondering how much longer we could keep our balance.

TWENTY-FOUR

Nova

I woke up alone, and for a moment I panicked, thinking of the last time Aleks had left me alone in the middle of the night, right before we'd clashed with the Void Order.

It proved to be unnecessary anxiety, this time; he stepped through the balcony door only a moment later, running a hand through his sleep-mussed hair. Despite the chilly morning, he wore only what he'd fallen asleep in: a pair of loose trousers slung low on his hips.

I allowed myself to exhale. Tried to let the tension drain from my shoulders. But my eyes were drawn to the scars on his chest, shining in the morning light. Scars that made me think of his early life in Elarith.

A life I now had to admit I knew entirely too little about.

I only knew he'd suffered as a child. That there were scars on his back, too—violent marks that always filled me with sorrow whenever I ran my fingers over them. What he'd actually endured, though, and for what real purpose...I couldn't say. Which made it hard to outright deny the things Orin had told me.

But gods, I *wanted* to deny them.

Judging by the dark circles under his eyes, Aleks hadn't slept much, if at all. I offered him a sleepy smile. He didn't return it. Instead, he stayed by the glass door, staring out at the pale dawn.

"...Is something wrong?"

He started to shake his head but then hesitated, picking up his discarded shirt from the nearby chair, turning his back to me. "Your brother stopped by earlier. He wanted to speak with you."

"What about?"

"I don't know. He seemed to forget when I asked if there was a message I could pass along." He kept his back to me, but I saw his grip on the shirt tighten.

I fumbled for words. For an explanation. For something, *anything*, that would loosen the tense grip of uncertainty closing around us. "...He's having a hard time trusting anyone right now."

"Yes. There seems to be a lot of paranoia going around."

My chest tightened at the edge in his voice.

The silence seemed to stretch for an uncomfortable eternity before he spoke again. "And what about you?" he asked, pulling his shirt on and finally turning to face me. "Do you still trust me?"

"Yes," I said immediately. "Of course I do."

It wasn't a lie.

But it still felt like one.

How could I explain that, though? How could I tell him that I was irrevocably in love with him, that I trusted him more than I trusted myself...and yet I was also afraid. Afraid of what he was becoming—or maybe what he'd always been. Terrified that every step I took to put the world back together was unraveling him. Unraveling *us*.

He looked to the door, and panic flared in my chest again. I was relieved when he sat down beside me instead of leaving, even though he didn't speak right away.

I reached for his hand. "I trust you," I insisted.

I'm not sure which of us I was trying to convince more.

He pulled his hand back slightly. "And yet you're clearly keeping something from me."

I started to my feet, but he caught my wrist and held me in place. His grip was strong enough to hurt.

"Nova." He squeezed even tighter. "You know something about what's happening to my magic."

Shadows rose instinctively around my free hand—a reflexive response to being cornered.

Then it happened: A thread of his magic reached out to meet mine like it had so many times before. Only it had...changed. It felt wrong. It *looked* wrong. It twisted itself into my shadows and began to pull them apart and then toward him, reducing them to a single point of twilight-hued energy before they vanished entirely.

It was the same thing that had happened during our battle with the Order.

I hadn't imagined it then.

I wasn't imagining it now.

And there was something so much more horrifying about it happening *here*, in the quiet of my room, rather than in the chaos of battle. Something more deliberate. Undeniable.

Aleks released my arm and stood up abruptly, backing away from me.

I stared at the space where my shadows had been, now just empty air.

He shook his head, a hint of panic in his eyes, as he quietly said, "Tell me what you know."

I wanted to. But gods, I *couldn't*. I couldn't tell him about the things Orin had told me, or the supporting evidence I'd found alongside my brother and Eamon over the past few days. If I did, I was afraid he'd leave.

He'd want to protect me. He'd be gone before I could stop him.

My lungs ached. My throat burned as if alcohol had been poured down it, reminding me of those dark weeks when we'd been separated.

I couldn't lose him again.

I *couldn't*.

"It…it's not that I'm keeping things," I said. "It's just a lot has happened these past few days. There's a lot of information I'm still trying to make sense of, and I just…"

He waited for me to finish.

I didn't.

Because I didn't know what else to say.

He moved toward the door.

"Aleks, please wait—"

"When you're ready to talk about this openly and honestly, come find me." He paused in the doorway, lifting his face toward the ceiling, one hand bracing against the frame. He looked like he didn't want to leave.

He still did.

Slowly, I sank onto the bed, pressing my palms against my eyes, trying to stave off both tears and an impending headache.

Phantom slipped in from the balcony, trotting to my side and nudging his cold nose against my arm until I lifted my head and scratched behind his ears.

He licked my hand—a rare display of open affection

from him. Then he circled the space where my shadows had been obliterated, vigorously sniffing the air and whining as he did.

(*His magic smells different.*)

More evidence I couldn't ignore.

"What…what does it smell like?"

Phantom tilted his head, considering. (*Cold. Metallic. Like blood.*)

I drew in a shuddering, uneven breath.

I had to go talk to Aleks. I had to fix this before it had time to fester into a wound we couldn't heal.

But as soon as I stood, my plans were derailed by a knock at the door. I opened it to find Eamon standing there, practically vibrating with nervous energy. I knew that look in his eyes—he'd discovered something.

Breathlessly, he said, "We know where the second shard is."

LESS THAN AN HOUR LATER, I WAS CLEAN, DRESSED, AND standing in one of the palace's smaller sitting rooms.

My argument with Aleks had been shoved to the background out of necessity, though it still hovered at the edges of my mind like a bruise I kept painfully bumping against.

We were waiting on my brother to finish with

another meeting before we could begin. Only Thalia, Phantom, and I were in the small room where Eamon had already piled his stacks upon stacks of research materials across every available surface. I tried my best to browse through the nearest pile, to prepare for what was coming, but the words and images only blurred together.

"Your focus seems to be elsewhere," Thalia commented from her seat by the door.

I picked up a tattered scroll, eyes scanning it without really seeing it. "It's been a difficult morning."

"Aleks?" she guessed.

I tilted my head toward her.

She shrugged. "Aveline saw him leaving your room in a rush this morning. She asked me if I knew anything —if everything was all right. She's concerned about you." A pause. "We're *all* concerned about you."

Before I could find the words to try and alleviate any of that concern, Bastian and Eamon entered the room and locked the door behind them.

Again, I tried to focus on the task at hand.

But all I could think about was the last time we'd gathered to make plans like this, before our last expedition to the Above. Aleks had been with me, then. He should have been with me now.

I hadn't been able to find him on my way to this meeting, though.

And part of me—a part that felt traitorous and wrong—wondered if that was for the best.

"Let's be quick," Bastian said, taking a seat at the head of the polished, ornately carved table that took up most of the room.

Eamon needed no more encouragement than this. He plucked three large books and a leather portfolio from his stacks, moving as if he'd spent the past hour rehearsing this presentation. Knowing him, there was a good chance he had.

"Here is our target," he said, picking up the tome bound in dark cloth and flipping to a page he'd marked with a scrap of parchment. "A place known as *Memoria Resonare*. Or, more commonly, the Chamber of Echoes."

The yellowed page showed an illustration of a chamber filled with row after row of tall stone slabs. They looked like gravestones, in a way—except that more than just names and epitaphs were etched across their faces; every inch of them seemed to be covered in carved words. He flipped to the next page, which showed several more rooms with walls that were equally carved up, one of which had a pool of water in the center of it.

"I know that place," I said, surprising myself.

The others turned to look at me.

"I saw that pool in the vision the sentier gave me. And Lorien also mentioned the chamber to Calista in the last vision I saw, when I was holding the shard of his cursed soul." I concentrated, trying to recall his exact words. "*You've committed your sins and vows to the Chamber of Echoes*…that's what he said to her, I think."

"…Interesting." Eamon's eyes lit up with scholarly excitement. "And what he said aligns with what I've discovered in these texts." He tapped the open book. "Every Vaelora once carved their truths into the walls of this chamber. Confessions, fears, regrets, all the darkest parts of themselves—things they had to acknowledge and let go of before ascending to their full power."

"Like a purging ritual?" Thalia asked.

"Exactly."

"Mind carved into one realm…" I thought aloud. "That's the line from the curse we've been trying to decipher. This must be what it was referring to."

"It all fits," Bastian agreed.

"So, where is this place?" Thalia asked.

Eamon consulted his notes, his eyes darting over piles of materials, calculating. "Most texts I've been referencing seem to agree that it's located underneath the temple where the Vaelora once spoke their vows and received the blessings of kings and queens. And that temple is at the absolute center of the realms—built where the gods first granted the Vaelora their power, according to legend."

"In Nerithys, then?" my brother asked.

Eamon nodded. "In the Kingdom of Midna, to be precise, but outside the royal city proper. In a neighboring village known as Vestral."

Concern flickered across Bastian's face. "We haven't been able to explore beyond the royal city's ruins.

There's a chance this other village and its temple don't even exist anymore, like so much of the middle realm."

"It's divine-touched architecture." Eamon spoke with his usual certainty, even as a frown threatened to drag down the corners of his lips. "If anything is still standing among the rubble and decay, it will be that temple."

"But if it's a sacred site meant only for Vaelora, does that mean we won't be able to enter?" Thalia glanced between Eamon and me. "That Nova will have to face whatever is inside the chamber on her own?"

Eamon didn't seem to have an answer for this.

My gaze fell to the empty chair beside me, where Aleks should have been sitting. The growing distance between us felt like a physical thing, suddenly, its weight heavier than any crown or other duty I was trying to balance underneath.

And I had a bad feeling that whatever we found in this Chamber of Echoes was only going to make it worse.

Maybe that was why I so desperately wanted to pretend nothing had changed; that we would face this trial together like all the others we'd faced. I wasn't alone. He was still with me, even if things between us were strained.

So I said, "Aleks might be able to enter as well."

My brother bowed his head slightly, massaging the space between his eyes.

Thalia folded her arms across her chest, a deep, uncertain frown overtaking her features.

Eamon gave no outward sign of either approval or dismissal. As usual, he offered the most even, measured reply. "He *is* the closest embodiment of a Light Vaelora we have. Even given his…ah…*complications* that we've been discussing, he's still clearly connected to Lorien's power in some way or another. He still might be able to open passages and bypass wards, as he's done in the past—as he did in the Midna Palace, for example. It would be worth a try."

Assuming he's still able to summon pure Light magic.

I didn't say it out loud. But my mind was full of images from this morning, of his wrong-looking magic consuming my shadows. What if that happened again? What if something even *worse* happened?

The thought was terrifying.

The thought of going into that chamber alone was infinitely worse, though.

"I'll speak with him about joining us," I said quietly.

No one seemed overly enthusiastic about this plan, but no one could muster up any clear objections, either. So it was decided: we would leave that very evening for the middle realm.

I didn't linger after this decision was made. I wanted —*needed*—an afternoon alone to prepare for what lay ahead.

But though I tried to slip away unnoticed, my brother caught up to me at the end of the hallway.

"Nova."

I stopped but didn't look his way, my gaze instead fixing on a portrait of Calista hanging to my right. The artist had depicted her with a stern, almost cold expression—so much different from the fiery, youthful version of her that I'd witnessed in Lorien's memory.

Bastian cleared his throat. "I know things are difficult between you and Aleks at the moment."

I glanced over my shoulder. "And?"

He met my eyes, unflinching. "And I'm just...I'm sorry."

He said it like he was apologizing for a death. As if Aleks was already gone, and I was the only one who hadn't admitted it yet.

Denial surged through my veins, hot and fierce. I turned to face him more fully, my head lifted high. "There's nothing to be sorry about. He and I have weathered worse storms."

We are not a tragedy.

"We'll survive this storm, too."

Bastian held my gaze for a long moment. "Yes." He nodded slowly. "You will."

It didn't escape my notice how he had emphasized me and not Aleks. His typical, overprotective brother behavior, but it stung nonetheless.

"We both will," I told him, firmly. But the words felt heavy on my tongue, weighted down with a fear I couldn't seem to shake off.

I turned and walked away before Bastian could see the cracks forming in my armor.

Nova

Evening arrived too quickly for my liking. I moved through the day like a puppet on strings, some unseen hand pulling me along, moving my limbs and putting words in my mouth that felt hollow and disconnected from my mind.

I'd found Aleks and discussed our plan, as I'd told the others I would. But he hadn't agreed easily, and I didn't see him for hours afterward—not until the sun was sinking below the horizon and I stood near the western gates, preparing to leave for Nerithys.

The sight of him coming toward me made my stomach flutter and my chest tighten from an odd combination of relief and anxiety. I stepped to meet him, my mind racing with all the things I wanted to tell him, the conversations I'd been rehearsing in my head all day.

But when I reached him, I only managed two words: "You came."

"You asked me to." Despite his reassuring tone, his gaze was troubled, fixed on something in the distance. "Did you honestly think I would let you face this alone?"

"Aleks, about what happened this morning…"

"It doesn't matter."

"It does."

He cut his eyes toward me. "Not right now, it doesn't. Let's survive this next ordeal. Then we'll talk."

I didn't want to wait. And I was tired of the two of us merely surviving. But before I could object to anything he'd said, we were joined by the rest of our company.

It was time to move.

The four of us—myself, Aleks, Zayn, and Thalia—made our way into the middle realm just as we had last time, and just as Thalia and I had so many times over the past month; I'd created a portal that was more or less reliable by establishing two points of similar magical energy, one in both Noctaris and Nerithys. They called to one another, forging a path between those realms that we could follow like a thread through the darkness.

We landed in our familiar spot, right at the base of a crumbling watchtower, in the shadow of the twisted and broken remains of the Midna Palace gates. But instead of turning toward the palace as we always had before, we turned to the road that ran between that palace and the village of Vestral.

It had been easier to move through this realm's chaotic energies the last time we visited—during our trip to the library at the palace—with Aleks at my side, his magic helping to balance the chaos.

He had a similar effect, this time, too. More subtle, but still there. Still helping rather than hurting. I took it as a hopeful sign that we would figure out some way to regain our equilibrium, and I clung to that hope with everything I had—even though it was difficult to be optimistic in a place like this.

A bleak landscape stretched before us, a dismal painting in varying shades of grey and brown. Lifeless earth, skeletal trees, crumbling stone. The sky above it all was a sickly yellow-grey, as if the sun itself were diseased. The ground occasionally rumbled, testing our balance. I didn't know the exact cause of that shaking, but it was common here; I'd always imagined it as a side effect of the Above and Below pulling apart, leaving the realm of Nerithys quaking in between them.

"I forgot how cheerful and inviting this place was," Zayn muttered, his hand resting on his sword hilt.

Thalia tossed him a look but said nothing, only gripped her own weapon more tightly. She'd been quieter, less combative than usual since Orin's death, her grief now manifesting as a cold, sharp focus that didn't break now.

Aleks walked slightly apart from the rest of us, his expression guarded. I caught him glancing at his hands more than once, as if checking to make sure they were still his own. Or making certain no wayward magic was leaking from them, maybe.

We walked the road into Vestral in silence. Once there, we moved through the ruins of that village with a similar wariness, past homes reduced to hollow shells, doors that hung crooked on broken hinges, empty food stores and wells that had long since run dry. In more than one of the collapsed buildings, I saw scattered bones—human and animal alike, bleached white by time.

The farther we walked, the more dramatic the destruction seemed to become. On the far side of the village, entire streets had been swallowed by fissures in the earth.

"The temple should be at the very edge of the city," I said, consulting the map Eamon had given us. "Past the old market district and through what's left of the merchant's quarters."

"Assuming that temple still exists at all," Zayn said doubtfully.

"It does," said Aleks. His gaze shifted to me as he quietly asked, "Can't you sense it?"

I hesitated, closing my eyes and focusing for a

moment, before nodding. "A concentration of magic. It feels muted—old, residual—but like there's lots of it."

We pressed on.

The market district was a maze of collapsed stalls, broken pottery, and rusted scraps that crunched beneath our boots. As we cleared a path through the debris, I continued trying to feel out that concentration of magic ahead of us, to get some sense of what we were getting ourselves into.

Something soon rose over the initial impression of muted power: Something more...*alive*, but unsteady. Like a dying heartbeat.

I moved to the front of our group, leading the others toward that faintly beating heart, until finally we rounded a corner and there it was: a structure known in Vaeloran legend as the Temple of Ascension.

And the Chamber of Echoes awaited us down below, hopefully.

Unlike everything else in this realm, the temple itself stood untouched by decay. Burnished gold walls glowed with their own inner light—not reflecting the sickly sun above, but radiating something warm and reddish. Jagged towers rose on either side like stalagmites jutting from a cave floor. Between them stood a central structure, solid and imposing, its pillars supporting a domed roof over an open-air platform. I could easily picture ceremonies unfolding on that high platform, crowds gathered in the courtyard below to bear witness.

Carved into every wall were symbols I recognized from my studies: the ancient language of the gods. I couldn't read much of it reliably, but most of the etchings seemed to be prayers of some sort, maybe blessings offered by the people of Vestral in an attempt to garner favor with the gods and their chosen Vaelora.

And at the center of it all, an imposing door of solid black stone awaited us.

"Well," Zayn said, breaking the uneasy silence. "That door's not ominous-looking at all."

The unsteady heartbeat seemed to be coming from that door. As I stared at it, it grew stronger. Faster. My shadows stirred beneath my skin, restless and eager. Light rippled along Aleks's arms in response.

"It's…reacting to us," I realized. "It feels like it's demanding our attention, doesn't it? Like it's trying to pull us forward."

Aleks looked at the light dancing across his palm, studying the brightness and the hand holding it as if again making sure it was all his own. His expression darkened. "Let's not keep it waiting, then."

A path of white stones led us through the temple grounds, past withered gardens and fountains that held only dust and more dry bones. I tried not to look too closely at those bones. Tried not to think about all the things that had died when this realm had fallen into ruin, knowing that Noctaris could very well meet the same fate. The desolation here felt horribly…*different*. In Noctaris, there was death and darkness, sure—but it had always felt more like a world sleeping, just waiting for the right moment to wake.

Here, the ruin felt more permanent. Final.

Aleks moved toward the door without hesitation. I hurried to follow, with Thalia and Zayn close behind.

As we approached, I could see that the doorframe was covered in more carvings—names. Dozens of them. The names of every Vaeloran who had ever entered this place.

And near the top, two that made my breath catch: Lorien Blackvale. Calista Mireth.

Aleks reached out, running a hand over the smooth black door, which had no handle. "How do we open it?"

The answer came not in words but in sensation— the strongest pulse of magic yet. It seemed to hook into my heart and pull. Beside me, Aleks pressed his hand to his chest as if he'd felt the same thing.

But I didn't know what it wanted from us. Tendrils of our magic continued to rise, drifting forward and swirling chaotically around it, but the door itself never so much as trembled.

"Blood," Thalia said suddenly. She was examining the wall to the left of the door, where a shallow basin had been carved into the gold plating. Her fingertips traced a faint etched scene above it—a figure standing before the door, their hand outstretched. Drops falling from their fingertips. "I think it requires blood."

I looked at Aleks. He met my gaze and nodded.

Together, we approached the basin. I gathered

shadows into my hand, letting them solidify and shift into a sharp point that I then drew across my other hand. A few drops of blood welled up, dark and hot. Beside me, Aleks did the same with a blade of Light magic, cutting his palm open. I tried not to stare at the light pooling in his hand alongside the crimson, but I couldn't help noticing the color.

Still the familiar whitish-gold of his Light magic.

For now, at least.

As our blood dripped down, mingling in the stone bowl, I exhaled a soft sigh, some of the tension leaving my shoulders...

Only to jump as the door swung open, revealing a staircase leading down into absolute darkness.

From the depths came a sound like whispering—thousands of voices speaking at once, too low to make out individual words but loud enough to raise goosebumps on my skin.

I couldn't seem to make myself move.

Zayn found his courage first, stepping forward with his hand on his sword. Courage wasn't enough, though; the temple rejected him before he'd even taken two steps inside, engulfing him in pressure that nearly made him crumple to his knees. The whispering briefly rose into a high-pitched wail as he stumbled back. Thalia barely managed to catch him before he fell.

"So much for the valiant charge I had planned," he said with a shaky laugh.

Thalia snorted at this, shoving him back upright.

She considered the entrance for a moment before swiftly following our lead with a blood offering, taking out a small knife and whipping it across the heel of her hand.

The drops sizzled and hissed as they landed in the basin. Another wail rose from inside the temple.

Frowning, she tried reaching her hand across the threshold, but jerked it back almost immediately.

"It's as we expected," she said, wincing and shaking her hand. "No one is charging into this place except those with Vaeloran blood." Her gaze trailed to Aleks. "And hopefully those with very deep ties to the Vaelora, too," she added.

I cautiously stepped closer to the entrance. When I reached over the doorway, the whispers seemed to quiet, as if the spirits inside were drawing back, watching to see what I would do next. I glanced over my shoulder and found that Aleks had taken several steps away from the door. His face was pale, his expression difficult to read.

Zayn went to speak with him while Thalia pulled me aside, her grip gentle but firm.

"Assuming he can make it across the threshold," she said, low enough that only I could hear her, "are you *sure* you want to go in there alone with him?"

I frowned. "He isn't going to hurt me."

"That isn't the only thing I'm worried about."

I looked back to the waiting stairs. The whispers

were getting louder again; I would have sworn I heard my name lifting clearly among them more than once.

"You were listening to Eamon's warnings, weren't you?" Thalia asked. "According to legend, the chamber beneath this temple doesn't just demand you to carve your truths into its walls—it can force you to speak them. Every truth you have can be exposed. You can't lie here; people have gone mad trying to do so."

I glanced at Aleks, my stomach twisting into knots.

Every truth you have.

I might end up telling him everything Orin had said. Everything I'd learned alongside my brother and Eamon. Everything I'd been too afraid to say.

I turned back to Thalia, forcing my voice to remain steady. "We'll be fine," I assured her, even as doubt coiled tight around my heart. "What choice do we have?"

She shook her head and mumbled, "I wish I could go with you instead."

I smiled sadly at her. Then I offered her that sign of affection we'd created, just for the two of us, months ago—my hand over my heart, tapping twice.

Her mouth remained fixed in a tight line, but she returned the gesture, adding the usual affectionate eye roll and slight smile that was typical from her.

"We'll be back," I promised.

"In one piece," she commanded. "Mind and all."

"In one piece," I agreed as Zayn and Aleks rejoined us.

All trace of amusement was gone from Zayn's face. Aleks was still impossible to read, but there was no hesitation in his movements anymore.

He apologized for his moment of doubt, and then his hand found mine, squeezing once. "Are you ready?"

No. I wasn't ready. But when had I ever been ready for any of this?

"Let's go," I said.

We descended into the dark together, like we had so many times before.

The stairs seemed endless, spiraling down into the earth, lit only by occasional flickers of pale light, the source of which I could never seem to pinpoint. We passed several cave-like rooms that held the stone slabs I'd seen both in my vision and in Eamon's book. Graveyard after graveyard full of them, all arranged in neat little rows. It was tempting to get closer, to try and get a better look at the things carved on them. But I was afraid I wouldn't be able to start again if I stopped, so our relentless descent continued.

The whispers grew louder with each downward step, some transforming into distinct voices—some pleading, some angry, some broken by grief.

I lied to them.

I should have saved them.

It was my fault.

I couldn't stop it.

I loved them more than the world—

The confessions of every Vaelora who had ever carved their truth into this place. I should have tried to block them out. It would have been safer. But I couldn't help listening. Couldn't help wondering about the ones that had walked before me, and how I measured up to them and their sins.

Finally, the stairs ended.

We stepped into a vast circular chamber that took my breath away. The walls here were covered—completely covered—in carvings. Scenes and symbols and words in several different languages, cut by dozens of different hands over countless centuries. Some carvings were shallow and hasty, others deep and ornate. All of them pulsed with a faint, ghostly light.

"We're here," Aleks said in a hushed tone. "Now, where do we start looking for the piece of Lorien that's supposedly here as well?"

I withdrew Grimnor and studied it for a moment, hoping the entity sleeping within its blade might make himself useful again, as he had in the Hollow Grove.

But the sword remained cold and lifeless in my grip—and it felt strangely heavy, too.

Aleks read the disappointment on my face. "Nothing?"

"Not this time. It seems like whatever energy saturates this place is completely crushing any magic Grimnor holds. Which includes Lorien's power too, I guess."

"Just our luck."

"It feels like the air in here is suffocating our own magic too, doesn't it?"

Aleks summoned a small flicker of light to his palm, with obvious effort.

"…You're right," he agreed—though he didn't seem disappointed by this.

I guess it was somewhat of a relief, to not have to think about our magic and the way the bond between us was changing. But it made me feel oddly vulnerable, too. I was no stranger to fighting the battle of us and our magic, whatever form it took. And without that familiar fight to focus on, I felt…exposed.

Like there was one less thing insulating us from the truths that threatened to condemn us in here.

"…*Mind carved into one realm*," I recited, trying to keep moving. "I wonder if we need to look for whatever thoughts or confessions Lorien carved here?"

It was as good a plan as any, so we split up and started to do just that.

I had only been searching for a few minutes when, out of the corner of my eye, I noticed Aleks had stopped moving.

"Nova. Look."

I hurried to his side, gaze trailing up to where he was pointing.

Lorien's name was carved there—a hasty signature I could barely recognize. Above it, several lines of text stretched across the wall.

His confessions.

But they were crossed out, struck through with several deeply carved lines that made it impossible to read what he'd written.

"That's…strange. Who would want to cover up whatever he confessed?"

After a moment of considering it, Aleks said, "…Why do I feel like the Order had a hand in this, too?"

I didn't reply. Couldn't reply. My attention had snagged on the mere mention of the Order, and now my thoughts were racing, all the truths I was trying to bury about that clandestine organization threatening to rise up.

Confront him, something whispered. *Confront him with the truth.*

When I spoke again, my voice didn't sound like my own. "You should know."

He gave me a curious look.

The words surged out of me, harsh and quick, even as I tried to hold them back. "You know about the Order and the hands they have on all these different things. The hands they control. The lives they manipulate like pieces on a board. Deep down, you know. You've always known, even if you don't remember."

Aleks had gone very still, his eyes widening with something between confusion and dawning horror.

I pressed my lips together, fighting the compulsion to keep speaking, to spill every secret I'd been holding. I bowed my head, shaking it as pain radiated through my clenched jaw.

I would keep my mouth shut.

I wouldn't give in to this place so easily.

The whispers around us grew louder, swelling like a tide rushing in to fill the silence I was desperately trying to keep.

Then, a singular voice rose above them, not from any one direction, but from everywhere at once. Maybe from the walls themselves. It said only one word: *TRUTH.*

The word reverberated around the chamber. The carvings on the walls began to glow brighter, light pouring out of them and spinning into a cyclone that reached nearly to the ceiling.

A woman stepped out of the swirling mass of light.

She wore a white silk dress with swaths of gossamer fabric that trailed behind her like folded wings. A gold ribbon was tied around her face, hiding her eyes, but she moved with grace and precision, all the same. She held a small crystal dagger on a cushion of blue velvet, offering it as she stopped before us.

Again, a disembodied voice spoke, filling the room and vibrating through the very core of my being: *Those who seek the path forward must first shed falsehoods. Carve your confessions or let them destroy you. The choice is yours.*

I stared at her. I wanted to rip off her blindfold, for some reason; the urge was so strong, my hand cramped from my efforts to fight against it.

Aleks looked between me and the blade she held for a long moment before he seemed to make up his mind. He stepped forward.

"I'll go first."

TWENTY-SIX

Nova

Aleks picked up the dagger before I could disagree, making his way to a stretch of blank wall that the woman indicated.

Speak, said the floating voice.

After a pause, he spoke—only to have his voice swept into the current of whispers once more rising around us.

But then I noticed faint words appearing on the wall before him.

With trancelike movements, Aleks lifted the knife and began to carve, following the lines and curves of the ghostly letters. The blade cut into the surface as if it was made of clay rather than stone.

I held my breath as I stepped closer, reading what eventually blazed clear and bright before us.

I'm afraid of what I'm becoming.

The blindfolded woman followed his every movement. As he finished carving the last letter, her lips twisted—a frightening smile. Then came that voice that floated high above all the other whispers: *Deeper.*

Aleks spoke again, but this time, as his words flickered onto the wall, he clenched the dagger to his chest, fighting the urge to carve his second truth into permanence.

His breathing grew labored. His balance swayed as he tried to turn away only to freeze mid-step, as if bound by an invisible chain. Every attempt to move away from the wall ended the same way. The dagger shook in his hand, its tip tilting dangerously close to his chest; I worried he might carve straight into his heart in an attempt to free himself.

Thalia's somber warning rushed to the front of my mind—

People have gone mad trying to resist it.

"You don't have to do this," I said, hurriedly moving closer to him. "We can turn around. We can find another way to get what we need."

The woman in white looked at me. Even though I

couldn't see her eyes, I felt as if her gaze was spearing me straight through.

Aleks placed a hand on my arm, stepping between me and the woman as if to protect me, even as he continued to struggle against the compulsions tearing through him.

"Aleks, I…"

He stilled at the sound of my wavering voice. "I'm fine."

Concern continued to gnaw at my insides, but I didn't try to stop him as he stepped forward, his movements slow but turning steady once more as he reached toward the wall.

More words appeared, each letter like a drop of blood forcibly squeezed from his veins:

I had a dream. A vision where I hurt her. I hurt all of them. The dead were too many to count.

I watched his hand moving over the confession. The way the knife trembled in his hold, his knuckles white with the force of his grip.

Softly, I said, "It's not true, Aleks. The future is impossible to predict with certainty, you know that. This is all just your fear talking."

But he didn't seem to hear me.

He just kept carving, oblivious to the horrified expression overtaking my face as he dug deeper and more violently into the wall.

Dead. So many dead. She isn't safe. I can't keep her safe. I have to leave her.

The sense of dread radiating from him was suffocating. He clenched the knife tighter still. His tracings of the glowing letters grew messier and messier, but he kept going with terrible determination.

He carved every last word.

When he'd finished, the blindfolded woman gave a slight bow of her head. Smiled again. The voice seemed to come directly from her, and only her, this time—though it still shook my entire body as if rushing in from everywhere, all at once: *Truth spoken. Truth accepted.*

The words Aleks had carved flashed like fire before fading to a dull glow. He dropped to one knee, gasping for breath.

Then the woman turned to me.

Another dagger had appeared in her hand, this one darker than the one Aleks had used—black crystal that seemed to drink in the light around it, much like Grimnor did.

I took it but shook my head. "This is manipulation.

Just because you forced him to voice his fears doesn't make them his truths."

The woman canted her head. *Why do you fear the truth so loudly, Daughter of Shadow?*

"I don't," I snapped.

But it was a lie.

And the chamber *knew* it was a lie, and it seemed to be punishing me for telling it; the pressure in the air doubled, tripled, making it hard to breathe.

The dagger in my hand grew hot.

Compulsion seized me; my lips were moving before I could stop them.

The knife seemed to lift of its own accord, guiding my hand to a blank section of wall. Words flashed upon it before I could turn away.

I was cutting into the stone an instant later.

I KNOW WHAT HE IS.

Deeper, said the blindfolded woman.

My body shook with resistance, but the words kept appearing, and my hand kept carving against my will.

A MONSTER—

The knife slipped from my shaking grasp. I caught it awkwardly, the blade slicing across my palm. I didn't think to drop it, didn't think to pull away. I just kept carving, even as the edge of it dug into my skin, filling my palm with blood.

A MONSTER THEY CREATED TO
DESTROY—

It felt like my chest was caving in. My body locked up, fighting the final word. The knife clattered to the ground. I couldn't carve the last word.

I *wouldn't*.

I felt the woman watching me. The whispers rose to a deafening crescendo. The walls seemed to shift and writhe, the carvings moving like living things.

TRUTH.

The command slammed into me like a physical blow.

"...Me," I gasped the word out, and the chamber snatched it up like a dragon seizing prey. It was blazing on the wall in the next breath, completing the sentence I'd so desperately tried to leave unfinished.

A MONSTER THEY CREATED TO
DESTROY ME.

I didn't pick up the dagger. Didn't carve the last word. I just stared at it, my vision blurring with tears I refused to shed.

Aleks rose unsteadily to his feet, his gaze fixing on the wall as well.

I opened my mouth to lie, to offer false comfort. But I couldn't manage it, of course—the chamber wouldn't allow it. I stopped myself from even trying.

"I…I'm sorry," I whispered. "I should have told you before now. I just…"

The words hung between us, heavy with all the things I couldn't say, all the truths still locked inside me, waiting for their turn to be carved into stone.

Aleks didn't reply. Didn't look at me. The blind-folded woman glided around us with ghostlike movements, bending gracefully to pick up the daggers we'd used. She inspected them, as well as the things we'd carved, for several moments. Then she turned back to us.

Her eyes were still hidden. Her mouth remained perfectly emotionless. Yet I could sense the expectation in her tilted head, her patient stillness.

She said, *Nothing breaks, nor binds, so completely as the truth.*

I leaned against the wall, unsure of how to reply.

Aleks paced the room, studying my carved words, occasionally trailing his fingers along them.

It could have been minutes that passed. Hours. An entire day. I don't know how long it took before I couldn't stand the silence any longer. I turned to the woman, desperate for guidance, for some sign of what came next.

She only repeated, *Nothing breaks, nor binds, so completely as the truth.*

The only response I felt this time was *anger*. Anger at her, at this place, at the way things were and how impossible everything seemed. I sank back against the wall and closed my eyes tightly, my entire body trembling.

But anger soon brought clarity with it, as if that fury had burned a path through my fear and uncertainty to reveal the revelation I'd been hoping for.

Nothing breaks, nor binds, so completely as the truth.

Broken or bound. Maybe *this* was the true test— how would Aleks and I leave this place? We had walked side by side into the darkness, over and over, but could we walk in the light together, too? Even when that light revealed ugly things? Frightening things?

So many things were trying to break us.

The last words Aleks had carved flared like a warning sign on the wall across from me, making my heart race.

I have to leave her.

"Nova."

I flinched at his voice, afraid of what he was going to say next. It was the Hollow Grove all over again—I was in the middle of a nightmare, and I knew it, but I still didn't want to move into whatever future awaited me; there was something oddly comforting about familiar terrors.

But I hadn't stayed in that forest.

And I couldn't stay in this chamber, either.

So I pushed away from the wall and met Aleks in the center of the room. My heart pounded. My palms were slick with sweat. The whispers rose eagerly with my footsteps, as if in anticipation, while a hundred painful truths burned brighter and brighter on the walls all around us.

Aleks ignored all the noise and all the flashing, fiery words as I approached him. His gaze fixed on mine, unwavering as he said, "There's one more truth you should know before we leave this place."

I held my breath.

"I love you," he said.

The suffocating pressure in the air seemed to lessen—enough that faint threads of golden light soon lifted from his arms. My shadows rose in answer, thin ribbons that intertwined with his magic.

He watched them dance together for a moment before settling his gaze back on mine. "I love you," he repeated. "No matter how the light and shadows shift."

I reached my hand toward his. He took it without hesitation, his warm grasp closing over the dried blood covering my palm.

"I love you, too," I replied, my voice soft yet certain, the declaration somehow not swallowed up even as the ghostly voices continued to storm around us. It was not a revelation, but it still felt like a confession as much as anything I'd said thus far—the deepest, most desperate truth I was clinging to. I'm not sure if I actually said it out loud, if the words were swept away by the whispers, or if they appeared on the walls as bright and bold as all our other confessions...

I didn't care.

I didn't need to carve this truth into stone. Because it was already carved into my very being, deeper than any blade could cut.

I loved him, and I wouldn't let him go.

No matter how the light and shadows shift.

The storm around us slowly calmed as Aleks and I turned to face the blindfolded woman, our magic fading but our fingers still laced together.

The woman held up the first dagger.

Truth spoken.

The black dagger followed, clasped in her other hand.

Truth accepted.

She held the blades up as if comparing their weight, balancing them on a scale. An eerie sound funneled toward us, like wind howling through a narrow mountain pass, and a door I hadn't noticed before slid open on the opposite side of the room, revealing a smaller inner sanctum. There were words carved on its walls, too, but they seemed to be vows, not confessions.

In the very center of the room stood a large, deep basin of stone. My heart skipped several beats as I realized it was the very same one I'd seen in my vision from the sentier—except it was drained of the turquoise water that had once filled it.

Cautiously, we approached it.

And there, resting at the bottom, was the piece of soul we'd come to collect.

TWENTY-SEVEN

Nova

"If looks could kill, that soul shard would be obliterated by now," Zayn said from his perch on the cushioned window seat of the parlor.

I blinked, dragging my stare away from the shard in question, which I'd spent the past hour trying to divine visions from. This was my fourth attempt in as many days, and they'd all been unsuccessful.

"I'm just…frustrated," I muttered.

Phantom, who had been keeping watch by the door, padded over and shoved his head under my hand.

I absently scratched his favorite spot between his tapered ears as I said, "The last one yielded so easily. It gave me such a clear vision of Lorien—a better understanding of him. I was hoping to continue putting the puzzle together."

Zayn picked through the platter of fruit and cheese beside him, popping a grape into his mouth. "Do we honestly *want* to get to know the man better? You've met the guy. I've met the guy. I'm still not convinced that there's any vision you could have that would change my perception of him as a monumental bastard."

I absently ran my fingers over the scars in my palm —a lasting reminder of the words I'd carved into the Chamber of Echoes.

Four days since our ordeal. And every night, I'd woken up from nightmares of blood in my palm and words burning on the walls all around me.

Aleks had been there to comfort me, at least; we were back on speaking—and sleeping—terms, the vows we'd put forth in that chamber of truth helping to mend what had started to fracture between us. But things were still strained. He still kept to himself more than I would have liked, even if I understood his need for space. And we still had far too many questions about what lay ahead.

"I just feel like the truth is more complicated than we previously thought," I said, looking back to the shard.

What had Lorien carved into the walls of that chamber?

What other truths were we missing about him?

"It's like the magic in that place is still bearing down on me, even now. And I can't help being obsessed with untangling things."

Zayn conceded with a shrug, stretching out, tucking his hands behind his head, and closing his eyes. Only he could relax at a time like this.

"It's not just about changing our perception of Lorien, either," I pressed. "There's power in understanding our enemies."

"Fair point, I suppose."

"It seems like we might have a common enemy in the Order, too, if they truly are the ones who came between him and Calista. I wonder what he knows about them? About their operations, their structure, their—"

The door started to open, interrupting us.

Phantom growled. Zayn bolted upright. I tensed, hand instinctively moving toward Grimnor; there were countless guards surrounding this room, and I'd asked them all to make sure I wasn't disturbed by anyone aside from my inner circle.

I breathed a sigh of relief when it was one of those trusted few—Captain Voss—who stepped inside.

"Your Highness." He gave a small bow. "I apologize for interrupting."

"It's fine." I cast a forlorn look at the shard. "You're not interrupting anything particularly productive."

"I see. Could you follow me, then?" There was an

urgency in his usually stoic tone that had me immediately rising to my feet and pulling on my coat.

"Where to?" I asked, tucking the shard of soul carefully into my pocket.

He merely beckoned and hurried out of the room; I wasn't sure he'd even heard me.

I grabbed my sword and rushed after him.

Phantom followed after he'd shifted into a slightly larger, more imposing canine form—a form he'd been taking much more often as he escorted me through the halls these days, keeping any potential threats and overly curious courtiers at bay.

Zayn followed us as well, looking far more alert, suddenly. There was a nervous energy thrumming through the palace that I guess even he couldn't relax underneath. We'd been insulated from it in the private parlor, but now it hit us in full force.

Much of that energy was because of the event looming just two days ahead—my coronation. An affair I'd somehow forgotten was imminent while we were dealing with everything else.

It was impossible to deny it was happening now, though; the preparations were all being made. Servants rushed through corridors with linens and flower arrangements. Guards rehearsed formations and security protocols. More guests of all ranks had started to arrive, joining the ones we'd already been hosting for weeks. The scent of food and wine drifted from the kitchens at all hours.

It was overwhelming, and yet...I felt oddly calm about the actual ceremony. We'd all discussed it at great length in between our other missions—the necessity of giving this realm a strong figurehead at the center of its strongest kingdom. Though I had my share of detractors, I was still the gods-blessed Vaelora and the rightful heir to Rivenholt's throne. One who had clawed this world back from the edge of complete annihilation, even if the job was still incomplete.

In the grander scheme of things, a crown on my head seemed almost like an afterthought to me. But I knew it was an important symbol to my people.

There was something else brewing under the surface of all the ceremony preparations, though. Something that made Captain Voss's jaw tight and his steps quicker than usual—and *that* had me worried.

Finally, I couldn't suppress my curiosity any longer; I placed a hand on his arm, drawing him to a stop. "What's wrong?"

His eyes darted from side to side, checking for eavesdroppers. "The regent requested I not speak of it until we were in a safer location. Not much farther, come along..."

He took us outside, down the lantern-lined path that cut through the main gardens, past the training grounds and our largest greenhouses, and then farther still. Leading us toward the private, royal stables, I soon realized; there was a small, hidden space connected to the tack room that we had occasionally used as a secure meeting place, and I assumed this was our ultimate destination.

As we approached the stable yard, I noticed a wagon parked near the entrance. Nothing terribly out of the ordinary in appearance, but the closer we got, the more uneasy I felt.

Phantom growled at the exact moment I caught a hint of what smelled like blood.

My shadows writhed restlessly beneath my skin. The energy they were reacting to…I knew exactly what it was.

The energy of the newly-deceased.

"This way," Captain Voss urged, pointing us toward the tack room while he circled back, making certain we weren't being followed.

When we stepped inside, my brother, Eamon, and Thalia were already there to greet us. We waited for Voss to give the all clear, then we secured the room and made our way toward the entrance to the hidden annex, which was located behind a false wall disguised as shelving for bridles and saddles.

We paused before this false wall, exchanging few words at first. I was thoroughly confused and growing more anxious by the second when Thalia cleared her throat and asked, "Have you eaten today?"

"…What?"

"Because this might turn your stomach. Fair warning."

Before I could ask any more questions, Bastian opened the wall to the annex.

Inside were two dead bodies sprawled out on tattered blankets, both of them young men with pale skin already mottled with the first signs of decay. The stench of death hung heavy in the confined space.

"Look at their necks," my brother instructed.

Wrinkling my nose, I stepped closer and did as he asked, as did Zayn.

Both men had matching brands burned into the skin just below their jawlines—circles with thorn-wrapped swords cutting diagonally through their centers. Faint but unmistakable marks.

"…Fuck," said Zayn.

"Order members," I breathed. "Here?"

"They were killed in Tarnath, to be more specific," Captain Voss said, and my heart clenched with fear for that royal city and the people within it. "A group of my patrolling soldiers found them in an alley near the eastern district just before dawn. They seemed suspicious, and turned violent when questioned—violence that led to, well, *this*."

Bastian pulled the wall partially closed. It blocked some of the stench, but did little to stifle my magic and its interest in the dead energy drifting off the bodies.

"We have two thoughts," my brother said. "Either they're here for Aleks, if he truly is a wayward weapon of theirs… Or they're here because they know we have two pieces of Lorien's soul in our possession—that we are dangerously close to having both Vaeloran souls in one place, for better or worse."

"Or for both reasons," Thalia said grimly. She shook her head, clearly biting back several violent, choice words about that organization that had killed her father. "This shouldn't have caught us by surprise. We already suspected that the Order is as tangled into all of our affairs as it's possible to be."

"Yes..." Eamon agreed slowly. "But most of their operations have been centered in the Above for so long, with some minor movements in Nerithys. All evidence suggests that this supposed 'new world order' that they're trying to bring about would be in Soltaris, not here."

"Because they assumed this realm was finished," added Bastian. "And they left it for dead."

Zayn huffed out a humorless laugh. "Well, the bastards assumed wrong, didn't they? They'll regret underestimating this realm."

"I wish they had *continued* to underestimate us," Thalia mumbled.

My brother frowned. "The questions I have now are: How long have they been operating in Noctaris? How many? And how deeply have they infiltrated and influenced this palace and the political happenings of our kingdoms?"

I stared through the partially open wall, at what I could still see of the dead. "I wonder how many of the arguments we've endured these past months were orchestrated by the Order?"

"I wouldn't be at all surprised to learn they've been influencing some of the leaders who have opposed and questioned you," my brother said. "A unified and revived Noctaris poses a greater threat, after all; the stronger you get, and the more allies you have, the more difficult it will be for them to destroy you."

"So, that's a third reason for them to show their ugly faces here." Zayn clasped his hands behind his head and sighed. "Honestly kind of surprised they haven't already descended on us in force."

"That might be imminent," said Thalia.

"It's regrettable that these two ended up dead before we had a chance to force information out of them," Voss said. "I've spoken to the ones who battled with them, as well as some of my more trusted soldiers; orders have been given to try and capture any other suspicious individuals alive."

"All well and good," said Eamon, "but we could also get at least *some* information from the dead, could we not?" He gave me an expectant look.

I nodded, even as a cold sweat washed over me. "Let me see what I can divine."

I nudged the wall open farther, bracing myself against the renewed assault of death's stench. Everyone stood back except for Phantom, who insisted on staying close to my side, his form tense and protective as we both crept over and crouched by the corpses.

My hand shook only slightly as I moved it over the decaying men, focusing on the one adorned in finer clothing; he struck me as a higher-ranked member who would likely have more useful secrets.

Shadows dripped from my fingertips, pooling in the air above the corpse. I pressed those shadows down into the man's chest, closing my eyes.

An explosion of images followed in rapid succession; it took me a minute to calm my racing pulse and the magic surging through me, to be able to clearly parse through the chaotic visions and find what I was looking for.

I saw the memory I needed through the eyes of the dead man himself—a meeting in a darkened room, where he seemed to be receiving orders. He wasn't alone, either; at least a dozen others were circled around him, all of their eyes fixed on the hooded figure who stood at the back of the room.

The air was tense, rippling with a combination of suppressed fear and fanatical fervor.

"More are descending into this forsaken realm as we speak," said the hooded man. "They'll join the numbers we already have stationed in the shadows. It's only a matter of time before we'll be ready to move in earnest, and we'll be expecting you all to be prepared..."

His voice sounded vaguely familiar.

Then he leaned into the light of the single candle burning on the table between them, partially revealing his features, and my chest tightened as I recognized him.

Cold, greyish-blue eyes. Dark hair streaked with silver. That man…he was the one who had led the attack on us in the Above.

Severin Thane.

Memories of the night we'd met crashed over me with painful clarity. Of the way he'd taunted Aleks, leaving that tormented expression on his face. Of Orin's body crumpling against the ground. Thalia's scream. And all the questions, the unanswered mysteries surrounding that entire ambush…

I opened my eyes, trying to keep the memories from overwhelming me. But it was useless. It wasn't just grief and confusion that distracted me, but *fury*.

As rage coursed through me, my shadows responded violently, coiling and striking out. Grimnor rattled at my hip, eager for me to use it. I *wanted* to use it. I wanted to resurrect this corpse beneath me, only so that I could kill him again—feel his life drain away just as I'd felt Orin's life draining away.

An instant after I had this morbid thought, the man's eyes…*opened*. His body twitched. His pallid, cracked lips parted, a low moan escaping them.

I jerked my hand away, falling back against Phantom.

The man went still again, but his eyes remained open, staring lifelessly at the ceiling.

My allies were all silent behind me, but I could sense

their astonishment, along with a hint of fear, even with my back to them.

"…Remarkable," Eamon whispered.

"It's the same thing that happened with the sentier," I said quietly, clenching my fists into Phantom's fur, leaning against him until the last wisps of shadow settled back beneath my skin. "An accident. I wasn't actually trying to reanimate him."

"But you *could*," said Eamon.

I swiped a slightly shaky hand over the man's eyes, closing them once more. Then I got to my feet, turning and slowly making my way back to the group.

"You could revive him," Eamon repeated. "And in time, I think you will. The most powerful of your persuasion have demonstrated that ability in the ancient texts. You could ask anything of the dead. Anything at all, and then force them back to life so that they can give it to you. Calista herself—"

"We're short on time, unfortunately," Thalia said, coming to my rescue, "so let's focus on what she can already comfortably do. It's not like she doesn't have enough to worry about."

"Agreed," my brother said, pulling the wall partially shut once more. "So, what were you able to see?"

I told them about the meeting—what little I'd been able to see before my emotions had gotten the better of me.

"I should have stay focused," I said. "I'm sorry.

Maybe I could try again…" I glanced toward the annex, but Bastian put a hand on my shoulder and squeezed.

"You've confirmed our suspicions that they're planning something; that's enough for us to concern ourselves with at the moment."

"We're a relatively easy target, admittedly," Thalia added. "They likely saw the chaos of the reviving realm and decided they needed to move against us before we managed to better organize and consolidate our power."

"Before I officially become queen?" I wondered.

Voss shifted uncomfortably. "Do you think they intend to attack during the coronation itself?"

My brother considered this carefully. "As I said before, if the kingdoms of Noctaris are in chaos and fighting amongst themselves, drawing her attention toward them, Nova can't focus on her Vaeloran destiny. More time for the Order to work toward their ultimate goal of destroying the cycle and remaking the world in their image."

"Maybe we should cancel the ceremony?" Voss suggested. "It might be safer."

"No," I said quickly. "That will only make them think I'm afraid of them. If they're trying to interfere with my rise to power and influence, canceling is exactly what they would want me to do."

The fury was back in my bones, suddenly, hardening into cold determination.

"Let them continue to creep through the shadows and try to scheme against me. I don't care."

Thalia studied me for a moment, then her lips curved into a slightly savage smile. "And let them be reminded that we *control* the shadows here. We don't fear them."

I mirrored her savage expression. "They're afraid of what I'm becoming—that's all the proof I need that I'm on the right path. Wait until they see me in a crown."

I felt the mood of the circle shift with my words, determination and resolve slowly replacing fear.

"All the same, I want every soldier on high alert and ready for anything," my brother said. He closed the annex door, his hand resting against the false wall for a heavy moment before he turned and regarded us all with a grave look. "Because if they decide to step into the light and face us, then we need to be ready for that, too."

TWENTY-EIGHT

Nova

While Captain Voss oversaw the cleanup and disposal of the dead Order members, the rest of us went our separate ways.

Zayn went to find Aleks. Thalia and Bastian went to make sure the guard rotations were properly set, and that every entrance to the palace grounds was being monitored. Eamon didn't say where he was going, but judging by the furrow of his brow and the telltale way he was whispering, debating with himself, I guessed he was off to bury himself in the library archives. Again.

Phantom and I made our way toward my room, but I eventually lost him, too; we ran into Eamon's little sister, Brynn, and she lured him back outside with a promise of fresh treats from the kitchens and a game of fetch. For all his steadfast determination to protect me and remain vigilant, it was always amusing to see how quickly he transformed back into a typical dog when food and play were involved.

And it was just as well; I wanted to be alone with my thoughts. Between the soul shard in my pocket and the images I'd seen in the stable, I had no shortage of things I needed to process without any distractions.

I reached my room and promptly locked the door behind me, wasting no time taking out the shard and returning all my focus to it. My frustration from earlier immediately tried to resurface, but I tamped it down.

You could ask anything of the dead. Anything at all, and then force them back to life so that they can give it to you...

If I could do that, then it should have been easy to see what I needed from this mere fragment of a person, right?

I could do this. I simply needed to focus on what I truly needed to ask, maybe; this was a piece of Lorien's very soul—the possible things it could show me were endless, and the things I wanted to know were equally vast.

After a bit of thought, one question rose above all the rest while I tapped my fingertips against the shard's smooth surface.

"Show me what you know of the Order, why don't you?"

The crystal remained cold and unresponsive.

Then another idea occurred to me.

I grabbed Grimnor from the chair I'd rested it against, unsheathing it and studying it for a long moment. As it often had these past weeks, the blade pulsed with a faint, ghostly light. Proof that Lorien was still in there, biding his time. Waiting on me to finish putting him back together, as agreed.

Not for the first time, I found myself wondering about what he would truly do once I managed to uphold my end of the bargain. And would the re-emergence of the Order change his plans, whatever they were? Would it make him more cooperative?

Did we have a common enemy in them, as I'd mentioned to Zayn earlier?

"I know you could help me if you wanted to. You can strengthen my abilities. You did it when we met in the Palace of Midna." I spoke the words over the blade, letting my shadows curl around the steel and tangle with the ghostly light of Lorien. Watching the powers weave together made my stomach twist and turn—the same nauseous feeling I always got whenever I had to acknowledge the connection the two of us shared.

But I was determined to get answers, no matter the cost. So I let my shadows continue to wrap around Grimnor, to coax a response from the stubborn demon trapped within. I narrowed my eyes on the blade, pouring more of my will into the connection.

"Come on, you insufferable bastard—*help me.*"

His light flickered, then pulsed brighter, as if in answer. Unmistakable power and awareness vibrated through the sword.

I wasted no time.

I stabbed Grimnor into the shard, my balance teetering slightly as the point sank through the hard crystal as easily as piercing water.

The light of Lorien surged violently along the blade, racing toward its point. The shard reacted in kind, its surface fracturing with veins of brilliant luminescence. A synthesis of power—two pieces of the same fractured whole coming together, enveloping me in blinding brightness as they did.

I held tight to Grimnor's handle, letting its blade channel and reinforce the magic flowing between me and the fragment, until we were both swallowed up in the familiar-by-now fog that came before a deeper, more immersive vision.

The fog rolled away, momentarily taking my breath with it. I didn't recognize the place I stepped into, this time, but wherever it was...

I was *here.*

I'd finally done it.

I was in a small house, standing at the head of a narrow corridor. Bits of fog still hovered along the edges of my vision, but there was less of it at the end of the hall, as if my magic was trying to guide me to that clearer spot. I followed its suggestion and found myself standing before a closed door. I passed through it like a specter and took in the scene unfolding inside.

Lorien leaned in a corner of a small, warmly-lit study. A book was propped open in his hands, but his stare was glazed over, likely not processing a single word on the page. He looked haggard, shadows under his eyes, his clothes rumpled as if he'd barely slept. He soon gave up on the book, snapping it shut and instead pacing the length of the room, occasionally glancing toward the door.

Waiting for someone.

Finally, the door opened. A white-haired man entered, his expression carefully neutral. I noted little else about his appearance—the vision seemed to be blurring many details out—save for one other thing: The golden pin he wore, which was shaped like a circle with a sword cutting through it. White gemstones adorned the top half of the circle, while black ones lined the bottom.

"Master Gareth," Lorien said, straightening. "Did you deliver my message to Calista? When will she arrive?"

Gareth slowly closed the door behind him. "I'm afraid Lady Calista won't be coming, Lorien."

"What? Why not? Is she unwell?" Concern flooded Lorien's face. He moved toward the door. "I should go to her—"

"She's perfectly well." Gareth's voice stopped him mid-step. "She simply...declined your invitation."

Lorien frowned. "That doesn't make sense. We were supposed to meet three days ago, and she never came. I've sent four messages since then—"

"All of which she received." Gareth pulled a folded letter from his robes, holding it out. "She asked me to deliver this to you. I'm sorry, Lorien. I truly am."

With slightly trembling hands, Lorien took the letter. I watched his face as he read, saw the color draining from his cheeks.

"No," he whispered. "No, this can't be right."

"I'm afraid it's her handwriting, is it not?"

"Yes, but..." Lorien stared at the letter, his throat working. "She says she's chosen to join Argoth at his court in the northern territories. That he's offered her..." He trailed off, seemingly unable to force the words out. He tried several more times to read it out loud before giving up and crumpling the paper in his hand instead.

"I'm sorry," Gareth repeated, his tone oozing false sympathy. "I know how much she meant to you."

"She wouldn't abandon me for that power-hungry mortal king," Lorien said, but his voice wavered with uncertainty. "She wouldn't."

"Wouldn't she?" Gareth paused deliberately. "You told me she's been spending a lot of time visiting his northern stronghold."

"For political reasons. She was investigating reports

of unrest in the region, monitoring the balance between Light and Shadow—"

Gareth shrugged. The gesture was far too casual, almost cruel. "It seems there was something more to these visits than her Vaeloran duties."

Lorien sank into a chair, the letter still clutched in his hand. For a long moment, he said nothing. Then: "I want to see her. Talk to her face to face."

"I don't think that's wise."

Lorien's voice hardened. "I don't care what you think is wise."

Gareth studied him for a moment, then shrugged again. "Very well. But don't say I didn't warn you when it all comes crashing down." There was a gleam of anticipation in the man's dark eyes, I thought. As if he would have been all too happy to see it all come crashing down.

Lorien didn't seem to notice it; he was already gathering his coat and heading for the door.

The scene shifted.

Lorien stood in the shadows of an opulent ballroom, looking entirely out of place in travelers' garb and dirty boots, like some common wanderer who'd clearly snuck in through a side door. The room before him glittered with candlelight and the jewels of Soltaris's elite. Music and laughter—much of it fake and high-pitched—filled the air.

And there, at the center of attention, was Calista.

She wore a gown of midnight blue that seemed to

shimmer with captured starlight. Her dark hair was swept up, adorned with a delicate silver headpiece. And on her left hand, catching the light with every movement, was a black diamond ring. There were black diamonds along the bottom of several of the banners hanging throughout the hall, too; it must have been a symbol of Argoth's royal house.

Beside her stood a man who commanded the room without seeming to try. King Argoth himself. He was handsome in a cold, precise way—sharp features, calculating eyes, a smile that never quite reached those eyes. I could see features he shared with Aleks, even though they were several generations removed from one another, and the resemblance made my chest feel tight. He held Calista's hand possessively, speaking to a circle of nobles who hung on his every word.

The more I studied the way Calista stood next to him, the more I couldn't help thinking she seemed… *diminished*, somehow. Her smile was perfect but empty. Her posture was immaculate but rigid. And her eyes— usually so bright and blazing—seemed distant. Hollow.

"Something's wrong," Lorien muttered, taking a step forward.

He pushed through the crowd, jostling several people aside and ignoring their indignant protests and sharp gasps of offense.

"Calista," he called out.

She turned. For just an instant, emotion flashed across her face—was it fear? Relief? Desperation? But then Argoth's hand tightened on hers, and her expression smoothed into something blank and unreadable.

"Lorien." Her voice was measured. "I wasn't expecting you."

"Can we talk? Privately?"

She averted her eyes. "I have nothing to talk about with you, I'm afraid."

Lorien's magic was starting to glow beneath his skin, his control slipping. "Calista. Just one moment. That's all I ask."

Calista glanced at Argoth, almost as if seeking permission. He studied her for a long beat, then released her hand with deliberate slowness.

"Just for a moment, then," he said pleasantly. "No more. We have guests to attend to."

She led Lorien to a balcony overlooking the gardens. The moment they were alone, he grabbed her arms and spun her around to face him.

"What are you doing here with that dangerous man?" He reached for her hand, lifting it—and the black diamond ring adorning it—up between them. "And wearing *this*, no less?"

Her voice was cold as she pulled out of his grasp and clenched her hands into fists at her sides. "I've made a choice, Lorien. You need to respect that."

"I can't. I won't." He moved closer, lowering his voice. "Something's wrong. You're not acting like yourself. Are they threatening you? Using magic on you? Just tell me what's happening."

"Nothing's happening except that I'm choosing my own future." Her voice was fierce, but I could hear the brittleness underneath. The fear edging in.

"What about our plans?"

"The ones you would have abandoned the second you got what you wanted from me, you mean?"

"What are you talking about?"

"I know about your dealings with the Order. They've told me everything. All the compromises you've made, the counsel you took from them, the—"

"They *lied*. Can't you see? *All* of this—" he gestured to the glittering palace "—is a lie."

She stared at him, her expression hard. Shaking her head with a bitter little laugh, she whispered, "How can you sound so certain, even now?"

"Because I know what to believe in." He closed some of the distance between them. "You and I are the only truth in this mad world."

For a moment, her mask cracked. Her eyes burned with emotion, her lips trembling. She opened her mouth as if to say something.

Lorien cupped her face in his hand.

Then Argoth appeared in the doorway.

"Time's up, I'm afraid," he said, speaking just as pleasantly as before. But there was unmistakable steel beneath the courtesy. He moved to Calista's side, placing a hand on her shoulder. "Lady Calista has other guests to greet."

Calista's face went blank again, the moment of

vulnerability vanishing. She let Argoth guide her back toward the ballroom, glancing over her shoulder only long enough to mouth two final words.

Goodbye, Lorien.

I felt something shatter in Lorien's chest—felt the pain of it echoing through the sudden darkness that settled over the vision, a torment that clenched my own heart and lungs and made it hard to breathe.

Magic surged violently through him, light exploding outward in waves. There was a call for guards. The balcony shook beneath the force of his power. The storm of his grief and rage tore through the gathered nobility like a physical wind—and it seemed to destabilize the vision itself, too, causing the images to shatter and scatter.

I blinked back to the present and nearly let out a scream.

A ghostly apparition of Lorien stood in front of my balcony doors, silently watching me.

He said nothing, only pointed down at the shard lying on the floor beside Grimnor. The fractures that had appeared on its surface were gone; somehow, it was still in one piece.

I picked it up.

It was cold again. Lifeless. But the vision it had shown me still burned behind my eyes.

Heart racing, I tried to reconcile this latest vision with all the ones before it. With all the different versions of Lorien I now had swirling through my mind—the idealistic young man, the trapped demigod, the betrayed lover, the bitter architect of his own destruction…

A knock at the door jerked my gaze toward it.

When I looked back, Lorien was gone.

I still found myself quietly asking my questions out loud, as if he were actually there to puzzle them out with me. "Do you think it was true?" I asked. "Whatever was written in the letter? Do you think she truly chose Argoth? Or was she manipulated into it?"

Another knock. "Lady Nova?"

Aveline.

The sound of her kind yet firm voice helped settle my nerves and ground me more fully back in the present.

"Come in," I called, hoarsely.

She swept inside with two servants in tow. They carried a dress of rippling midnight silk, along with what looked like the rest of my coronation regalia—a cloak of deep charcoal grey lined with silver, intricate pieces of jewelry, and countless other accessories I couldn't quite focus on, given what had just happened in this room.

"Time for your final fitting before the ceremony," Aveline announced with gentle authority.

I wasn't exactly in the mood to stand still and be fussed over, but I didn't complain as they carefully removed my clothing and began draping the gown over me.

The dress itself was breathtaking—fashioned from layers of silk that appeared black until I moved, at which point shades of slate grey and deep purple peeked through, like shadows dancing within shadows. The bodice was fitted, embroidered with dark silver thread that revealed branch-like patterns when the light hit it just so. More delicate embroidery decorated the floor-length hem, forming silvered images of moths and nightshade flowers. The shoulder line was finished with a subtle ombré effect, making the fabric seemingly dissolve into wisps of translucent black organza, like smoke curling off my shoulders. Or shadows; it would blend well with any I happened to summon.

"Arms up, please," one of the servants mumbled around a mouth full of pins.

I obeyed, standing numbly upon the stool while they worked to make minor adjustments to the hem and the way the layers fell. They pinned and tucked, debated the length of a certain panel, tested how the fabric moved when I turned.

I tried to pay attention to their whispered consultations and suggestions, to keep my eyes on my reflection in the trifold mirror set up before me. But my gaze kept sliding toward Grimnor, to the shard, and to the place where Lorien had been standing only minutes ago…

Had I imagined him?

No.

I was certain I hadn't. Somehow, he'd momentarily broken through—pulled himself partially into this room using...what? Were we truly so connected? Had I made a mistake, asking for his help? Dread coiled in my stomach. It somehow felt like I'd officially reached a point of no return with him, with all of this.

"My lady?"

I was suddenly aware of a hand on my arm. I gave my head a little shake, forcing myself to refocus. Aveline's eyes were shining with emotion when I finally met her gaze.

I managed a small smile. "Well? How do I look?"

She stepped back, gesturing for the servants to do the same so I could see the full effect in the mirror.

The dress had transformed me into something otherworldly—something I didn't quite recognize at first. The dark silk made my pale skin seem to glow. My raven hair, which one of the servants had quickly pinned up to check the neckline, framed my face in a way that emphasized my features—the sharp line of my jaw, the intensity of my eyes, the set of my shoulders that spoke of a strength that I hadn't possessed just months ago.

"You look like a queen," Aveline said softly.

I looked at my reflection again, closer this time. Everything else faded into the background as I inhaled deeply, watching the way the movement made the dress shimmer. With my exhale came faint shadows, curling across my collarbones and down my bare arms. As expected, they looked like they could have been an extension of the dress itself—exactly as I'd hoped for when Aveline and I had planned this design.

A dress fit for a queen who walked comfortably alongside darkness and death.

Staring into my reflection's eyes, unflinching, I realized I truly didn't fear those things any longer. Because I'd learned to carry my shadows—to wear them like armor and wield them as weapons rather than hiding them away.

And now, I would use them to survive whatever came next.

TWENTY-NINE

Nova

The next day and a half passed in a whirlwind of planning and preparing, with frequent, harried meetings about security measures and ceremonial protocols. Excitement was the dominant emotion throughout most of my palace, among the servants and visitors alike. Because they only saw the celebration in the making—the glittering decorations going up, the boisterous conversations, the food and drinks flowing more and more freely.

They weren't thinking beyond this historical moment. And they weren't haunted by the things I'd witnessed. The faces of dead Order members; Lorien's ghostly apparition; Aleksander's wrong-looking and odd-feeling magic—just to name a few.

Which was what I wanted, of course.

I had agreed to wear a crown and bring them hope, and keeping that fragile hope alive meant shielding them from all the questions and fears that kept me awake at night.

It was exhausting, constantly being on guard. But I kept moving, walking through the halls of my palace with power and purpose, my head held high and Phantom stalking alongside me with all his senses honed and alert.

There were more sightings and encounters with possible Order members. More suspicious activity. But, although my soldiers made several attempts to apprehend possible suspects, none were successful. One more died—taking her own life with a quick blade to the throat rather than submitting to capture and questioning—and the others all slipped out of our grasp at the last instant.

With every encounter, Captain Voss and a few of my advisors continued to urge me to reconsider going through with the public coronation. I refused. The palace, the royal city, and all the reviving settlements throughout Rivenholt were abuzz with expectation. I wasn't going to let them down. I wouldn't show fear.

There was a darker reason I refused, too. Though I wouldn't admit it to anyone, part of me *wanted* the Order to attempt to crash this coronation party.

Because I wanted revenge.

I'd frozen in place after witnessing Orin's murder, but that wouldn't happen this time. I was stronger now. More prepared. And we were in my territory, too, where my shadows were easier to summon and wield.

So let them come.

Finally, the evening of the main event arrived. I insisted on getting ready on my own, savoring the last few moments of solitude before I would be thrust into the glaring spotlight of the public eye.

My dress hung beside the window, dark and beautifully ominous in the setting sunlight. Aveline had left a plate of cinnamon and honey cakes alongside it—my favorite of the many delicious things she baked. I nibbled at the corner of one as I gathered my accessories and contemplated what to do with my hair.

My gaze kept lifting to the balcony doors, to the spot where Lorien's ghost had appeared. He hadn't returned since our brief encounter the other day—perhaps because the second shard we'd obtained was now locked away with the first, several floors below me and Grimnor.

While I styled my hair in loose curls that I pinned up and away from my face, I kept one eye on that legendary sword, thinking.

What had triggered Lorien's appearance?

Would he continue to find more ways to manifest, now that we had two pieces of his soul?

And where was the third, final piece?

A soft knock interrupted my thoughts. Two quick taps, one long—like he always did to let me know it was him. I quickly slid the last pin into my hair and went to answer.

Aleks stood on the other side, as expected. He was already dressed, looking the part of an effortlessly gorgeous noble in a black coat embroidered with silver thread, perfectly tailored pants, and polished black boots that gleamed in the light.

My tense muscles relaxed a bit at the sight of him. He was the only person I would have let into my sanctuary just then, and I was relieved that he'd actually shown up; though we'd spent last night together, and our conversations had been easy and unguarded, part of me remained convinced that I was losing him.

The last words he'd carved into the Chamber of Echoes still haunted me.

I have to leave her.

I grabbed his hand before my memory of that ordeal could sink its claws into me. I needed to feel it—the way he locked his fingers into mine and squeezed. Solid. Real. Still here.

He pulled me closer and kissed me, slow and deep and savoring. When he drew his lips away, he didn't go far, leaning his forehead against mine for a long moment. "Ready for tonight?"

"As I'll ever be."

He finally stepped back, his gaze shifting between

me and my waiting gown. He nodded encouragingly toward it.

With slow but determined motions, I made my way over and slipped it on. Lifting the heavy skirts, I went to the gold-rimmed mirror standing in the corner of the room and stood perfectly still before it, staring at my reflection without really seeing it.

A thousand thoughts rushed through my head.

I couldn't focus on any of them.

Aleks was at my back a moment later, fingers working carefully over the buttons between my shoulder blades, helping to secure the dress. When he was finished, he pushed the waves of my hair to one side, pressing his lips to the curve of my neck and watching my reaction in the mirror—the way my body curved toward his, eager to turn that light brush of his lips into something deeper, more consuming.

He wrapped his arms around my waist, resting his chin on my shoulder. "You look stunning," he said.

"Good to know. I can barely breathe in this thing, so at least the end result is worth the suffering."

He chuckled, a mischievous glint in his eyes. "I look forward to helping you take it off later," he said, his fingers trailing over the buttons he'd fastened. "Because I hate the thought of you being uncomfortable in any way, of course."

"Such a gentleman."

He straightened a bit, bringing his mouth toward my ear. His lips grazed the shell of it as he murmured,

"None of my thoughts are particularly gentlemanly at the moment."

Heat flooded me, skating from the top of my head down to my toes. "Is it too late to postpone the ceremony and just stay here with you?"

"I'd say so." He let out another soft laugh, taking my hand and twirling me around to face him. "But I'll make it worth the wait when we get back here, later tonight. So you have something to look forward to."

"Deal," I said. "I'll be holding you to it."

"I hope so," he replied, offering his arm.

I took it, and we left my room, making our way down the torch-lit corridors toward the grand hall.

"Nervous?" he asked as we reached the first floor. It was surprisingly quiet; our shoes clicked loudly against the polished floors, each step making me think of a clock ticking down to our destiny.

I kept my eyes straight ahead. "Why would I be nervous? I'm merely being crowned queen of a half-dead kingdom filled with unstable and unpredictable energy, while surrounded by diplomats who are uneasy allies at best, and with a murderous, mysterious cult watching from the shadows, just waiting for their opportunity to move against me."

I heard the crooked smile in his voice as he said, "I suppose it was a dumb question."

I let out an anxious little laugh, slowing to a stop and turning to look at him. "No—thank you for asking."

He was still smiling that crooked little smile of his,

but it wasn't reaching his eyes, suddenly; their golden color seemed duller, tarnished by the dark uncertainties circling around us.

My stomach sank. I couldn't help feeling as if we were coming to an ending of some kind. Like I was leaving for an entirely different kingdom, and he was showing me only as far as the border before we went our separate ways.

Maybe he could sense this fear—or even heard it, despite our fraying mental bond—because he blinked, forcing a brightness back into his gaze. "I'll be keeping watch for any threats," he said. "So don't worry." He brushed a hand across my cheek, warm and reassuring light circling around his fingertips and sinking into my skin. "I'll keep you safe. Always."

I nodded in spite of my fear. "I know."

I wanted to mean it—to believe it, more than anything.

We walked a little farther in silence, until I heard someone calling my name. I turned to find my brother approaching, Phantom at his side.

Phantom wore a navy, diamond-studded collar, while Bastian was dressed in his full regalia of deep blue and silver. My eyes lingered on the silver tree pinned at his chest, the main emblem of our kingdom.

Bastian and Aleks exchanged a wordless nod in greeting, and then Bastian told him, "Captain Voss could use your input on some security matters. You'll find him at the gate by the grand hall."

Aleks kissed my hand, squeezing it tightly before walking away without another word. Maybe it was my imagination, but he seemed eager to leave, his eyes even more troubled than before.

I tried to shake off the growing sense of dread as my brother, Phantom, and I made our way outside, to the covered walkway that connected the palace to the grand hall and ballroom where the night's festivities would take place. Instead of heading into that hall as I'd anticipated, Bastian steered me toward one of the smaller, quieter courtyards a short distance away. It was empty. Peaceful. I made my way to a stone bench shielded by trees with silver-green leaves, sweeping my skirts to the side as I sat down.

My brother sat beside me, while Phantom entertained himself by sniffing and pawing through the flower beds. After a minute, it occurred to me that this was the very same place where my brother and I had first sat together months ago, when he'd told me of my true identity. Of his. Of my true kingdom, and the crown that was mine by birthright.

So much had changed since then, but sitting with him, I was reminded of the constants—his steadfast, stoic presence throughout all of this. The way he had protected me, even if he drove me slightly crazy while doing it. We'd lost so many years to separation and lies, but in that moment I felt like he'd always been there, right by my side. Like he always would be.

I leaned my head on his shoulder, staring into the

windows of the grand hall. I could make out the vague shapes of figures moving through the decoratively frosted glass. The number of them was multiplying at an alarming rate, and I could hear more carriages arriving at the gate Aleks had headed toward; the guests were truly piling in, now. It was almost time to face them.

"I didn't think I'd ever see this day," my brother said. "Though I never stopped hoping you would come home."

Home.

The word didn't make me recoil as it once had. It was still a complicated thing to me. But I'd always thought home was less of a specific place and more of a feeling. And the people who stirred that feeling in you were what truly mattered. So home was here, at my brother's side. At Thalia's. At Eamon and Zayn's, even.

Home was Aleks, and it always would be, no matter how our light and shadows shifted.

And sometimes, you had to fight to protect your home—a fact I was reminded of as a group of guards approached, halting at a respective distance until my brother waved them closer.

"The perimeter is secured," the lead guard informed us. "We have a company ready to escort you inside, whenever you're ready."

"Thank you," Bastian said.

They bowed and stepped back to their respective places.

My brother stood and offered me his hand. A strange emotion overcame me as I looked between it and the guards waiting for us, and then finally to the bustling grand hall. I couldn't have named the emotion—maybe because it was a combination of so many different things. Fear. Anger. Determination. Hope.

"You know this remains your choice until the very end," Bastian said.

"I do." I took his hand, rising to my feet. "And I choose it."

Aleksander

I'd witnessed more than my share of elaborate royal ceremonies throughout my life, but none had made my heart pound quite like this one.

Nova stood upon the raised platform at one end of the grand hall, bathed in the light of a hundred candles from both the ornate silver sconces lining the marble walls and the glittering crystal chandeliers dangling above. A crowd of at least two-hundred looked on as she faced Lord Carrick Brennan, the man who served as ruler of the royal city of Tarnath, and as Master of Ceremonies for occasions such as this. Her brother, Eamon, and Thalia stood off to one side, while several foreign dignitaries stood as witnesses on the other.

I kept watch from the bottom of the steps that led up to the platform, Phantom sitting at my side, his body tense.

I never ceased scanning the crowd for threats, my magic humming beneath my skin in constant readiness. But I kept finding my gaze drawn back to Nova. To the regal silhouette she cut in that midnight gown. The way she held her head high despite the weight of what was to come. The fierce determination burning in her bright eyes.

She took my breath away every time.

Focus, I told myself. *Keep her safe first. Admire her later.*

The ceremony pressed on and on.

Zayn caught my attention from his position near the eastern entrance, his hand resting casually on his sword hilt, though his expression was anything but casual as he gave me a barely perceptible nod—all clear, for now.

I returned the nod, then let my attention drift once more across the faces in the crowd, studying them. The nobles who had crawled out of hiding now that there was a throne worth groveling toward. The commoners who were in awe of the queen rising before them, especially since she'd taken the time to personally invite many of them to this event. The red-faced men and women from all ranks who were mostly here to enjoy the celebration, politics be damned…

Most looked harmless enough.

I hadn't spotted any obvious Order members—yet.

But that didn't mean they weren't here.

Lord Brennan's voice resonated through the room, ancient words in an old tongue that I imagined spoke of duty and sacrifice, of power and responsibility.

Nova's expression remained serene, composed, though I could see the tension in her shoulders, the way her fingers curled slightly at her sides, wanting to anxiously twist into the layers of her dress. Subtle things that most of the room wouldn't notice. I almost overlooked them myself.

She might have been terrified beneath the surface, but she was magnificent nonetheless. Even her more vocal detractors—such as Lord Renvar—remained quiet and respectful as they watched. I kept a close eye on both him and the Drynland King, Marius. If the Order had truly infiltrated this kingdom's politics, those two seemed like the sort they might have targeted.

They did nothing to arouse any suspicion for the moment, though. All was calm. Everything proceeded according to plan, and eventually, the ending of the ceremony arrived.

Bastian moved from his place at the edge of the platform, carrying the crown of Rivenholt.

For a reverent moment, Lord Brennan studied that crown—an elegant circlet of dark metal intertwined with silver—before he lifted it from its velvet cushion.

The room grew unnaturally still as he spoke his next words in the common tongue that transcended realms: "Do you accept the burden of this crown, and all that comes with it? Do you pledge to protect this realm and its people, to guide them through darkness and into dawn?"

"I do." Nova's voice rang out clear and strong.

I held my breath as the circlet was placed upon her head, watching the deep red stones in its center catch the light and shimmer like captured flames.

The room erupted in applause and cheers. Relief swept through me in a dizzying wave. We'd made it through the ceremony without incident, at least. No assassins leaping from the rafters. No poison in the ceremonial wine. No blades flying through the air.

Nova's eyes found mine, and the smile she gave me was small but genuine, meant only for me. The tension eased slightly in my chest, even as I continued to scan for threats all around us.

The musicians struck up a waltz. Nova descended from the platform and moved into the adjoining ball-room alongside her brother, with whom she shared a quick dance. When it ended to warm applause, she turned and made her way toward me, parting the crowd as she came.

"I've been told the people expect plenty of dancing at these festivities," she said, extending her hand. "If you'd do me the honors."

I took her hand, bowing slightly. "Your Majesty."

She rolled her eyes but smiled at the formal address. I felt her pulse quicken beneath my fingers as I led her toward the middle of the room, spinning her beneath the grandest of the chandeliers, watching her shine under the lights and being briefly, utterly struck dumb by the very sight of her.

As we began to dance, the crowd formed a curious circle around us, watching. Whispering. I wondered what they thought of the two of us together—what new, creative rumors about me and my magic were flying as of late. We certainly didn't draw the same warm reception that she and her brother had.

But I didn't care.

I'd promised to keep her safe, and I preferred to do it while keeping her within reaching distance. I would have danced with her all damn night if I could have gotten away with it.

"Still managing to breathe in this thing?" I asked, trailing a hand along the back of her dress.

"Barely." She leaned slightly closer, lowering her voice. "Any signs of trouble?"

"Nothing yet. But the night is young." I tried to keep my voice light.

As we swayed and spun to the music, I caught another glimpse of Zayn as he repositioned himself to maintain a clear line of sight. Captain Voss stood near the main entrance of the ballroom, alertly scanning the crowd. Soldiers were stationed at every exit, every window, every possible point of entry.

And still, I couldn't shake the feeling that we'd missed something.

"You're tense," Nova observed, her fingers tightening on my shoulder.

"So are you."

"Well, I'd likely move with more grace if I wasn't wearing a dress that weighs approximately fifty pounds, and heels that are slowly but surely killing me."

I grinned. "My beautiful, formidable queen, finally vanquished by a pair of shoes, of all things."

"Not how I thought I'd ultimately go, but here we are."

"I have the utmost faith that you'll pull through. Because you are an undeniable force of nature and majestic willpower."

"Remind me of that when I collapse into an undignified heap later."

The song was ending, and I knew other nobles would be clamoring for their chance to dance with the new queen. To curry favor, to make their petitions, to assess whether she was truly as powerful as the rumors claimed.

I spun her again before drawing her close—scandalously close, judging by the gasps and whispers that rippled through the crowd—and subtly lifting her toward me to take some of the pressure off her feet.

"Remember what I promised you earlier?" I murmured, ignoring the crowd and their continued whispers.

Color bloomed across her cheeks. "I'm counting on it."

"Then survive the politics and the shoes for a few more hours, and—"

I stopped mid-sentence, going perfectly still as a cold sensation swept through me, like ice water splashing across exposed nerves. It wasn't painful, exactly, but my magic still reacted, crawling to life beneath my skin.

"Aleks?" Nova's concerned voice sounded oddly garbled, like I was hearing it from underwater.

I forced myself to resume dancing, to not cause a scene, but my attention was no longer on her. I was focusing on my magic. On the way it had started to twist and writhe, to create that itching sensation that I had learned to hate. To fear. I only just managed to keep the power contained, forcing it down by repeating the promise I'd made to Nova hours ago.

I'll keep you safe.

I had to keep her safe, even if that meant putting distance between myself—my magic—and her.

"I need to go check on something," I said quietly. "Stay here. Stay close to Zayn and the others."

"What's going on?"

"I'm not sure yet. But something's not right." I caught Zayn's eye and jerked my head toward Nova—a silent command to watch over her. He straightened, immediately moving closer.

The song ended. I bowed to Nova, pressing a quick kiss to her knuckles before handing her off to Zayn for the next dance. "I'll be back soon."

"Aleks, wait—"

But I was already moving, slipping through the crowd with practiced ease, ignoring anyone trying to catch my attention.

I crossed back through the grand hall and headed for the main palace before veering down a partially-hidden path that led to what had once been the former queen's impressive rose garden.

Nova had intended to restore the area, but the project had understandably fallen by the wayside, given everything else demanding her attention. Tonight, it had been roped off to prevent guests from wandering into it, as most of the fountains were dry and in need of repair, the paths between them unlit and slightly overgrown.

After making sure I was alone, I sank against the only garden wall not covered in ivy, leaning my head back against the cool brick and closing my eyes. I breathed steadily in and out through my nose, trying to regain control, lifting my hands and studying them. No magic escaped my control, but my veins were glowing, the light much darker than it should have been.

A shiver crawled down my spine.

I had a sudden, distinct feeling that I was being watched.

I lowered my hands and focused on listening, quickly picking up on the sound of soft footsteps moving away from me and heading deeper into the garden. Cautiously, I followed the sound. My magic seemed to settle as I drew closer to it, so I didn't think beyond this; I just kept going, following a pull I couldn't readily explain, moving farther and faster until all the noise of the coronation festivities had faded behind me.

I strode all the way to the back of the garden, to where no lantern light reached me. Only faint moonlight filtered through the branches of trees, washing over weathered stone statues and painting everything in eerie patterns of silver and white—but it was enough to see by.

And there, keeping perfectly still beside a dry fountain, stood a figure in a dark cloak.

They weren't trying to hide. That was the first thing that struck me—how they were simply standing there, waiting, as if they'd known I would come.

I slowed to a stop, keeping a safe distance between us.

"Remove your hood," I commanded.

The figure still didn't move. Didn't speak.

"Remove your hood and show your face, *coward.*" Light gathered around my hands. I tried to guide it toward them, to use it to illuminate their features…only to watch it flicker erratically, like a candle in the wind. Its color deepened, pale gold giving way to that horrid shade of violet.

I balled my hand into a fist and drew it back, pulling most of my magic back and extinguishing it with a tight squeeze of my fingers. But a few errant embers of violet continued to dance in the air before me—damning, irrefutable evidence of my instability.

The figure tilted their head toward that evidence. And then they finally spoke, their voice muffled by the hood, distorted in a way that made it impossible to determine gender or age.

"So it's true," they said. "The Void King manifests."

The words made no sense, but they filled me with a mixture of cold terror and an anger I didn't understand. *"Who are you?"*

"We are patience. We are inevitability." The figure took a single step back, deeper into shadow. They had something in their hand, something that glimmered faintly with the same color as my wayward magic. "We are the servants of that Void. The—"

"The Order," I snarled.

It wasn't a question any longer.

"The Order is…one name among many. One face of a much larger movement of truth." Another step back. The shadows seemed to thicken around them, growing darker and more substantial. "A truth whose time is fast approaching."

The object in their hand pulsed brighter. It was pulling the flickers of my wrong magic in, I realized, growing more brilliant with every trace it absorbed. There was an odd humming in the air, too—the same sort of hum that had accompanied the spells we'd encountered in the Hollow Grove.

"Are you ready to prove yourself, Aleksander?"

Instead of answering, I lunged forward to apprehend them, prepared to rip clearer answers from them by force if necessary.

But the moment I moved, they let out a sharp, barking laugh. The air around them rippled. Then they disappeared—not fleeing, not running, but simply *dissipating* into the night, their body turning to smoke that scattered into nothing within the span of a heartbeat.

No trace of them remained except for a lingering feeling of wrongness in the air, a heaviness that settled like an oily residue over my senses.

"Damn it." I spun in a circle, scanning every shadow, every corner. But it was useless. They were gone, though the laugh they'd let out still echoed in my ears. And their words…

The Void King manifests.

What the fuck did that mean?

My magic seemed to have settled, at least. I wondered if that strange figure had been the reason for the initial pull I'd felt in the ballroom—what was that strange, spelled object they'd carried? Had it really absorbed my magic? The thought had me desperately circling the garden, searching one last time for any trace of the intruder.

But again, it was in vain.

Finally, reluctantly, I turned back toward the celebration. Toward Nova. The sounds of music and laughter grew louder as I approached the ballroom. I paused in the doorway, taking in the scene: the new Queen of Rivenholt surrounded by admirers, smiling and gracious despite her obvious exhaustion and concerns. Zayn was still by her side, maintaining his vigilant watch. Her brother was nearby as well, his protective gaze fixed on her. Thalia and Phantom paced through the crowd. Soldiers stood at every exit.

Everything looked normal. Safe. Under control.

But as I stepped back into the warmth and light of the celebration, I couldn't shake the chill that had settled into my bones. Couldn't stop mentally reciting everything we had learned about the Order. All the things Nova had told me about my connection to them, starting with the confession she'd carved into the walls in the Chamber of Echoes.

A monster they created to destroy...

My jaw clenched. I cursed myself again for not being fast enough to catch that bastard in the garden.

Nova caught my eye from across the room and smiled, relieved to see me return. I smiled back, forcing myself to look relaxed, unbothered.

Unsurprisingly, she saw right through it.

With an impressive display of tact and grace, she managed to shake off her circle of admirers and make her way toward me. Phantom caught up to her as she walked, and Thalia and Zayn weren't far behind. Bastian eyed us from across the room, clearly concerned, but forced himself to keep talking to their guests, keeping them happy and distracted.

Nova wasted no time with pleasantries. "You found something."

"Someone," I corrected, and then I quietly recounted what had happened.

Our circle was quiet for a moment after I'd finished, our hushed tension a strange juxtaposition against the music and laughter swirling around us.

"I'll inform Captain Voss," Thalia finally said before rushing away.

Zayn grabbed goblets of wine from a passing servant, handing one to each of us. Nobody actually drank, but the goblets served as props to make our gathering look more casual.

"The magic they used to disappear is troubling," Nova said quietly. "If they have spells that can allow them to come and go so easily, it means nearly everywhere is vulnerable." She glanced toward the crowd, her concern for her guests obvious on her face—at least until one of those guests made eye contact with her, at which point she immediately smiled and slid on a mask of serene confidence.

"It feels more like they're biding their time rather than planning to exploit vulnerabilities." I tried to sound reassuring, despite the unease coiling in my gut. "I can't explain it, but I don't get the sense they're planning a large-scale attack. More that they're here for something specific."

Nova hugged her arms around herself. She was clearly doing her best to fight off a frown as more guests wandered closer to us, but she couldn't keep the slight tremor from her voice as she asked, "For you?"

I shook my head. "They aren't getting me. I'm not going anywhere."

But I couldn't deny how I'd followed the pull of my magic straight to them—a pull I was increasingly certain had been purposefully put into place.

They'd baited me.

And I'd fallen for it.

Nova's concerned gaze held mine until Zayn cleared his throat, alerting us to the crowd drawing nearer.

"I think they want to see you two dance again," he said.

I took Nova's hand and led her away from the overly curious onlookers, guiding her to the center of the room once more. I don't think either of us felt much like dancing, but it was an excuse to keep close, to keep talking where no one was likely to interrupt us.

But it was different than our last dance.

We moved without missing a step. My thoughts were elsewhere, though—still in that shadowy garden, scanning the darkness for answers that weren't there to find. The itch beneath my skin had faded, yet I still didn't trust my magic. I trusted nothing about myself in that moment. Not my mind, not my heart, not even the hands that held onto Nova, that dipped and spun her across the dance floor…it all seemed suspect.

It all seemed capable of hurting her.

And I didn't know how much longer I could risk staying by her side.

THIRTY-ONE

Nova

The evening of my coronation came and went without incident, save for a few guests who overindulged and had to be shown the door.

It was nearing midnight when I finally escaped the celebrations myself. The party continued on without me, which I didn't mind at all; it was nice to hear the sounds of genuine joy echoing across the grounds. It sounded like the normal revelry of a normal palace, with no hint of all the catastrophic possibilities pressing in.

I tried to savor the scene while making my exit, gazing back one last time at the crowded ballroom, breathing in the warmth and laughter, before I slipped away with Aleks and a small company of guards escorting me.

Aveline had been informed I was retiring to my room, and she had taken the initiative to prepare accordingly. We stepped into the space to find a fire already roaring in the hearth; clean, comfortable clothing laid across the bed; and trays of food and drink set on the table near the window. The latter was especially welcome, as I suddenly realized I'd been too busy to eat anything all evening. A bath had been drawn as well, the scent of lavender and rose oils wafting into the bedroom and tempting me toward the steaming water.

I sighed happily as I took it all in. "Remind me to tell Aveline how much I love her."

"I'll add writing a thank you card to your to-do list," Aleks said, taking the coat from my shoulders—his own coat, which he'd draped on me earlier—and hanging it on the hook by the door.

My thoughts briefly stumbled over that extensive to-do list, making my body tense. It made me all the more eager to melt into that hot bath and forget about everything for a while. I grabbed a few bites of food to sustain me, but then wasted no time shedding my crown and the heavy coronation gown and slipping into the water.

Aleks declined my invitation to join. He insisted on patrolling my room and the hall outside, instead, and then speaking at length to the guards on duty. He returned some time later, his expression troubled. Distant. There had been nothing unusual reported by the guards, but that had obviously done nothing to settle his nerves.

He moved between my bedroom and the bath in a sort of trance, bringing me a glass of champagne at one point, but otherwise keeping to himself.

I sipped the fizzy liquid as I watched him, trying and failing to hear his troubled thoughts. Our mental bond had been entirely too short-lived; how could we get it back?

After downing the rest of the glass in a few quick gulps, I set it aside and sank lower into the water. "You're making it difficult to relax."

"Sorry." He stopped his pacing and leaned against the door of the linen closet, folding his arms across his chest. He remained lost in thought for another moment before he finally met my eyes as he said, "It's been a long night, hasn't it?"

I extended a sudsy hand toward him. "Come join me."

His gaze trailed over the tub, lingering on the places where the bubbles were thinning out, just barely obscuring my body. But he kept still.

Quietly, I said, "We're safe for the moment, aren't we?"

He didn't reply.

I pulled my hand back into the water, swirling the bubbles and floating rose petals around. "It's been hours with no sightings or disturbances of any kind. My room is surrounded by guards and wards alike. I'm tired, Aleks. I just need to relax. And so do you."

He shook his head. "The way that figure disappeared so easily in the garden is still haunting me. Just knowing they might find a way to break through all of our defenses…"

I picked up a rose petal, twisting it between my fingers. "Well, you know how I feel about my bath time being interrupted. If they *do* manage to manifest in here and ruin it, then the gods themselves won't be able to save them from the wrath that I will rain down upon them."

This coaxed a small smile onto his troubled face.

"I'm serious."

"*Serious,*" he repeated, chuckling, "about your naked, bubbly, wrath?"

"Can you think of anything more terrifying?"

He hesitated, but then sauntered closer, sitting down on the stool beside the tub. "Nothing comes to mind."

"Exactly. Now, get in here or you'll be subject to that naked wrath yourself."

He considered me for a long moment, rolling up his sleeves and trailing his fingers through the water, grazing them along my hip and thigh. Then he braced a hand on either side of the tub and leaned in close, his lips brushing against mine as he said, "I could think of worse ways to go."

I grabbed a fistful of his shirt and pulled him into a proper kiss. It took an enormous amount of willpower to stop myself from pulling the rest of him into the tub, clothes and all.

"Relentless," he said under his breath, his eyes shining with a combination of lust and amusement as he drew back and started to unbutton his shirt.

"A queen must be tireless in her duties," I countered.

"You've got that part of the job down, no doubt." He shrugged out of the shirt, and the rest of his clothing swiftly followed, ending up in a neat pile on the floor. "Your enemies will never out-stubborn you," he said, slipping into the water so we were facing one another.

I slid toward him, pressing myself between his legs, the tingling effects of the champagne making me bolder. "I'm glad you've finally learned when to admit defeat."

He kept one arm on the rim of the tub and wrapped the other around my waist, dragging me flush against his hard body. "This doesn't really feel like *defeat.*" His lips found mine again, his soft kisses soon giving way to deeper, hungrier ones. "Feels more like I've won you."

"Really?" I rolled my hips against him, a teasing motion that made his fingers dig more possessively into my side. "You have me right where you want me, do you?"

"Not exactly."

Before I could ask what he meant, he flipped me around, cupping a hand between my legs and pulling my back against his chest. His other hand reached around to grab one of my breasts, his arm pressing in and pinning me to him as he pinched and tugged at its satiny tip.

"That's better," he mumbled, the words falling hot against my ear. "Now: Relax."

My pulse was far from *relaxed*, but I closed my eyes and sank completely against him, surrendering as his hands worked their magic, the one between my legs massaging in gentle circles while the other continued to play with my breasts.

I moaned softly, and his touch grew quicker. Rougher. He kissed a slow, seductive trail along the curve of my shoulder, up along my neck. As his teeth found my earlobe and nipped, his name escaped me in a gasp. He responded by slipping one finger inside me, then another.

It was pure bliss—the combination of his sure hands and the warm water lapping against my body. Of my heart pounding in time with his. Of his firm muscles against my skin that had been made softer and silkier by the oils in the water.

And when that water began to grow cold, he moved smoothly from the tub, helping me out alongside him, his hands never straying far from my body. He dried every inch of my damp skin with slow, attentive strokes, following the soft brush of the towel with tantalizing touches that made me forget about any chill my nakedness might have brought on.

I watched us in the mirror above the sink, just as I'd watched him when he was helping me into my coronation dress; the confident way he kissed and caressed every inch of my body was mesmerizing.

He caught me staring, and his mouth pulled into a smirk. "You like watching what I'm doing to you, don't you?"

Instead of answering with words, I leaned back against him just as I'd done before, eager for his lips to keep staking their claim on me. He watched me for a moment, smiling at the impatient way I rubbed myself against him, then he took my hand and led me to that mirror we'd used earlier.

It was taller, reaching all the way to the floor, fully exposing every act we committed before it. We resumed our session from the bathroom—him behind me, my body curving against him, desperately trying to eliminate any space between us. He smoothed a hand over my stomach and then went lower, plunging two fingers inside of me once more. As he slid them in and out, I felt my orgasm building, my body losing control and starting to contort wildly, trying to chase the shivers of pleasure winding through it.

But he withdrew his fingers before I could catch any sort of release, his breathing coming in ragged gasps as he kissed the nape of my neck. "Not yet."

He grabbed a blanket, spreading it on the floor in front of the mirror. Pulling me down and into his lap, he arranged us into a position similar to the one we'd had in the tub.

"Spread your legs," he ordered, his hand tapping encouragingly along my inner thigh.

I started to, only to have him grab them and push them wider himself, his grip digging into the flesh of my thighs as his cock throbbed against my back.

"Now," he breathed against my neck, "touch yourself for me."

The words alone were enough to send another shiver of near-release spiraling through me. Actually doing as he commanded made me dizzy in the best possible way—a heady combination of heat and desire and *power*. He might have been the one giving the commands, but there was no question about whether or not I had any power; I could make his breath catch with just a single, purposeful swipe of my fingers. I could control the pounding of his heart with only a deliberate look at his reflection, locking my eyes on him as I pleasured myself.

We were both at each other's mercy. Both starving for release, both hungry in a messy, heated way that didn't fit with any proper, royal agenda. So when I decided I needed him inside of me, I didn't speak, didn't need to; I merely rose onto my knees and positioned myself so I was hovering over his lap. He rose with me, his hands moving under my ass, supporting me as I rocked myself back and forth along his hardened length.

"Keep watching," he whispered, and I did—and so did he, his eyes heavy with lust as he finally guided himself into me. He took me slowly, gaze burning into the reflection of us in the mirror, savoring every reaction as he pushed inside inch by inch.

He was so controlled. So composed. It was both maddening and unspeakably arousing, how focused he seemed to be on making me feel every sensation to the fullest extent. Maybe it was the fear, the uncertainty that loomed over every decision we made lately—and that need to keep control so that our magic didn't spiral into something dangerous.

I'll keep you safe, he'd promised me.

But after a night spent carefully watching every step, every word, every move that I made as I balanced a new crown on my head, I didn't care about *safe* any longer.

I lowered myself more fully onto him, drawing a groan and a curse as he throbbed against the deepest parts of me. I leaned back, pressing as much of my body to his as possible. Stretching my arms back as well, I hooked them around his neck, holding on as I worked my hips in an increasingly eager dance.

For a moment, he barely moved. He just let me grind against him, his hands on my hips, helping me balance. I watched him in the mirror—his head falling back, lips moving with silent curses. His fingers digging deeper and deeper into my skin. His composure slipping, bit by bit, until he reached his breaking point.

He abruptly adjusted his position, stretching his legs out to give him better leverage. Then he grabbed my arms from around his neck and twisted them against my back instead, pushing my breasts out, displaying them front and center in the mirror as he started to thrust, to control the way I rose and fell against him.

He buried his face in the crook of my neck, alternating between soft kisses and devouring ones, and occasionally just letting his lips rest against my skin as he breathed me in.

But he never went long without lifting his eyes and taking in the sight of what he was doing to me.

His gaze was wild with desire whenever it swept over the mirror image of my body—so completely, obviously enraptured by me that it pushed me a little closer to the edge every time I watched him drink me in.

"Now you get to see the beautiful sight I do whenever I'm moving inside of you like this. Do you see why I'm obsessed with you?" His voice was low, each word sending heat coiling through me, making me clench more tightly around him. He gave several quick thrusts in response to that tightening, keeping my arms pinned behind my back so my breasts heaved up and down with the force of his pounding. His gaze followed their movement—and soon mine did, too.

A wicked smile curved his lips. "Does it turn you on, watching them bounce while I fuck you?"

My reply was somewhere between a breathless *yes* and a whimper.

Because gods, it *did*. But it was more than a physical desire burning through me. It was the freedom of it that I craved. The way I felt exposed, yet safe. There was nothing proper or expected about what we were doing—all thought of royal duties and divine destinies faded whenever we were together like this—yet it felt indescribably, undeniably *right*. Even as our magic stirred beneath our skin, and I held my breath and hoped it wouldn't turn into a more violent storm.

But even if we were consumed by that storm, I don't think it would have mattered.

I don't think I would have stopped.

Because there was nothing I wanted more than this.

Nothing more than *him*.

He didn't stop as the first swirls of shadow lifted from my skin, but his thrusts did grow gentler, more deliberate. He guided me into the more intimate position we'd started in, both of us on our knees with him filling me inch by throbbing inch. I reached back again, this time wrapping my arms around his waist, relaxing against his firm body and leaving myself completely at his mercy.

The slower pace he set made it easier to watch what he was doing. To study the commanding grip he took on my shoulder with one hand, pushing me down to meet each of his thrusts, while his other hand roamed over my front side, teasing every inch he could reach before finally sliding between my legs.

He continued driving into me with slow, deep motions, but his fingers quickly worked up to a rougher, more insistent rhythm. His mouth was equally rough, sucking on my neck until I was squirming, desperate for release.

Every part of my body was aflame by this point. My thighs squeezed tighter together with every building wave of my orgasm, with every balance-rocking clench of my insides.

"Eyes open and face forward," Aleks rasped, his hand moving from my shoulder to my jaw, lifting my gaze. "So you can see how beautiful you look when I make you come."

I hadn't even realized I'd closed them. My awareness was slipping, giving way to hazy bliss. But I did as he said, fixing my eyes on the mirror.

And that was all it took: one last glimpse of him at my back. Of his fingers falling from my jaw to bracket my throat, all of him clearly just a breath away from coming completely undone…

I shattered.

He quickly followed, holding me against him until he'd given every last drop of himself to me—and then for several minutes after, until my body finally stopped shaking.

He lifted me up, twisting me around so we were facing one another, before dragging me back into his lap. I pulled the blanket up around us. We sat like that for several minutes, tangled up in one another, hearts still pounding as we slowly came down from our high.

With a sigh, I leaned my head against his chest and closed my eyes, the exhausting activities of the day finally catching up to me.

"You should go to sleep."

"I *am* sleeping," I grumbled against him.

His chest shook with a quiet laugh. "In an actual bed, Chaos."

Still grumbling, I untangled myself from him and let him help me to my feet, and then through the motions of cleaning ourselves up. I dressed for bed, but he pulled on a proper shirt and pants and went to check in with the guards around my room.

He was gone for no less than a half hour. Despite my exhaustion, I couldn't fall asleep without him in the room, and I was moments away from getting up and going to patrol the halls myself when he finally returned.

I shot upright as he closed the door and locked it behind him. "Anything to report?"

He shook his head. But just as before, he didn't seem convinced that all was as well as it appeared on the surface.

Did he sense something that my guards couldn't?

I clutched the sheets to my chest, working the silk anxiously between my fingers, thinking.

"Rest," Aleks urged.

"…What about you?"

"I'm not tired."

"Me either," I yawned.

His lips quirked in a small smile. "Liar."

I was too tired to argue.

He settled down in the nearby chair—close enough to provide some measure of comfort. I watched him for a minute more before giving in and curling up with my pillow.

I drifted in and out of sleep.

Every time my eyes fluttered open, I saw Aleks still sitting up, wide awake and staring at the door. No matter what I said to him, our conversation always ended the same way: with him reassuring me, over and over, that he was fine, that he wasn't tired, until I lost the battle to stay awake.

The fourth time I woke, I found him on the other side of the room, pulling on his coat.

"...Aleks?"

He didn't answer me this time.

I rubbed the sleep from my eyes, looking toward the window, trying to gauge the hour. It felt like it was still the middle of the night.

"Where are you going?" I asked, sitting up.

He paused only for a moment before continuing to fasten the buttons of his coat, then moving on to his boots, which he pulled on with methodical detachment.

"Look at me, Aleks." I got out of bed and started toward him, but lost my courage after only a few steps, bracing my hand against the dresser as my balance swayed. "Please?"

Finally, he finished dressing and turned in my direction. It was almost more painful than him keeping his back to me—the way his gaze slid past mine, either unable or unwilling to hold it.

I was barely breathing as he walked over to me. As he took my hand, his thumb stroking my palm for a moment. My lungs felt like they might shrivel up completely when he finally glanced up and met my eyes.

"I would give anything to keep you safe," he said.

"...I'm safe with *you*," I whispered.

"I don't think so, Nova. Not anymore."

I started to disagree.

Then, I noticed his wrists. The faint, twilight-hued magic circling them. He rolled up the sleeves of his coat to reveal veins glowing with the same purplish light, all of it darker than I'd seen it thus far; it was impossible not to think of a void as I stared at it, of a cold nothingness waiting to consume everything. And the scars on his chest—what I could see peeking through the open collar of his shirt and coat—had darkened as well, like fresh bruises blossoming all across his skin.

He stared at his palm, watching a strand of violet-black magic coil and writhe against it.

Clenching his hand into a fist, he met my eyes again. "If I'm the reason they're here, if they're planning on triggering something dangerous through me, then I think…I think it's better if we keep our distance. At least until I figure out what's going on. And if I leave, then perhaps I can lure them away from you." His voice was chillingly calm.

I tried to mirror that composure.

But my shadows were rising, unbidden, curling around my arms and legs. Like they sensed a threat. And no matter how I tried to push them down, they wouldn't settle.

Aleks turned away, making it halfway to the door before I finally found my voice.

"You've fought it this long," I said, taking a step after him. "You're stronger than whatever they did to you. Stronger than whatever they're still trying to do to you. I *know* you are."

He paused with his hand on the doorknob.

The moment stretched between us like a drawn blade, sharp and poised to cut through my heart.

He looked back at me.

But whatever his reply would have been, I never heard it—because we were interrupted by shouting in the hallway outside, followed by the unmistakable sound of a body hitting the door.

THIRTY-TWO

Nova

The scene outside my room was worse than anything I could have imagined.

Three guards lay dead near my door. Two with a clean slash mark and a sticky waterfall of crimson across their throats, the third slumped against the wall, a gaping puncture wound in his stomach. The stench of blood was overwhelming.

The other five who had been marching up and down the hallway all night were frozen in various states of attack and defense, some with their swords still clutched tightly in their hands.

There were no culprits to be seen.

Somehow, the assailants had pulled this off in near silence. And then, for whatever reason, they had chosen not to attack me.

Yet.

It felt like they were only trying to lure me out, just as they'd lured Aleks into the garden earlier. Toying with us. Trying to get us right where they wanted us—wherever that was.

But what choice did we have but to follow the trail of carnage they'd left?

"These aren't dead," Aleks muttered, feeling the pulse of one of the guards frozen in the hall.

"They look like my mother and the others did at Rose Point."

"A spell, then."

"And we know exactly who's capable of this sort of spell, don't we?" My stomach twisted at the thought, eyes glazing over as memories of that trial in the Above came crashing in. I still didn't understand how the Order could create such strange, powerful spells like the one they'd anchored in the Hollow Grove—but here was more evidence of what we were truly up against, glaring right at us.

I gave my head a little shake and hurried back into my room, throwing on clothing and grabbing my sword. Aleks grabbed his weapon as well, and we set off without a word for the main part of the palace, fearing the worst.

We passed no one and nothing, eventually descending into the entry hall that was eerily silent.

We searched the space carefully, but it was entirely deserted, which made no sense; the coronation revelry had likely ended hours ago, but there should have been servants still moving about, cleaning and otherwise putting the palace back together. Drunk and exhausted guests stumbling through the hallways. Guards making their rounds. Some sign of life. *Any* sign—

"Nova."

I turned toward Aleks, who stood by one of the tall windows flanking the front door, his hand pulling back the heavy curtain to show me something.

My hand flew to my mouth as I noticed the figure at his feet—a young woman I quickly recognized as Aveline's niece, Sylvia. One of the servants who had frequently tended to me since my return to the palace, who had made this palace feel warm and inviting even when I'd felt like an imposter within its walls.

How many more familiar faces were dead and stashed in shadowed corners and behind elegant drapery?

And where was her aunt?

I walked over and knelt at her side, stroking her hair —which was matted with blood—out of her face. There was a gruesome wound gouged into the side of her head. A tremor went through me as I noticed how similar her dark blue eyes were to Aveline's. She'd died with them wide open in shock. Looking out this very window, maybe, unaware of her assassin until it was too late.

Probably because she was too busy staring at the horror on the other side of the foggy glass.

There were several more dead bodies strewn across the lawn. Some wore the colors of my guard. Others were dressed in the fine clothes of nobles and dignitaries who hadn't made it far enough to escape.

Hands shaking, I pulled the curtain back over Sylvia and took a step back. "We have to find the others. My brother, and…"

I heard a voice in my head, calling my name, and I spun around.

Phantom—who had spent the evening at Captain Voss's side, helping him patrol—had appeared in the foyer. He gave an anxious whimper and raced toward us, his movements clumsier than usual. He collided with me in a tangle of limbs and fur, body wiggling and tail thrashing despite his obvious distress. Clearly relieved to see me, even if he would never admit it.

Thankfully, he was in one piece with no obvious injuries. But there was someone else's blood splattered across his fur, turning it darker and shinier in places. His paws were stained as well; he'd left a faint trail of prints across the pearlescent grey floor.

"What's happened, Phantom?"

He fixed his bright eyes on mine, and he pressed only one word into my mind at first: (*Marius.*)

It took some work to calm him down—I'd never

seen him rattled like this—but eventually I managed to sort through the rambling words he was pushing into my mind, to put together a fractured picture of how the attack had unfolded. How the Drynland King had turned on us the moment the opportunity presented itself, his soldiers joining forces with Order figures who had seemingly materialized from nowhere.

Many of our guests had evacuated, at least; most of them had fled into Tarnath, following the lead of Lord Brennan. Some of our soldiers had gone with them, establishing a more solid defensive perimeter around that city's gates. Others had scattered, fleeing into the night—with plans to return with reinforcements, I hoped.

Captain Voss had personally led a company of soldiers to come find me, but where that company had ended up was unclear; Phantom had lost track of them in the chaos, when he'd moved to help protect Eamon and his little sister as they fought their way toward safety. He'd followed them to where they'd taken shelter, but then he'd caught my scent and made his way to me.

I went to the massive front doors, throwing them open with a violent motion made more powerful by the adrenaline rushing through me. Stepping outside, the eerie quiet was replaced by the sounds of distant screaming and clashing weapons, along with odd cracks and wails that I suspected might have been more of the Order's corrupted spells going off.

Aleks followed me, standing close at my shoulder, his hand on his sword.

"Our fears are confirmed, then," he said, after I had quickly shared all that Phantom had told me. "I wonder who else the Order has tried to sway? And what did they promise them in exchange for their help infiltrating this palace?"

"No telling."

"Fucking traitors."

The word burned through me, filling me with rage. But it wasn't only toward those traitors. Part of it was fury toward myself, too—for not navigating the emerging political situation more carefully, for not seeing the warning signs. For not being able to convince my detractors of my ability to control our world's magic into something strong enough to save them all.

A crown was merely a symbol.

I had so much left to prove.

"Marius, and others like him, are desperate for power," I thought aloud. "It's no wonder they bought into whatever lies the Void Order fed them. My brother and I didn't lie to them. We spoke of sacrifice and hard-won victories to come, not false promises of easy conquest and unlimited power."

"And one is infinitely more tempting than the other for weaklings like Marius," Aleks muttered. His gaze narrowed, scanning the yard.

I swallowed hard, thinking of all the times I'd

dismissed Marius as merely irritating rather than genuinely dangerous.

But it wouldn't do me any good, standing here lamenting my mistakes and trying to determine all the places where I'd made wrong choices. I needed to focus on my next step. And, after me, I knew that my brother would be the next biggest target of our enemies.

I had to find him.

And make sure he's still alive.

I shook this last, morbid thought from my mind and knelt before Phantom, running a soothing hand over his trembling body.

"Can you lead me to Bastian?"

He hesitated a moment, fur bristling as those sounds of distant fighting grew louder. A cold wind blew, low and haunting, as if mourning the dead scattered around us. Phantom lifted his pointed nose into the frigid breeze and started hunting for my brother's scent. After a few false starts, he seemed to find what he was looking for and shot off into the dark.

We sprinted after him, trying not to get distracted by the sounds and smells of the battle unfolding in the distance, pressing toward us like a rising tide.

Phantom took us to one of the side entrances, through the formal dining room it led into, and then into the hall beyond and up a narrow, twisting staircase to the second floor. On the landing, we were met by a small group of soldiers, most of whom looked ragged and battle-worn.

They wore the emblem of the Drynlands—a black lion standing on two legs with its claws extended, mouth open in a roar.

I didn't ask questions. I didn't care what they were doing this deep in my palace, in a wing that should have been secure. Thoughts of their disgusting king flooded my mind, mixing with images of the night's mounting collection of dead bodies. The blood on these soldiers' own swords looked fresh, too. Abundant. They raised those swords, as if they intended to add my blood to them.

One of them stepped forward.

The next thing I knew, Grimnor had pierced him in the throat. Dark wisps of energy bled from the steel as I pressed it through, becoming solid, sharp barbs that helped me cut a path that was viciously wider and deeper.

As the man crumpled at my feet, it set off a predictable chain reaction. The soldiers didn't bother with questions or words of any kind, either; they moved as one to avenge their fallen comrade, charging toward me with a recklessness that might have frightened me if I hadn't been so furious and numb.

More were flooding in from the hallway behind them.

I didn't take the time to count them all. I only noted how outnumbered we were, and then I flicked the excess gore from Grimnor and readied it for my next swing.

I took a single deep breath. Exhaled it with power and purpose. Shadows rose around my body, writhing in a violent dance, blocking out the light from the flickering lamps along the walls.

Phantom drew closer to me, shadows of his own flickering around his form. His darkness blended with mine, until the only clear thing setting him apart was the terrifying gleam of his eyes and teeth.

Most of the soldiers stumbled back at the sight of us.

Aleks intercepted the first soldier who found the courage to attack me. He grabbed him by the front of his coat, spinning him around and shoving his sword between the man's shoulder blades, then dislodged it by kicking him down the stairs.

As the body thumped and rolled down the steps, Phantom and my shadows surged forward. I moved in their wake, cutting through the line of enemies with brutal efficiency.

More and more blood coated Grimnor's blade. It began to hum, its ghostly white energy joined by twisting tendrils of pale blue—Lorien, making himself known. My shadows seemed to respond to his presence, growing darker and more aggressive. Power surged in a dizzying spiral around me. I wasn't entirely sure where it was coming from, but I grabbed hold of it all the same, letting it flow through my body and into every strike.

It was a quick massacre after that.

Aleks and Phantom still moved alongside me, relentlessly tearing our enemies down, but I lost track of them and everything else as I slashed, parried, and stabbed.

When I finally stopped, chest heaving and blood staining most of my clothing, a pile of bodies littered the landing and the stairs below it.

Eerie silence settled once more.

I was still too numb to think about what I'd done. About the lives I'd taken. I just kept hurrying onward—until I noticed Aleks wasn't following me.

Skidding to a stop, I twisted around to find him still standing over the ones we'd slain.

He was perfectly still, his sword held loosely at his side, his head tilted as though listening to something only he could hear. The veins in his wrists and neck were glowing faintly through his skin, that same cold shade of violet I'd seen earlier.

Grimnor shook in my hand.

My breath caught in my throat as I realized where we were in the palace—how close we were to the vault where the two shards of Lorien's soul had been placed for safekeeping. A chill raced through me; it felt like Lorien's ghost was watching me from beside the balcony doors again.

But there was no one here except Aleks and me, the corridor so empty and silent that my footsteps echoed as I moved uncertainly back toward him.

"Aleks? Are you okay?"

He waved off my concern, rebalancing the sword in his hand and turning to follow me. He never met my eyes. Images of our last conversation in my bedroom flared in my mind. He'd been so close to leaving. So ready to sacrifice whatever he had to in order to keep me safe.

But he was still here. Still fighting at my side. There was another war still clearly being waged within him— one that seemed to be growing louder. More violent. It was a war I couldn't focus on, though, because a breath later, Phantom came to an abrupt halt at the end of the hallway and let out a sharp bark. He was urging my attention forward, toward whatever he'd seen around the corner.

I rounded that corner and immediately spotted Bastian. He was surrounded, as was Thalia. Both of them bound in chains, kneeling, with no less than a dozen Order members on either side of them.

And Severin Thane stood at the center of them all, holding a knife to my brother's throat.

THIRTY-THREE

Nova

Severin gave a mocking little bow as he caught sight of me. "Your Majesty. How nice of you to join us."

The knife in his hand looked like the same one he'd used to impale Orin, glowing with the same strange light that had been haunting my nightmares ever since our last encounter.

I composed myself and started toward them with measured steps, my hand on Grimnor, Phantom at my side.

Aleks followed farther behind us. He seemed determined to stay close to me, but the proximity of the soul shards—even though they were still locked inside the secure chamber—was making this more and more difficult for him. More and more dangerous. I saw it out of the corner of my eye, the way the wrong-looking magic writhed more wildly than ever beneath his skin.

It made my stomach twist with a painful combination of fear and fury.

But it wasn't as painful as the sight of the blade currently resting against my brother's skin, or the chains binding him and Thalia, or the sheer number of enemies surrounding them.

They all stood just to the side of the heavy metal doors sealing the chamber shut. We'd secured the shards within that chamber because very few could work the magic necessary to open it, aside from my brother and me, but now, I found myself wondering if it was safe enough—if *anywhere* could be safe enough to keep these Order bastards from finding their way in.

I forced myself to keep my eyes on Severin and ignore everything else.

He tilted his head, studying me as I approached. "It's good to see you again, Nova."

"You made a mistake, coming here," I replied in a low, dangerous voice.

"On the contrary; I only wish we could have been here sooner."

I took another step forward. "You don't belong here. This is my territory, and you're going to find out very soon that you are not welcome in it."

"Is it really *yours*, though? If tonight's activities are any indication, your subjects don't seem particularly loyal to you."

"No." I lifted my hand, pulling forth a swarm of darkness, forming it into a blade that mirrored the legendary sword in my other hand. "But the shadows still are."

Phantom growled in agreement, tendrils of dark energy rising around him and bolstering the ones swirling around me.

"Set them upon us, then." Severin's smile sharpened, his cool grey eyes glistening with a dangerous challenge. "And let's see what happens." He signaled with a barely perceptible nod.

One of his followers pressed a sword to the back of Thalia's neck.

She closed her eyes, her mouth setting into a hard line. Angrily resigned to her fate.

But I wasn't accepting any such fate.

My voice remained low, cold as the shadows twisted around me. "What do you want, Severin?"

"Ah, *there's* the hospitality Rivenholt is known for, finally."

I didn't dignify this sarcastic comment with a reply.

"You've all been playing a very dangerous game, haven't you?" He looked down at my brother, then back to me. "Did you honestly think we were going to let you keep trying to restore the full extent of Vaeloran power without us intervening?"

Bastian's eyes fixed on me, steady and unwavering despite the blade at his throat. His head twitched the tiniest bit—barely a shake of his head—but his message was clear enough.

Don't listen to him. Don't let him control you.

"We managed to torture enough useful information out of several of your servants." Severin's gaze swept toward the sealed chamber doors. "So we know the pieces are here. We know they've been locked away, and we were in the process of helping ourselves to them, as guests of your fine palace. But then we were rudely interrupted." He tapped the knife against my brother's throat.

My pulse skipped several beats, but I kept my face impassive.

Don't let him control you.

"It's just as well, though, because it seems this door is sealed with an impressive amount of Vaeloran magic. Given enough time, we could probably figure out its secrets. But why do that, when you're here to do it for us?"

"So you've come here to take them, have you?" I made my voice as calm as his, despite feeling like my heart might pound its way out of my chest at any moment.

"Yes," he replied, simply. "And we appreciate you finding them for us, by the way, as we now finally have the means to destroy them—something we didn't have when our dear Calista first made the powerful but questionable decision to spare Lorien's life and create those shards. It's taken some time, but now we have a questionably powerful tool of our own, don't we?" His eyes were on Aleks as he spoke those last, chilling words.

Aleks, who remained several feet behind me. He was kneeling, his sword braced against the ground, his head bowed. I felt my composure crumpling a bit as I took in the sight.

I tried to take a deep breath.

Don't let him control you.

I jerked my head back toward Severin. Too quickly. My mask slipping, only for an instant—but he noticed it.

He smiled like a gambler who'd just won a bet. "Surrender the pieces to us, and maybe we can work something out. And, if he does as we ask, maybe he survives this ordeal. Maybe you all do." With a casually cruel shrug, he added, "Or maybe you don't."

I swallowed hard, my throat tight.

Every choice before me seemed impossible.

"Don't listen to him," came a voice from behind me —from Aleks, though I didn't recognize it at first. It sounded strange. Close to breaking, clearly strained from fighting whatever the shards' proximity was doing to him. I didn't meet his gaze, but I could feel his eyes burning into the back of my head.

Pleading with me.

"Nova. Don't do this."

When I finally glanced back, I saw more Order members flooding in, blocking the only path that led out of this dead-end corridor.

He couldn't escape this.

We couldn't escape this.

"If you open that door, I don't know what happens next." His voice remained quiet, strained—yet it was the only thing I was aware of for a long moment. Louder than the frantic pounding of my heart. More painful than the shallow rasp of my breath. More powerful than the cold caress of my shadows.

"But if you *don't* open it, you already know what will happen," Severin chimed in, as though I needed the reminder.

Clenching tighter to Grimnor and my makeshift blade of shadows, I moved closer to the door. Close enough that I could have reached out and touched it. I could feel the soul shards on the other side waking up. Their essence was somehow slipping through the thick metal, wave after wave washing toward me and seeping into my skin like poison, or like power...it was hard to decide what it felt like. Grimnor hummed in eager response, the black blade practically vibrating in my grip.

"Go on, then," said Severin.

I didn't move.

My brother lunged forward, suddenly, struggling against his bindings and nearly managing to drag several of his captors with him before they regained their balance. He was far too outnumbered, though; they wrestled him back into submission. Severin's knife slipped across Bastian's face during the scuffle, leaving a deep cut that stretched from his chin up to the corner of his eye.

I stared at the blood dripping from the wound, thinking of the guards I'd found outside my room. Their scarlet-stained throats and dead, vacant stares.

I shook the hand holding my makeshift blade, causing the shadows to separate and rejoin the ones circling protectively around me.

Then I reached out and braced my hand against the cold metal door.

A memory flashed in my mind as I did. One that had plagued me for months. A memory of how I'd opened this chamber back when it had been keeping Grimnor and its counterpart, Luminor, safe. I'd let Lorien inside by mistake. He'd stolen so much from me that day—and it had only been the beginning of so many losses to come.

But this time, it would be my own decision.

Not a trick I'd fallen for.

There were only bad options before me now, but maybe there was power in deciding which one I would choose to face.

"I'm growing impatient." Severin's words coiled around me like a noose, making it hard to breathe.

Aleks shook his head. Bastian and Thalia were both silently urging me not to give in, their expressions identically desperate and defiant. Phantom's eyes were trained on the chamber door, his teeth bared, as if he too could sense the poisoned power seeping through it.

Severin's smile disappeared. He rolled up his sleeves and readjusted his grip on his knife, moving with the same calm grace he had before slaying Orin.

"Just remember, this was your choice, Nova."

He sliced toward my brother's throat.

"WAIT!"

At the last possible instant, his hand stopped.

The blade still hovered entirely too close to Bastian, burning with whatever corrupted magic gave it that unsettling glow.

I kept my glare leveled on Severin as my fingers moved over the door, finding the symbols etched into it. The markings turned warm beneath my touch. The ancient Vaeloran connection was soon waking within me, and it took only an instant of concentration to sink fully into that bond, to let the Vaeloran memories imprinted on this door guide my hand's movements.

Slowly, Severin pulled the knife back to his side.

"Her too," I ordered, nodding toward Thalia.

I waited until the Order member pulled his sword away from Thalia's neck before I put my hand more firmly against the markings and continued tracing them. Faint shadows lifted from my wrist, reaching out like extra fingers, tapping and pressing, then sinking into the symbols when they started to glow.

A groan of metal and stone echoed through the corridor as the doors began to move.

Bastian hung his head—whether from relief that his life had been spared, or disappointment in my decision, I didn't know. Thalia looked furious. Maybe at me. Maybe at everyone. But I didn't care what they thought. What they wanted. I couldn't sacrifice them.

I couldn't watch anyone else I loved die.

Not if there was any chance I could save them.

I looked back to Aleks one last time, and I found him watching me and my shadows as he had so many times before—with a slightly awed expression in his eyes and a hint of a smile curving his lips.

But there was something else in that expression, something as wrong as the bruise-colored magic twisting beneath his skin.

A…*hunger*, almost.

I couldn't speak over the lump that had formed in my throat. I could only think the same words over and over, hoping that he might somehow hear them through our battered bond.

You won't betray me. I know you won't.

The doors shook before slowly swinging open.

Several Order members immediately moved to enter the chamber, but Severin held up his hand, bringing them all to a halt. He canted his head toward Aleks.

"Take them," he commanded.

I held my breath.

Aleks didn't move at first.

Please don't move, I thought, desperately.

He met my gaze. And he saw me. I know he did. His eyes held the same clear, golden warmth I'd fallen in love with; it wasn't like before, when Lorien had possessed him and turned his gaze into something darker, something blood-tinged and violent.

Several tense heartbeats later, his eyes still hadn't changed, and I began to hope that *nothing* had changed —the Order had gotten this wrong. Whatever they'd done to him, he'd managed to heal from it. To shake off their corrupted hold. I was certain of it.

Until he rose to his feet and strode forward, calmly moving into the chamber without giving me a second glance. Our enemies all made room, drawing back and watching him pass without a word.

I stepped after him in a daze.

Phantom slinked into the chamber as well, his ears flat against his head as he glanced between Aleks and me, whining and waiting for me to give him a command.

I had no commands to give.

I still couldn't speak. I didn't know what to say. What to do. My gaze fixed on the pedestal in the center of the room, on the shards resting on its grooved top.

Aleks was walking straight toward them.

Grimnor lifted as power surged toward its tip, yanking me forward as if it wanted to intervene with or without my consent. I had to run to keep from falling, and after I'd started, I didn't stop, moving to position myself between the pedestal and Aleks.

He slowed without comment, looking to the sword in his own hand as if sizing it up, considering the best way to attack.

A cold sweat washed over me.

"Going back on our deal so quickly?" Severin called from the doorway.

My gaze darted to my brother and Thalia, still bound by the other Order members. "Let them go," I snarled, pointing Grimnor at Aleks. "Fulfill your part of the deal first."

"Or else what?" Severin asked. "Are you really going to stop him from following my command, no matter what it takes?"

Cool, clammy sweat continued to build, drenching my palms and the back of my neck. The room spun.

But I didn't lower my weapon.

"You're willing to put your blade through the man you allegedly love?"

This elicited several cruel chuckles from the crowd around him. My shadows grew more furious at the sound, arching up around me before twisting into several sharp points that all took aim at Aleks.

I looked again to my brother and Thalia. "No one touches the shards until you release them."

"We'll see." Severin made a gesture with his hand. Something lit within his palm, a symbol glowing against his skin. He clenched his fingers over it just as quickly, hiding it before I could make out any distinct shape.

Aleks rolled the tension from his shoulders. His voice was achingly normal, familiar—his and no one else's—as he growled out a single command: "Move."

"Aleks, I know this isn't what you want to do." Somehow, my stance remained steady, as did my voice. "You don't have to do this."

Again, he looked right at me, his golden eyes bright and aware. He didn't seem any different than he had in my room such a short time ago, when he'd told me he would give anything to keep me safe.

Then he swung at me so violently I barely managed to dodge it.

I heard more cold laughter from outside, followed by sounds of a struggle—my brother and Thalia trying once more to fight their way free, I assumed.

I ignored it, scrambling to set my feet, moving Grimnor into a guard position just in time to block another violent swing. Aleks didn't back away as his blade hit mine; he leaned into the collision, shoving until I lost my balance.

I stumbled, overpowered and too stunned to think about properly countering his attack.

Aleks drew back, preparing to strike again.

Phantom reached him first, his fangs sinking into Aleks's arm and dragging him to the ground. They tumbled across the stone floor, blade and claws flashing in a violent tangle.

Magic flew from Aleks's free hand, silver-violet and dangerously precise. It wrapped around Phantom and immediately began constricting, strangling away the shadows surrounding his form. Once those shadows were gone, the ropes of magic didn't stop; they only wrapped around the solidness underneath, squeezing into Phantom's body until he was forced to shift into something smaller in a desperate, clumsy attempt to squirm out of reach.

The sight of him struggling brought me quickly to my feet. I swung at Aleks without any thought of holding back, causing his magic to scatter as his focus shifted to parrying.

Phantom lay still, whimpering, even as the magic around him dissipated. Each pained cry sent another shot of heat through my blood, driving me into increasingly ruthless attacks.

Again and again, Aleks met my furious blows, until the sound of clashing steel entirely filled the small space, and a particularly sharp *clang* brought me back to my senses.

I kept attacking, but not at full force; I was merely trying to distract him for as long as I could—long enough to figure out what the hell I was going to do next.

But it soon became impossible to merely defend; he was swinging harder and harder, forcing me to do the same if I wanted to avoid ending up on the ground beside Phantom.

"Aleks, stop!"

He didn't stop.

More magic burst from his palm, curling around my shadows, choking them into submission.

I stumbled, once again knocked off balance by the unsettling sensation of my magic being absorbed by his. As I struggled to regain my footing, he struck toward my grip on Grimnor, trying to disarm me. I sidestepped, but not fast enough; his blade sliced across my fingers.

The sword slipped from my grasp. He followed his attack with an elbow to my face, forcing me to abandon my weapon and stagger backward.

The pain was blinding.

Aleks considered the blood dripping from my hand with a cold, detached expression. Then he turned and walked away, reaching for the pieces he'd been instructed to collect.

I clutched my bleeding hand to my chest.

My heart pounded in my throat.

Something ancient and primal rose within me. An instinct I couldn't suppress, reminding me of who I was. *What* I was. I was Death. Darkness. One half of a cycle that could not be broken, no matter what it took to preserve it. No matter what it cost.

The man before me was a threat to that cycle.

And I had to make him *stop*.

He picked up the first shard.

The magic that exploded from my body in the next

instant was unlike anything I'd ever summoned before. Shadows completely filled the chamber, and I was aware and in control of every last tendril of them.

I hadn't simply summoned the darkness, I *was* the darkness. A primordial beast with enough awareness to send a single, precise shadow snaking toward the one threatening my purpose, my power. That snaking shadow wrapped around the shard Aleks held and ripped it from his hold.

The other shard was swooped up just as easily, and both were dropped into my physical hands a moment later. My fingers closed around them with poise and purpose beyond my understanding—another instinct leading me to squeeze tighter and tighter.

They shattered.

White light streaked into the darkness I'd created, blinding bolts cutting jagged lines across the shadows. At first, they seemed at odds with one another. But soon they were twisting into a unified whole, light and dark becoming inseparable.

The maelstrom of magic billowed around me, dark clouds flashing with occasional bursts of brightness. I stood perfectly still in the center of it all, feeling oddly serene as the storm whipped at my hair and clothing, lashing against my skin with a violence that felt like it was permanently branding me. Reshaping me.

When it finally settled, it was like emerging into an entirely new world. One the gods had only just birthed from the chaos. Power thrummed through every fiber of my being. All of my senses were heightened.

I caught sight of Aleks backing away from me, no sign of his magic—corrupted or otherwise—visible across his skin.

But I couldn't focus on him for long.

Because Lorien Blackvale had just appeared beside him, his body as solid as mine.

Not a ghost.

Not a memory.

An actual, living being who picked up my sword and handed it back to me.

THIRTY-FOUR

Nova

I took hold of Grimnor in a daze.

Its weight settled in my hand, undeniably real, but even then, I couldn't believe what was happening.

Lorien didn't speak, merely studied me for a moment before turning away.

Phantom got to his feet, giving himself a hard shake. He limped to my side, his ears flat against his head and teeth bared as he observed the threats around us.

Lorien moved to the center of the room, inspecting the place where the shards of his soul had rested. There were bits of both light and shadow twisting through the air above the empty pedestal. With a wave of his hand, he bound them together and then pulled them into himself.

Aleks stood against the back wall, his sword hanging loosely in his grip, his expression eerily vacant as he watched the scene unfolding between us.

The seconds pounded by. My chest felt like it was caving in a little deeper every time I looked at Lorien, my heart oddly heavy and sinking. I kept expecting him to disappear. To go back to being that ghost that had haunted my room just days ago.

But he didn't. He remained solid and real, rolling the tension from his neck and shoulders. As if he'd just woken from a quick nap, rather than from a centuries-long curse.

"…Impossible," came Severin's voice—completely devoid of its usual cockiness. Genuinely shocked. Maybe even afraid. Several more Order members crowded the doorway behind him, trying to catch a glimpse of what had happened.

Lorien glanced toward them. His dark eyes took on a murderous gleam, a look that seemed terrifyingly at odds with the slight smile that curved his lips a moment later. White light gathered around his fingertips, crackling with barely contained fury.

A few had enough sense to quickly back away, scurrying and tripping over one another as they retreated into the hall. The ones that didn't move paid for it an instant later, when lances of bright light speared toward their eyes, blinding them.

Severin moved with almost inhuman speed, avoiding the attack and rolling into the chamber itself. Several others joined him, drawing their weapons and preparing to fight despite their obvious fear.

I finally broke out of my daze.

While they were all distracted by Lorien, I moved, ducking and weaving through bodies and blades, racing toward the ones holding my brother and Thalia captive.

Ignoring the burning pain radiating through my bloody hand, I swung Grimnor in a sweeping, powerful arc. Shadows flew outward, wrapping around the throats of the men guarding Bastian. I didn't have to put much pressure on them before they were falling backwards, clawing at the darkness, trying to shake off my attack.

Phantom followed my lead. Even with a slight limp, he was still deadly fast as he charged toward Thalia, slamming into the two men holding her arms and knocking them both to the ground.

With our help, both Thalia and Bastian managed to twist entirely free of their captors. They staggered to their feet and ran, hands still bound in chains behind their backs, shouting for me to follow.

I took a few steps after them, but I couldn't help pausing and looking back toward the vault.

Aleks was still in there.

And Lorien…what the hell was he going to do next?

Phantom whined. (*We should regroup someplace safer.*)

When I hesitated, his whining turned to insistent growls. He stepped between me and the vault, shifting his form into something larger and more imposing.

As magic flashed and shouts echoed from the vault, I turned and fled. Tears stung my eyes, blurring my vision. It made it difficult to pay attention to where I was running, so I just followed Phantom's lead through the twisting corridors.

When I finally managed to blink the tears away, I looked up just in time to avoid running into a familiar figure—Zayn.

"There you are." I breathed a sigh of relief once I'd caught my balance. "Are you okay?"

He glanced from my blood-covered hand to my tear-stained cheeks, frowning. "I could ask you the same question."

"We don't have time for small talk," Thalia said, having doubled back toward us. She gave the chains still around her wrists a little shake. "We need somewhere to hide while we deal with these."

"...Nova's office was empty when I checked it a few moments ago," Zayn said, already starting toward it.

We followed him, finding both that office and the hall outside of it still empty, and we decided to temporarily barricade ourselves inside.

Every instinct screamed at me to go back for Aleks, but I made myself focus on the chains binding my brother and Thalia. I blinked furiously until I summoned the magical sight that allowed me to see the energy around the metal bindings. I guided a shadow toward that energy, intertwining the two, then tightened the darker strand until the bindings began to pop. They were relatively thin, weak chains; it didn't take much manipulation to shatter them.

As soon as he and Thalia were free, my brother grabbed me and pulled me into a bone-crushing embrace.

"We tried to get to you," he said when he finally leaned away. "But we ran into Severin and his followers before we could."

"Phantom said Captain Voss attempted to come back for me, too," I told them. "But I haven't seen him, either."

We fell silent for a moment, wondering what trouble he might have run into. It was hard not to fear the worst.

Zayn straightened suddenly, obvious fear gripping him. "Wait—where is Aleks?"

I couldn't bring myself to meet his eyes.

Zayn looked to the door, as though considering whether to rush back out there, but my brother placed a hand on his shoulder, stopping him.

Bastian's voice was carefully measured. "Aleks is busy. Distracted by Lorien, along with the rest of the Order."

"...Lorien?"

With a trembling voice, I recounted what had happened in the vault.

"He's *back?*" Zayn asked. "As in flesh-and-bones back?"

I nodded.

"*How?*"

We were all silent, still trying to process it ourselves. Finally, my brother said, "Mind and body…those were the two shards we'd collected thus far…"

"And apparently that was enough to give him life, when coupled with Nova's powers," Thalia finished.

Silence stretched between us once more, heavy with questions nobody really wanted to ask.

Zayn broke it with a bitter laugh. "So we've revived the bastard, *and* he's quite literally heartless. Fantastic." He folded his arms across his chest, leaning back against my desk and shaking his head. "I mean, what could possibly go wrong with this scenario?"

Thalia cut her eyes toward me. "It *was* an impressive bit of magic, for what it's worth."

I managed a weak, humorless smile. "And yet, for some reason, I don't feel like celebrating my accomplishments."

"Will it last, is the question," Bastian said. "And what happens if he and his magic prove unstable? We don't know exactly what those shards contained, or how they all work together, but I assume the fact that he's still missing a piece of himself will make him even more unpredictable."

Thalia's expression darkened. "Between him, and whatever the hell is going on with Aleks's magic, the fallout this palace might suffer could be catastrophic."

I went to the window, searching the grounds below for any sign of movement. Phantom came to stand beside me, leaning his weight into me. Anchoring me. It was becoming a habit of his, I'd noticed—and the gods knew I needed it just then.

At least a half hour passed while we discussed our next steps, arguing about how to deal with the Order infiltration and control the bleeding. It felt like we were taking hours to discuss these things. Days. Entirely too long to be safe behind a barricaded door while chaos reigned beyond it.

I was seconds away from picking up my sword and charging back into the fray, plans be damned, when a commotion in the hallway made us all freeze.

Slowly, I moved toward the door, listening closer.

Then I heard a voice I recognized: *Eamon.*

I didn't wait for the others, throwing open the door and rushing out of the room.

A battle was raging in the corridor. I was relieved to see that most of the ones surrounding Eamon were palace guards fighting on our side, but the situation looked far from under control. They were struggling against more Drynland soldiers. Two women bearing Order marks had joined these enemy soldiers as well, wielding curved swords that glowed and crackled dangerously in the confined space.

I stormed forward, followed quickly by the others.

Bastian and Thalia both commandeered swords from fallen figures on the outskirts of the skirmish. Zayn was already armed, and he wasted no time slamming his blade into the first soldier he reached. His fear for Aleks must have been simmering toward something explosive beneath the surface; I'd never seen him move with such violence.

Our victory was swift.

Only one of the Order members managed to escape our onslaught; I followed her halfway down the hall before I managed to rein in my fury and shadows, begrudgingly letting her go so I could turn my attention back to a bloodied and shaken Eamon.

I ordered our guards to each end of the hall, having them keep an eye out while the rest of us talked.

It was unsettling to see Eamon's usually neat appearance so disheveled, with red spattered across his fine clothes and a bruise covering a large swath of his face, swelling up his left eye and marring its usual brightness.

"I thought you'd evacuated," I said.

"I did. But I decided to come back."

"Why wouldn't you?" Zayn muttered dryly, gesturing to the carnage around us. "Clearly the party is still in full swing."

Eamon gave him a sharp look, smoothing the rumpled fabric of his shirt. "I made sure Brynn was safe first. I left her with Aveline, at one of the shelters we've established in Tarnath."

My relief was immediate, knowing they were both safe. It was short-lived, though, because no part of me was certain I could *keep* them safe.

"But I had to come back, I had to see if…" Eamon cleared his throat, as if trying to rid it of the uncharacteristic emotion building in it. He was back to his usual controlled demeanor when he continued, "I had to witness for myself what was happening, and I wanted to help more people if I could. And then, on my way back to the palace, I saw…I saw something impossible."

I knew what he was going to say before he found the words.

"Lorien Blackvale." He lifted his gaze to me, searching for confirmation. "My eyes weren't deceiving me, were they?"

I shook my head slowly. "No. They weren't."

Eamon propped a hand under his chin, his brow furrowing in thought. "He was fleeing toward the woods beyond the South Gate, it looked like."

"He…fled?"

"He was outnumbered. I saw more Order symbols than I could count on the ones pursuing him." He paused. "And those Order members…Aleks was among them."

My heart plummeted.

Zayn spoke up, his voice tight. "So, Lorien escaped?"

"For now, it seems."

"And what did Aleks do after that? Where did he go?"

Eamon shook his head, clearly frustrated by his inability to make sense of what he'd seen. "I followed him for a time, trying to figure out what he was still chasing after. I didn't approach him, but I saw him asking questions, demanding information from anyone he encountered…"

I held my breath as he fixed his gaze on me.

"He was looking for you, Nova."

The words settled like brands over my skin, igniting a burning need to move. I didn't even know which direction I was going, but I sheathed Grimnor and started to walk. I couldn't keep still.

"Nova, wait a moment," came my brother's stern voice.

I ignored him, walking faster.

I could feel everyone watching me, shifting uncertainly, but it was Eamon who actually caught up to me and jerked me to a stop.

"We need to be careful. He's acting…strange."

I tried to shrug out of his hold. "I know he is, but there's an explanation, a chance we could—"

"He *killed* them, Nova." The words left him in a breathless rush.

I stopped trying to fight my way out of his grip, my gaze flying to his, certain I'd misheard.

He dug his fingers into my arm. He seemed to be trying to keep his hand from shaking. "The ones who didn't know where you were, or who refused to tell him anything, he was just…he was just slaughtering them left and right."

The room spun. Bile rose in the back of my throat. I swallowed it down, bracing a hand against Phantom's back as he brushed against my leg, whimpering softly.

"And he's…he's looking for me," I whispered.

My brother stepped forward, shaking his head. "No, the *Order* is looking for you. Aleks is only doing what they've commanded him to do. And you can't just keep throwing yourself so willingly at him."

I leveled a glare in his direction, but there was little fire behind it.

Because I knew he was right.

He'd been right all along, I guessed. Aleks was dangerous, had *always* been dangerous, and I couldn't go to him now without potentially triggering something even more cataclysmic than what we'd already witnessed tonight. He was looking for me because of my magic. Because of what I was, and what *he* was— what he'd been molded into.

A monster they created to destroy me.

But if I didn't stop him…

"He'll tear this palace apart to get to me." I swallowed hard, trying to keep my voice from breaking. "What am I supposed to do? I can't let everyone else suffer while I hide."

Bastian opened his mouth to argue, but he seemed

to be struggling to find the words. He only shook his head again, still refusing to agree with me.

Months ago, I might have deferred to his judgment. But I had changed. Maybe it was the weight of the crown I now carried, or maybe it was simply that I'd lost too much to keep still. I was surrounded by so much loss and chaos that the only option seemed to be pushing through—to keep moving so I didn't drown.

I lifted my chin. "I'm going to face him."

The declaration hung like a death sentence in the air.

Zayn moved first, breaking through the settling dread as he stepped to my side. "And I'm going with you."

Thalia moved to my other side, catching my eye as she silently tapped her hand over her heart.

The conflict was clear on my brother's face—the desire to protect me warring with the realization that I had already made my choice, and there was nothing he could do to change it.

Finally, he turned to Eamon and said, "Continue evacuating as many as you can, and make sure riders have been sent to the soldiers we have stationed throughout the outer establishments. We're going to need reinforcements before this is done."

Eamon nodded grimly and departed along with the guards who had been keeping watch for us.

Taking a deep breath, Bastian turned back to me. "Lead the way."

I looked to Phantom and his nose for the second time that evening. "I know it will be difficult with the chaos and all the conflicting scents, but if anyone can find him quickly, it's you."

His tail gave a single thump—clearly pleased by the praise and unable to suppress it even in these awful conditions. He gave me his typical, critical huff, followed by a sneeze, but then he put his nose to the ground and started to work.

It took longer to find the trail we needed, this time, but eventually he managed it.

My eyes were no longer blurring with tears, but I still kept them fixed only on Phantom as he led the charge through the palace. I didn't want to look too closely at the things we were passing. The proudly-hanging banners of Rivenholt. The paintings of Noctaris's wider history, and opulent artifacts tied to the Vaeloran who had protected them in ages past...all these things that had felt normal for a fraction of a moment last night, when I'd walked past them as a new queen with the sounds of celebration still ringing in my ears.

Maybe it had always been an impossible dream, to think that I could walk so easily into the next part of this story. That taking up a crown and pledging myself and my magic to this realm would be enough to fix such a broken world.

I'd dreamed it like a fool, just the same.

And I wasn't ready to wake up, to give up on that

dream, just yet—but the nightmare that greeted me when we came to the edge of the training grounds opened my eyes wider than ever.

This was where the worst of the battles and chaos seemed to have converged. And this was where we finally found Captain Voss: He was still alive, but holding his clearly-wounded side as he shouted orders at his exhausted soldiers, who were just barely standing their ground.

My brother ran to help him.

I strode forward as well, scanning the grounds, searching for Aleks. Desperately, I tried to settle the emotions erupting inside me. To not give in to the grief, the rage, the helplessness. Things that would pull me under if I let them latch on too tightly.

I knew the Order was creating carnage for the sole purpose of trying to drag me down, to give me no choice but to react with emotion. They had been baiting me from the moment they'd left those bodies outside my room. Making it impossible for me to walk away from their trap.

Because no one who called themselves *Queen* could have walked away from this.

There were so many dead bodies.

My servants. My soldiers. My supporters. Enemy soldiers, too, but even they caused a painful twist in my gut, because their deaths felt like the death of something much bigger—snapping my plans of unity like a neck snapping at a gallows. The execution of *hope*.

The worst trail of brokenness and blood led right through the center of the dusty training yard.

Aleks waited at the head of this trail, his back to me, his hands surrounded by flickering violet light.

How many of these bodies was he personally responsible for?

How could he have done this?

He turned as I approached. His gaze didn't meet mine at first, staring instead at the tendrils of shadow that had started to lift like smoke from my skin. When he finally did meet my eyes, there was only the barest hint of recognition from him. Then came cold assessment, nothing more.

"Tell me you didn't do any of this," I said, my voice strangled as I swept a shaky hand toward the fallen bodies around us. "*Please* tell me you didn't do any of this."

He didn't deny anything. He only said, "You shouldn't have run from me."

My breath caught. My shadows swarmed more violently, sensing my fear, my growing desperation.

Aleks followed their motions. The light around his hands intensified. He wasn't even moving—he was barely breathing—but I could feel the pull against my magic already, the void he was creating. The emptiness. Impossibly cold and fathomless, like it could swallow both me and my magic up with no more than a nod from him.

Phantom and Thalia intervened before he could

attack, both drawing from those shadows surrounding me, pulling them into something larger, more formidable. Phantom's body shifted and grew, while Thalia wielded the darkness like whips, lashing at Aleks's legs. They came at him from opposite sides, drawing him away from me, at least for a moment—at least until he aimed that violet-tinged magic at their shadows, ripping the darker magic apart and sending them both tumbling across the dirt.

Zayn rushed forward then, his sword gleaming in the early morning light. Aleks met him with a quick draw of his own blade. They circled each other, steel clashing again and again, while Phantom and Thalia continued to try and distract Aleks, to level the odds.

My brother was still rallying the soldiers alongside Captain Voss behind me. All around them, the battle was growing louder, deadlier.

And I stood like a statue in the middle of an earthquake, my foundation rocked, little fissures spreading through my composure.

Every possible move felt perilous.

"I told you it was a dangerous game you were playing," came a low, satisfied voice.

I twisted around to find Severin approaching me.

"How did you do this to him?" My voice was low and shaking, a tremor of rage running through it. "Whatever tricks you've used, they won't last. We will find a way to break them. And to break *you*."

"*Tricks*." He chuckled darkly. "You know, for a being

capable of such impressive magic, your understanding of it—and the gods who grant it—is very poor."

I gritted my teeth.

"But you just keep stumbling forward anyway, don't you? Admirable in a tragic sort of way."

I withdrew Grimnor from its sheath.

Severin didn't so much as flinch. "Violence is always easier than understanding, isn't it?"

His mocking tone only made me want to drive my blade more *violently* into him.

A terrible, pained cry distracted me before I could.

Thalia and Phantom were busy battling encroaching Drynland soldiers, while Zayn was on the ground, clutching his chest.

Aleks stood a few feet away from Zayn, his sword dripping red. Perfectly still. Perfectly poised. As if he didn't know—or care—what he'd just done. He eventually looked back at his fallen cousin, lifting his sword and giving it a lazy twirl, as if casually trying to decide whether or not it was worth the effort to finish Zayn off.

"Can you make him stop, I wonder?" Severin mused aloud. It seemed like an actual question—not a taunt, but a test. An experiment. I was nothing more than a pawn in the game he was creating, and I hated it. But I kept playing because I had no choice, because I couldn't just stand there letting myself fall apart while people died around me.

I hurried to Zayn's side, kneeling beside him. His

eyes were unfocused, his breathing rapid and shallow. But he said my name…so he recognized me, at least. And the wound seemed less critical up close, involving his shoulder more than his chest.

Grabbing the knife at my ankle, I ripped off the bottom half of his shirt, then used it to wipe aside the blood and better assess the wound.

"I appreciate your interest," he rasped, running a hand over the skin I'd exposed. "But now isn't really the time for us to be getting naked."

"Shut up," I muttered, arranging the fabric squarely over the cut, trying to stem the bleeding.

He huffed out a laugh that quickly shifted into a pained groan. "Also, you'd think I'd have learned by now to…to…"

"To what?"

"To stop following your reckless ass into battle."

"Not my fault you're a slow learner," I said, guiding his hand to the fabric and forcing him to press firmly despite his discomfort.

A shadow overtook us.

Aleks.

I repositioned myself, shielding Zayn with my body. Staring up at Aleks, at his body silhouetted by the sun, violet magic crackling around him…it was the first time he truly looked like something…*other.*

It didn't last. As he moved closer, stepping out of the direct sunlight, he looked just like Aleks once more—and I didn't know which was worse.

I wanted to scream at him.

To shake him until he woke up, until he managed to slip free of whatever spells were binding us to this horror.

Grimnor hummed beside me, its blade lighting with its true magic. No longer tainted with Lorien's power. The ghostly twists against the black steel called to my shadows, reminding me of the ancient strength that I carried within me.

For a moment—just a horrible, breathless moment—I wondered if that strength could be enough.

What would happen to Aleks if I managed to overpower him? If my shadows managed to fill up that awful emptiness his magic created? To somehow undo it?

I wrapped my fingers around Grimnor's handle, but I couldn't seem to lift it.

"Get up," he said, coldly.

"Aleks, please…"

"*Up.*"

Zayn's hand closed around my wrist, as if to stop me. His grip was surprisingly strong. He'd managed to sit upright, too, and Thalia and Phantom were drawing closer as well, all of them clearly prepared to hold me back.

Out of the corner of my eye, I saw my brother running toward me. Soldiers preceded him, their weapons at the ready; as soon as they drew too close,

Aleks immediately turned to deal with them, lifting his bloody sword with smooth, deadly grace.

"Stop!" I jumped up, closing the distance between us in a few long, panicked strides. "You don't have any orders to do anything to them." My balance wavered as he looked at me, but I didn't back down. "It's me you're after, right?"

With slow, calculated movements, he turned to fully face me once more.

"It's me you're after," I repeated. "And I'm here now." My voice grew softer toward the end, the words struggling to rise over the lump in my throat.

He took a step closer.

"I'm right here," I whispered.

Can't you see me?

He tilted his head, as if considering the question I hadn't asked out loud.

The world narrowed to just the two of us. Everything else seemed to fade away into the background. Grimnor pulsed in my hand, but I didn't swing it.

Why would I swing it?

Every other time, Aleks had fought to get back to me. Against Lorien's possession, against all the tortures he'd endured, all the terrible things that had tried to rip us apart. Against all odds, *he loved me*. He would have done anything to keep me safe. To keep us from becoming a tragedy.

But there were limits, I supposed.

Endings that became inevitable, cliffs that eventually gave way when you danced too often, too recklessly, upon their edges.

I realized, too late, that this was the way it ended for us.

Aleks lifted his hand, cold magic gathering around it. My shadows reacted immediately, squirming under my skin, trying to resist being drawn to him. It felt like I was being pulled apart from the inside out. The pain was immeasurable.

The look of satisfaction on his face was worse.

As I stared at him, I started to drift into a cold, empty space that I could only guess was somewhere between life and death.

Death seemed so much easier than life in that moment.

I wanted it to claim me.

And the only reason it didn't was because Lorien moved faster than Aleks did. He materialized from thin air, scooping me into his arms and racing toward a rippling patch of air a short distance away—a portal.

We were leaping through it and tumbling into darkness before I even had a chance to scream.

THIRTY-FIVE

Nova

I landed in the rubble in front of Midna Palace with Lorien's arms wrapped tightly around me.

He'd...*saved me.*

But he'd also taken me away from all the people I loved. Forced me to abandon them in the middle of battle, and the gods only knew how the Order would retaliate to losing *both* me and Lorien. I was safe, but numb. Beyond confused. I didn't even have my sword; I'd dropped it when Lorien had essentially tackled me.

This was wrong.

All wrong.

Lorien shifted, his body pressing closer to mine.

My reflexes took over—I kicked wildly, shoving him away and landing a boot just below his ribcage. He rolled out of my reach, cursing as he grabbed his stomach.

He watched me for a moment, eyes narrowed, before shaking his head and getting gingerly to his feet. "You're welcome for saving you, by the way."

"Why did you do it?" I demanded. *Why did you take me away from him?*"

"Should I have let him kill you instead?"

"He wouldn't have killed me."

"You're a fool if you really think that."

"And you're a bastard."

"Yes, I am, but at least I'm not an idiot, unlike you."

A sharp pain radiated through my chest, as if my heart was shrinking away, hiding rather than admitting the actual danger I'd been in.

I *wouldn't* admit it.

But I couldn't bring myself to keep arguing, either.

My vision blurred. I tucked my head toward my chest, trying to fight off my building nausea.

Lorien loomed over me. "If I'd been a second later, he would have ripped you in half. I could feel the strength of the magic he was wielding, even from a distance. He clearly intended to destroy you."

I lifted my head, glaring at him until I found the energy to stagger to my feet.

Then I punched him, hitting him squarely in the face with as much strength as I could muster. Blood was streaming from my fist as I pulled it back, the wound Aleks had left aggravated by the strike.

Lorien opened his mouth to speak.

I swung again before he could get another word out.

He caught me by the wrist this time, gripping it so tightly I was certain his next move would be to snap my bones in half.

He brought his other hand up to cover my bloody fist. He glared at me the entire time he was doing it—as if some part of him *did* want to break my bones—but warmth flowed from his palm, soothing away the pain instead of making it worse. A soft glow and a tingling sensation followed.

When he let me go, the bleeding had ceased. My skin had knitted itself back together, leaving only dried blood and a faint scar across the back of my hand as evidence of what Aleks had done.

"Stop it." I took a step away from Lorien, my entire body trembling. "Stop fucking *helping* me!"

He glanced at a few of the other scrapes and bruises I'd picked up during the night's battles, as if he was considering healing those too, just to spite me.

"I will hit you again," I hissed. "If you touch me again, I swear to the gods I will hit you hard enough to knock you back into Noctaris."

"Right," he said. "I'm going to give you a minute to deal with this." He gestured to my clenched fists and the rest of my furious, trembling body. "Then we need to make a plan."

"I'm not making any *plans* with you."

"No? You already have everything all figured out, do you?"

I started to snap out a response, but the words died in my throat.

"That's what I thought."

He turned toward the palace, considering it for a moment before letting out a sigh and heading up the cracked and crumbling front steps.

I grabbed him and yanked him back. "We don't have time to just sit around. We have to go back. My brother, my friends, Aleks—"

"They'll survive long enough for us to figure some things out."

"And if they *don't?*"

"Then it will be less we have to worry about, won't it?" He pried my fingers from his arm and shoved my grip away with infuriatingly calm precision.

I just stared at him.

"I'm giving you a minute," he repeated. And then he turned and continued up the steps.

My anger only grew as I watched him disappear into the palace. Grew and grew until it consumed me, blinded me, made me so hotheaded and delirious I didn't even know what I was angry about anymore. *So many things.* I couldn't have possibly picked one to focus on.

I thought about following Lorien, demanding him to take me back to the Below.

I thought about just trying to go back myself, even though I knew I was in no state to attempt it. Crossing the realms was dangerous even when I could focus—it would be asking for disaster in my current condition. *More* disaster.

And what was the point of going back if I didn't know how to fix anything?

In the end, I simply collapsed on the steps.

I sat with my anger for far longer than a minute. Long enough that it had time to turn into grief, into regrets that wound so tightly around me I could barely breathe. I kept trying, though.

In.

Out.

In.

Out.

I lasted only a few minutes more before finally breaking down, burying my face in my hands and letting sobs wrack my body. All my mistakes, all my losses, hit me in merciless waves, each one forcing my body to curl a little more tightly into my grief.

I should have tried harder to figure out what Aleks was truly fighting against. We'd buried too many things, avoided too many difficult conversations. I'd convinced myself that I could fix everything if I just kept pushing forward, unflinching. I loved him, and that was the beginning and end of everything, the truth that had carried me to this point, but now…

Now, I understood that love alone was not enough.

Whatever vows we'd made, whatever feelings we shared…none of it mattered without action. Without the courage to face what was broken, rather than just marching stubbornly forward. None of it counted if I couldn't save him from the Order's control.

And if I couldn't save him, then what *could* I save?

I might have stayed there for hours, letting that question torment me into a comatose state, if not for the gnawing worry that eventually made me lift up my head.

I couldn't just curl up here and weep forever.

I had to get back to Noctaris.

My body felt like it weighed ten times what it should, but I forced myself to stand. On shaky feet, I climbed the steps and walked through the ruins of the palace, trying to see it all with new eyes. Trying to understand more of what I'd missed.

The heaviness in my bones persisted, but I could learn to walk with it, just as I'd learned to walk with all the other heavy things I'd collected throughout my life.

I found Lorien sitting on the broken bridge that led into the Aetherstone's chamber, staring at the mountains in the distance.

I hesitated before approaching him.

I was finally calm enough to truly look at him—to see a strange combination of the monster I'd first met, woven together with all the different memories I'd witnessed. He still had an undeniably cruel, calculating look in his eyes, but they no longer burned with the same reddish tint as before; they were closer to his natural shade of deep brown. His lips curved up in a way that almost looked thoughtful—yet I still shivered when I looked at them, knowing how readily that smile could turn feral.

I'd once heard a legend that the blood of gods ran in his veins. That he had been such a powerful Vaelora because he was already divinely-touched, even before the gods had granted him the dominion of Light.

Sitting there under the overcast sky, with the soft glow of magic warming his beige skin, highlighting every sharp and powerful line of his body, he almost looked the part.

But I could also see the toll the past centuries had taken on him. The haunted expression that flickered over his face any time he started to let his guard down. The way power radiated off him, yet he was still gripping the stone edge of the bridge like he was afraid of tumbling over. Like a fallen god who had yet to figure out how to carry the weight of his broken wings.

Whatever he was, as I stared at him, I finally, truly admitted to myself that he was *real*, even if he was still a mystery I couldn't make sense of. And I had revived him, somehow. Was that why he'd saved me? So that we were even?

And what the hell did he intend to do next?

We need to make a plan, he'd said.

As if it was really so simple.

As if I could just trust him now, after everything he'd done.

"I was beginning to wonder about you," he called, without looking at me.

I steeled myself and walked forward, my steps echoing in the still air.

"You said you wanted to make plans." I swept a hand toward the crumbling entrance to the chamber that had served as our battleground not so long ago. "But what happened to your *plans* to take control of the stone in there?" I demanded. "Your scheme to control all of its magic and destroy Noctaris?"

He kept his gaze on the distant peaks. "They were never my plans. Just lies I bought into because I wanted revenge against your realm. Because I didn't realize what the Order had done to Calista. How they poisoned her and turned us against one another."

I was silent for a long time, waiting for him to elaborate.

He didn't. It almost seemed like he *couldn't*, and it was unsettling to see him rendered into such a helpless state.

I folded my arms across my chest. Reconsidered the words I'd planned to say, the angry demands I'd planned to make of him.

Quietly, I said, "You truly did love her, didn't you?"

He still didn't look at me. "I killed her in the end. Nothing else really matters."

Probably against my better judgment, I sat down

beside him, keeping a careful distance. "Then you tried to kill me, because I carry her legacy."

"And because Severin urged me to do it. To finish what I'd started. And because it was easier than admitting to myself that *what I'd started* might have been a mistake—especially after spending centuries trying to justify what I'd done."

It was the strangest part of this ordeal yet, to hear him admit that he'd been wrong.

"Of course, I didn't manage to kill you." He tilted his face toward me, as if he still couldn't believe I'd survived, and he needed to see me for himself. "Something protected you and your brother that night, and I still don't know what it was. Only that it broke me into pieces. Then the Order—the Light Keepers, or whatever masks they wore at the time—they took those pieces and tried to feed them into the weapon they were building."

"…They wanted you to possess him."

"Just another experiment they subjected your dear Aleks to."

I fought the urge to bury my face in my hands again. The last person I wanted to witness another breakdown would be the man sitting beside me. But it was so tempting to just give in to the despair threatening to drown me.

I just wanted all these revelations to *stop*.

I fixed my eyes on the remains of a fallen statue far

below us—a severed head of some lesser god I didn't recognize—and I forced myself to keep talking.

"That's the real reason he has some of the power of a Light Vaelora." It wasn't really a question; just the theory I'd always suspected but never wanted to fully believe.

"I don't think it was part of the Order's plans," Lorien said. "They hoped he would just neutralize my magic, I'm sure. But he rejected the possession, and then hung on to fragments of my power and found a way to channel it instead. So, to answer your question…yes. He has it because he stole it from me."

I thought of all the times Aleks had made my shadows disappear over the past weeks.

Was he neutralizing them, or collecting them?

Could he ultimately wield my own power against me, too?

"He might have been able to balance your magic temporarily, but it was never going to be the true Vaeloran bond," Lorien said. "He was never going to be your true counterpart."

I snorted. "And you are?"

He shrugged. "You don't have to like it."

"I don't."

"Well, that makes two of us. But unless you intend to go against the divine plans of the gods themselves…"

"Fuck the gods," I muttered.

He let out a quiet, bitter little laugh. "And once

again, you remind me of her." He went quiet for a moment. "Or who she was in the beginning, at least."

It was obvious that something very painful was playing out behind his dark eyes—a specific memory of some kind.

I didn't dwell on what it might have been. "How can you be sure of all of this?" I asked instead. "The Order's involvement, I mean?"

"Because Aleks knew it all himself, deep in the back of his mind, even if he wasn't consciously aware of it. And so I saw it, too, during that last possession. I had him much longer this time than I did when he was a child, and he knows much more of the Order's schemes than he did back then. It was a very eye-opening few weeks. Not only because of his knowledge, but because I could feel the power that had gathered in him since our last encounter. I was fighting for control as much as he was, if I'm being honest. And after all of that, what choice did I have but to continue to dig, to find out the truth about the Order? And about myself, and the things I lost when I was cursed?"

"Find out the truth?" I shook my head. "By manipulating me into doing it for you, you mean."

His mouth curved with a hint of a smirk. "And you performed magnificently, by the way."

I scowled.

We sat in prickly silence for a moment before I said, "Aleks…he changed so quickly. So completely."

Lorien considered my words while absently

summoning a ball of light between his palms. "The events of these past months have shifted everything. Your powers awakening more fully, the battle we had over the Aetherstone…all things that also spurred the Order into movement again. It seems quick, but they've been biding their time for years now, waiting for opportunities to strike. And they infiltrated your palace, didn't they? I suspect they've been there for months, if not longer. And once Aleks returned to that palace himself…" He trailed off, allowing me to fill in the rest.

The thought that they might have been creeping through my halls all this time made my skin crawl. I felt disgusted. Violated.

Worse, though, were the new, even more painful questions flooding my mind.

How much of Aleks was truly…*Aleks*?

How much of what he'd said and done these past weeks was merely him trying to get closer to me for the sake of completing the Order's mission?

I swallowed hard. "I still don't understand how they're controlling him in the first place."

Lorien cut his eyes toward me. "You've seen the markings on his body."

"…His scars, you mean?"

"They aren't normal scars. And wherever he told you he got them from…he almost certainly wasn't telling the truth."

"No. He wouldn't have lied about that, he—"

"Maybe not on purpose. I'm sure his tormentors did all they could to hide their true purpose from him."

I hugged my arms tightly around myself, thinking of those scars. Of how precisely carved so many of them were. They'd always made me feel sick whenever I touched them, but I'd always associated them with his abusive past—so of course they'd felt wrong to me.

I never once thought they might have been the source of something far worse.

"Each one is a spell woven into his flesh. *Runes,* some call them. Corrupted magic. Nothing divine about it. Very few people in any of the realms would have recognized them for what they are; I doubt even most of the Order members fully understand what they've done to him. Only Severin and the other higher-ups, the ones capable of carving such enchantments, know the true power of such things."

"But where did they even learn how to do that?"

"Your guess is as good as mine. But this world has had no shortage of beings that have tried to rival the gods we serve. We both know that the Vaeloran Cycle was birthed into a chaotic world, meant to be its saving grace. But darker things have a way of taking root in broken places."

I fell quiet for a minute, summoning a shadow and watching it coil around my fingers. "How were we ever supposed to balance anything in such a world?"

He huffed out a laugh. "Still so concerned with trying to bring balance and peace?"

"We were made for that, weren't we?"

"Yes. And look where it's gotten us."

I had no response to this.

"Maybe it's time you tried worrying about power instead." He stood, stretching.

I shifted the shadow into a dagger-like shape, twisting it around in my hand as I considered his words. I could sense him looking down at me, but I didn't meet his gaze when he spoke again; I just kept walking the sharpened shadow between my fingers.

"I doubt Aleks would be strong enough to destroy us both, if we were to face him together as one. That's why the Order tried to sow as much discord between you and I as possible, and why they wanted to stop me from being revived. Because their little weapon isn't as perfect as they'd like it to be. Not yet, anyway."

With that, he left me alone with my thoughts once more, heading into what was left of the Aetherstone's destroyed chamber.

I let the shadow dagger dissipate as I studied all the other destruction surrounding me. The cracked ground. The tattered banners. The broken bridge I sat upon. A world gone so incredibly wrong because of lies and manipulation.

But it occurred to me, then, that nothing was breaking in that moment.

Not a single rumble had occurred since we touched down here. The sky was overcast, but something about the sunlight diffusing through the ash-colored sky was oddly calming. The air was crisp, almost clean smelling.

Perhaps peace was not a viable option, as he'd said.

But there was no denying that this was the most peaceful I'd ever seen Nerithys. Just as there was no denying that I had truly revived Lorien. That our magic represented two halves of the same whole, that we were connected, and that *something* had prevented him from killing me twenty-five years ago.

And as I sat there, considering everything, I realized I knew why all of these things were true.

Understanding bloomed like a slow ache through my chest, bringing me to my feet. Even then, it took me a moment to summon the courage to step forward. To actually make a plan with him.

I couldn't believe I was even thinking about allying with this dangerous, unpredictable man.

The same villain who had haunted so many of my nightmares.

I was desperate, though. I knew I needed help. It wasn't the way I would have written my story, but that didn't change the way things were unfolding. Our magic was stronger together and, if the legends about our kind were true, there was very little that it couldn't accomplish.

So it was time to make another deal.

Without any more hesitation, I made my way over to him. "If I get you your heart, will you swear to help me take the Order down? That you'll help me take Aleks back from them?"

He slowly looked back at me. That cold, dangerous calculation was back in his eyes. A look that told me he no longer saw me as another living being, but merely as a piece in some greater, more deadly scheme he was playing out in his mind.

I didn't flinch. "Well?"

"…You know where it is?"

"Answer my question."

His eyes narrowed. Suspicion was an even more dangerous look on his face—a blink away from violent refusal.

Still, I persisted. "You want your revenge against the Order, don't you? You made your mistakes, but now you know the truth about what they did."

"Some of it. There's more to uncover."

"We have a common enemy, though. That much is undeniable."

"It is, isn't it?" He canted his head, his calculating suspicion twisting into something slightly more… *unhinged*. A corner of his mouth curved up.

"Take it or leave it," I said.

"You know I love a good bargain," he said, holding out his hand.

THIRTY-SIX

Nova

We returned to find Rivenholt Palace and its grounds eerily quiet.

A thousand explanations for the silence crossed my mind, each more horrifying than the last.

What if we were too late? What if everyone was dead? What if Aleks had kept killing, even after my magic and I had left this realm?

"Focus," Lorien muttered.

Somehow, I forced myself to, though the pit in my stomach continued to grow.

We had emerged on the very outskirts of the palace grounds, and the plan was not to get any closer than this; I knew my brother well enough to know that he wouldn't keep battling to the death if he could help it. He was far more likely to have pulled back once I'd disappeared, his focus shifting to protecting the royal city and the ones who had evacuated to it. He would be cautious, regrouping and waiting for reinforcements before he attempted to reclaim our overrun palace. The eerie quiet all but confirmed this was what had happened.

Or that's what I was choosing to believe, at least.

After a quick scouting of the immediate area, we made our way into Tarnath. The sun was relatively high in the sky by this point, but a thick fog hung over the streets, obscuring the buildings around us.

Though I couldn't see everything clearly, the city bore obvious signs of the night's chaos. The usually bustling market square was eerily empty, its colorful awnings hanging limp in the damp air. Overturned carts and scattered belongings littered the cobblestones, abandoned in the rush to flee.

I cloaked Lorien and myself in shadows as we crept through the streets, hiding us. The dark shroud stifled our footsteps as well, allowing us to pass by the few people we saw with little more than the occasional confused glance in our direction.

The first place I went was the old barracks at the edge of the main square, a large building that had been empty ever since my return to Rivenholt, but which I knew had housed refugees and soldiers in past emergencies; I wasn't surprised to see plenty of activity bustling around it. Supplies were being carried in and out. Wounded soldiers were being helped into waiting hands. Small clusters of people huddled around the edges, talking in hushed voices and casting worried glances about.

I cut my eyes toward Lorien as we approached the entrance. "Not many will recognize you, but it's still probably best if you wait outside while I find the others."

"Are you planning on enlightening me about the rest of your plan before you tell it to them?"

"No."

"Wonderful."

"Just don't do anything rash while you wait."

"Hurry up," he replied, "and I won't need to."

The words were less than comforting, but I didn't waste time debating with him. I slipped inside the barracks, passing several soldiers who did double-takes before dropping into hasty bows and then trying to clear a path for me.

Even with escorts, it was overwhelming to push through it all. The troubled voices, the moans of pain, the metallic scent of blood mixed with herbs and smoke…it pressed in on me from all sides, making me slightly dizzy.

There were so many wounded.

My appearance seemed to be a welcome sight for most of them, at least. It wasn't the main reason I was here—and I didn't truly have time to spare—but I couldn't help pausing to grasp the hands that reached for me. Stopping to greet the ones who called out my name. Kneeling beside some of the more distraught survivors. I was still scanning the crowd for my brother and the others, but I was constantly being pulled in other directions, and after several minutes, I still hadn't found anyone I was looking for.

Lorien remained outside as I'd asked, but I would have sworn I could sense his growing impatience with me. His irritation bleeding into my thoughts, a mental prod that felt distinctly annoyed…and then I realized I truly *was* hearing and feeling those things, because he was sending them through our Vaeloran connection.

Annoyed at the intrusion, I twisted around and started to march back toward the exit.

A familiar face caught my attention before I made it back to the door.

"Aveline!"

She stopped in the middle of her task, tossing a basket of bandages onto an empty bed and rushing to embrace me. Her usual scent of soft rose and clean linen was marred by the strong scent of disinfecting alcohol, but it was comforting, nonetheless. I sank into her warmth, letting myself relax for just a moment.

"I knew the rumors weren't true," she said, her arms tightening around me. "People talking as if you were gone…" She leaned back, studying my face, tucking a strand of hair behind my ear. Her fingers didn't seem to be able to keep still. She kept adjusting my collar and hair, going so far as to redo the loose end of my braid, clearly flustered even as she smiled encouragingly at me. "They don't know my queen like I do, do they?"

I breathed in deep, trying to inhale her steadiness, her unwavering faith in me.

But all I could think about as I stared into her eyes was her niece, who, as far as I knew, was still lying dead in the palace entryway.

I averted my gaze, attempting to keep her from seeing the pain in it.

She cupped a hand against my cheek. "You'll be wanting to speak with your brother, I suspect." Gently, she forced my eyes back to hers. "I can show you to him."

I was so overwhelmed with relief I forgot to breathe for a moment. "He…he's safe?"

She nodded, her hand moving from my cheek to the apron she wore, taking out a handkerchief and wiping something from my forehead. Blood, or dirt, or the gods knew what else. Then she switched abruptly into her commanding mode, carving a path through the chaos, guiding me out of the building and pointing to a run-down house at the end of the street.

"Straight on to that house with the faded red door." She glanced between it and the barracks behind us, fighting off a frown. "You'll be all right, now?"

It was an affirmation as much as a question, but I still nodded. "I'll be fine."

"Good. I'll need to get back in there before someone bleeds out on my watch."

I grasped her hands one last time. She gave them a tight squeeze, commanded me to be careful, and then she was back to the business of ordering everyone else around.

I hurried on toward the house she'd indicated, Lorien secretly following in my wake.

Phantom sensed me coming before anyone else; his bark was a beautiful sound. He appeared a moment later, shifting into dark mist and squeezing through a cracked window, then materializing back into his familiar canine shape as he hit the cobblestone street. He raced to greet me, but his wagging tail turned to raised hackles and bared teeth as Lorien stepped out of the shadows alongside me.

"It's fine," I assured Phantom. "I can explain."

A growl rumbled in his chest. (*I have doubts.*)

"Still doubting me after all this time? Really?"

Another growl turned into an uncertain whine, but before he could say anything else, the door was opened by two guards who ushered us inside. They both cast wary looks at the man accompanying me, but neither dared to question what I was doing.

Captain Voss stood in the back of the entry hall. His face brightened a bit at the sight of me. "Your Highness." He bowed his head, and as he lifted it, his gaze fell on Lorien, and he briefly froze—one of the only times I'd seen him speechless with uncertainty. He clearly recognized who he was, though; my brother had likely filled him in on the details.

Lorien held up a hand. "No titles necessary for me."

The captain's lip curled. "I didn't intend to address you with one."

I cleared my throat. "Is my brother here?"

With one last cautious look at Lorien, Voss slowly made his way toward a narrow door flanked by two more guards, motioning for me to follow.

The room it opened into was much larger than I would have guessed from the other side. No less than a dozen high-ranking soldiers moved about the space, exchanging information and discussing strategy in low voices.

Thalia and I spotted each other at the same time. She went perfectly still for a moment, blinking in disbelief, before crossing the room in a few frantic strides. She caught me by surprise when she threw her arms around me—surprising herself, too, judging by how quickly she let me go.

She tried to compose herself, to fall back into her usual stoic demeanor. But her eyes were shining with emotion when she said, "I *really* wish you would stop coming up with new, creative ways to scare me."

I gave her a sheepish smile.

"And new, creative ways to test your brother's patience," she added, glancing at Lorien.

"It's a necessary evil, I'm afraid."

"...Come on, then," she said, ushering me toward a smaller room off to the side, where my brother was deep in conversation with several of his advisors.

Zayn sat in the corner of this room with a tankard in his hand, his shoulder heavily bandaged, his eyes drooping slightly; I suspected whatever was in his cup contained strong pain relief of some sort. He rose at the sight of me—only to sink back into his chair when he noticed who I'd entered the room with.

It was a grim reminder of the complicated pasts that haunted every step and decision we made. Doubt crept into my chest as I watched Zayn turn away, all trace of his usual good humor and optimism gone from his expression. The weight of what I was planning—what I would be asking them all to accept—hit me in full force, making it hard to breathe.

But it wasn't as if I could turn back now.

Bastian finally looked up from his conversation, stopping mid-sentence at the sight of me. He hastily finished giving a few orders and then excused himself, shaking his head as he stepped to my side.

His eyes darted to Lorien, who lingered by the doorway. "Why is it that every time I let you out of my sight, you come back with more trouble in tow?"

I shrugged. "It's habit at this point."

He wrapped me in a loose embrace, planting a kiss on top of my head and then letting his chin rest there, taking a moment to collect himself.

"Eamon should be arriving shortly," he informed me, pulling away. "I had some questions for him." His gaze flicked again to Lorien. "And now I suspect we'll all have quite a few more."

While we waited for his arrival, my brother and Thalia filled me in on the aftermath of the battle. Zayn eventually managed to offer me a friendly, relieved greeting, but he continued to keep to himself after that.

"The number of dead could have been a lot higher, all things considered," Thalia said quietly.

"The most concerning things at the moment are actually the borders of the palace and Tarnath. The protections that Calista erected centuries ago seem to be weakening. A side effect of Aleksander's strange power, we think."

Lorien tilted his head at the mention of Calista's name, but he didn't move from the spot he'd taken by the unlit fireplace. His expression remained carefully neutral.

"Those wards have stood for over five hundred years," Thalia said. "I don't think they're going to fail overnight."

"We don't know what Aleks is capable of. If we don't stop him soon—"

"I will."

Bastian started to reply, only to press his lips together and take a deep breath through his nose.

"I'm going to stop him," I said, quietly.

He and Thalia exchanged a soft, uncertain look, but they said nothing else until Eamon arrived.

Once we were all assembled in the smaller room, we took a moment to make sure the space was secure from eavesdroppers. Zayn finally joined us, and we all gathered around the rugged table in the corner, save for Lorien, who continued to brood by the cold hearth.

I wasted no time laying out my plan. "You took me to Calista's grave not so long ago, during one of our trainings," I said to Eamon.

His gaze darted uncertainly toward Lorien before looking back to me. "...I did."

I didn't look at Lorien myself, but I would have sworn I could *feel* the color draining from his face, the sudden tension radiating from him. Not surprising—and this was why I'd kept my plan close to my chest. I'd been afraid he wouldn't follow me back here, otherwise.

Because, according to most stories, Calista's grave lay in the same place where he'd killed her.

It was also the point from which her protective spells flowed. A sacred place of sacrifice and ancient power—and, hopefully, the resting spot of one final secret that I needed to unravel.

"My magic felt stronger there than it has anywhere else in this kingdom," I told the others. "So we're going to invite the Order to meet us there...and tell them it's where we want to negotiate."

My brother straightened. "*Negotiate?*"

"We'll tell them they can have the last piece of Lorien's cursed soul—his heart—in exchange for leaving this realm in peace. We'll agree to stop pursuing the rebirth of the Vaeloran Cycle so long as the dome of protection that Calista created is allowed to endure."

Thalia leaned forward. "You aren't *actually* going to give it to them, are you?"

I met her skeptical gaze with a slight smile; she knew me well, at this point. "Of course not."

"Good."

"I'm going to give it to him," I said, nodding toward Lorien.

The silence that followed this statement was thick enough to choke on.

Zayn shifted in his seat. "...Can we take a vote on this?"

"No," I said, flatly. "It's our only chance to keep things from spiraling completely out of control. We have to trust that Lorien and I together—both of us at our full power—will be too much for Aleks to handle. And once the threat of him is neutralized..." My breath hitched. I hated this. *Hated* talking about Aleks like he was the enemy. But I pushed through. "Once we can focus on...other things...then we can take out the Order members. Starting with Severin, hopefully."

"And what happens if Aleks proves too strong to *neutralize*?" Zayn asked.

I had no answer for that.

Lorien finally spoke. "Then you still take out the

Order members, while we have the full focus of their weapon on us."

I nodded. "They're controlling Aleks by using rune magic, we think. If we kill some of the more powerful spell casters among them, then it might help him break free of their hold."

"Severin should be your main target," Lorien told them. "But tell your soldiers to be on the lookout for anyone bearing rune marks. They likely won't glow as bright as the one's on Aleks, but you can still see them, if you're paying attention."

The others all turned to me for confirmation. I breathed in deep, nodding. "This is our best chance to end this without losing everything."

A hush fell over the room.

A minute passed, then another, with everyone deep in thought. I rose from the table, unable to sit still any longer. There were few places to go in the small space; I ended up wandering to the wall next to the fireplace, where a banner featuring the silver tree of Rivenholt had been hung.

My brother soon came to stand beside me, his presence providing the usual calm air I'd come to depend on. But there was a tightness in his shoulders—and his voice—that betrayed his worry.

"You're sure you know where the heart is?" he asked.

I kept my eyes on the tree, studying its sprawling, twisting limbs. They made me think of paths. Of choices we had to make, and all the ways they twisted together. "This ends at Calista's grave. I'm certain of it."

He was quiet for a long moment. I wondered if he could read the doubt lurking beneath my confidence. If he sensed my fear...and then decided to trust me anyway.

"I can do this, Bastian," I assured him.

He nodded. "We'll arrange a messenger, then."

THE HOURS TICKED BY WITH AGONIZING SLOWNESS. Thalia and Bastian left to oversee the preparations with the soldiers. The rest of us remained hidden in that back room, waiting for the messenger to return with the Order's response.

We tried to rest. To eat and replenish our strength. Nobody managed much of either of those things—except Zayn, who I was becoming convinced could sleep under any and all circumstances. Eamon worked at the table, making notes on spare scraps of parchment and muttering occasionally to himself. Lorien busied himself with building a fire, and then sat down before it and proceeded to ignore all of us.

I was trying to keep my distance from my *counterpart*. But the small room was dismally cold, and the warmth of the flames proved too enticing, so I eventually gave in and ended up sitting opposite of him on the faded rug in front of the fireplace.

His gaze was haunted again, lost in distant thought. I wondered if I could use that damnable bond of ours to listen to those thoughts. I didn't try, but even without prying deeper something told me he was reliving one of his darkest memories—and it wasn't hard to guess which one.

I'd avoided asking about his memories in Midna, but after a few minutes of sitting there beside him, I couldn't help my curiosity. I felt like I'd already walked so much of their story at this point...I wanted to know more.

Especially since I would soon be walking upon the bloodiest part of their history.

I took a deep breath. "...Do you remember the day it happened?"

Lorien blinked. His tormented gaze turned hard and cold, his eyes taking on a look of polished stone. A muscle worked in his jaw, but he didn't speak, didn't acknowledge me for several moments.

I frowned, starting to turn my attention to the flames.

Then he said, "I forgot so many things after that curse broke me. They started flooding back after you recovered the mind shard. But that day..."

The fire popped and crackled in the silence.

"I never forgot that day." The words were flat with practiced detachment. He picked up a small piece of wood, adding it to the fire and watching the flames consume it entirely before he continued. "My body only lasted a few hours after she cursed me. I was deteriorating in every possible way, but I used my last breaths to hunt her down. All these centuries later, and I'm still surprised I was able to find her and finish her off. It was…it was almost like she *wanted* me to."

"Maybe she didn't want to live with the weight of the curse she'd cast?" I suggested.

He huffed out a bitter, disbelieving laugh—an automatic reaction, maybe, after centuries of ruminating on their violent end. He didn't refute what I'd said, though, and his gaze eventually turned thoughtful again.

"There might have been a practical reason she chose to die," Eamon cut in. He was still sitting at the table, all the way across the room, but I wasn't surprised he'd been listening in with his usual, insatiable inquisitiveness.

"A practical death?" Zayn said, yawning as he stirred from the restless nap he'd been taking in the corner. "That's a new one."

Eamon was insistent. "There's a sacrificial element to the most powerful Vaeloran magic, isn't there? We see it in the Cycle itself—how the Vaelora were expected to ritualistically impale themselves after their part in the Turning was completed. So it makes sense that Calista would have willingly given her life. It might have granted her the power she needed to cast her protections over the palace and its surroundings. A shield that's lasted ever since."

Until now.

I pressed a hand to my chest, trying to breathe through the unsteady pounding of my heart.

We fell into silence again. Lorien didn't seem to want to talk anymore, despite Eamon's repeated attempts to engage him in theoretical discussion, so I got up and went to sit beside Zayn instead, because I was worried about him; he was clearly still not his normal self, his usual energy dampened by both his injury and Lorien's presence.

"How's the shoulder?" I asked—because that seemed the easier topic.

"I could use another drink."

"It really helps to dull the pain, doesn't it?"

"Not especially, no. I'd just prefer to be drunk for this next part of our adventure."

I rolled my eyes but managed a weak smile.

He shifted slightly, wincing. "This rune magic…" he began after a moment. "I've heard of it in passing. Wicked stuff."

"The spells can give the bearer immense power, Lorien said." I paused, my throat tightening. "But they also take a lot of the user, apparently. Sacrifices of mind and body…of their entire self." Just saying the words made me feel sick.

There was no doubt that the spells in Aleks's body were fully active now. It was bad enough, the destruction he was causing to my realm. But what about the destruction he was doing to *himself*?

What was he losing?

I'd been replaying it with vivid clarity all day—the last time we'd faced one another on the battlefield. How he'd hardly seemed to recognize me.

I didn't say it out loud, but Zayn seemed to pick up on my fear. He placed a comforting hand on mine. "I don't think even the darkest magic could erase you from his mind."

I wrapped myself around his arm and leaned against his uninjured shoulder with a sigh. "I hope you're right," I whispered.

He tilted his head back against the wall. He seemed to be drifting off again, until suddenly he spoke. "I've been thinking."

"I didn't know you were capable of that."

He chuckled. "I make a point of not doing it unless I have to."

"Well…what were you thinking about?"

A pause, and then: "How I should have fought harder to protect him when we were younger. I was there. I saw the Light Keepers pushing him out of sight, stealing him away for lessons, for supposedly routine training and disciplining. He never talked about what they did to him, but the signs were there, if I'd cared to see them."

"You weren't fully yourself," I reminded him.

"No. But I had moments of awareness. I was still me,

sometimes, even with Lorien's presence always coiled in the back of my mind. I could have tried harder. And when I finally broke free..."

I looked up, urging him to continue.

"I don't remember a lot from those years. But I don't think it's magic that stole those memories, in my case. I think it's my own mind, blocking out the truth of it. Because I don't want to think about how easily I went along with terrible exploitation. How many people I let down, just so I could avoid difficult things. Not just Aleks, but other family as well."

"...You have a younger sister, don't you?" I recalled.

"Not that it matters. She won't remember me; she was too young when I left. And I doubt I'll ever bother trying to meet her again. Why would I force myself back into her life? I hope I can see her one day, from afar, just to make sure she's okay. To see who she's become. But I'm not going to subject her to all the darkness I'm guessing I'll still be carrying with me."

I laid my head back on his shoulder, trying to come up with the right words to say.

"If I could go back in time, I'd like to think I could change something. That I could look closer at Aleks and see what they were doing to him. That I wouldn't be such a coward, this time."

"We do what we have to do to protect ourselves," I said quietly. "You can't save anyone when you're drowning yourself."

His body rose and fell with a deep sigh. "Well, I'm not drowning anymore."

"So now we save him," I said.

He let out another quiet laugh. "Easy as that, huh?"

"Easy as that."

He didn't seem convinced—and neither was I—but some of the tension did eventually slip from his body. We sat in silence, watching the shadows on the walls shift with the firelight. I'd started to doze off against him when the door opened, jolting me awake.

My brother stepped inside, armor damp from the rain that had started to fall outside. Without a word, he handed me a folded piece of parchment.

I scanned it quickly, feeling the eyes of everyone in the room fixed on me. I couldn't meet anyone's gaze as I lowered the letter. But I forced myself to lift my head, to don a mask of confidence.

Because Severin had agreed to meet me, and now all that remained was to see my plan through to the bitter end.

THIRTY-SEVEN

Nova

We traveled on foot toward the woods that lay just beyond the northern edge of Tarnath.

My brother, Thalia, and Phantom walked alongside me. Severin had insisted on a more intimate meeting, so we'd kept our numbers low; Eamon had stayed behind, as had Zayn—after finally admitting that his injury would make him more of a liability than an asset.

We'd brought several of our most skilled soldiers to

round out our party, though, and we also had others who would be waiting not too far in the distance, should we signal for more help; I didn't trust Severin to keep to the agreed-upon terms. Voss waited with this second regiment, positioned where he could keep one eye on the city and one eye on whatever was happening in our direction.

Lorien walked at the very back of our group, his hood drawn up to hide his face. We'd agreed he would stay out of sight until the last possible moment, doing all he could to cloak his power—the Order couldn't know he had returned with me. Not until I was ready to reveal him. Not until we were both ready to unleash our final attempt to undo them.

The last time I'd walked this path, it had been daytime. It seemed like an entirely different landscape as I passed through it now—a much more lively one. Glowing insects buzzed between the trees. Creatures scurried in the brush, tempting Phantom more than once. And perhaps it was the proximity of Calista's grave and the echo of her magic, or maybe just my imagination, but the shadows seemed to be as alive as everything else, twisting and turning in a spellbinding dance.

Welcoming me in, almost.

Strange flowers bloomed along the forest floor, their color like translucent starlight, the petals neither fully solid nor fully spectral. They swayed without wind, their movement hypnotic, their soft radiance lining a path that led deeper into the woods.

As we started down this path, Phantom pressed close to my side, his ears flat against his skull. (*This place still smells like death. But it's teeming with life, too. I don't like it.*)

I gave him a comforting pat on the head. It made my senses uneasy as well—the way death and life intertwined so strangely here. I would have sworn I occasionally glimpsed the blood that I knew had once coated the ground, yet the wards Calista had created were also at their strongest here, a reminder that life and death were forever bound in this world.

As the first glimpse of her grave came into view, I drew to a stop.

"I need to handle this next step on my own," I reminded the others.

My brother looked hesitant to leave my side, even though this was part of the plan we'd all decided on. I would go first, because there were things my magic and I needed to do. Answers I needed to divine from the sacred ground. He and the others would keep watch while I gathered these last pieces of the puzzle I was putting together and prepared myself for what came next.

Thalia put a hand on Bastian's shoulder. "You know the plan. Let's not stray from it." She gave me a meaningful look, and two taps on her heart, before turning away. Phantom huffed in reluctant agreement before bounding after her.

Bastian lingered a moment longer. "Be wary," he said quietly. "And listen for our warning signal."

"I will."

He turned back and began giving orders for our company to spread out and take their defensive positions.

I walked the last stretch of the path alone, and with each step, the world became quieter.

Calista's gravesite sat in the heart of a depression in the earth, as if the land itself had bowed in reverence—or recoiled in horror—from what had happened here. The trees that ringed the clearing around it were curved in unnatural shapes, their trunks smooth and black. Almost like twisting shadows that had petrified over the years.

As for the memorial itself…it seemed smaller than I'd remembered. Less imposing. Just a circle of dark rocks, its widest point barely twenty feet across. The ground within this circle was covered in a carpet of black moss that released tiny puffs of luminescent spores when I stepped onto it, making the air around me sparkle with ghostly light. In the center, a grave marker rose almost haphazardly from the moss—white stone, rough-cut, unadorned except for a single dark symbol carved deep into its face.

The mark of the Shadow Vaelora.

A myriad of feelings washed over me as I stared at

that mark—grief, reverence, doubt, determination. All the many things I'd lived through since realizing my part in the ancient cycle of magic.

Focus, I told myself. *You came here for a reason.*

I knelt before the grave marker, placing both hands on the cold stone. Closing my eyes, I called on my shadows to reach once more into the past.

I had mastered this over these last months, if nothing else; even with my unsettled feelings, it was easy to concentrate on letting darkness seep into the stone and the ground around it, coaxing those whispers of the past up to the surface. I pictured Calista's face as I did, making sure to think specifically about what I needed to see.

Please, I thought. *I need to understand. I need to know if I'm right about what you did.*

Resistance came—as if her spirit was testing me—but I quickly pushed through it.

The world shifted.

I wasn't in my body anymore. I was watching from a different perspective, seeing through eyes that weren't my own.

Calista's eyes.

She was kneeling in this very spot, her hands pressed against the ground, blood seeping between her fingers from wounds I couldn't see. The forest around her was on fire—not with normal flames, but with Light magic turned wild and destructive...

Lorien's power, tearing through everything in his grief-fueled rage.

I don't have much time, she thought, her consciousness bleeding into mine. *I have to finish this. I have to make sure the pieces go where they need to go.*

Her magic was pulsing outward, creating that dome of protection that surrounded the palace and the royal city. But at the same time, another tangle of magic was rising inside of her, another complicated spell blooming into existence.

Mind to the place where knowledge sleeps. Body to the place where gods forget. Heart...

She hesitated, her hands moving to her own chest.

I felt her magic gathering there. Shadows responding to her call. They reached out from her body like dark appendages, beckoning toward the sky. And then I saw it: The last piece of Lorien's shattered soul. The piece the sentier hadn't revealed to me. It fell as the others had—streaking down like a falling star—and landed directly in front of Calista.

She picked it up with trembling fingers and clasped it to her chest. It gave off one last powerful burst of light before she covered it completely with her hands, pressing it more tightly against her. When she pulled her hands away and looked down, the shard was gone.

Blood stained her tunic. I wasn't sure if it had been there before, but now fresh pain radiated through her body, through our shared consciousness. Her heart pounded frantically fast and loud for a few seconds, and then…

Nothing.

The vision fractured as she took her last breath.

I gasped, pulling back from the stone so hard I nearly lost my balance. My own heart was pounding, my hands shaking as I realized…my theory had been correct.

I took a deep breath, willing steadiness back into my body with concentrated effort.

"I thought you might like this back," came a voice from behind me, casually cold and devastatingly familiar.

I twisted around to find Aleks watching me. He was alone, as far as I could see—but he also held Grimnor; he must have taken it from the battlefield after I'd dropped it.

I leapt to my feet. "How…how did you…"

"Get past your allies?" His eyes gleamed with dark amusement. "You underestimate me, Chaos." He glanced over his shoulder, toward the rising sounds of a skirmish. Muffled by the magic of this place, but obvious just the same. "They'll be busy for a moment, at least."

I tried not to let my panic show. "My sword," I said, evenly. "Hand it over."

"Like he did, you mean?" He sauntered forward with easy, predatory grace. "When the two of you moved against me back in the palace vault?"

"Together…" I kept my voice steady, trying not to think about those frightening moments when I'd brought Lorien back to life. "Is that what they told you? That Lorien and I conspired against you?"

"No one needed to tell me anything. The Vaelora bond is well documented."

"You know it's more complicated than that," I breathed. "Even if they've twisted your perception of it."

He said nothing, just watched me for a moment, his golden eyes like a wolf's in the dark.

I swallowed hard. "Give me back my sword, Aleks."

He looked the blade up and down, as if considering, then shook his head. "Why don't you summon your ally to help you get it back, as you did before?"

"Lorien and I are not allies. Our destiny may have been written by the gods, but I'm not walking that path willingly. I'm not like Calista."

"Really?" He took a step closer to me. Then another, and another, until we were nearly face-to-face. He could have reached out and touched me, and for a moment I thought he might.

Hoped he might.

My body couldn't tell the difference between this Aleks and the one that had memorized every inch of my skin; all those inches craved his touch. His reassuring closeness. His warmth.

"I find that statement odd," he said quietly, "considering how you practically *reek* of him."

I went still.

"Did you think I wouldn't be able to tell that his magical signature is all over you?" He finally touched me, then, dragging his fingers over my throat—but only so he could draw shadows from my skin and crush them in a quick, violent display of his rune-forged magic. "Did you think that I wouldn't know he's close by, even now?"

I forced myself to breathe normally.

"These chaotic schemes of yours were always going to be the end of you."

The familiarity in his tone, in his words, nearly made me sink to my knees. My voice shook when I spoke. "I'm not your enemy, Aleks."

He glanced at the shadows rising defensively around me, the darkness settling against my skin like armor. "Your shadows say otherwise."

The sounds of fighting grew closer. The situation was deteriorating quickly—too quickly—and I needed to strike.

I knew I needed to strike.

So why couldn't I move?

"Let's not waste time on denials," Aleks said. "I was told you wanted to negotiate. To trade something valuable for peace. I'm just here to make sure the exchange goes smoothly." His gaze drifted to the grave behind me. "So," he continued, lifting my own sword and pointing it at my chest, "where is it?"

I didn't answer, my vision blurring as I stared down at the blade between us.

"Are you going to make me spill your blood?"

"Do it." The words trembled through my lips. My vision blurred further, hazy from unshed tears. I stepped closer to him, until Grimnor's tip pressed painfully into my ribcage. "Just do it," I whispered, shaking my head. "It would be easier."

His hand gripped my sword more tightly; he seemed to be confused.

It was a short-lived hesitation. Even through the haze, I saw the exact moment the Order's magic surged through him to steal him back—the markings on his chest beginning to glow beneath his shirt. The way that glow spread up his neck and into his face, turning his expression from something raw and uncertain to something terrifyingly blank. And then came the cold awareness, which was worse.

He opened his mouth to speak—

A curved beam of light cut through the clearing like the blade of an axe, slamming into Aleks and sending him stumbling backward.

Lorien emerged from the treeline, his hood thrown back, power radiating from him in visible waves as he leveled a glare in my direction. "What the hell are you waiting for?"

My reply didn't make it out.

Severin appeared on the path leading into the clearing, distracting us. He moved with the calm, unhurried poise I'd come to expect from him.

More Order members surged in around him, spilling into the clearing from all sides.

My shadows rose automatically to meet them all. The dark ribbons seemed sentient, almost, fighting on my behalf while I was still trying to come to terms with what was happening around me, inside of me.

I heard my brother shouting orders, felt the pounding of boots, and then a displacement of air as Thalia's magic joined mine, dark tendrils of gathered shadows lashing out at the enemies nearest to me.

"Whatever the next part of your grand plan is," she called, whipping her staff in front of her, drawing darkness into a protective barrier around herself, "now would be a *brilliant* time to execute it!"

My focus shifted back to Aleks.

He moved with inhuman speed, closing the distance between us. Grimnor flashed in his hand, arcing toward my throat.

But I knew that blade too well to be so easily cut down by it. With little effort, I sent a stream of shadows toward it, braiding them into its familiar energy and then tightening my hold, jerking Aleks's swing off-balance.

He retaliated with a snarl, grabbing hold of one of the shadows with what looked like his bare hand at first; there was a rune glowing on his palm, I realized. It flared violet as he seized my magic and crushed it. I should have been used to the pull of him draining my power by now, but it seemed stronger than ever before, leaving me feeling like I'd been kicked in the stomach.

I couldn't breathe.

Couldn't think.

Lorien was there in the next instant, light blazing around his hands. "If you aren't going to truly fight him, then *stand the fuck back,*" he growled at me, and then sent a lance of pure white magic toward Aleks.

Aleks deflected it with Grimnor, scattering the light.

But the deflection still gave me time to wake up. To shake off my shock, and then to summon more shadows and join Lorien in his next attack. We moved together as if guided by the collective memory of all the Vaelora who had come before us. Where my shadows struck, his light followed, a seamless barrage that *should* have overwhelmed any opponent.

And for a few moments, we had Aleks on the defensive, driving him back across the clearing.

But all around us, the battle continued to intensify. My brother was locked in combat with three different Order members, his sword flashing as he fought to keep them from overwhelming him. Thalia had drawn a circle of shadows around herself and was driving spears of darkness at anyone who came close, but I could see the strain on her face. Phantom tore through enemy ranks in his massive shadow-hound form, his jaws closing around throats and limbs, but there were too many. And they kept coming.

We were far past outnumbered.

I was sure Bastian had already signaled for reinforcements; I doubted they would arrive in time to make a difference.

Lorien and I divided, sending streams of magic toward Aleks from both sides, forcing him to try and defend from two directions at once. Grimnor deflected what it could. The powerful void Aleks summoned handled the rest. He stood far too easily in the eye of our storm, his magic continuing to drink ours in, distorting the air all around him.

Lorien's gaze met mine across the chaos, and though he didn't growl any commands at me this time, I could hear his words snapping through our bond.

End. This.

I hesitated for an instant too long, trying to decide how to orchestrate that ending.

Aleks was suddenly *there*. He spun, and Grimnor came down in a brutal overhead strike that I barely blocked with a shield of solidified darkness. The impact sent shockwaves through my arms, dropping me to my knees.

He raised the blade for another strike.

With desperate focus, I reached out for Grimnor's essence, for the bond we'd forged. *Come back to me*, I commanded, rising to my feet. *You're mine. Not his.*

The sword trembled in his hands.

Aleks's expression flickered with doubt. He put distance between us as he gripped the hilt tighter, fighting to maintain control. But Grimnor was responding to my call, the ancient magic within it recognizing its true wielder.

With a surge of determination, I yanked it toward me with only a thought.

The sword flew from Aleks's hands and sailed across the clearing, landing perfectly in my grip. Power raced through me as our connection reestablished, shadows pouring out from both me and the blade like a burning house belching smoke.

For a heartbeat, I thought we'd gained the advantage.

Then I saw Aleks smiling through the darkness between us, and I was reminded of the cruel truth: that he didn't need a weapon to destroy me.

His hands began to glow with that cold light, and before I could react, he was upon me again. One hand locked around my wrist, the other pressed flat against my chest, and I felt it immediately—the pull. The drain. Grimnor fell from my hand. Shadows still rushed from it, desperate to protect me, but they weren't enough.

Aleks simply devoured them, pulling them into his body like they were nothing more than air, like they promised life rather than death.

Lorien raced to my side, summoning a sphere of brilliant white light that he thrust toward Aleks's chest. Aleks countered by summoning his own sphere of void magic, violet and cold. The powers collided, remaining immovable for several heartbeats, neither giving an inch.

Grimnor continued to expel waves of shadows. Once I caught my breath, I joined its efforts, weaving magic into the assault Lorien was maintaining. Our Vaeloran powers began to combine in earnest, twisting into something unprecedented—Light and Shadow corded together like an unbreakable chain that wound itself around the void in front of Aleks, squeezing it.

It all felt different, now.

Maybe because I'd truly made up my mind to end this.

End this. End this. End this—

Tears filled my eyes with each surge of magic I released, but the words continued to pound through my brain, and little by little, the balance of power began to shift.

Our different magics battled on and on, twisting, breaking, rebuilding with increasingly bright and violent surges. It was like watching a world fighting to be born from the chaos of a dying star. Light and dark both vying for dominance, then settling into equal forces while the void Aleks commanded began closing, the gaping mouth of cold getting smaller and smaller.

Overwhelming him.

We were already overwhelming him.

Maybe we wouldn't even need to restore Lorien's heart. Maybe things weren't as desperate as I'd thought. I could see the runes on Aleks's chest beginning to fade as his magic did, I thought; was it possible that we could purify those markings, somehow? That we could remake him, just as the Vaeloran could remake entire realms?

Ragged, desperate hope spurred me on.

I poured everything I had into one more surge of magic.

End this. End this. End this—

The power built and built, its pressure mounting until the air itself seemed in danger of cracking, its howling lifting into a crescendo that made my ears feel like they were bleeding.

Then I caught something out of the corner of my eye—a flash of movement from Severin's direction. A spell that must have been tethered to the ones carved into Aleks, because a moment later, the runes on his body blazed back to full, terrible brightness.

The void yawned wider once more, swallowing up the Vaeloran magic, distilling it down to a single point that wavered for a moment before bursting.

The force of it sent Lorien flying backward.

I managed to dig in my heels, anchoring myself with a few last wisps of shadow that I guided into a less abrupt finish. Aleks and I remained locked together for one more terrible moment.

Then we both collapsed, falling toward each other in a tangle of limbs and spent magic. I rolled out of his reach, grabbing Calista's gravestone and trying to pull myself back upright.

Aleks clawed toward me, throwing his weight onto mine, holding me down.

My body ached so badly I almost gave in right then and there. In the fog of pain and exhaustion, it seemed like it could have been just another battle we were fighting side-by-side, him crawling toward me to make sure I was okay. How many times had his body wrapped around mine like this, protecting me in the middle of the wreckage?

Why couldn't this be one of those times?

I dug my grip tighter into the stone, starting to twist myself around and upright—until I realized there was a knife pressed to my side.

I sank against the stone, turning my back to it and settling with slow, careful movements.

Aleks moved with equal deliberation, bringing the knife up to my chest. His breathing was ragged. His eyes were struggling to focus. His body shook with the effort of holding the blade steady, but the knife didn't waver.

We'd ended up where we'd started this battle, with him digging sharpness into my skin.

Circling, always circling back to the edge of ruin.

The battle had come to a halt around us, almost everyone knocked to the ground by the force of the magic we'd been throwing off. Several didn't appear to be moving. I heard my brother say my name—enough to know he was alive, thankfully, though I didn't dare look at him.

Lorien was kneeling a few feet away, breathing hard. But he was still conscious. His magic was still flickering around him. Power still burned in the gaze he fixed on me. Ancient and undeniable.

Despite the pain of this last failed attempt, I was certain, now, that the two of us at full strength would be enough.

That there was no other way to end this.

I wrapped my hand around Aleks's grip on the knife.

"Your only hope now bound to shadow's forfeit…" I recited those words from the curse that had shattered Lorien so long ago, my voice steady despite the emotion welling up in my throat. "Mind carved into one realm, heart into the next…" Shadows rose from my arms, snaking around the knife, binding our hands together.

Into the next Shadow Vaelora.

That was what she'd meant.

That was the real reason why Lorien hadn't been able to kill me as a child—because destroying me would have meant destroying a piece of himself. And it was why I'd been able to revive him when I shattered the other two shards.

Because I had the third one.

I'd *always* had it.

My brother called my name again, and this time I met his horrified gaze. Saw him silently begging me to escape, to run, to do anything except pull that knife closer.

But I'd already made up my mind.

"It's in me," I said, holding his stare for a moment, trying to make him understand even though I knew he was too far away to hear the words.

I looked back to Aleks. He was so close, but I didn't know if he could hear me, either. If he ever would again. My lips still moved, one last whisper among the wreckage.

"I love you," I told him. "No matter how the light and shadows shift."

And then I jerked his hand toward me, plunging his knife into my chest.

THIRTY-EIGHT

Nova

At first, all I felt was *power*.

It was awakening inside of me, unraveling the shadows coiled around the knife, drawing them deep into my chest.

And it was gathering outside of me, too, darkness rising all over the gravesite, as if whatever remained of Calista had stirred at my sacrifice, and now she was reaching up through the soil, grasping for my shivering body.

Everything converged toward the blade buried in my chest. Toward the shard it had pierced—a fragment that had been hidden there for twenty-five years. As the shadows sank in, that pierced fragment began to beat like a second heart.

Then it was moving, twisting and turning, trying to break free.

I sank into the ocean of ancient power surrounding me, trusting the shadows to guide the fragment out.

Seconds later, they managed it.

My vision flickered as I watched its extraction. Pain quickly followed, white-hot and all-consuming. I tried to scream, but no sound came out. Blood filled my mouth, warm and coppery; I'd convulsed, I thought, and bitten my tongue. I dug my fingers into the cold dirt, trying to keep still.

Tremors continued to shake my body, but eventually, I managed to lift my head and see what was happening.

Aleks had gotten to his feet and taken several steps back. No longer attacking. Just watching me with a mixture of horror and confusion.

The shard floated in the air between us.

It took excruciating effort, but I fought my way up into a kneeling position, preparing to reach for it, to hand it over to Lorien as we'd agreed.

But something was wrong.

It didn't look like it should have.

The shape was different—like an actual human heart, grotesque and beautiful, and somehow still beating. And its light…it wasn't glowing with pure, radiant white like the other shards.

It was black.

As black as the shadows I commanded.

As the seconds ticked by without it inside of me, waves of weakness began to overtake my body, building and building until my balance swayed. I knew the knife had only pierced a small portion of my flesh, but it felt like my entire chest had been splayed open. Like every part of me was in danger of tumbling out, leaving me entirely hollow and empty.

I'd only thought about getting rid of the fragment of my old enemy; I hadn't thought about the space it would leave behind.

Clearly, it had tangled more completely with my own life-force than I'd realized.

And without it, I suddenly couldn't *breathe*.

The world tilted sideways.

Lorien caught me as I fell, his grip more ruthless than supportive, forcing me to keep staring at the floating fragment—as if he was waiting for me to explain, to tell him the next part of my plan.

But I didn't have anything left to tell him.

Nothing left to give.

I only knew that my goals hadn't changed: I wanted to save my world. My magic. And, more than anything else in that moment, I wanted to save the man standing before me, to somehow heal his scars.

I would give anything to keep you safe.

His words, first. But now, they were mine as well. A

shared vow. The only thing tethering me to reality. I had to keep fighting. To keep breathing.

I inhaled as deeply as I could, blinking hard, trying to focus.

As I did, a fracture formed in the center of the heart.

And then it *broke*, splitting in two with a sound that echoed like a crack of thunder.

One of the pieces flew outward, slamming into Aleks. He staggered back as it sank into his chest, a strangled sound tearing from his throat. His eyes went wide. The runes on his body flared…but then began to dim.

The second piece of the heart fell toward me, hovering just out of my reach, pulsing with a soft, steady darkness. It was hard to focus on.

Everything was getting harder and harder to focus on.

Lorien's grip tightened on my shoulders, holding me upright.

I knew the bargain we'd made. Knew I couldn't go back on it now—if only because I was too weak to stop him from taking what was promised. The very thought of trying to fight him off was agonizing.

Just take it, I thought, my vision darkening at the edges. *Please. End this.*

A moment later, my back hit the ground. Lorien had released me. Let me fall. He was reaching for the remaining half of the fragment—his outstretched hand was the last thing I saw before I closed my eyes and let the exhaustion claim me.

I drifted in and out of awareness for some time. The crooked black trees wheeled above me every time I opened my eyes. *Closer.* They seemed to be leaning closer with each blink. I started to see their long branches as fingers, as if the dark hands of Death itself were reaching down to claim me. I welcomed it in like an old friend.

Then came pressure against my chest, firm and deliberate.

I heard myself gasping. Choking. I didn't actually *feel* these things, though, because I was detached from my body, floating somewhere up above…

Until a massive weight settled into the hollow place where the fragment had been. It sank deeper, expanding into the cracks of my broken body until all of the emptiness was gone.

A rush of power overcame me, and I realized what had happened.

The broken heart piece…

Lorien had given it back to me.

The pain of it sinking in proved worse than the knife, worse than the heart's extraction. It felt like it was twisting into my actual heart, knitting itself more tightly into the very fabric of my existence, and it was all so much heavier than before.

But despite the weight, I could breathe again. And I could move. I reached a hand up, feeling across my chest. Blood soon covered my fingers, but beneath them, my sewn-together heart was beating steadily. Powerful, insistent beats that thundered with the force of everything I'd endured. Everything I'd survived. A heavy but beautiful burden.

I felt someone lifting me up off the cold ground, and I opened my eyes, expecting to see Lorien or my brother.

Instead, Aleks was there, watching me with an odd look on his face—a soft, wondering look. Like he'd just woken up, and he was trying to decide if he was still dreaming. His hand found mine, interlacing our fingers as he cradled me against him.

I squeezed his hand until I was certain of it: The recognition taking hold in his gaze. Proof of something that ran deeper than the darkest magic, that burned brighter than any curse they could carve into his skin.

"You…you see me." The words scraped through my cracked, dry lips.

He exhaled a shaky breath. Nodded. "I see you."

The world went still. Like a gasp held between life and death, with everything waiting to see whether or not we would manage to keep breathing.

That stillness shattered with the violent sound of clashing steel.

Aleks pulled me closer, curving his body protectively around mine as we tried to see what was happening. A wall of shadows had been surrounding us, but now it was beginning to fade, revealing the full extent of the chaos still unfolding in the clearing.

Reinforcements, led by Captain Voss, were emerging from every direction.

The Order members were scattering, some engaging with my soldiers, but most of them converging toward a rippling point at the edge of the gravesite; a portal that hadn't been there moments before. Rune marks glowed in the air and on the ground around its edges, violet and pulsing.

Aleks stared at that rippling gateway for far too long.

I grabbed his arm, trying to force his attention back to me. But Severin appeared beside the portal in the same moment, his expression triumphant, despite the chaos, and Aleks didn't seem able to look away from him.

"This won't be the end of their plans," Aleks said quietly.

He rose to his feet, pulling me up with him. As we helped one another balance, I noticed a mark on his bicep—a scar that hadn't been there before, I was certain. Upon it glowed an obvious shape, a spiraling sigil hovering just above the skin.

The other runes were barely glowing, even as Severin's gaze fixed in our direction. But they were clearly still there. Like embers buried in ash, waiting for their moment to burn, to consume.

"...I still feel their pull." He pressed a hand to his

temple, as if struck by a sudden headache. His eyes closed as he tried to steady himself through it. I would have sworn his body swayed toward the portal, like a compass needle drawn to magnetic north.

I held my breath, terror clawing through me.

Then his hand moved down to his chest, right over the spot where the broken shard had sunken in.

His eyes flew open. He managed to turn away from Severin, though he still didn't look at me as he said, "I'm going to keep fighting them."

The declaration should have brought relief. It didn't. There was something in the way his fist clenched as he said it, as if he were trying to hold onto sand slipping through his fingers. Something that told me I knew what he was going to say next, that shattered me before the words had even left his mouth—

"But I can't do it here…beside you," he finished quietly.

The portal shimmered, too bright to ignore, no matter how desperately I wanted to.

"You can't follow me this time," he said, taking my hand and finally meeting my gaze again. "You understand that, right?"

I shook my head, but he kept talking anyway.

"Promise me, Nova. Promise me you won't do anything foolish. Trust that I'll find you again, when I can."

The words lodged in my throat.

There was no time to get them out.

A pained cry rang out across the clearing, distracting me. As soon as I looked away from him, Aleks was pulling his hand from mine, striding quickly toward the portal without looking back.

Severin watched him approaching, a slow smile spreading across his face.

I picked up Grimnor and ran after him.

An Order member cut me off, tossing a sphere of something that exploded into chokingly thick smoke. I coughed and stumbled forward, trying to wave it away.

By the time I made it to clearer air, it was too late.

Aleks had reached the threshold of the portal.

"*NO!*" The scream tore from my throat, raw and desperate.

He paused to look back at me, one last time—

Then he stepped through, Severin following with a slow, deliberate bow in my direction, just before the portal collapsed.

THIRTY-NINE

Nova

Nearly four days had passed since the battle at Calista's grave.

My kingdom had needed me every second of those days—to guide them through their grief, to reassure them, to help them pick up our latest broken pieces and continue to rebuild. And they *still* needed me, of course. But on the afternoon of the fourth day, my brother offered to run interference so that I could have a brief chance to escape. A chance to breathe.

Because he knew as well as I did how I desperately needed time to think outside of the spotlight, to find a quiet place where I could sit and make sense of Aleks's last words to me.

You can't follow me this time. You understand that, right?

And I did.

But that didn't mean that my heart wasn't breaking. Or that I could just move forward, as if nothing had changed. As if he wasn't gone.

And not taken, this time...he'd *chosen* to leave. Which made it all the more painful, whatever his reasons for doing it.

I already had a destination in mind when I slipped out of the palace by way of a rarely-used servant's passage. Phantom hadn't let me out of his sight these past three days, and today was no exception; he offered to join me, and to carry me, before I could even ask.

I huddled close to his back, my hair loose and flying behind me as we raced across the blooming landscape. The day was warm, the air sweet with spring blossoms, the sky clear.

That sky was also brighter than I'd ever seen it, thanks to a visit Lorien and I had paid to the Aetherstone yesterday. It had been an experiment, an attempt to see how stable his magic could be, now that he'd been, in a sense, reborn. That was how I'd managed to talk him into helping me bring some more of the life back to my realm—because he was as curious as I was about what he could and couldn't do, magically speaking.

Whether or not he'd help me with this next chapter

of my story remained to be seen, though; I still couldn't make sense of him, even after all we'd been through.

But he'd been hanging around the palace these last few days, making use of the library and studying all the notes and artifacts from our adventures thus far, which Eamon had been carefully archiving. Making plans, I think—but keeping them to himself. We'd scarcely talked outside of our brief trip to the Midna Palace, though, and I didn't know where we were supposed to go from here.

He'd both saved my life and tried to take it away, and now a shard of his soul quite literally resided in my body. Even if my own magic had overtaken it, it didn't change the fact that it had originally been his. And he'd let me...*keep it.*

We were tied together, whether we liked it or not, like threads woven into the same piece of fate's tapestry.

Phantom raced into the forest where Calista had been laid to rest, and I instantly felt a shift in the air— that lingering sense of ancient magic prickling over me. As unsettling as I'd initially found it, part of me welcomed it, now; it made me feel closer to my Vaeloran legacy than anywhere else in the kingdom. Like I was coming into a place I could someday call home, even if I wasn't entirely settled yet.

Calista's gravestone had clearly been visited recently. My eyes were drawn to the offerings left there —smooth stones arranged in careful little stacks, alongside several carved wooden tokens, each one unique. Someone had tended to the ground as well, clearing away the weeds and smoothing the earth into gentle curves.

All of it was Lorien's doing, I assumed.

I knelt before the stone, placing my palm against its cool surface. The marble had been worn smooth by weather and time, but her name remained clear.

So many secrets still buried with her.

Would we ever know the whole truth?

Sighing, I moved to a lush patch of grass nearby and settled down to think. I crossed my hands behind my head and leaned back against Phantom's warm side, tilting my face toward the sky. Those black, shadowy trees loomed overhead, their twisted branches still reminding me of Death's hand—although they seemed less threatening in the daylight. Far less ominous, especially with such a bright circle of sky breaking through at the center of them.

As I stared at that bright circle, I found myself remembering what Thalia had said to me, weeks ago.

Never underestimate what a drop of hope can do in an ocean of despair.

The broken heart in my chest seemed to pulse as I recalled the words, stronger than even my truly beating one.

Another bit of hope.

I closed my eyes, focusing on that beat of hope as it echoed through even the darkest, most wounded parts of me. It was comforting enough that I soon drifted off while Phantom kept watch.

When I woke up some time later, Lorien was crouched beside Calista's grave, tending to it once more. He had brought flowers this time—white roses and blue thistle, bundled together with a thin ribbon.

I watched him for a moment, still not ready to try and figure out what would become of us, but unable to look away, either.

Eventually, I cleared my throat and said, "You never told me why you didn't take your heart back."

He stilled, pausing in the middle of arranging one of the roses against the stone.

"We had a deal," I said.

"We did."

"So why didn't you take it?"

"It was broken."

"A broken half is better than nothing at all."

"Is it?" He returned to his task, letting the question hang in the air. His movements were painstakingly precise, as if he'd spent centuries imagining how he might decorate this gravestone, and now he was deter-mined to do his vision justice.

I sat up slowly, brushing grass from my hair.

As he laid the last of the roses in place, he spoke again—almost more to himself than to me. "Let's call it atonement, then."

"…Well, thank you," I said. "For giving it back."

He didn't answer right away, studying the stone for a long moment, his hand braced against it for balance.

"I have one goal before me now," he finally said, rising back to his full height. "To find the ones who destroyed us. And trust me when I say I won't need a heart for that."

With that, he left, disappearing into the trees without a backward glance.

There was something final about his exit; he'd clearly decided on his next plans and purpose, and I suspected it would be some time before I saw him again.

Now all that remained was for me to face my own plans and purpose.

I took a steadying breath and got to my feet, resting a hand against Phantom's head as he nuzzled my side.

The sunlight shifted, drawing my eyes upward once more, and the broken heart inside of me seemed to wake in response, pulsing with a steady, insistent rhythm.

And as warmth washed over my upturned face, I would have sworn I felt the other half of that heart beating across the realms, as if in answer.